Embassie Susberry is a recovering attorney in Chicago, but when she's not doing her day job, she's reading or writing what she wants to read.

Code Name Butterfly was Embassie's first traditionally published novel. She has over 2000 reviews for her self-published novels on Amazon with average ratings of 4.7 stars. *The Game Changer* is her second traditionally published novel.

THE GAME CHANGER

EMBASSIE SUSBERRY

avon.

Published by AVON
A division of HarperCollins*Publishers*
1 London Bridge Street
London SE1 9GF

www.harpercollins.co.uk

HarperCollins*Publishers*
Macken House, 39/40 Mayor Street Upper
Dublin 1, D01 C9W8
Ireland

A Paperback Original 2024
1

First published in Great Britain by HarperCollins*Publishers* 2024

A catalogue copy of this book is available from the British Library.

ISBN: 978-0-00-869759-4

Set in Bembo by HarperCollins*Publishers* India

Printed and bound in the UK using 100% Renewable Electricity by CPI Group (UK) Ltd

This book contains FSC™ certified paper and other controlled sources to ensure responsible forest management.

For more information visit: www.harpercollins.co.uk/green

To all of those who wish to leave their mark on the world. I see you.

AUTHOR'S NOTE

Please be advised that historically accurate terminology has been used, which by today's standards would be considered offensive.

PROLOGUE

1950, Forest Hills

Despite being the main attraction, the young woman stood off to the side, clutching her tennis rackets tightly against her chest as she waited for her name to be announced. Next to her stood her opponent, a woman four years her senior, America's number-two female player, a three-time Wimbledon champion, and a previous winner of this very game.

As they waited for the announcer to state their names, the two women shared a quick glance and then looked away, both quietly wishing that the game could be played without the cameras and the reporters and the weight of expectations that lay heavy on their shoulders.

The younger woman did her best to keep her gaze somewhere not quite on the ground but neither on the spectators. She felt as though she had already lived that morning, having taken two trains and made a short trek just to get there. Upon her arrival, she'd been forced to run through a gauntlet of well-wishers and gawkers as she tried to get ready. To imagine that it took all of this just to play a game.

Their names were announced and they waved to the crowd surrounding them before separating, each walking to their assigned portion of the tennis court.

The set started with the older woman leaping in the air, serving the tennis ball first. The younger woman ran to meet it, just barely raising her tennis racket in time to send the ball over the net. The veteran player returned it easily but this time the younger player wasn't fast enough. "Love fifteen," the announcer called amidst cheers and silent groans.

There was no groan louder than the one released by the younger player. Again and again the veteran served the ball; again and again the younger player made one mistake after another, trying to drown out the hecklers' voices, trying to ignore the weight of an entire human race on her back, trying to remember all the years of blood, sweat, and tears that she had poured into this pursuit people called a sport.

The set was called, the young woman lost. The second set began. Almost immediately, the young woman made a silly mistake, earning the veteran player an easy point. Then she volleyed way out of court. She could feel it, the glee of her opponents, and the quiet, distressed pleas of her supporters. With her chest rising and falling, and her breath exiting her mouth in short, desperate gasps, she made a decision.

The game started again and this time she was ready. She met the ball each time it was sent her way, returning it with forceful, almost violent strokes. She was younger, lighter, faster and she used that to her advantage, tiring out the veteran player on the other side of the net. She won the next set.

So focused on the tournament before them, the sea of onlookers barely noticed the dark clouds that were slowly rolling in.

The third set began and even though there had been a short break, the young woman was ready for it. The two players fought it out, sending the ball back and forth, and back and forth. They slid, they dove, they spun, fighting an intense battle and yet, the winner was becoming startlingly clear.

And that's when the young woman finally felt it: the wind, blowing at an alarming rate; and then she heard it: the thunder growling in the distance. But she kept playing until she felt, first, a trickle of steady droplets, then a deluge of water. The sky grew ominously dark, making it impossible to remember that there had been a sun in the sky only moments earlier. None of it bothered her at all; she'd trained in worse conditions. As she stood ready and waiting for the final game to get started, as water soaked into her clothes and slid down her face, she looked up at the sky just in time to see lightning tear through the sky, striking one of the tall, proud frozen eagles that guarded the stadium. Everyone there watched as it fell slowly from its perch, rushing toward the ground and smashing into hundreds of pieces, taking the young woman's victory with it.

CHAPTER 1

Baseline—the line indicating the back boundary of the court

Summer might be dying a slow death all around her, but Hester J. Carlin had still slipped on her best woolen suit of armor—gloves and all—before coming to face down the elongated, seven-story red-brick dragon of a building that held her very future in its hands.

"Excuse me, Miss!" Two small boys, carrying the scent of the outdoors with them, ran past Hester, chasing something only they could see and nearly knocking her from the spotted sidewalk, and then sped into the bustling traffic behind her. As she caught her balance, planting the heels of her black shoes into the cement ground, she pondered whether this was a sign. Perhaps things would be better if she kept going backwards. She could flag one of the many taxis that were circling the block in desperate search of needy customers. She could return to the train station she'd just left a half hour ago and purchase a one-way ticket to nowhere. She could disappear into the great beyond, reinventing herself all over again where no one had ever heard her name.

But that was not Hester Carlin's way. Hester, known to friends and family alike as Hettie, had faced bigger giants and slain uglier monsters than the one before her now. This was not going to be pretty, she knew, as she pressed her bright red lips tightly together. In fact, she'd be lucky if she walked away with all of her limbs intact. But she would walk away.

Still, she could not seem to make herself move forward. There was something soothing in the lullaby of honking horns and squealing tires that surrounded her and she didn't want to leave. Releasing a low exhalation, Hettie removed one white glove and swiped at the bead of sweat that was sliding down the side of her face. Dropping her hand to her throat, she tugged on the chain of the necklace that was tucked under her blouse, setting the silver charm free. Then, replacing the glove, she straightened her shoulders, lifted her chin—and a small body slammed into her side. Since she had already been bracing herself, the child barely moved her an inch.

"Hey! Watch it, lady!" The boy had to be around seven or eight and he glared up at her with dark, annoyed eyes, irritated that she had momentarily stopped him from getting to where he was going. Well. She was definitely back in New York. "Is your daddy Michelangelo? He carve you out of marble? 'Cause you still ain't moving!"

Hettie closed her eyes for a long second. She'd just spent the past three months in the land of false niceties and politeness, where children wouldn't dare look an adult in the eyes without permission. She knew this boy's kind, though. She'd been raised right next door to his type. Those other children had been a little frightening at first, with their sweet manners. But this blatant rudeness was a welcome home. Hettie sneered down at the child before her. "Yo mama."

The boy took a step back, and rolled his neck, offended. "Oh, we about to talk about people's mamas?"

"No, we ain't, 'cause yo mama is such a snore, I nearly fall asleep thinking about her and I'm not ready to go to bed just yet." Her mind on much bigger things than playing the dozens with a pint-sized male, Hettie stuck her tongue out at the child and sashayed through the entrance of her office building before the boy could edge in another word.

She didn't make it to the front desk. The familiar click-click sound of her shoes against the marble entryway, the silent rush of elevators as they made their way up and down, pausing at different floors, the lingering odor of lemon cleaning solution in the air all hit her at once. She rushed to the nearest ladies' room and lost the small breakfast she'd eaten that morning. When she was almost certain that her stomach was settled, she flushed the toilet, went to the porcelain sink, rinsed out her mouth, and splashed water onto her cheeks and forehead.

Looking up at her reflection, she noticed that there was a slight crack in the mirror, which distorted her face, making it look as though there were two different Hetties standing there. Both were enrobed in the black suit. Both were wearing the fancy wide-brimmed black hat—a secondhand gift from Miz Ce-Ce. Both had warm brown skin and wide brown eyes. But while one looked as though she could handle anything that was thrown her way, the other looked as though she'd give anything to find a safe lap to crawl into until the approaching storm passed by.

There was a firm knock on the bathroom door.

"Miss Hettie? Is that you?"

Hettie brought wet hands up, covering her face. She released a soft exhalation and cleared her throat. "Yes, Mr. Thompson. It's me."

"I thought so. Girl, I ain't never seen a face turn such a color before. You sick in there? You need me to fetch help?"

Pulling out her handkerchief, Hettie dabbed at her face. "Thank you, Mr. Thompson, but I'm all right." As though to prove it, Hettie returned the damp cloth to her pocket, grabbed her bag, which she had tossed aside in haste, and exited the small washroom.

Mr. Isaiah Thompson, whose job it was to monitor the front desk and check different people in and out the building, stood there waiting. Older than her parents by many years, which was evidenced in the slight ring of gray hair that surrounded his otherwise balding head, he peered at her through dark, narrowed eyes. "They done treat you bad down there, Miss Hettie?"

Mr. Thompson might only work on the ground floor of the office building but he knew everyone and everything that happened within its four corners, no matter what company you worked for. Which meant that somehow he'd learned that she'd been sent to Montgomery, Alabama, to cover the bus boycott. The boycott that was not over yet.

"No, sir. It was . . . interesting to be sure but I was treated just fine." No one had harmed a hair on Hettie's head. It was she who had, arguably, created a ruckus. She, who had created danger when at first there had been none. She clutched the handle of her bag with both hands to hide their shaking.

"Well, that's good to hear. Just a stomach thing?"

"Yes, sir. Just a little unsettled. I've done a lot of traveling in the past two days," she said, forcing herself to smile. It wasn't a complete lie. She'd been told to catch the first train out of Montgomery and to return to New York within the next forty-eight hours or don't ever return again. The contents of her stomach flipped as they always did when she thought about the telegram she'd received. She'd only read it once, but the letters were imprinted on her mind.

"Well, come on. Let me get you into the elevator. I already called upstairs and told Mr. Edgar that you're here."

Sometimes Isaiah Thompson was too helpful. "Thank you, Mr. Thompson."

With a false smile plastered on her face, she followed where Mr. Thompson led and waved until the elevator doors closed before her. As the metal box began to climb up, Hettie felt her eyes fill with sudden tears. And she was about to enter a place where she could ill afford to cry. With only a few seconds to spare, she puffed up her cheeks with air and then exhaled slowly.

"Get it together, Hettie," she whispered to herself. "If you want to keep this job, you've got to be ready to fight for it." But did she want this job? A week ago, she'd rather have died than leave. Now, for the first time in her life, there was a small wiggle of doubt.

The elevator dinged and when the doors slid open, Hettie stepped onto the floor with her head held high, and her gaze cool. Only on the inside did she feel like her namesake, who had once left a prison with a baby in her arms and entered a yard filled with gathering gossipy goodwives and the scarlet letter stitched across her chest.

On the floor that belonged to the *Harlem Heights* newspaper office, noise filled every crevice of the wide-open room that held several clusters of desk, arranged in such a way that the occupants of each desk faced at least one other person. Filing cabinets outlined the entirety of the space, stopped only by windows and the occasional table piled high with paper. Telephones rang, typewriters clacked, unintelligible chatter seemed to fill the air, but then her colleagues caught sight of her and suddenly the only thing Hettie could hear was someone's pencil rolling across the surface of a desk and then hitting the floor.

Hettie produced a tight smile that earned not a single reaction. They knew. They might not know the details but they knew enough of what she'd done. A loud alarm rang through Hettie's head, warning her to turn around and flee. Instead, she took a step to the right toward the long hall that led to Edgar's office.

"He's waiting for you, Hettie," Gayle—Edgar's longtime secretary—said from behind her desk as Hettie slowly reached her destination. Gayle had one eyebrow raised and Hettie read both consternation and compassion in her face. "Welcome back."

"Thank you, Gayle." Hettie's artificial smile was beginning to hurt. She supposed she should be happy that Gayle was trying to signal kindness to her, but it was only making Hettie feel irrationally angry. "I'm going to leave my suitcase here, if that's all right?"

"Of course it is, dear." Hettie had always thought that Gayle resembled a snake she'd once seen in the zoo, with the intense way she liked to home in on whoever she was talking to. All Gayle needed to do was wiggle her tongue and she'd never be mistaken for human again. "Go on inside, Hettie. Edgar doesn't like to wait."

Hettie shook her head. Her imagination always ran away from her when she was in stressful situations. Edgar's door was already open and Hettie entered a room that was probably the size of her parents' living room, but you'd never know it from all the clutter. Stacks of paper were everywhere: on the floor, on bookshelves, on top of cabinets, and precariously balanced on his desk. But beware if you knocked one over or shifted a pile to the side. He'd know and he'd rage. Edgar Stewart was aware of every item that lodged within his castle.

As the editor of *Harlem Heights*—or the double H, as they called it—he was the only person on the floor with a corner office giving him four windows to look out. He stood at one now, eyeing the world beneath them with a cigarette slowly shrinking between two of his fingers.

Hettie closed the door of his office behind her and stood there, eyeing her boss. He was not a tall man, but neither was he short. He was nearly twenty years older than her, twice divorced, and losing his hair—except on his face, where he sported a furry mustache that nearly overtook his mouth. He stood on skinny legs, carrying all of his weight around his middle and forever putting Hettie in mind of a walrus. He was kinder in the mornings and a wretch to work with as the sun went down. His opinions were mercurial. One day he'd love an idea, and the next day he'd hate it and blame you for the change in his mind. But he knew his craft and he tried to be a fair man—which gave Hettie hope.

"I've never been so embarrassed in my life." Edgar's smoke-filled voice made Hettie flinch. "To think that those folks in Montgomery had to pause in their fight against injustice to write me a letter about someone on my staff." Still not looking at her, Edgar brought his cigarette to his mouth, causing ash to dance around his form.

Hettie dropped her gaze to the carpet, her face hot with shame. But she only let herself dwell in it for a second. She wanted this job—needed this job—and if she let herself wallow in regret and guilt she'd lose everything she'd worked so hard for. She clenched her fists at her sides and lifted her head.

"You were literally supposed to report what you see. What you see, Hettie," he stressed. "Not what you create in that ridiculous head of yours." He turned now, facing her with a tight mouth and flaring nostrils. "Now, give me one good reason why I shouldn't fire you and have you blackballed by every newspaper in the country!"

Hettie inhaled and exhaled. "Have you heard of Althea Gibson?"

CHAPTER 2

Drop shot—when a tennis player hits the ball just over the net

Hettie had known that she'd have to defend herself. She'd known that she was going to have to stand before the man who had been her mentor all these years and justify her value. She'd been beside herself on the train ride north, trying to figure out just what she should say. And then she'd seen it. It was a paper in North Carolina that had reminded Hettie of something—of someone—from her past. Someone she'd purposefully forgotten, if she was being honest, but she was out of options. This was the only card she had left to play.

"Althea Gibson?" Edgar repeated, momentarily thrown. There was a pause as he blinked a few times and Hettie knew that she had played a winning hand. But then, as though he could not let go of the speech he'd prepared, he rebounded.

"What you did . . . this ain't work turned in late, Hettie," Edgar muttered. "This ain't a typo or a fact that you forgot to check."

Hettie knew her boss. She knew what upset him and what calmed him down. She knew how to get him to see things her way and she knew when she'd gone too far. The fact that he was even meeting with her told her that she had not yet crossed the line of no return. He wasn't ready to let her go, but he needed a reason to keep her. "I've risen through the ranks quicker than any other journalist here because I put out good, reliable work."

"You also create work."

"I messed up. I acknowledge that. I'm willing to fall on my sword, Mr. Edgar. But you know me. I never make the same mistake twice."

"I should hope not."

Hettie ignored his comment. For all of his comebacks, he was listening. "If you keep me on, I will go above and beyond what I've already done to add to the double H's reputation."

"Ain't nothin' you put out that can't be got somewhere else. You're not special, Hettie."

She nearly took a step back. Her armor had taken a direct hit to the heart. Sometimes Edgar Stewart was a spiteful old man. Placing both hands on her hips, Hettie took a step forward. "I am the best journalist you've ever had. Better even than you." All things considered, she really shouldn't have added that last part, but if you were going to hurt her, Hettie had only one response and that was to inflict greater pain on whoever had wounded her.

Edgar stared at her and she stared back, holding his gaze. "Pride comes before a fall, Carlin."

"I'm already on the ground, Mr. Edgar. Would it make you feel better if I rolled around in the mud?"

A long moment passed and then he waved a hand, done with this line of conversation. Hettie dropped her hands to her sides as he made his way to his seat behind his desk and sat down. The old chair groaned beneath his weight and then settled. He pointed to the chair opposite him and Hettie took a seat on the edge. She was too jittery to get comfortable. "Althea Gibson," he said slowly. The words were an invitation.

"When I first applied for this job, didn't I indicate that I could write on a variety of topics?" Hettie had initially applied for the entertainment beat. That was the position that had been advertised and, well, Hettie needed a position anywhere that was willing to hire a girl fresh out of school. She'd always figured that once she got in the door, she'd eventually maneuver herself to where she wanted to be. And she had.

"You should have been applying to be an assistant or a fact-checker but no, you wanted to be thrown right in." Edgar's voice was gruff but Hettie heard a hint of marvel.

"I said that if you did not think I suited entertainment, I could write on local news, or business, or even on politics." Truthfully, at the time, she'd sort of been reaching for that last one. But if she'd been given the assignment, she'd have done it and she'd have done it well. "And also sports."

"Sports." The expression on his face was thoughtful and she could see that he was beginning to see where she was taking him. It still amazed her that she'd written down sports. Her interest in watching other people toss balls around was almost nonexistent. But Edgar didn't need to know that.

"I don't know if you know this but I grew up in Harlem." Most colored people born in New York had grown up in Harlem. But Edgar was not originally from New York. "Born and raised. Just like Althea Gibson."

Edgar leaned forward, his eyes on her. Hettie thought she could see a hint of wonder and awe filling them. Edgar wasn't just interested in Althea Gibson, he was a fan. "Are you saying that you know Althea Gibson? Personally, I mean. Everyone knows Althea Gibson," he said slowly, watching her the same way Gayle had earlier, as though she were prey that may or may not be devoured, depending on which move she made next.

"Yes." Hettie nodded once, firmly. Yes, she did know Althea Gibson. Fortunately or unfortunately. "And if you keep me on, I can get a scoop on Althea that no other reporter has managed to get." Hettie had no clue what that would look like or entail—it wasn't as though she'd had time to do any research—but Althea was famous. Surely there must be something about her that people wanted to know.

There was a long moment of silence as Edgar sat back in his chair, pondering her words.

"She's been giving Harmon the flux for years." Harmon was the official sports journalist at the double H. "And as much as I'd like to blame him, she is not an easy woman to deal with." He tugged on his chin. "If rumors are to be believed, she'll be back in New York by Saturday. She's competing at Forest Hills again this year. I'm not a praying man but Lord knows I hope this match goes better than the first." Edgar reached for a pile of papers and began shuffling things around. He paused, his eyes narrowing. "And you're sure you can get her to talk to you?"

"Mr. Edgar, Big—Althea will talk to me." Her words were

calm but her stomach was once again feeling unsettled as she sat there, selling her history with Althea as an advantage. It would not be an advantage. In fact, it would be a huge disadvantage. The years may have rolled by but Big Al's memory had been long when they were children. There was no reason to doubt its capabilities now.

"It's just that I thought your end goal was *The Crisis*? They don't even have a sports section." *The Crisis* was the official publication for the National Association for the Advancement of Colored People and it was far more widely read than where she currently worked. The staff that worked for *The Crisis* weren't your run-of-the-mill journalists. They were household names and widely respected writers—just like Hettie wanted to be. And she'd never hidden her ambitions from her boss. The double H was a mere stepping stone. But a stone that Hettie nevertheless needed if she was ever going to write something good enough to get the NAACP's attention.

"I still want to work at *The Crisis* and I think Althea Gibson will help me get there." Why else would she have mentioned Althea in the first place?

Edgar hummed, not in the least bit fooled. "It *would* be really bad if you applied for a job at *The Crisis* and had to explain how you got fired for writing a made-up story. If you had to explain how you nearly got a family killed with your thoughtless words. If you had to explain how—"

"Okay," Hettie said quickly, unwilling and unable to hear any more. She didn't have to take this. She didn't have to go this route. But she didn't leave. How could she, when leaving meant the end of everything she'd planned and dreamed of since as long as she could remember?

Edgar licked his thumb and turned a page from the pile

before him. It was settled now in his mind. Hettie would write on Althea Gibson. She only felt a little like vomiting. Reaching for the thin chain of her necklace, she tugged it lightly. "Connection or no connection, Althea is not a fan of Negro journalists. At all. She thinks we all write with an agenda." Edgar released a snort. "Of course, we do. But the short of it is, she won't entertain any interviews from the double H anymore. Harmon ticked her off one time too many. Nevertheless, Forest Hills is coming up and I do want something good."

"Forest Hills?" Hettie knew it was the wrong thing to say as soon as the words exited her mouth. Edgar paused and stared at her.

She scrambled for something, unwilling to admit that her knowledge of tennis was nonexistent. "She hasn't won Wimbledon yet." That was a tennis event, wasn't it? If Big Al had won that, she'd have remembered.

Edgar's eyes returned to the paper in front of him. "No." He paused. "She did win that French one this year. What's it called?" He asked the question lightly, his eyes resting on her as he tested her knowledge.

"Oh, um, uh . . ."

There was a knock on the door. Thank God for small favors. Although God was probably not thinking about her at the moment, what with all the trouble she'd caused in the past week, and here she sat steadily lying through her teeth. *I'll fix it, Lord*, she promised. How? She didn't know. But she rather liked to stand before her maker with peace in her heart. "Come in."

Edgar lowered the paper he was reviewing as Gayle informed him of a phone call he needed to make in ten minutes. Hettie leaned forward slightly, trying to catch sight of the words on the page and feeling like a child copying another student's test in school.

When Gayle left, closing the door behind her, Hettie said, "Roland-Garros."

"Huh?"

"She won Roland-Garros on May 26th of this year."

"Yes," Edgar said, pleased. "She can win. She's just not consistent, except for in the ATA." Hettie nodded even though she had no clue what any of his words meant. There was so much she needed to learn and quickly. "You're going to have to convince Althea to let you in. I don't want you just reporting her stats. Our readers want to know the human side of her. I want to know how she feels when she loses. I want to know who she's dating and planning to marry. I want to know if her parents are proud of her. I want to know if she expects to win big next year and how. And you're my ticket in because you're both girls." *Women*, Hettie corrected in her mind. They were both women, although she had no idea what being the same gender had anything to do with anything. "And, of course, the pair of you know each other."

Hettie blinked once, long and slow.

"It would be an absolute boon if that woman changed her thinking and you were there to capture it all." Hettie frowned. Edgar saw it. And mistook it as Hettie having working knowledge of the situation. "It's a whole mess, is what it is. But you need to be there if she starts singing a different tune."

What was this man talking about? Her mind was filled with questions but she could not ask a single one of them unless she wanted to reveal her ignorance.

"Put together a proposal for me on Monday, with Althea and tennis being the focus. If you do a good job, we can discuss your future."

"What does that mean? Do a good job?" Hettie had lived long enough to know that all vague terms in a contract should be defined clearly.

"I want you to turn the tide in Althea's favor. Negro journalists don't like Althea much and it shows in their writing. That means that folks who have never gotten to see her play think poorly of her. Change the way things are going. Help her see that she's got a role in fixing this. I am, admittedly, a huge fan."

In other words, he wanted her to have a hand in creating the story—the very thing she'd done in Montgomery. Hettie brought a tired hand to her face.

"If you get Althea on the same page with everybody else, all of your past mistakes will be forgiven. Just completely wiped under a rug. Understand?"

Not having a single word left in her, Hettie dipped her head in acknowledgment, rose to her feet, and left Edgar's office. She released a long exhalation after closing the door behind her.

"Not so bad, huh?" Gayle whispered, smiling as though she'd known Edgar would give Hettie a second chance.

Hettie eyed the other woman warily, unwilling to say anything she didn't want getting around. "Thank you for watching my bag."

Hettie grabbed her things and once again entered the space where her co-workers were gathered, waiting. She ignored the more pointed looks. "Tilly?"

"Yes, ma'am?" The young college assistant she shared with two other journalists rose to her feet with a notebook in hand.

"Where's Harmon?"

"At a baseball game."

"Please leave a message for him on my behalf. When he gets in, I need him to call me. I'll see you on Monday."

Without speaking to another person in the room, Hettie left the double H. She should feel more solid now, more settled. No, she did not want to write about tennis and Althea Gibson, but she still had a job and if she did it well, there was an opportunity to switch back to writing on national news. But she did not feel better. As she stepped into the elevator that would return her to the ground floor, for the first time in her life, she found herself giving serious thought to quitting.

CHAPTER 3

Singles—a game played by two players

Upon leaving her office building, Hettie could have flagged down a taxi, but her bank account was not as full as she would have liked at the moment. Thus, she took the subway, standing the whole time even though she was fighting waves of exhaustion. It had been a very long day.

It was a slow trek she made down the three blocks to the three-story, brown-brick apartment building where she'd been living for the past six years. Inside, she marched up the stairs until she reached the third-floor landing. She didn't have to wonder if her roommates were home, because Frankie Lymon was inside singing loudly about fools falling in love. There was no point in knocking to give a warning. Hettie unlocked the door and entered the small living room, which held a weathered but clean couch, two armchairs, a coffee table, and two lampstands. Debbie and Faye were in the small kitchen belting out lyrics, both of them slightly off-key.

Faye caught sight of her first and jumped back from the stove where she was stirring something that made Hettie's stomach growl with hunger. "Jeepers creepers, Hettie!"

Debbie turned around in her chair. "Hettie!"

"I sent you a telegram," Hettie said pointedly as she closed the door behind her.

"So, you did. I still didn't expect you here today."

"You've returned in one piece, I see." Over the years, Hettie had lived with a number of girls. Some, she'd been very glad to see the back of. Others, she still very much missed. But now, she was content with Debbie, a no-nonsense nurse who could be counted on for paying her portion of the rent on time. Eager beaver that she was, everything she did was planned in great detail and if Debbie was involved, all your t's were crossed and your i's dotted. Faye was a waitress at a local restaurant and moonlighted as a dancer in a local club. She was a tall, pretty girl with legs so long they sometimes put Hettie in mind of a flamingo. Faye was the brightness and energy of the place; the one most likely to hang up a painting or add a new plant.

Hettie dropped her bag at her feet and motioned toward herself. "All in one piece." Except she wasn't. But she'd had enough of thinking deeply. Entering the kitchen, Hettie took a seat at the table next to Debbie and removed her hat as Faye reached over and turned off the radio.

"Oh, that's lovely. A gift from Miz Celestine?"

Anything Hettie wore that was of the latest fashion was a gift from Miz Celestine, or Miz Ce-Ce as Hettie called her. "Of course. How've you been?"

"Just fine. Thanks for keeping up with your portion of the bills even though you weren't here," Debbie said. Before her were a pile of letters that she was in the process of responding to. "I've put your mail on your bed."

"Thanks, Deb."

"I'd invite you to eat but today is pasta day." Faye's look was bemused as she returned to whatever she was cooking in the pot. From what Hettie could smell, it was some kind of chicken soup and probably the reason why both of her roommates were wearing shorts. The heat from the stove was just a bit too much and Hettie began unbuttoning her suit jacket.

"I've been gone so long I don't know if pasta day is still in place." There was something about returning home and being in the company of people who had no expectations of you. Hettie was beginning to feel a bit more energy coursing through her.

"It's still in place," Debbie said bluntly before leveling an amused look at Hettie. "Mr. Pasta has called twice to ensure that you reach out to him once you return."

Hettie felt a reluctant grin cross her face. "Has he?"

"Mr. Steak also called—this very week—looking for you," Faye offered.

This week? Hettie's eyes grew wide with understanding as her gaze drifted to the calendar they had hanging next to the refrigerator. So, it had reached that date already? "How about Mr. Seafood?"

"I think he called a few weeks back." Faye reached for the notebook where they kept their messages.

"Mr. Fried Rice did not call but he did ask for an address to reach you."

"He sent me flowers on my birthday," Hettie said, sounding

smug as she rose to her feet. "Maybe I do feel like pasta tonight."

"Oh, Hettie, how you keep these men on a chain like you do is beyond me," Debbie muttered as she signed one of the letters with a flourish.

"Well, none of them are serious, are they?" Faye asked, already knowing the answer. "It's easy to have male friendships that go nowhere. It's the ones you want to take places that are hard."

Ignoring their conversation, Hettie crossed the room to where the telephone hung on the wall. Sticking her finger in one of the loops, she carefully dialed a number that she'd memorized long ago. "Hello, Eileen? This is Hettie Carlin. Is Howard in? If so, please tell him I've returned home and I'd love to meet him for dinner if he's available."

In no way had Hettie set out to have an address book specifically filled with men's names. What had started out as a simple dinner date between two friends had blossomed into something that—when she was tired—felt alarmingly like a second job.

Several years ago, she'd met Dr. Howard Greeley at a Christmas event that the journalists of the double H had been invited to attend. They'd gotten along so well that when he asked her out for pasta on a Thursday evening, it somehow turned into a regular event. Howard, a fresh widower who had no interest in remarrying, had introduced her to Reuben. Reuben, a rather successful loan officer in his late forties who was several times divorced and paying more alimony than a small country collected in taxes, claimed he had no desire to ever tie the parson's knot again. Yet, he still enjoyed an evening out with a woman and good seafood. It was through Reuben that she had met Tony. Tony had no interest in marriage with a woman whatsoever, but as a local politician, he occasionally needed to be seen with a date. They always ate at his favorite Chinese restaurant. These men were her standing dates, meeting with her every Monday, Tuesday, and Thursday evening. Through them she had met others who had come and gone, filling her Friday and Saturday spots. As it stood, her Saturdays were currently open and available, as Owen, a dentist, had recently moved to Iowa. But her Fridays did appear to still be booked, which Hettie was somewhat relieved to discover.

As it was Thursday and Howard was free, albeit for an early dinner, Hettie changed into a black and white checkered swing dress—another hand-me-down from Miz Ce-Ce—and met her old friend inside his favorite Italian restaurant just outside of Sugar Hill.

"Hester!" Howard was the only person Hettie knew who insisted on calling her by her legal name. With his high yellow skin color and his calm and gentle ways, he put Hettie in mind of a bear. Winnie-the-Pooh bear to be exact, but she'd never say such a thing out loud. A distinguished man, Howard would not appreciate the comparison. In his late fifties, he held a little weight around his middle, but was tall and quite striking. Salt and pepper were sprinkled throughout his short-cut hair and light beard. Rising to his feet from their favorite booth, Howard leaned down and kissed first Hettie's right cheek and then her left. So upper class, so European. Hettie loved it.

"Howard, so wonderful to see you!" Hettie found herself smiling the first genuine smile to cross her face that day. It was always nice to see Howard.

"You've lost weight, dear."

"All the walking. We don't take buses in Montgomery,"

Hettie said lightly and then wished she hadn't said it at all. She didn't want to think of Montgomery tonight.

"Sit, my dear, and tell me all about it. That young reverend . . . what's his name? The one named after the Reformation fellow?"

"Martin Luther King Jr.?" One day she'd be able to say his name without wincing. Today was not that day. She could barely look Howard in the eye as she slid into her seat.

"Yes, that one. I'm very interested to see how this plays out." Howard's words exited his mouth slowly. Like her father, Howard believed that change would come to America only when Negroes showed that they could accomplish the same things as whites, and thus earn their right to be treated civilly and equally. Purposefully angering the majority was not an idea that they thought was wise. And thus, Dr. King was making a lot of people—Negro and white—mad.

"Welcome back, Miss Carlin." It was their waiter, Joseph. Ready for a distraction, Hettie ordered the special Joseph recommended, while Howard stuck with his tried-and-true chicken parmesan.

"I called but I honestly didn't expect you back so soon." Howard was beaming at her from across the table. Debbie and Faye often wondered what it was that Hettie got out of these dinners, besides free food, since she was not chasing after a wedding ring. Hettie had no one specific answer for them. Howard, Reuben, Tony, and even Owen were men who moved in different circles than Hettie and more often than not had their finger on the pulse of whatever was happening behind the scenes in America. On more than one occasion she'd gotten a hot tip after one of her dates. But, it was more than that.

"Life has a way of changing things. How are your children?"

"Same as always." Howard's children were in their twenties

and thirties, and while they did not particularly like Hettie, they had slowly come around to the fact that neither Howard nor Hettie had any intentions of making her their stepmother. "Michael is getting married."

"Oh my! Tell me all about it." That was all Howard needed to hear.

Over a salad and pasta, Hettie listened very intently to Howard as he walked her through the most recent tests and trials of his family members. Usually, Hettie would speak more, adding her two cents to the conversation, but the long day was catching up with her. She said very little as she cleaned her plate and waited patiently for dessert.

"I did tell Louisa that she should give some thought to signing up my granddaughter for tennis but she said—"

"Do you watch tennis, Howard?" Hettie interrupted as the thoughts in her mind shifted quickly.

But Howard didn't seem bothered by the subject change. "Do I? I follow it religiously. I played it in college, you know."

"I did not know. Do you follow Althea Gibson's career?"

Howard made a face, before reaching for the cup of coffee that he'd requested so he could drink it with cake. "Who doesn't?"

"What was that look for? I heard she won the French thing so she must be a good tennis player." Hettie did remember seeing Althea's name splashed across the papers six years ago. She remembered half-heartedly listening to a sports broadcast when Althea played in some tournament that had America up in arms. If she recalled correctly, Althea lost and then Hettie hadn't paid much attention to anything else she did.

Howard grinned as he gave his cup a stir. "The French thing? Yes, she won at Roland-Garros. She is good, but not terribly consistent, except when she plays in the ATA."

Hettie leveled a finger at Howard. "That is nearly word for word what Mr. Edgar told me today and I didn't understand a thing he was saying."

"Then shall I explain it to you, my dear?"

"Would you please?" Hettie leaned forward as Howard moved their silverware to the side and set between them his coffee cup and a glass of water.

"Like everything in this country, there are two tennis organizations. There is the United States Lawn Tennis Association or the USLTA." Howard tapped his glass of water. "This is the tennis association for white people. Then there is the American Tennis Association." He touched the rim of his coffee cup. "This association is for Negroes. Although white people have played in our tournaments before, we are simply locked out of theirs. For the most part. There have been a few exceptions, for certain specific tournaments and certain specific players. Althea Gibson is one of them."

Hettie sat back in her seat, thinking. "She's good, isn't she?" That had to be an understatement. Althea must be a fabulous tennis player to have broken the color barrier. Hettie reluctantly smiled. That Big Al had risen to the top of a sport was not surprising at all.

"Oh, yes. Marvelous to watch, Hester. I've been fortunate enough to see her play a number of times. I have also seen her lose." Howard's mouth tightened a bit. "She's a bit . . . uncouth," he said stiffly. The thing about the people who lived in the fancy three-storied homes in Sugar Hill was that they really were in a different class than the rest of the Negroes in Harlem. But at the end of the day, they were just as colored. Class didn't matter as much when your future was tied to the shoe-polish boy down the street.

"She's still a bit rough around the edges?"

"To be fair to Miss Gibson, she gets better every year," Howard said tiredly. "But it's hard to countenance someone like her representing the Negro race. Oh, don't look at me like that, Hester. Tennis is a dignified sport. One should carry themselves . . . properly. Even Jackie Robinson knew how to behave and he played baseball. Althea comes to practice wearing blue jeans." Miz Ce-Ce also shuddered when she saw women wearing blue jeans outside the home. "It's the uniform of rebels," she whispered every time.

But there it was again, hidden in Althea's lack of class and wardrobe: that sense and belief that Negroes must act a certain way to obtain certain results. Life was already so exhausting. Hettie thanked God every day that that was not a burden she felt she had to bear. For a second, her heart went out to Althea. "She must be doing it well if she plays overseas and in the white people league."

Howard rolled his eyes. "The USLTA," he corrected pointedly. "She is . . . passable. It's just that I wish it were someone else standing in her place. You don't know Althea." Oh, but she did. "Anyway, Althea has been the one to beat in women's tennis with the ATA but not in the USLTA."

"Why do you think that is?" Hettie asked, genuinely curious.

Howard reached for his cup of coffee and took a long sip. "Experience. It all comes down to experience. The more she plays with the USLTA, the better she'll become. But it's hard to get through those doors, Hester. They don't mind the occasional Negro at Forest Hills. They enjoy watching the best of the best play every now and then. But they don't want our kind at their clubhouses, using their facilities, and learning the best tactics for how the game is played. It's like they think the brown will rub off," Howard muttered, a look of deep irritation lining his face. "It's hard for a Negro girl to play under those conditions. And then, when she does get a chance, she's playing on foreign ground and before a crowd that mostly hates her." Howard hummed, meeting her gaze. "Now, you almost have me feeling sorry for her."

Howard said no more as the waiter arrived with slices of chocolate cake for the pair of them. Oh, but Hettie had missed this while she was away. When the waiter left, Hettie spoke: "What if I said I had been assigned to write on her?"

Howard's eyes flashed for a second. "Well, that's an entirely different matter altogether. Why would Edgar ask you to write about tennis?"

Hettie took a small bite of her cake. "I grew up with Althea," she admitted after a long second. "Although I have not spoken to her since I was about thirteen." It had been nearly sixteen years since the two of them had breathed the same air. Quite frankly, not enough time had passed to Hettie's thinking. She didn't have to do this. The thought flashed through her mind. She didn't have to return to the trenches. She could always walk away from the very thing she'd spent most of her life building toward. "Mr. Edgar is hoping that I can . . ." What was Edgar hoping for exactly? What had he said? Something about Negro journalists not liking Althea? Now all of a sudden, Hettie wanted to know why. That seemed very odd. She looked at Howard. It couldn't just be because Althea was a little rough around the edges. "He's hoping I can write pieces on Althea that contribute to making her universally liked."

Howard delicately cut into his cake. "I wish you the best of luck, my dear. You're absolutely going to need it."

CHAPTER 4

Fault—when a player serves in an erroneous manner

Hettie would have pushed Howard more on his cryptic statement, except that she caught sight of a familiar face wining and dining a pretty woman. It was enough to distract her. Besides, Howard wasn't going anywhere. She could follow up with him later.

With dinner eaten, Howard walked Hettie outside and flagged a taxi for her. When he started to give the driver her address, she interrupted, providing Miz Ce-Ce's address instead.

"Until next week, Hester." Hettie waved a hand and then the cab was off. She wasn't in it for long. Ten minutes later, Hettie was climbing up the stone steps that led to her grandmother's apartment. Miz Ce-Ce answered on the second knock.

Her grandmother—dressed in a pair of bright red slacks

and a black shirt—slowly eyeballed Hettie. Then, Miz Ce-Ce reached out and pinched at Hettie's waist. "Miz Ce-Ce!"

"You've gotten fat." With these kind words, her grandmother turned away from the door and stepped aside.

Releasing an annoyed sigh, Hettie entered the apartment, closing the door behind her. No one else could get away with saying something like that to Hettie, but she tried to have patience with the elderly. "Howard says I've *lost* weight."

Having lived in apartments all of her days, Hettie could say with absolute certainty that Miz Ce-Ce's apartment was tiny. And it didn't help that her grandmother was prone to clutter. The living room was overflowing with boxes and clothes and fabric and shoes. The woman collected the latest fashions like small children collected newly minted coins. Except she had no place to store them.

"Howard lies. If you can pinch an inch . . . I'm telling you that dress looked better on me when I wore it."

Her grandmother hated giving away her things but there were days when even Miz Ce-Ce felt overwhelmed by the sheer amount of clothing she'd amassed. Those days were some of the best of Hettie's life.

"I looked better than Dorothy Dandridge in that dress," Miz Ce-Ce murmured as she crossed the few feet of her living room and moved to stand in front of a mannequin. If she couldn't find what she wanted in the store, she was not opposed to purchasing cloth and designing her own creation. She appeared to be working on a mauve dress. "You look like one of those dumplings you like to eat: short and plump."

Well, this was beginning to be too much. Hettie reached for the top of the nearest box and lifted it. "Dorothy Dandridge is three shades lighter than you."

Miz Ce-Ce shot her an annoyed look. Hettie pretended

not to see it as she eyed a very smart-looking navy blue hat. "I wasn't talking about skin color."

"She's also three decades younger than you and she probably doesn't have to dye her hair to cover all the gray or hide her wrinkles behind thick plaster." It took her a bit longer to work up the nerve—this was her grandmother after all—but if Miz Ce-Ce wanted to start a fight, Hettie would darn well finish it.

Her grandmother dropped her hands from the mannequin's shoulder. "It's been months since I've seen you, but if you're in a nasty mood, you can just leave."

The thing was, at the ripe old age of sixty-five, her grandmother probably could give Dorothy Dandridge a run for her money. Celestine Murphy was a petite woman with the most perfect figure one could think of. All of her curves were still in the right places and she sported the tiniest of waists. Hettie had inherited her large eyes from her grandmother—eyes that made Hettie look like she was perpetually caught by surprise. The same eyes made Miz Ce-Ce look like an innocent, never-aging doll. Many a man still mistook Miz Ce-Ce for a woman twenty years younger.

Hettie returned the top of the hat box to where she'd found it. "Not trying to be nasty at all. Just making a comment. Can I have this?"

"Absolutely not! If I ever part with it—and I won't!—I'll give it to Rosa."

"What a waste. It'll rot in her closet." Hettie and her grandmother shared a knowing look. Hettie's mother's style was bland on top of bland on top of bland, with a little bit of the 1800s tossed in.

"Did you really go out looking like that?" Hettie looked down at her dress. She had taken out a few seams to make the dress easier to wear but Miz Ce-Ce was being ridiculous. "Not the dress. I'm talking about those dark circles under your eyes. You look exhausted."

"I put makeup on," Hettie said stiffly.

"It's not working. If it's that job of yours that has you looking old and ragged before you're thirty, you need to find something else to do. In all the years I've seen you dashing about with paper and pen, I've never once thought about how happy you looked while you did it. Here's some free advice: stop trying to anchor your life in something that's destroying you. I lived that way once; it nearly killed me. Now, I live for myself and I'm much happier."

Much happier than what? For all of her words, her grandmother never seemed to contain much joy. Hettie mentally batted away her words.

"You know what you should do? Get married." Hettie released a small grunt, refusing to voice the words that danced on her tongue. Miz Ce-Ce had been married five times and was currently single, so what was it that she was trying so hard to sell to Hettie? Hettie carefully stepped over a few boxes, continuing her perusal of the wares hidden within Miz Ce-Ce's couch. "I've changed my mind on Howard. He's old but he'd be a good husband because he'll be dead before you're forty and you'll have the rest of your life to spend his money."

There were two swift knocks on the front door that blessedly ended the conversation. "It's me, Mama."

Hettie moved quickly, nearly running to open the door for her uncle. "You," her uncle Morgan said bluntly as he caught sight of her. Morgan Jennings was a mere two years older than Hettie and had grown up more like a brother than an elder. He was the son of Miz Ce-Ce's third husband.

"Me."

Her uncle was the male version of his mother, which meant—in a word—that he was pretty. More than one of her roommates had lost their heart to her married uncle and so now Hettie didn't invite him over anymore. He had never met Debbie and Faye, and he never would. He was cantankerous and blunt—although charming when he wanted to be. Like most older brothers, he was not above sharing everything that was hers, but he didn't want to loan out a single thing that was his. He was Hettie's favorite person in their family. He was the only person whose education had taken them past high school. He was the only person who understood why she worked so hard and so long, and where she was trying to go. He was the only person who never told her she should get married and instead cheered her on to greatness. Three times in the past two days she'd almost called him but then changed her mind. She couldn't handle it if he ever told her that she'd let him down. And so she'd bottled up her thoughts and feelings on the matter, as she did most things that happened in her life.

"You're home early, aren't you?" Morgan's eyes were narrow with suspicion and when she looked away, unable to meet them any longer, they turned into slits.

"Long story," she mumbled, with a wave of her hand. If he kept looking at her like that she might crack, and she refused to bare her heart with Miz Ce-Ce in the background.

Morgan huffed. He was not the type to ask, a fact that Hettie was immensely grateful for. "Well, then move out of the way," he said rudely, but he paused long enough to brush his shoulder against hers. Hettie closed the door as he greeted his mother.

"I did come here for a reason. Miz Ce-Ce, while I was out with Howard I thought I caught sight of Thurston on a date." There was no thought. Hettie had definitely seen her grandmother's current beau with another woman.

Morgan grimaced while his mother waved an airy hand. "I ended things with him ages ago." Hettie wouldn't be surprised if ages ago was last night. "I bet she wasn't nearly as pretty as I am."

Irritated by this topic of conversation, Morgan rubbed a hand across his face. "Are you two ready? I'm hungry."

"Ready for what?" Hettie asked, curious.

"Rosa invited us for dinner," her uncle told her.

"My mother?" Hettie brought a hand to her chest.

"Probably to celebrate your return. She knows you're back, right?" She did. Hettie had asked Debbie to call her mother and let her know she was coming home. But her mother had not once mentioned having her over for dinner. Typical. If she'd returned to her apartment instead of coming here, she'd have been getting a phone call in about an hour demanding to know why she was late. Hettie pursed her lips. And here, she had already eaten. "Let's go."

"Where's Carol and the kids?" Hettie asked her uncle.

"Oh, someone has jokes!" And just like that she was brought up to speed on his family. Morgan's marriage was not even close to a happy one but he was bound and determined to prove to his mother that he could stay married longer than she could. It wasn't necessarily a hard feat. Miz Ce-Ce's longest marriage had lasted seven years. Hettie had been blessed with a great many men to call grandpa.

Within five minutes, the three of them had left Miz Ce-Ce's apartment and walked two blocks down to the apartment of Oral and Rosa Carlin. While Miz Ce-Ce knocked, Hettie took a step back so that she was shoulder to shoulder with Morgan. "I just love it when Mama throws a party and doesn't tell me about it."

"Your problem is that when it comes to this family, your expectations are here." Morgan raised his hand high. "When your expectations should be here." He dropped his hand to his waist. "Just take it as it is. She missed you."

The door opened and Hettie got a brief glimpse of her mother as she waved Miz Ce-Ce into the house. The two women got to chatting as though they didn't see each other at least every other day.

Several years ago, Hettie had come to the conclusion that her mother was bored out of her mind. Boredom was not a sentiment that Rosa Carlin would ever express aloud, but Hettie knew her mother woke each day with nothing to do. Miz Ce-Ce, at least, had the fashion world and the constant flow of men in her life to keep things interesting. But Rosa only had her husband and the hope that Hettie would one day get married and produce children. Unfortunately, the woman was being greatly let down on both fronts.

"Are we allowed in the house?" Morgan asked pointedly. Miz Ce-Ce shot her son an unamused look before disappearing inside the apartment. Morgan entered next and Hettie followed slowly behind.

Starting down the hallway, Hettie paused in front of a new cross-stitch hanging on the wall. *The Lord gave and the Lord hath taken away; blessed be the name of the Lord*. "Was there nothing cheerier?"

"Just because you don't like what's written in the Bible doesn't mean you can change it." And there stood Rosa Carlin, Morgan and Miz Ce-Ce having slipped away. Hettie's mother was the result of a dalliance between a maid and the son of her white employer. It was still hard for Hettie to believe that Celestine Murphy had started her life on a rundown plantation, cleaning and taking care of white folks, but she had. It did not surprise Hettie that Ce-Ce had had an affair with a white man. When it came to romance, Miz Ce-Ce did not discriminate.

In her youth, Rosa had greatly resembled the actress Fredi Washington. So fair was she that, had she wanted, she could have passed for white. But that was not Rosa's goal in life. Having been raised by the young and flighty Celestine, her mother's objective was to rebel against everything that put her in mind of Celestine. That meant that she had looked for a man who was stable and set in his ways. And when she'd met Oral Carlin, who was fifteen years her senior, she'd settled down faster than you could blink. She'd raised Hettie in the church, never allowing her to miss a Sunday service, a Bible study, or a choir rehearsal. And she'd allowed herself to age to match her husband's years. Rosa Carlin's hair was lined with gray. It was rarely styled, as she was keen to wear it pulled up in a bun like some woman from the turn of the century. Her dresses and skirts were long. She didn't dare reveal an ankle. And when her eyesight started going bad, she'd purchased thick bottle-cap-like glasses. When she stood next to Miz Ce-Ce, most people assumed she was the parent.

"If you could change what's in the Bible I guess that'd make you God and not Him." If there was one thing her mother lacked, it was a distinct sense of humor.

"I'm not trying to start an argument, Mama. It was just a comment."

Her mama's frown deepened and Hettie knew she was trying to decide how to respond. To give Rosa credit, she tried to understand Hettie. And Hettie tried to understand

Rosa. But they were always two ships passing in the night. Her mama sighed, giving up on the matter. "Come and eat. Food's getting cold. And say hi to your pa."

Rosa stepped away as Hettie entered the living room where her father was sitting in his favorite armchair, listening to the radio.

"Hey, Papa." Dad might be becoming the more fashionable term but her father—who had been raised in Georgia—preferred Papa.

"You're back." If there was one thing Hettie loved about her father, it was his voice. It was deep and raspy, putting Hettie in mind of a bullfrog trying to sing at night. But it was also slow and sticky, like molasses making its way down the side of a tree. She could be in the middle of a crowd on Fifth Avenue and if she heard his voice, she'd find him. Her father pushed himself up to his feet. He was not a large man. His frame was slender and he leaned toward thinness. He was also a few inches shorter than her mama but you never could tell because his quiet presence was so loud.

Her father took a step toward her. Oral Carlin's skin was dark and weathered by the sun. He had spent half of his life outside laboring over cotton before one day deciding he didn't want to do it anymore. He'd moved to New York, met her mama, and the rest was history. Nevertheless, those hard times of his younger years still lined his face and his character. He was not a soft man, her father, and he rarely had a gentle or kind word. Life for him had been filled with one disappointment after another. For instance, he'd been mightily disappointed when her mama had brought forth no more children, leaving him only with Hettie.

"Yes, sir."

"You was respectful?"

"Yes, sir." Hettie was not quite a mix of her parents. For one, she was shorter than the pair of them. For two, her skin color was nowhere near as light as her mother's but neither was it the rich, coffee color of her father. It was some other shade of brown that could be described as caramel or cinnamon or toffee, depending on the time of year and her proximity to the sun.

"Didn't cause no trouble, did you?"

It was all relative, wasn't it? "No, sir."

"Dinner's ready," her mama called from the kitchen. Her father laid one weathered hand on her shoulder. That was it. That was all the affection she was going to get from the man. It still didn't stop that tug in her heart that longed for just a bit more. She wanted something else from him, something else from her mother. More. Miserable comforters were they all.

But one day they'd realize that she was worth more than the grandchildren they wanted from her. One day they'd realize that she was worth her weight in gold all by herself. And just like that she was settled. She couldn't quit now. She'd sacrificed her younger years, working day and night so she could pay for college. She'd practically lived at the double H when she'd first got hired, editing and fact-checking and running errands and being everything to everybody just so someone would remember her and give her a chance.

She'd learn this game of tennis and she'd write those articles on Althea Gibson. Matter of fact, she'd do better than that. She'd change Althea however she needed to change. Slowly but surely, Hettie would once again be on top of her game.

CHAPTER 5

Passing shot—when the tennis ball is hit forcefully so that it passes by the opponent without them being able to hit it

At the kitchen table, Hettie sat before a plate filled to the brim with food she had no intention of eating. She loved a good meal and her mother was a good cook but even Hettie's stomach had its limits. She'd just have to pack up this plate and take it home with her.

"That bus boycott business isn't over yet, is it?" Morgan asked. He sat directly across from her. On his right was Miz Ce-Ce.

On Hettie's right and Morgan's left was her father, who sat at one end of the table. Opposite Oral Carlin was Rosa.

"No. The bus boycott isn't over." Next to Hettie, her father released a grunt of disapproval. Was he disapproving of the bus boycott itself or of her leaving early? Knowing her father, it was probably a little bit of both.

Hearing Oral, Morgan continued, "The days of living the Booker T. Washington life are over." Technically, her father and Morgan were brothers-in-law. But because her father was so much older than Morgan, the relationship was more akin to uncle and nephew. "We've been trying it since slavery ended and nothing has changed. Segregation was supposed to have ended two years ago with *Brown v. Board*. Being polite and nice does not work. White folks ain't gonna change unless you get in their face and make them."

Hettie's father released another grunt of disapproval, even though his eyes never left his plate.

"The only way things will change is if we burn the whole system down." It was the smallest of things that made them angry. Hettie and Morgan had not been raised in the South, where they were taken advantage of on a daily basis and forced to walk with their heads hung low every time they left the house. No, they had been raised in a colored neighborhood surrounded by people who looked and thought like them. But invisible lines ran through New York, clear as day. Take the subway this far and no further. Shop here but not there. Eat at this restaurant but never darken the doors of that one. Films were white. Beauty was white. Higher education was white. The bus drivers that drove around their city blocks were white. The police officers that patrolled their neighborhoods were white. And yet, according to the news, the only people who ever committed crimes were brown. Small slights and silent noes had formed a deep and abiding rage.

Oral dropped his fork and the silverware clanged loudly against his glass plate. Everyone at the kitchen table sat up. "Brave words from a Negro living in New York." As Oral Carlin rarely spoke at dinner, he'd just said a lot. And he wasn't finished. "I don't see you going down there to share your words of wisdom. If you want to start the fire, you better be willing to burn."

Hettie might not completely agree with her father's way of thinking, but he was not an easy man to argue with. He'd *lived* segregation. He'd seen men lynched for the slightest of offenses. He knew folks who had disappeared into the night never to be seen again. For him, New York was a sort of promised land. Across the table, Morgan was struggling with what to say next.

Hettie jumped when she felt a kick. "Change the subject," Miz Ce-Ce mouthed at her before sliding a perturbed look at her son.

Last time Hettie checked, Miz Ce-Ce's vocal cords worked just as well as hers. Nevertheless, she pushed the sweet potatoes around her plate for a second before saying, "I've been assigned to the sports beat."

"What?" Morgan's mouth dropped open. Thankfully, there was no food in there.

"You don't watch or listen to sports," her mama said helpfully. But there was a hint of relief in that statement. Everybody had wanted to talk and think about something other than what was happening in the South. "You didn't even play much when you were younger."

"Like baseball? Will you get to meet Jackie Robinson?" Miz Ce-Ce asked, her eyes wide with excitement. Miz Ce-Ce followed sports just like Hettie—which meant her knowledge was limited to famous athletes only.

"Jackie Robinson retired," Morgan said flatly, still plainly hurt over the matter.

"I'd still meet him if I could," his mother countered.

Morgan dipped his head in agreement. "Very valid point."

"Not baseball," Hettie said, interrupting their side conversation. "Tennis. I've been assigned to write on Althea Gibson." Across the table, Morgan released a strangled sound. Hettie couldn't tell if he was amused or horrified.

"Who?" Rosa asked, her brow furrowed in confusion.

"The woman tennis player." Morgan was laughing but then he sobered. "Sports?" His eyes searched Hettie's face. He knew something very bad had happened if Hettie was now writing on sports.

"Didn't you go to school with an Althea Gibson?" Her mama was pointing a fork in her direction and still harboring the same confused look.

"It's the same girl," Hettie and Morgan said together.

"You watch tennis?" Miz Ce-Ce asked her son. They'd grown up with baseball, football, and boxing in the background. Maybe they'd even hear about the occasional basketball game. But never tennis.

"Yes," he said smugly. "I have been to an ATA tournament. I have a professional job, you know." Morgan was a paralegal at a law firm. If he'd been invited to a tennis match it was probably because his boss couldn't go. "I even prefer women's tennis to men's tennis, because at least with women's tennis other things bounce besides the ball."

"Morgan." The three women at the table groaned.

"Such a vulgar boy," Miz Ce-Ce muttered aloud, as though she hadn't raised him.

Morgan grinned, always happy to offend. "But nothing bounces with Althea. That woman is flat, no matter what angle you watch her from."

"Morgan, hush." Rosa glared at her sibling. Then she looked at Hettie. "Althea always did like sports, didn't she?"

"On any given day she'd be outside in the street throwing a ball around." Baseball, basketball, football, Althea had loved anything that required physical exertion and winning. Apparently, she still did.

"Like a boy," Miz Ce-Ce added.

"Throwing a ball around doesn't make you a boy," Hettie said, trying to make herself sound patient.

"Tomboy," Miz Ce-Ce corrected, as though that made things better.

"It was worse than that," Morgan declared. "I went to the same school as Bubba."

"Who's Bubba?" Hettie asked Morgan.

"Althea's brother. He said her dad used to take her on the roof of their apartment building and make her box. He said they'd throw real punches at each other." Everyone at the table stared at him. "I'm serious. He wanted Althea to be a woman boxer."

At this comment, her father released a snort.

"Bubba said Mr. Gibson started training her when she was about twelve and the fights could get real bad. Mr. Gibson didn't treat her any different from a boy. He'd punch her and everything. Bubba said the fights only stopped when she knocked Mr. Gibson clear across a room a few years later."

The kitchen table went silent as they all quietly wrestled with this information. Good gracious, Hettie thought, as she stabbed a macaroni noodle. She'd heard rumors but she'd dismissed them as tall tales. "Now, that just sounds like—"

"Hush," Miz Ce-Ce said, cutting Hettie off. "Don't start commenting on other folks' problems." It was statements like these that always reminded Hettie that no matter how much her grandmother pretended, she was a woman of a certain generation. "That's none of our business."

"I just remember her always running the streets," Rosa murmured, looking a bit lost in her memories. "She never seemed to be at home. One time I had to stay late at the shop and I saw Althea on the subway, settled in and asleep." Rosa paused. "I remember she called the police on her pa. That happened right before we moved."

Oral released a small huff of disapproval. Calling the police was right up there with willingly inviting a viper into your home. But, if anything, that told Hettie just how bad the situation must have been. Sometimes, like now, she was grateful for a father who was mostly uninterested in her. Hettie would not trade Oral Carlin with Mr. Gibson for anything.

"The question is how did she even get into tennis?" Miz Ce-Ce asked. "That's a wealthy man's sport."

"I know the answer to this one," Hettie told her family. "Remember 143rd Street used to be closed off? There was a paddle tennis . . . court set up in the middle of the street. Althea would play every day. She got noticed by someone who had a country club membership. They invited her to play there and she wowed them." She'd scared them too. Hettie knew, because she'd also been there that time Althea had been invited into that fascinating world of money and class.

"Did she not go to school?" Miz Ce-Ce asked.

Hettie shrugged. "When we were at the same school, she missed more than she came."

"She was trouble," her mama interjected. "Too much idle time. She was always starting fights and always forgetting to behave like a lady."

"Did she ever try to fight you?" Morgan asked Hettie, a smirk dancing on the edges of his mouth. He knew Hettie.

Throwing a punch was not even on the list of things that would ever cross her mind—even if someone did try to get physical with her.

Hettie frowned in his direction. "She wasn't unnecessarily violent. We grew up in a rough neighborhood," she reminded her family, since they seemed to have forgotten. "You had to know how to take care of yourself or you'd be run over." She wasn't sure why she was defending Althea but it was the truth. Althea only fought fights if the other person had started something. Or if you paid her, but that was another story for another time. Althea had not roamed the streets like a lion seeking whom she could devour.

"From what I can tell, she is a good tennis player. I've seen her picture on magazine covers. It's too bad she's not prettier," Miz Ce-Ce offered.

Hettie brought a hand to her forehead. Was she well and truly related to each person at this table?

"I heard she'll be back in town tomorrow," Morgan said offhandedly. "Her boyfriend who's not her boyfriend is picking her up from the airport. When are you supposed to meet her?"

"Huh?" Hettie dropped her hand.

"Will Darben told me the other day. You know I'm part of that veterans group." Her uncle had been drafted to the army in the Second World War. The only time he ever talked about his experience was when he'd had one too many drinks and needed help getting home. It was always Hettie he called when such an occasion occurred. "Will was army. He's now an engineer and he's thick as thieves with Althea. He's always talking about her when he gets a chance. He picks her up from the airport all the time when she returns from one of her tennis trips."

Hettie leaned forward. "Morgan, you are my favorite uncle." In the back of her mind, she'd been wondering how and when she could meet Althea. Now, she knew. "Would you please do me the favor of calling Will Darben for me?"

"Get me tickets to one of her games and I'll believe you."

"Done," she said, not sure how she was going to make that happen but also sure she could.

"I'll call him tonight."

CHAPTER 6

Serve—a shot by the server, intended to start a point

Will Darben was a handsome man, tall, and—Hettie could tell almost immediately—mild-mannered. How interesting that Althea was drawn to such a man, but it sort of made sense if you subscribed to the opposites-attract theory. "Morgan said you've known Althea a long time?"

"Oh, we go way back," Hettie said, releasing a sound that was supposed to be a laugh but sounded a bit strangled to her way of thinking. "Way, way back." She was sitting in the passenger seat of Will's Packard and they were on their way to Idlewild to pick up Althea.

"She's going to be so happy to see an old friend," Will said, a smile on his face as he looked forward to surprising his girlfriend.

Hettie felt an instant rush of guilt. If Althea remembered her, she doubted this was going to be a happy surprise. But, this had not been her idea, she told herself. It had been his. Hettie had been standing right there when Morgan had called Will and asked if he could set up a time for his niece and Althea to reconnect. It had been Will's idea to bring Hettie to the airport with him the following morning.

"She's been gone so much this year. I'm sure she's always longing for a familiar face."

"Her family didn't want to come to meet her?"

A cloud drew over Will's face. "They love each other, you know. But they're not that close."

From the way his body seemed to hunch over the wheel in front of him, he clearly did not want to talk about the matter but Hettie was a journalist. It was her job to talk about it. "I believe she has three sisters and one brother?"

"Yep." Will nodded, close-mouthed. "That's right."

Hettie waited but he said no more. No wonder Althea liked him. "How long has she been gone?"

Will's face brightened again. "For this trip? Barely a month but altogether, nearly a year. The State Department called her right around Christmas of last year and asked her to play tennis on a goodwill tour in Southeast Asia." He lowered his voice. "Probably on account of Emmett Till."

"Too much bad press for America?" Hettie asked, understanding immediately. As always, her heart ached at the mention of the young boy who had been brutally murdered in Mississippi.

"Yes. They want to show their allies how not racist America is." Will glanced over at her and they shared a look. "Althea figures as much too. But it was a good opportunity so she jumped at the chance. It was only supposed to be a six-week tour. She played in Burma, India, and Pakistan," he said proudly. "And did really well too. But when it was over, rather than come home, she went to Europe. She played in Sweden, Germany, and France. Oh, and she went to Africa—Egypt! She loved seeing the pyramids." Who knew tennis could take you around the world? Hettie had never really given it much thought before but she was thinking now. Althea very well might not be the same person that she once knew. "She won that tournament in France."

"Roland-Garros," Hettie rattled off. She'd never forget that name.

"Yep. It was probably the clay." Hettie blinked. What was this man talking about? "Wimbledon's surface is grass, and Althea's foundation ain't grass. I think that's why she's struggling. Of course, Wimbledon is just plain not easy to win. I talked to her briefly after her loss and she was real down in the dumps about it. She even did an interview I know she wishes she could take back. Here." Stopping at a red light, Will reached back and snagged a book. He dropped it in Hettie's lap. "I save all of her articles. It's one of the last few." What a gold mine! Hettie had been planning to do some digging herself next week, but this was perfect. "I know she wanted to play in Europe real bad but I think maybe she should have skipped the London tournament. I was there."

"You were at Wimbledon?"

"Yep," Will said proudly. "I couldn't stay for the whole thing, though."

"You're a very good boyfriend, Mr. Darben."

Next to her, Will Darben squirmed. "Will's fine, Hettie. And I'm not her boyfriend," he said stiffly.

Hettie's eyes lifted off the book in front of her. Will's gaze was a bit flinty. She could be wrong, but she was pretty certain she could smell blood in the water.

"We're just friends. Very good friends." His grip on the steering wheel tightened and the muscle in his jaw ticked.

Oh, Hettie had questions. But she was already probably pushing things a bit. She'd leave Will Darben alone for now. Hettie began flipping the laminated pages of the book in front of her and stopped at one of the last few articles. This one was courtesy of the *Daily Mail.*

After ten years of it, I am still a poor Negress, as poor as when I was picked off the back streets of Harlem . . . I have no apartment or even a room of my own anywhere in America . . .

It was, as a whole, a startling display of vulnerability. The Althea she'd known would never have said so much to a stranger. Hettie flipped to the following article. This one had been written by the *Sunday Graphic.*

Shame on Centre Court . . . I accuse the Wimbledon crowd of showing bias against Miss Gibson. I say it was this bias that helped to rob Miss Gibson of a quarter-final round victory.

Hettie went on to read quite the interesting take on racism from the British point of view. But if half of what the man said was true—and it probably was—Hettie could only begin to imagine the weight that rested on Althea's shoulders. She carefully closed the handmade book of articles. She'd sort of begun to figure it out but now she knew—Althea was fighting more than tennis battles out here.

Above the car, a plane seemed to fly dangerously low to the ground. They had reached Idlewild.

Hettie read no more as the car followed the circuitous lanes of the airport to a large parking lot. Will Darben parked the car, fetched a lovely bouquet of flowers out of his trunk, and together they entered the airport to wait for Althea's plane to arrive.

Hettie had never flown before. To get where she needed to go, the train had always been more than sufficient so she found the quiet busyness to be fascinating. It was either think of that or all of the many ways that this reunion might go south. Either way, time went quickly and before Hettie knew it, she and Will were watching Althea's plane slowly pull up to the gate. Hettie made the wise decision to step back and let Will be the first person that Althea saw when she set foot on solid ground.

And that is why the first time that Hettie saw Althea in sixteen years, there was a smile on her face. She looked the same, Hettie thought, as the long-limbed Althea Gibson rushed over to hug her friend—who was not a boyfriend. She was taller than the last time Hettie had seen her and there still wasn't much meat on her bones. She was wearing a long skirt and a warm forest green sweater but moved as though all the fabric was in her way. Her hair was short and curly, a dark cap on her head. Some people managed to keep the face they'd been given as children and Althea was one of them. To Hettie, time had changed little.

"I say, Will, I think this is a bit too much," Althea said, speaking rapidly as she took the flowers from Will. Despite her words, Hettie could see that she was pleased. When she turned slightly, Hettie saw that she had two tennis rackets crisscrossed over her back. Hettie could only guess that she didn't want to subject them to baggage claim. "What am I going to do with these and where will I put them?"

"In your room at Mom's. Sydney wanted to come with me to pick you up but he had to work."

"Oh, that's fine. I'll meet up with Syd tomorrow. We've got much to discuss, him and me. Let's hurry to collect my bags. I'm ready to eat. I could inhale a cheeseburger right about now but I won't."

"You've settled on playing at Forest Hills?"

"Now, what kind of question is that, Will?" Barely giving him a second glance, Althea started moving, her long legs eating up space.

"Wait a minute, Al. I didn't come alone." At his words, Althea Gibson stopped and turned, her eyes quickly scanning the area around her before stopping on Hettie. It was most likely because Hettie was the only other colored person within her vicinity. "It's your friend. The one you had from when you were a girl."

Althea's eyes squinted and her brow furrowed. Her head tilted to the side as she tried to place Hettie. Hettie took several steps forward, until less than a foot separated her from her old classmate. "Hey, Big Al. It's been a minute, but it hasn't been that long."

Hettie saw the exact moment that Althea remembered her and she wondered if the memory that flashed through Althea's mind was of the first time that they'd ever really talked to each other.

Hettie and Althea may have attended the same elementary school starting from the age of five, but they had never spent time with each other because neither had any interest in doing so. Althea was more inclined to play with boys than to sit in the shade during recess and gossip like Hettie. Althea was the child unafraid to speak her mind to the teacher, even if it meant she had to take a public licking every week. Hettie was spanked once in school and once had been more than enough, thank you very much. She'd followed every rule laid down and hadn't cared to spend time around others who might drag her along in their troubles.

Like two magnets repelling each other, they managed to have little to do with one another until Hettie came into contact with a girl named Sue Ann. For reasons that were still unfathomable to Hettie, Sue Ann decided that she didn't like Hettie but, rather than say anything, she'd gotten physical. She would trip Hettie if they were standing next to each other. Hettie's response was to make sure that they never stood next to each other again. Then, Sue Ann shoved Hettie in the hallway for no good reason. So, Hettie made sure to never linger there. But when she pushed Hettie off a bike so that Hettie returned home with skinned, bloody knees and scraped hands, Oral Carlin had had a problem with it.

It was Hettie's hope that her father would make a trip down to the school and say a few scathing words to her bully. But that wasn't Oral's way. Instead, he'd told her she better not ever come back to his house looking like she'd lost a fight. It was the first time, but not the last time, that she'd realized that her father might not be the sharpest knife in the drawer.

Her mama was no help, telling her to avoid the girl. Morgan told her he didn't hit little girls, which Hettie hadn't believed for one second 'cause he sure didn't have any issues with pushing her around if he thought she was in the way.

And then one day on the playground, Hettie saw it: Althea Gibson, who was not very tall at the time, punched a much bigger girl in a class a whole grade level above them, just once, and that girl hit the ground, out cold. That was enough for Hettie. Hettie spent the next few weeks saving pennies until one day she approached Althea.

"Big Al," she'd called her that day because the name had seemed fitting. "I'd like to pay you for your services." Like Hettie, Althea spent her spare time collecting empty soda bottles just to shore up enough money to rent a bicycle for a few hours or to go to the theater or buy a hot dog. Money was precious and they both knew it. They made a plan. Althea would get paid if she knocked Sue Ann flat on her back and told Sue Ann to leave Hettie well enough alone. Althea did her one better: she hit Sue Ann so hard that her dark green pinafore dress flew up over her head, showing off her yellow underwear. That was when Hettie had stepped in. She fanned the story into flames until people were certain Sue Ann's underwear had been yellow because she peed herself in fear. To this day, Hettie didn't know if the girl transferred schools or just disappeared in the crowd, but she never heard of or came across Sue Ann again.

After that, Hettie and Althea were sort of friends—until that other incident happened a year later. Hettie hoped it wasn't that incident that ran through Althea's mind. But she knew it probably was when Althea took a step back, the bouquet of flowers in her hand now looking a bit like an unwieldy football. "Somebody call the ambulance. If Hettie Jo Carlin is in my face, there's trouble to be had. Girl, whatever reason you're here the answer is no."

CHAPTER 7

Double fault—two missed serves in a row, resulting in the server losing a point

"I wasn't sure you'd remember me."

Althea levelled the flowers at her. "I've been hit in the head with more than a few balls in my life but it'd take a whole tank division to knock you out of my memory. Will, what do you mean bringing this one by?"

Before Will could say anything, Hettie answered, "Will's friends with my uncle. I asked him if I could meet with you."

Althea was shaking her head. "I don't even want to know why." She turned on her heels, headed for the baggage claim. For every one step she took, Hettie took two.

Feeling a bit like a bird hopping along the sidewalk, Hettie said quickly, "I don't know if you know this, but I write articles for a living."

"Oh, Lord," Althea muttered. Hettie was tempted, oh so tempted, to say something just as rude back but she needed Althea to be on her side. As though reading her mind, Althea turned her head and side-eyed Hettie, a smirk on her face.

"I want to write on you."

"I should be so honored."

"You should be, I'm a very good writer." Her firm statement was slightly ruined as she ran into someone's luggage cart. "Sorry, excuse me," Hettie said politely before running to catch up with Althea.

"You've been surrounded by all these male journalists. Wouldn't it be nice to have a female journalist following your career? You know, woman to woman?"

"How long did it take you to think of that one? I hope it didn't bother your little brain too much 'cause it wasn't worth the effort." Althea hopped onto an escalator going down and Hettie leaped for the step above her.

"You know that if I'm doing it, then the job is being done well. I'm good at what I do, Althea."

"You still talking to me? Where's Will?"

Hettie turned around briefly to see Will dodging a group of people several yards behind them. "Don't be mad at Will—it's not his fault."

"How about you don't tell me what to do, Hettie Jo? Good gracious me. You're a journalist? Yep, that sounds about right. You just slither around gathering people's thoughts and making them yours, with your little lizard-like ways."

Hettie had heard far worse insults and dealt with far worse personalities. She liked to think that she had mastered the art of patience when it came to her job, but Althea's smugness was overriding every technique she'd ever learned.

Hettie wafted a hand under her nose. "Do you smell that, Althea? That's the smell of the malarkey you're trying to toss my way. I love how you're standing there, spraying yourself with the scent of eau de victimhood. At the end of the day, you're just poor Althea who was trounced and thrashed soundly by little Hettie Jo Carlin."

Althea did not turn around but with every word that exited her mouth, there was a thrust of the flowers. Several petals fell onto the metal stairwell leading down. "You ain't never in your God-given days trounced me."

"Oh . . . but I have. You've been mad at me for sixteen years, you sore loser." With those words, Hettie knew it was all over. She was going to mightily regret this an hour from now but Althea didn't get to stand there covered in self-righteousness while she threw mud at Hettie. No, if mud was about to be flung around, then they were both going to get dirty.

Althea hopped off the escalator and politely waited for Hettie to do the same before turning around. "You're a low-down dirty cheat, Hettie Jo."

The words were whispered. They weren't unaware of the fact that they were in public, surrounded by white folks. But it didn't matter how hushed Althea was speaking. It didn't matter that Hettie saw a flicker of doubt in Althea's eyes—after all these years, Althea wasn't certain the label of cheater fit. Still, the words packed a punch. They still left Hettie feeling like someone had imprinted their fist into her side. Well. If Hettie was going to be in pain, then those around her were going to bleed. "Or maybe you're just not as great as you think you are."

She saw her words hit true as the bouquet in Althea's hand nearly bent in half. "I think that this conversation is over." It was a warning and a testament to Althea's maturity. If they had been years younger, Hettie would have been knocked clean through the doors on her right.

Hettie raised her hands in surrender, even though she knew her eyes were hot with rage. "I'm leaving. But you should consider the fact that you need me. For all my lizard-like ways, I can turn the tide of public opinion in your favor and it sounds to me like you need it." She had not done her research yet but that did not mean that she wasn't picking up on the general undercurrents that flowed from Althea's tennis career.

Althea's smile was wide, toothy, and very unfriendly. "Whatever I need, it's not you, little girl. If you're still standing there begging me to work with you, then it must be the other way around. You must need me."

"I do," Hettie said bluntly, lowering her hands. "I need you to get ahead and we both know what I'm like when I need to win a thing." Althea's face twitched, the anger in her bones morphing slightly into reluctant amusement. That was the thing about Althea: she was never angry for long. She burned hot in the moment and then she burned out. Hettie, on the other hand, could burn quietly for years. But for this matter, Hettie doused her own candle. Althea had her reasons for not liking Hettie. And Hettie didn't like Althea. There was no sense in making it bigger than what it was.

"Althea!" Hettie looked up to see Will waving from the top of the escalator.

"He's a sweetheart. Very polite and soft-spoken. He probably doesn't anger easily and he forgives quickly."

"You got all of that from a car ride?" Althea's voice was flat as she stared down at her nearly destroyed flowers before glancing at Hettie. Hettie's response was a grin. Althea sighed. Deeply. "I don't do journalists, Hettie. I don't like them all up in my business and I really don't want *you* digging through my life and spinning fancy tales."

"Is your life really that . . . interesting?" Althea played tennis. She wasn't Marilyn Monroe.

Althea's eyes once again took on that flinty look. "See, this right here is why I'd never be able to work with you."

"Because I see straight through your nonsense?" No longer in the mood to go head to head, Hettie waved a hand, brushing away the question. "People who don't do journalists usually have a reason." The words were said gently. She began to back up slowly. Althea wasn't going to change her mind today . . . if ever. Hettie was going to have to get creative in some kind of way. "But if a journalist is even interested in you, then you don't have much of a choice. If you allowed me to spend some time with you and write about what you hope to do and accomplish, at least you'd have some say in the matter." Some, not all.

The look in Althea's eyes said that she was not convinced—just as Hettie had expected. "Tell Will I'll take a taxi back. Welcome home, Althea Gibson."

Friday nights were also known as steak nights, which meant that when Hettie was in town, she had a standing date with Lewis. Hettie didn't know whether that was his first name or his last. Lewis was the only man in her personal phone book whose entry was mostly blank.

Hettie had met Lewis six months ago and she still had almost no knowledge of his background. She did not know where he worked or what he did for a living. She did not know where he went to church or who his parents were. She did not know how old he was or the kind of company he kept. What she did know was that he had popped out of nowhere one Thursday evening after Howard had had to leave for an emergency surgery.

Lewis had slid into the booth in the seat directly across from her and made her a proposition of sorts. Having, apparently, frequented all of the same restaurants that Howard, Reuben, Owen, and Tony liked to visit, he'd seen her on her weekly dates and somehow put two and two together and decided that going out to eat with men was her job. She'd never bothered to correct him.

This was not how Hettie typically moved about things. It was in her to want to know as much about a person as possible but there was something about knowing so little about this man that strangely appealed to her. With Lewis, there were no expectations on either end. He asked her no questions, and she asked him none. She merely spent her Fridays inhaling steak as he cried into his filet over his wife, who had left him for his accountant. It had been a small price to pay, since she was getting a free meal in a restaurant that she could only afford on special occasions.

"The divorce is final." They were the first words Lewis said as Hettie slid into what was known as 'their' booth in the darkened steakhouse.

At first, she could not believe she was spending a couple hours a week listening to a man lament the loss of his marriage. On more than one occasion, she'd considered canceling their agreement but every time Friday rolled around, she showed up—and in style.

With Howard, Reuben, and Tony, Hettie always dressed well for their evenings out. With Lewis, she dressed up. Maybe it had to do with the fact that the first time they'd met, he'd flatly admitted that his confidence was taking an absolute beating and, feeling more than a little sorry for him, she'd made a greater effort. Maybe it was because after their fourth 'date' she'd begun to notice that Lewis was tall and slender and gifted with the most beautiful golden eyes that were always shadowed by thin, round glasses. Maybe it was because somewhere around their tenth 'date' she'd started wanting this beautiful man to stop thinking about the woman behind him and look at the one in front of him.

That afternoon, after leaving the airport and feeling more than a little despondent about how her meeting with Althea had gone, she'd decided to look forward to her date with Lewis. She even put up with a couple of hours of Miz Ce-Ce and her 'words of wisdom' just so she could borrow the long, black, extravagant quarter-sleeve velour gown that had a slit that ran up her thigh. The dress was set low, revealing the very swells of her bosom. And Lewis noticed it not at all.

"Today was the day that, with one stroke of a pen, some man with authority just completely wiped out a whole family." Hettie's hair was perfectly coiffed. Her ears were sparkling with faux diamonds. Her lips were bright red and Lewis was thirty seconds from tearing up.

And he just might cry. He had done so before. The first time tears had slid down his unshaven cheeks, she'd sat in her seat, uneasy. Men did not cry in her family. Oral Carlin would sooner fling himself off a cliff than be caught with moisture in his eyes. Hettie had once seen Morgan swipe at a tear but that was only after she'd come collect him from a bar where he'd drunk one glass too many and was lost somewhere in the horrors of war. They'd both pretended the next day that such a thing had never happened.

Yet, here sat this grown man who was willing to cry—more than once—over his love for a woman. Perhaps it was because they were strangers that he was so free. Perhaps in his day-to-day life, no one ever saw him cry. All Hettie knew was that she'd never, in all of her natural-born days, come across a man who seemed to love a woman as much as he did.

She'd missed him when she was away. After she'd received that telegram from Edgar, the only thing that had brought her any measure of peace was that at least she'd see him again. Hettie reached for the glass of water in front of her. Gripping it tightly against the palm of her hand, she came to the sudden realization that she'd fallen absolutely, unequivocally in love with the man sitting in front of her.

CHAPTER 8

Love—zero points

Across the table, Lewis sniffed once and then reached a hand up to pinch the bridge of his nose under his glasses. After a long moment, he cleared his throat. When he opened his eyes, Hettie knew there would be no tears today. "The part that absolutely gets me is how she completely handed over full custody of our daughter."

Hettie could see by the candlelight that he had not shaved. She wondered how he was sleeping. She was curious as to whether this steak was the first meal he'd be eating today. But she wasn't about to ask.

"I would not have given it to her," he said in such a firm way that she knew it was true. He often made declarative statements like this that led Hettie to think that whatever career he was in, he held a position of power. "That . . . fool doesn't get to walk away with both my wife and daughter. But I expected a fight. I had come to peace with the fact that I might lose my summers with Hyacinth Arabella, but no. Laverne didn't offer one word of protest. It's as if she's done with anything I might have touched. Except for my money. She did want alimony." Lewis started to sneer but then it was as if his face could not hold such an expression and Hettie watched a wave of sadness overtake him. He shoved a hand under his glasses so he could cover his eyes. He always tried to hold on to anger, but inevitably hurt won in these battles. Hettie clasped her hands together in her lap to keep from reaching across the table to comfort him.

"How am I going to explain to Hyacinth that her mama has decided to move clear across the country?" Lewis neither expected nor wanted an answer to his question. All of his questions were rhetorical. She was there to provide a listening ear as his world crumbled around him.

A waiter appeared. Hettie pointed to one of the steaks on the menu and held up two fingers. The waiter patiently took the silent order she placed for her and Lewis while Lewis stared dejectedly at the table. When the waiter left, he leaned forward, his bright eyes on her. "Do you want to know what the worst part of it all is? My mama has to move in." Lewis sat back, folding his arms over his chest as though daring her to make some kind of judgmental comment. "I left a whole state to get away from that woman. I picked New York because I knew she hated it up here. And now, she's moving in for a few months so Hyacinth has someone else in the house who loves her. Jesus be a fence." He reached for his glass of water and chugged it.

It was Hettie's turn to look down at the table. She sort of loved it when he made these wide-eyed confessions. Like when he'd told her that his wife had accused him of being boring and he'd admitted that he'd wanted to get married in part so he could be boring. He was not built like a wind-up toy, always ready to entertain, thank you very much. Or when he'd shyly confessed that he hadn't realized that having a child changed a woman on the inside too. But after his mama had given him a scolding, hadn't he straightened up? Or that time that he'd explained that Laverne was his high-school sweetheart and the only girl he'd ever kissed, and he would have been perfectly happy if she was the last woman he'd kissed so why couldn't she be happy? He reminded her of a Siamese cat Hettie's neighbor had once owned. Proud and lonely, daring you to try and stroke its fur and yet, wanting deeply to be petted.

"I'll never marry again," he said after a long moment. "I loved Laverne with everything in me. Did I make mistakes? Of course. I'm not perfect. No man is." Lewis jabbed a finger into the table. "But I did everything I knew to do to make her happy. I put a roof over that woman's head. And food on the table. We have maids," he said, stressing the s. Hettie had long since suspected that Lewis lived in one of those fancy mansions on Sugar Hill where Howard lived and Reuben resided. It was the neighborhood that held the homes of W. E. B. Du Bois and Duke Ellington. "Laverne didn't have to lift a finger. I'd have hired a cook if she had wanted me to. She didn't want any more children after we had Hyacinth and even though I wanted more, I told her I was all done too. I compromised when needed. And I only ever gave her the best. If she wanted a car, I bought it. If she wanted her hair done at that fancy overpriced shop every week, I paid for it. If she wanted to spend all day roaming around that expensive Marshall Field's, I arranged for a nanny."

"I doubt she . . ." Hettie paused, forgetting for a moment that she was not supposed to comment.

Lewis flicked his gaze to hers. Every now and then, when she got a real good glimpse of his golden eyes, she thought maybe comparing him to a house cat was the wrong analogy. Maybe something more predatory lurked there. She had that thought now as she had his complete and undivided attention for the first time that evening. "You doubt what?"

She began very slowly, very hesitantly. "I don't know of any colored women who would spend the day walking around Marshall Field's. They only recently let Negroes out of the basement and onto the first floor. It's much better to order what you want from a catalog and have it sent to your house."

Her words made his jaw tighten and his lips thin as he came to some sort of conclusion. "I suppose those were the times when she was meeting whatever-his-name-is," he hissed even though they both knew he knew what his name was. The accountant had been a very good friend of Lewis. Hettie had learned this at a previous crying session. Then his nose curled up as though he smelled something bad. "You still buy clothes from a store that made you shop in the basement?"

It was the first time—apart from their initial meeting—that he'd ever asked a question he expected her to answer. And she felt herself wiggling a bit underneath his stare. "I'm not saying I shop at any of those large department stores." She did if the price was good. Hettie had long since made peace with the fact that she was a cheapskate. "But . . . I mean . . . it's life, isn't it? We regularly give money to people who hate us because that is how the system is set up . . . which is why the bus boycotts are so fascinating."

Now, why had she brought that up? Lewis started to respond but the waiter appeared with a shrimp appetizer, momentarily cutting him off.

"When you speak of boycotts in the plural, you are

referencing the one in Louisiana a few years back and the one currently going on today?"

She knew it. He was a man who kept abreast of things. "Yes. Although I'm aware that technically, colored people have boycotted businesses for years, but these situations are different."

"They are," he commented as he reached for a shrimp on the plate before them. Was he for the bus boycotts or against them? She very much wanted to know his opinion, except that she didn't want to think about Montgomery at all right now. She could say nothing more and let the conversation drop. But she sort of had his attention. She didn't want to lose it. Her mind reached, grasping at something, and the question that came out was: "Do you watch sports?"

Lewis paused in his reach for a second shrimp. He drew his hand back, his eyes narrowing with suspicion. Was she crossing a line, asking such a question? Were questions about sports interest considered personal? Very slowly, he said, "I watch sports."

"Did my question offend you?" Theirs was a somewhat honest relationship, wasn't it? "All men watch sports so of course you watch sports?"

Lewis blinked once, long and slow. "No. That was not what I was thinking at all. Did you have a question about sports in particular?"

"Do you watch tennis?" With his passing acquaintance with Howard, his perfectly tailored clothing, the gray Bentley she'd once seen him drive up in, and his occasional reference to things that cost large sums of money, Hettie assumed that if he watched sports, tennis was probably on his radar. She wouldn't be surprised if he played golf too.

Lewis nodded slowly, his eyes searching her face. "Yes. My wife and I—"

His gaze dropped to the table, and his lips pressed together tightly as his thoughts returned to his ex-wife. This, Hettie would not allow. "What are your thoughts on Althea Gibson?"

Lewis looked up. "She's the best tennis player I've ever seen." The words were said solemnly, seriously. Morgan would never make such a comment without qualifying that Althea was a woman. Lewis reached for a shrimp, distracted.

"Have you seen a lot of tennis players?"

"I watch the ATA circuit when I can." Thanks to Howard, she knew exactly what he was referencing.

"You don't watch the USLTA?"

"Only when Althea is playing. USLTA is not my idea of a fair fight. Why? Are you planning to listen to Forest Hills?"

"Listen to Forest Hills?" What was Forest Hills? Why did people keep bringing it up? Was it some kind of fancy tournament? Why would they only listen and not watch?

Eyeing her in that way of his, Lewis hummed. "You're new to tennis, aren't you?"

"Very."

"Forest Hills is America's Wimbledon. Those spectators are not the friendliest crowd of people to watch a game with. If I take any interest in what happens at Forest Hills, I listen to the game on the radio." He hummed. "Of course I did just get a television for Hyacinth. Maybe I will watch it this year."

"Forest Hills is America's Wimbledon," Hettie said, repeating to herself. "Roland-Garros is the French Wimbledon. And Wimbledon is Wimbledon."

Lewis's mouth twitched and Hettie was positive it was the first time that she'd ever really seen him amused. To think a woman had willingly walked away from this. He must have greater flaws than what he'd revealed, she told herself. "There's an Australian Wimbledon too. Why the sudden interest in tennis?"

He did not know what a loaded question he'd just asked. "We're honest with each other, aren't we?"

"Yes. Although I'm not sure why tennis requires such a question." With one finger, Lewis pushed the plate of appetizers an inch toward her. "I'll eat all of these if you don't take one."

Hettie took a shrimp. "What if I said I was a journalist?"

Hettie watched a slow stillness overtake Lewis. He looked down, he looked up, he looked to the side and then he looked at her. Then he sighed. "I suppose you could have aired my dirty laundry anytime in the past six months if you had wanted to."

"I'm not always the kindest person in the world but I like to think that I'm not cruel," she said gently. "Besides, I don't know what you do or why anyone would care about the details of your divorce."

Lewis's eyebrows rose but she knew, in that instant, he was reassured. "All right. You're a journalist."

"And let's say I was recently assigned to write on sports—tennis and Althea Gibson in particular."

Without taking his eyes off of her, Lewis reached into his suit jacket and pulled out a small notebook and pen. "Hypothetically speaking, what paper do you work for?"

"Why?" Hettie asked as he flipped a few pages and uncapped his pen.

"I would like to make sure that I unsubscribe from this paper when I get home."

"What? That's not fair!" He grinned—actually revealed white teeth—before replacing his notebook and pen. Hettie couldn't help but smile, even as she defended herself. "I'm not writing the article tomorrow. Naturally, I've got to take some time to understand the game. I'm going to spend this weekend learning it all." She had some very serious plans with the library.

Their conversation was momentarily interrupted with the

arrival of their steaks. "You're going to learn all of tennis in a weekend? In case you were wondering, I took a class when I was in college."

"A class?" Hettie paused in cutting.

"Tennis has its own language." Lewis shrugged. "But maybe you can learn it in a weekend."

"Why would you need a class?"

"To learn the history of tennis, the rules of the game, and the point system."

"It's not one, two, three, four, five points on the scoreboard?"

"Oh, no." Lewis shook his head. "It's love, fifteen, thirty, forty, game."

"Love?"

"Love means zero."

Hettie stared. "Why not just say zero?" Of course the sport was more complicated than it should be.

"Then there are sets. You have to win so many sets to win the match." Hettie released a huff of air. This was going to take her longer than a weekend.

"About Althea Gibson . . . from what I've gathered she seems a tad . . . controversial."

"In what way?" he asked, cutting into his steak. Hettie wasn't sure she'd ever seen him approach his meal with such enthusiasm. When men liked sports, they really liked sports.

"Well, for one, there seem to be class issues."

Lewis paused in what he was doing long enough to roll his eyes. "Class issues? Who told you that? Howard?"

"Yes."

Lewis waved a hand. "Maybe when she was younger. But she attended the school of Eaton and Johnson. She's fine."

"Eaton and Johnson?" Hettie's fingers twitched. Why hadn't she brought a notebook and pen?

Lewis shook his head and she wasn't sure if he was disappointed with her or the newspaper she wrote for. "Dr. Hubert Eaton and Dr. Robert Johnson are *the* two men to train with in the United States if you want to play tennis and you're a Negro. Althea trained with them. I know for a fact that a part of that training is etiquette. She's fine. There's no dinner table she could sit at where she'd be an embarrassment."

"It's a whole 'nother world, isn't it?"

"A rich man's world," he quipped as though he wasn't one of them. "It's expensive to play tennis and there are no financial benefits attached to it. I bet you your bottom dollar that Althea is poor as Job's turkey."

Hettie thought about that article she'd read earlier that day where Althea had revealed her poverty. "Why is it expensive?"

"Tennis lawns are not easily accessible. I've only seen them on college campuses and within country clubs. It's a traveling sport. You have to be able to move across the nation and possibly to other nations to play in competitions. You need coaching—any tennis player worth their salt still needs advice and encouragement—and coaches aren't free. And if you win, you don't win much monetarily. Why you?"

"I'm sorry?"

"What did you write before this new transition into the sports world?"

Hettie hesitated. "I wrote on current events . . . national events."

"You messed up," Lewis said bluntly as he leaned forward, making Hettie feel as though she were some kind of interesting specimen he'd come across under a microscope.

"I did." Two very simple words, but they made her chest ache.

"How?"

"How did you miss that your wife was cheating on you?"

It was the question she'd been wanting to ask for ages. She'd learned something over these dinners. Lewis was not just a smart man, but a detailed one.

Lewis's eyes flashed gold for a second. He lowered his silverware, sat back in his seat, folded his arms over his chest, and retreated within himself. She wanted to know who he was when he wasn't fixated on Laverne. She wanted to see him happy. She wanted to hear his laughter. She didn't want to be another person who hurt him. But while he might be able to easily air his private matters before a stranger, Hettie couldn't. The love she had for him was safe and contained. In no way did she feel vulnerable. In no way could he disappoint her if they kept everything the way it was. "Forget the question."

"I knew almost immediately when the affair started. I know Laverne. I could tell. There had been some distance between us for a while but I knew the moment I was being replaced." The words were said softly. "I thought that I would ignore it and she would . . . move past it . . . and all would return to normal. We've known each other for just over twenty years. Of course, she'd get bored with me." His voice was low, barely discernible. "I'm not the most exciting fella around. But we have a six-year-old . . . I was willing to wait. I thought—"

"I was covering the Montgomery bus boycott." The words slipped out. She'd think about why later. "That's where I've been the past few months." Lewis had been staring off to the side but his eyes slid in her direction. "I blundered in a big way. So big, Reverend King sent a letter to my office."

"The young reverend?"

"Yes."

"The one who's in all the papers? The Dr. Reverend Martin Luther King Jr.? That one?"

"Yes."

Lewis gaped, horrified. Hettie felt her stomach flip. She lowered her fork. She'd lost her appetite. "That's embarrassing." He was whispering.

"Yes. I know."

"Really embarrassing."

"I'm aware."

"Almost more embarrassing than my wife leaving me for Morton Smalls."

Yes. "Not that embarrassing."

"I'm embarrassed just sitting in this booth with you." Hettie lowered her elbows onto the surface of the table and covered her face with her hands. He was going to make her cry. "But you must be good at what you do. You weren't fired. I would have fired you."

Hettie dropped her hands. "Are you always this honest with people you barely know?"

"Always. Just ask my . . ." There was a giant pause. They stared at each other. "I feel like I know what you could say but I'd appreciate it if you didn't."

"Can't handle it?" The laugh she released was a bit shaky.

"No." Lewis reached into his suit jacket once again. "Listen, I have to cancel for next week. I don't want to cancel, since this is starting to become very interesting, but Mama is arriving next Friday and I have to meet her train."

"Oh." She was disappointed. Massively disappointed. But she said nothing as he pulled out a thin silver case. Flipping open the case, he removed a card.

"It's best to learn tennis as you play the game. If it doesn't all come together this weekend, I'll be at my country club next week with Hyacinth. It's the last week before school starts. She said she wanted to ride horses, so that's what we're doing." Lewis slid the card across the table. "We can play an introductory game if you like."

Hettie clutched his card with both hands. She did not play sports. She probably would not go to his country club. But she recognized the offer for what it was. "Thank you."

"You're welcome. I'll give the front desk your name so they'll know to expect you and put you on my tab." While Lewis returned the case to his pocket, Hettie read the card. Lewis was not his first name. He was S. A. Lewis of Lewis Sporting Goods. In tiny letters were the words *founder* and *owner*.

Hettie gasped. "I know this store!"

"Do you?" Lewis raised a hand, signaling their waiter.

"I have younger cousins. Every birthday, every Christmas, I buy them something from there. You're Lewis of Lewis." She was talking too quickly but she couldn't believe who she was sitting across from. Lewis Sporting Goods had several locations scattered not just throughout New York but also in New Jersey and Pennsylvania. He owned a chain.

Lewis grinned, a quick, tired thing. "Yes." That explained the look she'd gotten when she'd asked if he liked sports. "And you're going to keep my personal business under wraps, just like I'm not going to spill the beans on your dustup in the South."

"Agreed. Which country club?"

"Shady Rest." Hettie felt her eyes go wide. "Where Althea beats all the colored players in the ATA and the same one she's probably practicing at right now."

CHAPTER 9

Rally—when players hit the ball back and forth to each other over a net

On Saturday, Hettie did as she told Lewis she would and spent the day at the library studying tennis. She spent hours brushing up on the history of the game, the rules, and the past few winners of the USLTA, ATA, and international tournaments.

But she realized something after hours of memorizing terms. It was one thing to know what an ace was, it was probably another thing to actually see and recognize one. She probably *should* go to Shady Rest. Not only would she get to play a game of tennis, she'd also be able to see tennis played. And hopefully by Althea.

Their first meeting after sixteen years had been a disaster. Hettie had lost her cool as she'd known she probably would and Althea was still as stubborn now as she was years ago.

Somehow Hettie was going to have to convince Althea to allow her access and opportunity to write about her. A hard thing to do when this woman already knew all of Hettie's tricks. Tricks Hettie had finessed, but tricks all the same.

Hettie flipped the card in her hand. And then there was Lewis. It wasn't as if she hadn't occasionally done more than just dinner with her dates. Howard, Reuben, Owen, and Tony sometimes needed a date for a party. Hettie always went when asked because it was her chance to meet new people and see how the other half of society lived. But this invitation from Lewis had her apprehensive.

"The ink is gonna come off, what with the way you keep fiddling with that card." It was Sunday morning and Hettie was supposed to be getting ready for church. She'd started. Her dress was ironed and laid out on her bed. She'd showered. But her hair was in rollers and she was still enshrouded in her robe. She flipped Lewis's card in her hand.

"Faye." Her roommate was at the stove, babying her oatmeal. "I've got a problem." Like her, Faye was in the process of getting ready for Sunday services but she was a bit further along, since she was dressed.

"Well, go on and let me hear it. Maybe I can help."

"What does one wear to a country club? White, right?"

"Which country club? There's that Cosmopolitan one on Convent Ave. I do believe it's on its last leg. Rumor has it the doors will be closing soon."

Hettie straightened. "The Cosmopolitan Tennis Club?"

"Yes! That's the one. Right here in Harlem. I never got a chance to go."

"I went. Once. When I was thirteen," Hettie admitted as she reached for her cup of coffee. She grimaced slightly as the cold liquid touched her lips. Just how long had she been sitting here daydreaming? "A girl from school invited me. Her parents were members." At thirteen, she hadn't known what to expect but it was that very visit that had shown Hettie that you didn't have to live in an apartment so small that you were bumping into someone every which way you turned. You didn't have to wear clothes that had been washed so many times the original color was something less than discernible. You didn't have to grow up with only one goal, and that was of securing a marriage and having children.

There was an entirely different world out there, a world Hettie had spent the past sixteen years trying to be a part of and somehow still only remained on its fringes. At the end of the day, it was who you knew. She touched a finger to Lewis's card.

"Did you play tennis?"

"Huh? Oh, gosh no. But Althea did." She had been more than a little piqued that day when she'd glanced down from the stands to see long-limbed Big Al on the tennis court in blue jeans and a cotton shirt, when Hettie had worked so hard to look the right way. She'd had to beg Miz Ce-Ce to refashion one of her dresses. She'd even risked her mama's heavy hand with the hot comb to make sure her hair would be nice and straight. She remembered her head had still been tingling as Big Al had walked out on the court looking like something the cat had dragged in, amidst a sea of folks in blinding white. There had been murmuring and Hettie remembered her friend's mother's slight dismay at the sight of the young teen standing before the tennis net. And then Althea had played. It was probably the last time Hettie had seen Althea—until the other day.

"Althea? You mean Althea Gibson? The tennis player? She played there for years."

"How do you think she afforded a membership?" Hettie asked honestly. She'd have given anything to be a member back then.

"People probably took up a collection." Debbie entered the kitchen, dressed and ready for church. "They always do for special ones. What country club have you been invited to?"

"Shady Rest." Both women paused. There were a lot of people who had never even heard of Shady Rest . . . like Hettie's parents. It was a club for elite Negroes and the membership was selective. Most Negroes didn't even know people who had access to Shady Rest. But if you lived a certain lifestyle, eventually Shady Rest came up.

"Shady Rest," Faye repeated excitedly. She pointed to herself. "I've been there! For a date. There was a dance."

"How was it?" Debbie asked as she crossed the small kitchen to pour herself a cup of coffee.

"Billie Holiday sang. Langston Hughes was in the crowd. Adam Clayton Powell was there with his wife." Hettie hadn't even considered that she might see famous people at Shady Rest. "I wore the most gorgeous gown. Borrowed, of course. I went with . . . what was my date's name?"

"He was a member?" Hettie asked.

Faye shook her head. "No. His uncle's cousin's husband. . . something like that. I had a wonderful time. There's a fancy white house, a restaurant, a big golf . . . area. I think there were horses. What was his name?"

"How did you get an invitation to Shady Rest?" Debbie asked Hettie. "Howard?"

Faye stopped pondering her date's name and stared at Hettie. "Howard invited you to Shady Rest? For fun?"

Hettie leaned back as both women stared at her as though she were about to produce a wedding invitation. "Not Howard. My Friday date. And it's not exactly for fun."

"The steak fella?" Hettie hadn't shared much about Lewis with them.

"Yes."

"Are you trying to marry rich, Hettie?" Debbie asked as she leaned back against the counter. "I've always wondered, except things have never gone anywhere with any of your men."

"How old is the steak guy?" Faye interrupted. "And what's wrong with trying to marry rich? Better than marrying poor."

Hettie grinned. She loved when they talked as though it was actually an option. "I'm not trying to marry rich, although I'm not totally against the idea. I agree with Faye. Better to marry a man with some coin in his pocket so he's not dipping into yours."

"Oh, yes, I forgot. You want to be a part of the talented tenth," Debbie teased. "You want your own exceptionalism to open doors for you."

It was true—Hettie was a proud disciple of Du Bois. "Without even having been there, I bet you fifty whole dollars that more than half of the women who are members of Shady Rest received an offer of membership due to their own merits." That was one of the things she'd learned from her brief stint at the Cosmopolitan. Negro women did not need men to attain greatness and respect. They were a little bit freer than their white counterparts in that way. Of course, at some point, men always tried to step in and take over, but that was a different problem altogether. "To simply marry rich is not enough. I have to accomplish something." Like Althea. "One day I will walk through the doors of Shady Rest and they'll be happy that they're breathing the same air as Hettie Carlin."

Faye released a snort. "Hettie, that's why I love you. Does Mr. Steak know you're not looking for anything romantic? Men with membership to Shady Rest don't invite women there out of the kindness of their hearts."

Hettie picked up Lewis's card. "He did not invite me for romance." He was still far too stuck on Laverne for that. "Anyway, I need advice on clothing."

"What are you going for? Dinner? Dancing?"

"A game of tennis." Both women stared at her again. They knew Hettie well enough to know that running after a ball was not her idea of fun.

"So are you going because you want to see Shady Rest? Or because you're hoping for a romance with the man?" Debbie demanded.

"I'm going for work and to see Shady Rest. The man is . . . I'm not thinking about the man." Except that she did think about the man. Too much, really. What if the more she got to know him, the less she liked him? What if he didn't like her? Especially since she'd confessed to her massive blunder in Montgomery. Of course, he'd still given her this card. She flipped it once again.

Faye's voice broke through Hettie's musings. "Too bad you won't splurge on one of those cute tennis outfits." Faye took a seat at the kitchen table with her bowl of oatmeal. "I almost took up tennis just for the clothes. I would definitely wear light colors but I don't think you have to limit yourself to white. Do you have a flowy skirt? Put some shorts on underneath and I think you'll be fine."

"I have a tennis outfit," Debbie declared, a murderous expression crossing her face. "I only wore it once, before Doug broke things off. I paid a pretty penny for it. You can borrow it, Hettie, although it might be a bit long on you."

"Don't be so angry, Deb," Faye said, teasing. "Did you really want to be Debbie and Doug for the rest of your life?"

Hettie leaned forward, grateful. "Thanks, Debbie. I'll wear it and I'll love it and I'll hang your laundry for you as a thank you." Hettie stood up. At this rate, her parents were going to level some serious frowns of disapproval at her when she slipped into their pew.

"Is Mr. Steak picking you up?"

"We didn't settle on a day so, no. There's a train . . . right?" They all imagined Hettie, tired and sweaty with bouffant hair, as she trudged through the golf course to reach the doors of Shady Rest.

"Can't you just ask him to pick you up?" Debbie asked.

"I don't know about this man," Faye said seriously. "He doesn't sound like a serious contender at all."

"As I said, he did not invite me because he has romantic notions. His divorce was just finalized." Both women gasped. Of course divorce happened. But it was still more than a little bit shocking when it did. Except for when Miz Ce-Ce was a party.

"How old is he?" Faye's voice was hushed.

"Somewhere in his thirties."

"What's he do?" Debbie demanded.

"He owns a store." It was the simplest way to describe it.

"Is he ugly?" Faye asked flatly, confusion filling her gaze.

"Very attractive. He wears glasses," Hettie murmured as she motioned toward her own eyes. They knew how she felt about bookish types.

"Children?" Debbie's question was a bit forceful.

"One. A six-year-old."

"The mother might be a problem down the line," Faye said, concerned, as though Hettie and Lewis were a done deal.

"The mother is moving to California."

Faye and Debbie exchanged a look. "What's wrong with him?" Debbie finally asked. "What woman leaves all of that?"

"Did he cheat?" Faye whispered.

"He's been faithful since they were fourteen."

"Did he hit her?"

"I have no way of knowing but I'd say absolutely not."

"Is he like . . . Countee?"

Hettie paused. Countee Cullen was an extremely talented writer and poet. He was also the former husband of Du Bois's daughter. The marriage had lasted only months after Countee confessed to his wife that he was attracted to his own gender. "Of course not."

"Are you sure?"

"He's not like Countee. I would know." She would know. "In truth, he's not looking for a replacement for his wife because he loved her very deeply." Hettie felt her own heart pinch at her words. Oh, to be loved that sincerely.

Faye released a rush of air. "His thoughts on the situation don't really matter. If all you say is true, there's going to be a replacement. No woman with a brain in her head is going to let all of that walk around footloose and fancy-free."

"Something is wrong with him," Debbie announced flatly. "I'm convinced."

"Don't look a gift horse in the mouth," Faye said, disagreeing with their roommate. "You'd better go to Shady Rest and bag that man before someone else tries to get the jump on you. I highly recommend doing your hair beforehand. I'll roller-set it for you if you want."

It was like they'd heard nothing she'd said. "Let's talk later—I'm late." She fled the kitchen, refusing to answer any more questions about Lewis or consider why it bothered her that there was truth in Faye's words. Regardless of what he said now, Lewis would probably remarry. Was she okay with the thought that it might be with someone else?

CHAPTER 10

Deep—refers to a shot that lands near the opponent's baseline

Monday morning, Hettie entered the double H's office almost before the sun was up. She loved to work when it was quiet and there was little to no chance of the phone ringing to distract her. On the floor were several sections of desks. Hettie's was in the center and at the head of the section. As she crossed the floor, she chanced a glance down the hall. There was a light on under Edgar's closed door. His presence there did not surprise her in the least.

She'd spent hours over the weekend learning about tennis but that morning it was time to learn about Althea Gibson and what had already been written about her. By the time Tilly and most of the other staff arrived, Hettie had lost her suit jacket and had read through articles leading all the way back to 1950, when Althea had made her first debut at Forest Hills. Hettie understood now what an accomplishment that was. She knew now that the Forest Hills tournament was starting once again this Friday and Althea would be playing at it. She was not at all a favorite to win.

"Good morning, Miss Hettie."

"Tilly, how are you?" Hettie removed her reading glasses and lowered them onto her desk. "When you get a chance, I need you to pull some articles for me."

"Yes, ma'am," her assistant said as she took a seat at her desk, which was just in front and to the right of Hettie's. Tilly's desk faced Hettie's resident fact-checker's desk. He was not yet in. "I called Mr. Harmon as asked and left a message."

"Thank you, dear." Hettie reached into a drawer and pulled out a notebook and a pen. There was another thing she'd noticed after reading through old papers. Althea did have a problem with journalists. She was entirely too private, leaving room for people to make all kinds of speculations about her thoughts and concerns on a matter. And her thoughts—or lack thereof—on race were a concern. If these articles were to be believed, Althea had no opinion on being a Negro in America. Her skin color didn't matter at all. She had no words to offer about segregation or boycotts or lynchings. Althea was only concerned about tennis. Althea may not have known it but she was walking a fine line. Hettie knew in her knower that this was the problem that Edgar wanted her to fix.

"Miss Hettie?"

"Yes?" Hettie looked up from the few things she'd written.

"Mr. Harmon is on the line for you."

Hettie reached over, taking the receiver from Tilly. "Hello, Harmon."

"Hettie. I've already spoken to Edgar. He says you're taking

Althea from me." Harmon's voice was gruff but Hettie only heard mild irritation there. Ted Harmon had about twenty years on Hettie and he'd been at the double H well before Hettie had been hired. But even still, due to their different assignments, they hadn't interacted much.

"Just for a bit, Harmon. I will gladly return her when the time is up."

Harmon laughed. "Oh, that's funny. Listen, Forest Hills starts Friday and I'm not only going, I'm also writing on it, but I'll take you along and show you the ropes." Hettie lifted her eyes to the ceiling. She almost asked him if he'd run this by Edgar, but if this was the worst he'd do—having lost out to her—she would say nothing.

"All right. I appreciate it."

"Let's meet at the office Friday morning and catch the subway out there together. In the meantime, have you caught up on my recent stuff?"

"Yes."

"Here's a piece of advice: when Althea tells you to take a long walk off a short pier—and she will—call Syd Llewellyn. He always has something to say."

"Her coach?"

"That's the one. His number should be in my phone book on my desk. See you Friday." And then all Hettie heard was dial tone.

Hettie handed the receiver back to Tilly and then stood up. After stretching from side to side, she crossed the now busy workroom and made her way to Harmon's desk. The big black phone book was easy to find. She left a message for Althea's coach and returned to catching up on all the news articles she could find on her target.

Tuesday morning, Sydney Llewellyn called her back and

told her to meet him outside at the end of the block just before noon. "You can come inside, Mr. Llewellyn."

Their office did have a small conference room where she could shut out the noise and speak with him one-on-one.

"I'm working," the man said quickly. "But I didn't want this moment to pass by. I'll see you then."

And so that was how Hettie found herself standing on the street corner, waiting patiently for Althea's tennis coach, when a bright yellow taxicab slid up in front of her and honked its horn. A dark-skinned man waved at her through the window.

Hettie took a hesitant step forward. "Mr. Llewellyn?"

He nodded, said something that was slightly muffled but Hettie got the picture. He wanted her in the back seat. Having learned a long time ago that being a journalist was never boring, she opened the back door and slid right in. Syd Llewellyn took off before she could get comfortable.

"Hello, Hettie Carlin, I am Sydney Llewellyn," the man said as the car began to circle the block. "The one and only coach of Althea Gibson."

"Hello, Mr. Llewellyn."

"Syd is fine." Hettie detected a slight accent but decided against asking where he was from.

Reading and writing in a moving car gave Hettie a powerful headache, but some things had to be done. Slipping a pencil and her notebook out of her purse, she looked around the inside of the very tidy taxicab. There was a cross dangling from the front mirror and a Bible verse was taped neatly on the dashboard.

The blessing of the Lord, it maketh rich, and he addeth no sorrow with it.

As far as Bible verses went, it was a much happier one than her mama's current favorite. "Syd, how long have you known Althea Gibson?"

"You must be new." She could hear the teasing in his voice. Here was another person who spent time with Althea, who appeared to be lighthearted and easygoing. Perhaps it was a prerequisite.

"I am. Please have patience with me. Can I ask another question first, Syd? How did you get into tennis?"

"I'm Jamaican. I came to America to dance."

"Dance?"

"I've got the best footwork you'll ever see. Do you dance?"

"Occasionally. What kind of dancing did you do?"

"Tap dancing and I was so good, someone took a look at my footwork and thought, tennis is for him. I started taking lessons at the Cosmopolitan. Do you know that place?"

"I do."

"My first coach was Fred Johnson, same as Althea's. Not to take anything from Fred, but he doesn't know all that much about tennis." Hettie had come across Fred Johnson's name. She knew the man had worked at the Cosmopolitan for years, coaching different tennis players. "Fred knows only one way to play tennis. That kind of playing will have you losing each and every time."

"Did you compete much yourself?"

"A little but I'll be honest with you, Hettie, because the Bible does tell us that he who deals truly is the Lord's delight. I wasn't nothing special out there on the field. But just because I couldn't play doesn't mean I didn't know what needed to be done. You understand?"

"Yes, sir."

"I have a theory called the 'Theory of Correct Returns'.

For every point played, if you use the right strategy to return the ball, you can call the shots of the game. But you have to study every opponent. Find their every weakness and maximize your strength. It's war out there on the tennis court and you've got to be prepared! I tell all of my students they've got to stay on their toes *and* read. Physical and spiritual preparedness makes you a winner."

Hettie wasn't sure what she'd been expecting but this wasn't it. Her head began a slow spin as she jotted down his words.

"I always advise reading poetry or other writings that make you think. Do you know what I tell Althea to read?"

"What?"

"The Bible, for one. You cannot go wrong with God's word. How do you feel about the book of Ecclesiastes?"

"There is a time for everything."

Syd released a bark of laughter as though Hettie had told the funniest joke. "Always read the words of a wise man and ponder them. That's why I also have her read *How to Win Friends and Influence People*. Have you heard of that book?"

"I have, although I have not read it myself. How did she take that piece of advice?"

"Oh, you sound like you know her?"

"I knew her once upon a time, yes."

"Let's just say, if she's read it, she hasn't told me yet. She has a personality problem. One I've been trying to work with her on for some time. It's only right that the press love her. She's phenomenal. And when you're phenomenal, people want to know why and how. This is something I've been trying to get her to understand from day one. No one is out to get you, Althea," he said as though she were in the car with them. "The press can be your best friend if you let them. But it just goes in one ear and out the other."

"What do you think about her chances at Forest Hills?"

"She can win. She can beat all of those other girls. But when she loses, it's because of this." Syd tapped a finger against his head as he turned a corner. "You can't win until you know who you are and you don't care about impressing anyone else out there but yourself. When you know who God made you to be—when you know you're a winner? You get winning results! If I had been able to travel with her for those overseas tournaments, things would've been different. She's been surrounded for too long by people who don't care about her and that is what you see on the field. I just don't know if I have enough time to get her ready mentally for the challenge up ahead. But she's absolutely capable of winning, yes."

"How long have you been her coach?"

"A complicated question with a complicated answer. Only in the past year or so has she been willing to listen to me. Fred taught her the Continental stroke—which allows you to hit both forehand and backhand with the same grip. But the Continental stroke is not going to win a game for Althea. She's quick and she favors flat shots. She needed the Eastern grip. It took her a while to believe me. So much damage I've had to undo because of Fred. Now, what did you say you wanted to write on?"

"I want to do more than just write a story. I would like to travel with Althea; to go to practice with Althea. I would like to write an exposé on Althea."

For a second their eyes met in the mirror. "Did you say you knew her?" He asked the question very politely.

"I did. I'm not here to ask you to plead my case. But I'm hoping that you'll support my role once I win Althea over."

Syd released a loud bark of laughter. "Only one thing wins Althea over and that's the game of tennis. If you manage to change her mind, you won't have to worry about me." If she won Althea over. As the feeling of dread slowly began to crawl over her, Hettie knew what she was going to have to do. The cab turned another corner and came to a stop. Hettie recognized her office building. A hand reached back between the seats, a clear ask for money. "You didn't think the ride was free, did you?"

Swallowing the words she wanted to say, Hettie reached for her purse and her wallet. After paying Syd for the ride around town that she hadn't wanted, Hettie exited the cab and went in search of the nearest payphone. She dialed a number that was very much familiar to her. "Hello, is Mr. Lewis in?"

"May I ask who is calling?"

"This is Hettie Carlin, a reporter with *Harlem Heights*."

"I'm sorry but Mr. Lewis is away on vacation. However, I do have his assistant here if you'd like to speak with her?"

Hettie tapped her foot lightly. He'd told her he was spending the week in Shady Rest, hadn't he? "No, that's all right. I'll call back later. Thank you."

Hettie hung up the phone. The change she'd slipped into the coin slot jangled inside the phone box. Well, that was that. She was out of excuses. It looked like she'd be headed to Shady Rest so she could challenge Althea Gibson to a game of tennis.

CHAPTER 11

Volley—a shot where the ball is hit by the player's racket before hitting the ground

Hettie pulled into the small parking lot that was situated right in front of old, yet well maintained, white buildings, one of which had a sign nestled in front of it that read *Shady Rest Clubhouse*. She was here. She had made it. She'd also sort of borrowed the relatively brand-new white 1955 Cadillac Coupe deVille that belonged to Morgan. After an evening of drinking, he'd been unable to drive himself home and so he'd called Hettie. Hettie had met him at the bar, took him home, and with his drunken permission, kept his car. She'd square up with him later.

Hettie stepped out of her uncle's car, wearing a navy blue dress and carrying the tennis outfit in a small suitcase. It was Faye who had told her that the country club had lockers and showers and a whole dressing room for women. Hettie would look out of place arriving in a tennis outfit.

In no hurry, she did a slow circle, taking in all of the greenery. She appeared to be in the middle of a golf course. In the distance, she saw small figures walking to and fro, with metal clubs in hand. Hearing a low hum, Hettie turned as a golf cart sped past, headed for another hole. Otherwise it was quiet, peaceful, tranquil even. She may as well have been transported back in time.

She crossed the small parking lot, climbed the two small stairs, and pushed open the red door of what had most likely been someone's house at some point. This thought was brought home further as she took in the old but shiny wood floors and the white walls that held pictures of the country club's most famous patrons.

"Good morning." Hettie turned to see a front desk manned by two young women.

"Hello, I'm here at the invitation of Mr. S. A. Lewis." It occurred to Hettie that she probably should have asked Lewis what his first name was. Hettie pulled out the card he'd given her and handed it to the girl directly in front of her. The young woman eyed Hettie intently, as though she were going to paint a picture later. She was younger than Hettie, but she left Hettie twitching and wondering whether her dress was out of fashion or if a hair was out of place. These rich people things had a way of reminding Hettie just where she'd come from.

"Name?"

"Hettie . . . Hester J. Carlin."

The girl looked down at some paper. "You're on the list. I believe I saw Mr. Lewis outside on the patio a half hour ago."

"Can you show me where I can change clothes?"

Alone in the locker room, Hettie quickly slipped into the tennis outfit and checked her hair. She had unbraided her cornrows that morning, which had left her with a curly style that she then wrestled into a nice bun. This way, if she overheated, there was a chance of still walking away looking nice. The borrowed tennis dress was a little long, falling just past her knees, but it fit perfectly elsewhere, cinching at the waist and showing off the figure she sometimes imagined that she'd inherited from Miz Ce-Ce. She felt pretty and distinctly feminine as the loose fabric of the skirt swirled around her legs. She touched up her lipstick, locked her locker, and headed for the back doorway.

Hettie slowly stepped out onto the wide, wooden patio. A number of tables were set up with large umbrellas erected atop for shade. There were quite a few people seated comfortably, talking or reading. But then she saw him, sitting alone at the table furthest from the doors and flipping through a newspaper. She did not rush over. It felt odd seeing him somewhere else that wasn't the steakhouse. It was even stranger seeing him wearing sunglasses and enrobed in a bright white shirt and matching pants.

It had been easy in the apartment to discuss Lewis as though he were a purchase she was considering making; to go through the pros and cons of this man. But all she could think was, this was her Lewis in a very unfamiliar habitat and what if he wasn't the same? She felt oddly nervous, as though he'd see that she didn't belong here amongst all this wealth and that their friendship—such as it was—was only conducive to Friday nights in darkened restaurants. As though feeling her eyes on him, he turned and rose to his feet. He was tall and his legs were long, his waist was slim, his chest was muscular. For the first time, she recognized that he had an athlete's body.

"Hettie! Good morning—come take a seat."

Her heart thudded once. He was the same, her Lewis. "Good morning," she said as she moved to sit down in the seat he pulled out for her.

"Don't take this the wrong way but I think you're smaller."

"You look like you've grown a few inches yourself."

"No, ma'am. I've been six foot three since high school." He returned to his seat, stretching out his legs and leaning back slightly in his chair. For a long moment, neither one of them spoke, although she could feel his gaze on her. Choosing to let him have the first word, Hettie looked around. There was more grass and greenery in the backyard, as expected of a golf course. Tucked up against the patio were brightly colored, empty golf carts. Further away, Hettie saw what looked to be a field of some sort for another sport. Tiny figures moved this way and that. She wondered where the tennis courts were; she could not see them anywhere.

"Did you have any trouble getting here? It dawned on me just this morning that I should have told you I could have a taxi waiting for you at the train station if you needed one."

"No trouble at all. I borrowed my uncle's car. Have you been waiting for me?"

Lewis clasped his hands together. "I'm not sure." It was such an honest comment that she laughed. To her surprise, he smiled back. It was the first time that she'd ever seen his eyes light up in such a mischievous way. "You called for me."

Hettie's eyebrows rose. She hadn't left a message. "They told you?"

"I have excellent staff. And you announced yourself as a

reporter. Of course, they told me." He tapped a finger against the edge of the table. "I had an inkling that I might see you today and by the looks of it—" his gaze might have been hidden by his sunglasses, but she felt his eyes sweep her form "—you've come for a game."

Hettie nodded. "I have, but answer me this: what is your first name?"

Lewis looked away. "At the risk of sounding unnecessarily mysterious, I save the first name for family. Just call me Lewis. I found myself thinking about you the other day." He'd changed the subject but she could accept this new topic.

"Oh?"

"There are a lot of people here who could talk tennis with you. People who know a little bit more about what happens behind the scenes than I do. I spoke briefly with Fred Johnson and he's willing to talk to you."

Fred Johnson. Althea's first coach and the one Syd disdained. He might be worth speaking with.

"Thank you, Lewis," she said, meaning it. "I appreciate all of your help. Even having me here today."

Lewis waved a hand. "Don't thank me. I never do anything without a reason."

Hettie raised an eyebrow. "What's your reason for inviting me here?"

His hand sliced through the air as though her question was irrelevant. "Althea is here. Are you going to try and meet with her?"

"I would like to."

"A friend of mine is here with his wife. She knows Althea and might be able to introduce you. I've shaken hands with Althea once, but I doubt she remembers me so I would be no help on that front."

"I don't need an introduction. I grew up just down the street from Althea. We attended the same elementary school."

Lewis shifted as though to get a better view of her. "You're from Harlem?"

"Yes."

"What happened after elementary school?"

"The school system is overcrowded. They don't allow every child to go to high school. I got accepted into high school and Althea was sent to trade school." If Hettie had to guess as to the reason why they had been separated, it probably had everything to do with Althea's truancy. The state of New York had decided Althea wasn't worth investing in educationally.

Lewis released a small grunt of irritation. "I guess I'll be leaving Hyacinth in private school for the rest of her days. And then you two what? Grew apart?"

"Well, it's a bit more complicated than that."

Hettie was beginning to love the way Lewis smiled slowly, first with his eyes and then with his mouth. "I'm beginning to think that everything with you is more complicated than it appears. I asked around about you."

Hettie suddenly wished that she had something she could fiddle with but she'd left her purse and her necklace in the locker room. Lowering her hands to her lap, she said, "Oh? Do I want to know?"

She watched him crack a few knuckles. "You really are a journalist."

"Did you think I lied?"

"No." He stretched the word out for longer than it needed to be. "Quick question: what is behind the laundry list of men that you dine with every week?"

"Are you referencing the laundry list that you're currently on?"

"Yes. That one."

Hettie pushed back her chair and stood up. "This is me changing the subject. Where is Althea? In one of these buildings or on the tennis court?"

"She's that way." He pointed left. "She's about to put on a show by beating anybody and everybody who thinks they know their way around a tennis racket. All right, I'll allow the subject change." He'd allow . . . there he was with that authoritative language again. Lewis stood up, carefully tucking his chair under the table, even though he probably didn't have to.

One day this would be Hettie, soaking in the benefits of a country club. "Has Althea been a member of Shady Rest since she started competing in the ATA?"

Lewis shook his head. "Only one thing gives you membership to Shady Rest and that's money. When and if she has a membership, it's because someone has paid for it for her. Her entire tennis career has been purchased by others."

Hettie cringed a bit on the inside. "Why?"

"You know why. She's going to be hard to speak to right now. Did you want to try your hand at tennis? My golf cart is right over there. We can shoot a couple balls while we wait for the show to be over. Just so you know, there are three tennis courts to the north of us and three to the south. She's north. I recommend we head south. Don't worry, we won't miss her. There'll be plenty of time to speak to her."

Hettie smiled, although she'd lost all humor. Speaking to Althea was exactly what she was worried about.

CHAPTER 12

Foot fault—when the server's foot touches the baseline while making a serve

Ten minutes later, Hettie was seated next to Lewis in a brightly colored three-wheeled motor cart headed south. It was not the smoothest of rides and Hettie couldn't resist holding on to the small rail next to her. "Did you get to study tennis like you planned?"

"Yes, you're now talking to an expert." His grin was quick to appear this time. "Where's Hyacinth?" Hettie was a little curious about the girl.

"Horseback-riding lessons." Lewis looked down at his watch. "You've got my full and undivided attention for an hour. Then I'll drop you off where Althea will be playing and go fetch my little duchess."

Hettie was somewhat disappointed that she wouldn't see

Hyacinth but also very much relieved. "How did you come to open a sports store? It seems a bit . . . unusual." Random was what she wanted to say.

"The first thing you have to know about me is that I'm one of those people who fixates on things. I can't control it. When something intrigues me, I have to know everything about it and I'll think about it constantly until I've figured it out. It used to drive Laverne . . . anyway it all goes back to when I was seven. My parents owned a general store that sold necessities only. Times were hard. Folks weren't buying superfluous things like footballs."

"So, running a business has always been in your blood?"

He glanced slightly in her direction. "Yes. I was sitting behind the counter long before I could talk properly. Anyway, I love sports. All sports, but there is one game that reigns as king in my heart."

"Oh, let me guess. Baseball?" From all that she had gathered about Lewis, he seemed like a person who took his time making decisions. There was no other sport that he would have played as a child that moved so slowly that you could sit and ponder—while playing the game—other than baseball. Basketball seemed too fast. Most people seemed to discover tennis in their teen years. And he did not have the look or feel of a football player.

He nodded twice, slowly, looking impressed at her guess. "Baseball. My family wasn't destitute but we couldn't afford extra things like baseball bats. We used a two-by-four whenever we wanted to play a game. To a seven-year-old, that was very disappointing. After complaining to my father, he told me it sounded like I needed a job. In hindsight, he was joking. But I didn't take it that way. I asked him for a loan and purchased a shoeshine kit from his store.

Then I sat outside and offered to shine men's shoes for a penny."

"A penny?"

"I was seven. It took me all of spring and most of the summer but I saved enough for a baseball bat. I walked several miles, dragging my large jar of pennies in a small wagon to the other store in town."

Hettie's lips twitched at the picture he was painting. "Were you worried about being robbed?"

"I have three brothers and they all tagged along. I'm the oldest and the youngest was four but we had that two-by-four with us. We were ready for anything." Four sons under the age of seven? His poor mother. "The other store, in case you were wondering, was white-owned. But I had heard that they sold baseball bats. I went inside, leaving my kith and kin outside. I waited my turn. Then I asked to buy a bat, knowing I had the exact amount needed for the cheapest one. I'll never forget how that man took a long look at me and said no."

Hettie shifted in her seat to get a better look at him.

"He was just contrary for no good reason. I asked him how come he wouldn't sell it to me and he said it was none of my business but he didn't sell to dirty . . . Negroes. Dirty, as though Talitha Lewis keeps filthy people in her house. I couldn't understand that. Even at seven I couldn't fathom what race had to do with the matter when I was offering him the color green."

Lewis leaned in her direction at the same time that the golf cart dipped. His shoulder brushed against hers, setting off little bitty firecrackers under her skin. When she got a whiff of his cologne, something in her stomach flipped. Her grip on the rail tightened because she was a little bit concerned that she might reach over and touch him. Completely oblivious to all he was stirring within her, he continued, "That right there is a prime example of how frightening racism is. I tell my brothers all the time, you can't reason with the devil. He's only going to think evil thoughts all the time."

Hettie jumped on this statement. Anything to think about something else. "You don't subscribe to the philosophy of Booker T. Washington?"

"Booker T. Washington was born a slave. I can understand his choice to not challenge segregation and voting rights. He just wanted us to survive in a time when Negroes weren't surviving. I can respect that. But it's been almost three generations since slavery. Things need to change."

"You're a proponent of the boycott, then?"

"I'm a proponent of every boycott everywhere. I don't like giving my hard-earned money to people who not only hate me, but would be happy to see me dead. That's bothersome to my soul."

"Which part of the South are you from?" she asked, because his dialect had changed. Lewis always spoke with a hint of the South in his voice but most colored folks did. Even Hettie was prone to hold on to a word too long every now and then. But somewhere in the middle of his story, his accent had thickened in the way only a native's would.

"Tennessee. My family stayed when Ida B. Wells left. That ought to tell you how deeply entrenched that land is to my people. But it never took root in me. I knew from the moment that man called me dirty that I was not staying where a person could talk to me like that."

"What happened next? After he denied you?"

"I told that white man it was his store to do of his will and his good pleasure, but one day I'd have my own store and when children came to me with their hard-earned money I wouldn't fashion nonsense. I'd sell them what they wanted. And matter of fact, I was gonna have so many baseball bats in my store, I'd be able to give them away if I so willed and desired."

"Was he offended?" Hettie had heard stories of white men taking hubris when colored children spoke their mind. She had heard stories of whole families packing up in fear and running in the night because a child had talked back to a white man.

"He laughed. I was hot, Hettie. I've never been a person who speaks with my fists but I still remember how badly I wanted to knock that look off his face. My mama always says, be angry but sin not. Well, I let myself settle into that anger. Every time someone would ask me what I was aiming to do when I got older, I'd tell them own a store that sells baseball bats. My daddy got sick of that answer. He told me I'd best think of something else. But I'm not built that way."

Beneath the cart, the ground leveled and an empty tennis court came into view.

"Did you ever get your baseball bat?"

"My parents had already purchased it for me but my daddy said I was taking the shoeshine business so seriously, he didn't want to interfere. And I did not tell them ahead of time when I finally realized I had enough money to buy it myself, otherwise they would have stopped me from going to the store." Lewis brought the golf cart to a stop and they both climbed out. Hettie watched as Lewis went to the trunk of the cart, lifting it and pulling out what could only be a tennis bag. She mentally kicked herself. She hadn't even thought about the fact that she'd need equipment.

Lewis unzipped the bag and handed her a tennis racket.

The handle carried his last name in small blocky letters at the bottom.

"To think that someone else's foolishness started this," Hettie murmured to herself as she turned over the racket.

But Lewis had heard her. "It's an interesting conundrum. Would I have always ended up making and selling my own sports equipment? Or did that incident make me who I am?"

"What do you mean by making?"

Lewis frowned at her. "I don't sell other people's stuff. I make my own. That," he said, pointing to her tennis racket, "is my design. Patented and everything. How else do you think I compete with Harry C. Lee? Everything I sell I made myself. By hand," he stressed in case it wasn't clear enough. "Now it's time to show off your knowledge. Explain to me the tennis court."

Happy to show off what she'd learned, Hettie pointed out the baseline. "This is the boundary of the court," she said, pointing to the outer white line of the field. "Sideline." She pointed to the white line that paralleled the length of the tennis court. "Service line, service box, and the net, of course."

"Someone's been hitting the books. Did you hear that, Fred?"

Hettie looked up to see an old, weathered man wearing all white sauntering over to them. His head was shadowed by a green visor that had seen better days. He had a tennis racket tucked under one arm . . . and he was missing a second arm. "Interesting grip you have there, young lady." Hettie looked down at the tennis racket in her hand. "You'll hurt your wrist if you hit a ball like that. All fingers should be on one side, with your thumb on the other."

Lewis took a step back and said nothing as Fred Johnson took ten minutes to instruct Hettie on the fundamentals of the game. Under his brief tutelage, she learned the proper way to stand when performing a flat serve and the correct way to use the racket when volleying.

Trying to catch her breath after only a few swings of the racket, Hettie paused to ask Althea's former coach a question. "How long did you work with Althea?"

The older man released a grunt. "He did say you were a reporter, didn't he?" Under his withering stare, Hettie almost looked away, but Fred sort of reminded her of her father. And Oral Carlin didn't take to people who backed down. Hettie straightened to her full height, holding his gaze. "I worked with her up until the time she first left New York so about four years, give or take a few months."

"When did you know she was good?"

"The moment I saw her walk out onto the court. I bought her her first racket. A Harry C. Lee. Sorry, kid, you weren't in business yet in those days," Fred said, nodding in Lewis's direction.

"How do you feel about her tennis now?"

"She's doing too much and stretching herself thin. She's allowing herself to be pulled in too many directions, trying to get famous when she needs to focus on a win. The ATA keeps placing their demands on her as though she can get the USLTA to open the doors for other Negroes. She could barely make it through. How is she going to hold the door open for others? And I can't believe they made her play in their tournament, knowing Forest Hills is this week. And then there's the USLTA. They're watching her every move, looking for a misstep. Don't even get me started on the government and the State Department, which likes to trot Althea out and show her off to the world like she's a trained puppy. It's too much and she needs to put her foot down. Mark my words, if she ever decides to pull away from the circus and put all her energy into the game, she'll be undefeated."

"As long as she plays in the USLTA, the circus is going to follow Althea," Lewis said from where he was sitting on the grass at the edge of the baseline.

"It's not easy being the first and that's a fact but if she wants to accomplish more with her career, she's going to have to cut some people and some things out. It was nice to meet you, reporter."

"Likewise, Mr. Johnson. Thank you for your time and your tips." Hettie dipped her head in respect as the older man walked off, headed to who knew where. When he disappeared from sight, Hettie pointed her racket at Lewis. "Don't get comfortable, sir. I need you to put me through my paces."

Other than plucking at the strings on the hoop of his racket, Lewis didn't move. "Put you through your paces? Are you planning on taking up the game?"

"I have to if I'm going to beat Althea."

"Beat Althea? At tennis? Why would you even think to do that?"

Hettie walked over to Lewis and sat down onto the grass. "Remember how I told you I am now writing on sports? Really, I have to focus on Althea."

Lewis leaned back, slowly lying onto the grass. Then he turned on his side, facing her. They were both going to be sporting some serious grass stains. "You're trying to get her attention?"

"Yes." He was so quick.

"Hettie?"

"Yes?"

"I was a good southern boy." Hettie blinked, not sure where he was going. "I can hunt with the best of them. Daddy would take us out in the woods in search for deer, elk, turkey, squirrel. We couldn't come home unless we caught something. If a man doesn't work, he doesn't eat. But sometimes we'd be sitting out there for hours. And you get so bored, you find yourself watching nature like it's a picture show. There was this one, very small, teeny-tiny bird out there. It was fierce and deeply territorial, chasing all other kinds of birds away. But you should have seen it when it was matched against a great horned owl. My little mockingbird, why are you trying to start a fight with an owl?"

Hettie stretched out her legs, leaning back on her arms. "I can win."

"No. You can't."

"It won't be a full game. Just . . . thirty seconds."

"You'll lose in ten. She is an expert at her craft. It is insulting to think that you could even touch an ounce of her greatness on the field." Hettie looked at Lewis and he lowered his sunglasses so that their eyes met. "I'm not going to baby you on this," he said as though they had a relationship where he babied her on other issues. "Find another way."

"I beat her once, you know."

There was a pause. "When?"

It was Hettie's turn to hesitate. "Sixteen years ago."

"Fourteen years ago, I could carry up to two hundred pounds on my back and run ten miles. I'd die if I tried that now."

"You were in the army?" She didn't know why this surprised her. Most men his age had served.

"Yes."

"WWII or Korea?"

Lewis shuddered and it reminded her of Morgan and how tense he'd been when the draft for Korea had started and how relieved he was to learn he didn't have to go. He too still shuddered at the mention of Korea. "The first one."

"How was it?"

"Miserable. Don't change the subject. What you did sixteen years ago isn't going to help you today."

She didn't like his answers, but he had a point. "What if I change the game?"

"Althea is good at everything. You can't name a sport she can't whip your tail at. What did you beat her at a century ago?"

Hettie tossed him a dirty look. "Table tennis."

"And you won?" he asked, disbelieving.

"Yes. And I'm going to win this game too. Just like I did back then. It doesn't even matter what sport it is." Lewis looked like he was two seconds from having a conniption so she continued, "It never matters when you cheat."

CHAPTER 13

Unforced error—a mistake made by a player that was not caused by their opponent

Lewis's gasp was so loud, Hettie was amazed that all of Shady Rest hadn't come running to find out what happened. "You can't do that," he whispered, profoundly disturbed at this revelation.

"Oh, yes, I can. And not how you think either. I'll still need to be able to play the game. But you're right. I can play table tennis, or I could at one point. So, that might be a better game to challenge her with."

"Hettie." He was still gasping for air. He brought a hand to his chest. "You're going to willingly destroy the sanctity of the game? Why?"

"Althea does not like journalists." She was not willing to go so far as to admit that Althea did not like her. "To convince her to accept me, I need to challenge her to a game and win. It's the only way." She'd come to that conclusion while talking to Syd. There was never going to be enough time for Hettie to convince Althea to change her mind. And Althea wasn't a changing-her-mind kind of person. But she was someone who could not say no to a challenge. "And she has to accept me, for me to keep my job. And . . ."

Lewis sat up. His sunglasses were folded in his hand so Hettie had no problems seeing his golden eyes gleaming. "There's an and? Lady . . ."

"And I have to convince her to take a formal stand for civil rights." It felt good to tell someone the whole of it. Hettie could not remember the last time she'd confided in someone. No wonder Lewis kept their Friday night dinner dates, even though he did all the talking. It was freeing.

Lewis began sputtering. "Althea? Althea Gibson? Take a stand for civil rights? She'd rather give up Wimbledon altogether."

"You're familiar with her views?"

"Mockingbird, is water wet? Is the sun bright? To love Althea Gibson is to know that she's not going to love you back. Althea loves no one else except Althea. And you're going to what? Swoop in and save the day? You're going to make it so colored people have another sports hero like Jackie or Joe or Jesse? What kind of journalism is happening over there at the double H?" Every word exiting Lewis's mouth was filled with judgment and consternation, and Hettie found herself fighting the rising shame that was filling her.

"How do you know where I work?"

"I told you. I've been looking into you. While I still don't know yet what it is that you did in Montgomery to get you kicked out of a whole city, I am now beginning to form ideas, and I must say, I don't think I like the ethics of your profession."

A small bird of some kind landed near the racket Hettie had been borrowing. She watched it hop and skip and poke at the ground. What exactly had she expected to happen by telling this almost-stranger about herself? She knew what she'd wanted to happen. She'd wanted him to try to understand; to help her work through the logistics and see if there were any other options. But maybe it was to his credit that he didn't. Maybe Hettie was meant to do life alone. Not ideal but she'd be all right. That still didn't stop the wave of overwhelming sorrow that crested over her. She really had sort of loved him.

Hettie sat up straight and brushed at the dirt on her hands. "I find it very interesting that I somehow managed to spend the past I-don't-know-how-many-months listening to you whine about a woman who doesn't want you anymore without passing any sort of judgment. Oh, how you wondered why she would pack her bags and leave. Let me tell you something, mister, you did something but you ain't gonna hear me say none of that. Nope. I just let you say your piece until I learned enough about you to realize that whatever Laverne didn't like about you doesn't bother me. I thought this was a two-way street," Hettie said, waving two index fingers back and forth to demonstrate. "You know, a friendship of sorts that allowed for us to confide our faults to each other. However, I see that this is not the case. Here." Picking up his tennis racket, Hettie startled the bird and it rushed off, headed for the blue sky. She thrust the racket at his chest. Mouth agape, he barely caught it.

Hettie pushed herself up to her feet, brushed off her backside and continued to speak. "Thank you for inviting me here today. Thank you for arranging the quick tennis lesson with Mr. Johnson. Thank you for all of those steak dinners you paid for. Thank you for the fantasy of those nights where I got to pretend to be out with a man who I liked, respected, and yes, maybe even lusted after, but consider this the last day that I take a penny from you, Mr. S. A. Lewis." When he started to move, Hettie held up a hand. "No. I will walk back. There's absolutely nothing you can say at this moment that would make me want to be around you."

And on those words, she turned on her heels and walked away, crossing the vast sports grounds. Fifteen minutes later, she momentarily regretted that she hadn't at least made him drop her at the building where they'd initially met that day. And then she gritted her teeth, changing her mind. Sweat might be sliding down the side of her face and pooling in unwanted places but she'd rather be uncomfortable than sitting next to someone looking down at her and pointing fingers. No, her methods were not always the right ones but it wasn't as if she was out here trying to hurt someone. A memory of Montgomery flashed through her mind and she winced. She brushed the thought aside. That wasn't relevant to now. Working with Althea would help her but it would help Althea as well. She wasn't whatever it was she'd seen on his face.

"I'm a good journalist," she whispered aloud to herself as Lewis's words about the morality of her work rang through her mind. "I do my job well." But the words didn't bring the comfort they usually brought. She marched forward, each step feeling heavier than the last.

"Excuse me! Yoo-hoo!" Hettie looked up as a golf cart zoomed into existence. Seated behind the wheel were a couple around her parents' age. "My dear," the wife said. "I realize you're still young but you should consider investing in a golf cart. It's entirely too hot to be crossing the savanna. Jonathan, we must give her a ride. Where are you going?"

"To see Althea Gibson play."

"How serendipitous! So are we. Hop on."

The very nice couple drove Hettie up to the northern tennis courts and then parked their golf cart in a makeshift parking lot filled with other golf carts. Hettie hopped down just as the crowd of people in the metal stands unleashed a roar of delight.

"You need a hat, young lady, or you'll turn dark as a berry out here in this sun." Hettie dipped her head politely at this admonishment. She should have brought a hat but not because of fears of growing darker. She was already tanned from her time in the South and unlikely to tan further. But if she did, Hettie didn't care. She had enough problems in life without taking on the mantle of worrying about how dark her skin was.

"Thank you for the ride." Hettie gave the couple a wave and ran over to the seating area, which was filled to the brim with people dressed in white, tan, and cream. She was too late to get a good seat, but she had no problems standing amidst another group of latecomers who watched as Althea tossed a ball in the air, leaped, and then slammed it forward. The woman on the other side of the net was smaller than Althea, but fast. She darted across the court, sliding a bit as her tennis racket rose to meet the ball. The ball went gliding back across the net and it was Althea's turn to run for it.

For the first time in Hettie's life, she realized that watching pure athleticism was like watching art. She forgot that she was supposed to be on the lookout for faults and double faults and slices and all the other ways that tennis was played. Instead, she took in the tennis players themselves, moving gracefully across the court as though in a synchronized dance. It almost made her wish that she could go back in time and take up a sport.

The tennis ball hit the ground. There was a whistle and the crowd roared again. From the way Althea raised her racket in the air and grinned, Hettie knew she'd won. But it was the other tennis player who blew a kiss to the crowd and curtseyed, showing off the layers of her skirt. Hettie looked back at Althea. She was wearing shorts. Several people left the stands, racing to hug and laugh with the other player. Althea walked past the baseline and off the field, alone. The losing player stepped away from her small entourage and turned this way and that, posing and hamming it up to the crowd as she showed off her figure. Althea was zipping up her tennis bag, clearly ready to move on to whatever came next.

Not sure what was okay and what was not, but absolutely certain that this was no 'real' game, Hettie pushed herself through the crowd, crossed the tennis field, and came to a stop next to Althea. "You need help?"

"Good gracious," Althea hissed as she hefted her tennis bag over her shoulder. The way her shoulders were sort of tucked in, Hettie could tell that Althea was tired. Althea started walking, her long legs carrying her away from the crowd behind them. "You again?"

"Me again. Good game there. That was an excellent slice at the end," Hettie said firmly. If you sounded knowledgeable, people believed you.

"I never sliced the ball once."

"Your Eastern grip is something else."

Althea's lips twitched. "I used the Continental."

"Althea! Althea!" Hettie watched as Althea closed her eyes, weary at the sound of her own name.

"Do you have a golf cart?" Hettie asked, eyeing the small machines that were lined up near them.

"Do I look like I have golf-cart money?"

Hettie let her eyes drift down Althea's long, slender form in all her white. "You sort of do."

"Well, I don't even have a membership here at the moment. I know you don't have one either. Whose idea was it to let you in? And why are you dressed like you're planning to play a match?"

"Althea!" Someone was yelling her name. "Come take pictures."

"Do you think I can pretend not to hear him?"

"Can you just borrow one of those carts or do they actually belong to someone?"

Althea pivoted and pointed a finger at Hettie. "They actually belong to people," she said, even as she marched toward a tan one and sat down behind the driver's seat. "For example, this one belongs to Bertram Baker. But I like your idea. We should definitely borrow one." She started up the engine. Hettie had ten seconds to decide. She didn't let herself think too much: she just jumped into the passenger seat as Althea took off at a speed faster than Hettie had thought the things could go.

"I take it we don't like Bertram Baker?"

"There is no 'we', Hettie Jo."

"I'm going to be kicked out and blacklisted for the rest of my life, aren't I?" Hettie asked as a man came tearing out of the tennis crowd, waving his hat.

"I doubt it. Nobody knows who you are." Althea's words carried no heat but Hettie still winced. "That man owes me at least a ride back to the locker rooms. Listen, I don't know how you even managed to get in here but I do admire your gumption. I'm still not having a reporter looking over my shoulder every which way and breathing down my neck."

"This might surprise you . . ." Hettie paused, holding on to the rail for dear life as the cart slid down a small hill at an alarming rate. "But I have no desire to breathe on you. I have a job. I report on people and events. And you are someone worthy of reporting on at the moment."

"Well, I don't like reporters and I really don't like you. You're a liar—"

"Big Al—"

"And possibly a cheat."

"You're just saying that because you can't handle the fact that you lost!"

"And I don't want you sniffing around."

Hettie gritted her teeth. "Big Al, I am a woman of infinite patience but this has already been a very trying day."

"Ha! Patience! I suppose if I look up the word in the dictionary, it'll be a picture of your face staring back at me?"

Why was Hettie doing this again? Oh, yes, because she didn't want to lose her job. "How about we make a bet?"

"No."

"If I can beat you at a game of table tennis . . . just like I did sixteen years ago, you've got to let me tag along behind you until the next Forest Hills tournament. The one that's occurring next year," Hettie said, in case it wasn't clear.

"Girl, I thought you wanted to do one story, now you're talking about following me around for a whole year? Figure the odds. And," she stressed, "you couldn't beat me in a game of table tennis if I played with one hand tied behind my back and my eyes closed." Althea's words were firm but Hettie had seen that quick flash of something at the mention of a possible game. Althea Gibson could not turn down a challenge.

"I have before."

"You got lucky!"

Hettie scoffed just as the golf cart came to a jerky stop outside the main building. "If that's what you have to tell yourself . . ."

"I don't have to tell myself nothing. It's the truth!"

"If it's so true, why not have a rematch? Prove that you really can beat me."

Althea slid out of the golf cart and then reached back in for her tennis rackets. "Get thee behind me, Satan."

"All this name-calling is really starting to irk my nerves." Hettie hopped down from the golf cart. "You ought to be thankful I'm almost thirty years old, otherwise I'd be calling you something along the lines of a lily-livered coward, 'cause it sounds to me like you're afraid of losing to me a second time."

Something dangerous flashed across Althea's eyes but then it disappeared as she straightened to her full height. "We're not children, Hettie Jo. If you think your tired challenges will move me then you never really knew me at all."

"If you win the game, I'll disappear, never to be seen again."

"Deal," Althea said quickly. "And don't follow me," she called over her shoulder. "The very sound of your voice is giving me a headache."

CHAPTER 14

Court—the area where a game of tennis is played

"I was there the first time she played at Forest Hills, you know," Harmon told Hettie. They were sitting side by side on the subway, being gently tossed to the left and the right as the train clack-clacked to their destination. "Oh, it was something to see," the older man murmured. There were stars in his eyes as he studied the ceiling of the car, because it wasn't the ceiling he was seeing but the events of 1950, the year that Althea first played in the US tournament.

Harmon was older and gray but long-legged and slender, still holding on to the athletic physique of his youth. If Hettie recalled correctly, basketball had been his game of choice. She was willing to bet her bottom dollar that Lewis would look the same when he aged. Then she shook her head. She wasn't thinking about Lewis ever again.

"I read about it."

Her words pulled Harmon out of his thoughts. "Reading about it does not do it justice." Curling his hands above each of his shoulders, he said, "The feeling in the air was electric. It was like Gibson was carrying all the hopes and dreams of the Negro race." Hettie internally winced, feeling a moment of pity for Althea. Goodness, but she could not even imagine such pressure. "They didn't think she'd do that well. I think they thought she'd be out in the first round, 'cause they had her playing in Court No. 14, far away from where the clubhouse and the main courts are. There wasn't even room for hardly any spectators. Court No. 14 is rarely used for games; they mostly use it for practice." Harmon tsked and shook his head as he lowered his arms. "They will try any way they can to insult us. Did you learn how she got in? You have to be invited to play at Forest Hills. Talent is not sufficient to get you through the door, no matter what they say."

"Another tennis player wrote a letter to the USLTA, correct? Alice Marble, I believe." Hettie had begun creating a timeline of events as it related to Althea, based entirely upon the articles written in the past. But everything that had happened behind the scenes was information she had to get from those who had been there.

"Marble wasn't the only one writing letters. She was the most famous one. Before Forest Hills, Gibson *was* invited to play in a few smaller USLTA tournaments and she did well. Like a steady drumbeat, she kept building up and up, and the very highest you can go here in the States is Forest Hills. And while the smaller USLTA tournaments had opened their doors to a few Negro tennis players, the very hallowed Forest Hills never had. Bertram Baker was writing them, Arthur Francis—"

"Bertram Baker?" This was the name of the person whose golf cart Althea had borrowed.

"The executive secretary of the ATA. Nice fella, but he thinks he owns Althea. That last year when she was trying to finish college was a doozy. I can't speak to how the young woman must have felt, but he was stressing me out. Baker and Francis have a clear goal in mind when it comes to Gibson."

"That goal would be?"

"That she open the door as wide as possible for other Negroes to get in. Everyone has an agenda. Don't you forget that. Most people think sports are naught but numbers and trophies. It's politics, too, Carlin. When black bodies are involved, it's never just a game. Anyway, Baker has his faults but it's quite possible Gibson wouldn't be where she is today if not for his heavy hand. He set up meetings with the USLTA, all but begging them to allow her in. Their answer was a very firm no. Then there was a letter-writing campaign. Then ATA cashed in on relationships with white folks who thought a bit more kindly to integrating the game. It was a whole thing. Finally, Alice Marble shows up. Marble is a fantastic tennis player and a real pistol. She's even played in the ATA. She defeated Gibson in 1947 but she took a liking to our girl."

"Alice Marble has a column in the *American Lawn Tennis* magazine," Hettie said slowly, probably telling Harmon what he already knew.

"She doesn't just stick to the game. You can't call the USLTA racist to their face if all you care about is winning. *Life* magazine heard her rallying cry and responded. *Time* magazine too. Of course, the problem was—"

"That they were asking only for Althea to be let in. It was not a call to integrate the sport." How had she missed how complicated sports were all these years? It was a whole civil rights movement within itself. Was it because sports seemed like entertainment? Something you enjoyed but did not need?

Harmon shifted a bit to get a better look at her. "You have been doing your homework, haven't you? Yes, letting Althea in is not letting everyone in. Will the USLTA close the doors behind Gibson the day after she retires? We'll have to wait and see. Anyway, thanks to Marble's letter, Gibson was invited to play in the National Clay Court Championships in Chicago and the Eastern Grass Court Championships in New Jersey. Not Forest Hills, but these were tournaments that would have never invited her before. And then, after waiting until almost the last minute, Forest Hills sent her an invitation. Oh, the excitement, Carlin. You could taste it in the air."

Hettie couldn't stop the uptick of her lips. This was a man who loved what he did.

"Gibson arrived at Forest Hills and she was like a racehorse coming out the gate. Come on, this is our stop. We have to take the express to Forest Hills." Harmon and Hettie didn't speak to each other as they crossed the train terminal, paid for another ticket, and got on another train. "Where was I?" Harmon asked as they took their seats.

"Althea's first game."

"She played against Barbara Knapp, a British player. She won the first two sets, 6–2. The next day, her opponent was Louise Brough."

"She was the Wimbledon champion that year, right?"

"Yes. She'd won Forest Hills the year before too. Brough is a tough player and this time everyone and their mama was sitting up in those stands, watching the game. It took a while for Althea to get her bearings but once she did, she was beating the stink out of her. It was a humdinger of a game.

White folks were yelling slurs and whatnot at Gibson, but it was only fueling her. You could tell. And then it was like God himself had a change of mind. Carlin, the sky had been perfectly blue, the heat level just right, the wind, a cool breeze and then, in a matter of minutes darkness rolled in, a storm started, and one of the statues at Forest Hills was struck by lightning. I kid you not. The game had to be delayed. When the game started up again the next day, Gibson lost."

Hettie had read about this game and just like Harmon, her shoulders fell at this statement. It seemed so unfair, when Althea clearly would have won had it not rained.

"Did you read her interview after the match?"

"The one where she said that she didn't think of herself as a Black woman breaking a color barrier and she wasn't thinking about any implications her role might have on the Negro race?"

"Gibson just crushes you with her indifference. Logically, I understand. She doesn't want the focus to be taken off tennis. She doesn't want to be a problem for the USLTA or to provide them with any reason to uninvite her but it always sounds like she's saying something to the effect of 'I'm not one of you dirty Negroes; I'm something else'. I'm not going to lie, the distance she's trying to create between sports and reality has gotten to me. That's why my last few articles have been less than flattering. As Edgar still loves her, the best thing is for me to be replaced. We're here."

They walked down the street of a long block while Harmon railed at Edgar's failure to provide them with a car. "Where would we park it?"

They were in a residential neighborhood. On each side of Hettie were large homes, perfect lawns, and the occasional decorative stone statue. They were not downtown, where you could circle a block or two before finding a spot. She felt out of place, and more than a little uncomfortable. She hated feeling like if she took the wrong step, someone might call the police. Reaching into the bottom of the bag slung over her shoulder, she placed a hand on her journalist credentials.

"These houses are the parking lot. You make arrangements with the owners ahead of time. It's a whole thing. They rent out space in their driveway or in front of their homes. See," he said, waving a finger at the cars that lined the streets. Now that Hettie looked at it, it did appear that everyone around them was throwing a party.

Hettie came to a stop, spinning around in a slow circle to see if she had missed a sign or two. "Who even knows to do that?"

"White people, dear. Please stop airing your ignorance. Also, I've realized it's not fair to leave you with the impression that Althea is the only Negro player to play at this event. That's not true. She was the first."

She'd known what he meant when he said it. "Lorraine Williams has played here." A week ago, she had never heard of that name. Now, her head was filled to the brim with tennis players.

"Yes," Harmon said, nodding at the mention of the young and up-and-coming Negro tennis star. "One year there was a record-breaking eight Negro players here. But you know what they're afraid of, don't you?" Harmon didn't give her a chance to answer before he spoke again. "They're afraid we're good. They're afraid that if they start opening the door for all talented players in the United States, tennis won't be a white sport anymore. Like boxing."

"What about baseball?" Harmon shook his head. "But Jackie . . ."

"I have a theory about baseball. Mark my words, fifty years from now you won't see a lot of Negro players in the big leagues and it won't be because they can't play."

"Really?" Hettie asked, astounded.

"Really."

"But you think tennis will change?"

"If it weren't so expensive and the players actually made some cash, the answer to that question would be unequivocally yes. But if things stay where they are with the amateurs only being allowed to play in the major tournaments, then I have grave doubts. Civil rights or not, sometimes people forget that lack of money is a real problem." He tapped her shoulder and pointed. "Look." Hettie obeyed and caught sight of a large, Tudor-style building, and blue and yellow awnings. "That is the West Side Tennis Club. Soak it in, sister. It's the only time they'll ever let your kind in. Did you bring your identification?"

The West Side Tennis clubhouse was very different from Shady Rest, in part because they were in New York. There was no expansive greenery all around. There was simply a massive house that looked like it could have belonged to Rockefeller and, in the backyard, tennis courts.

Hettie followed Harmon's lead as they entered the hushed and hallowed clubhouse. To her surprise, there were decorations everywhere announcing the Diamond Jubilee Seventy-Fifth National Championships. She couldn't help but look down at herself. She'd had a trying time picking out an outfit that morning. It needed to be professional and it had to fit into the crowd—even though she knew she was going to stick out like a sore thumb. Hettie had settled on a slim-fitting, solid-color tan summer suit. The sleeves stopped at her elbows and the belt cinched at the waist, but the fabric was light enough that she hadn't yet worked up a sweat, despite the multiple train rides and the walk in. Her hair was completely tucked under the brown cloche hat she was wearing and she had her brown work bag slung across her shoulder.

"Here's your press pass," the man at the front desk said, his voice just barely above a whisper as he handed a pass each to Harmon and Hettie. "Here's a copy of the events that will be taking place today. The tennis courts are that way."

Harmon and Hettie said little as they walked down a long hallway, passing dozens of photos of tennis champions looking down at them. The West Side Tennis clubhouse was certainly larger than the Shady Rest clubhouse but both places had the same feeling of elegance and wealth. They passed a parlor room where men in blazers and women in dresses conversed and laughed lightly. A piano was being played in the distance and every time Hettie inhaled, she got a faint whiff of alcohol and tobacco.

They reached the back of the building and Harmon opened the door, allowing for Hettie to step out onto the patio. She reached for the sunglasses in her bag as the rays of the morning sun seemed to hit her squarely on. Her view was one of tennis court after tennis court, with grass so green it hurt to stare at. She wondered what Lewis would think if he could see this place. Then she batted the thought away. Forget Lewis. What did Althea think when she saw this? Did it make her excited? Or nervous?

"She's not on Court No. 14 today," Harmon said, looking down at the schedule they'd been handed.

"Will she win?" Hettie was starting to consider herself to be fairly knowledgeable about tennis but not so knowledgeable that she could predict the outcome of a game.

"She's got a wrist injury. She's been playing nearly non-stop for a year. She did beat Brough in the Eastern finals but

Brough is old now. Gibson is the number-two seed, but this is her seventh try and she's never made it beyond the quarterfinals." Harmon raised his face to the sky, squinting as he pondered her question, still giving it serious thought. "Gibson is the kind of player who could get taken out in the first round for silly mistakes but she could also take it to the end. I can't say how she'll do today but this is Shirley Fry's year. All I know is that if I was a betting man, I'd put my money on Fry, who has been beautifully consistent at nine out of ten matches for the past few months."

"Should we go find Althea and see what her thoughts are on the matter?"

Harmon released a dry laugh. "She doesn't talk to the press before matches but we can try and catch up with her today after her match with Nell Hopman. Welcome to covering Gibson and learning to live life on the edge."

CHAPTER 15

Poaching—a strategy played in doubles where the player at the net attempts to volley a shot hit to their partner on the baseline

"She destroyed her first opponent," Hettie explained to Tony as they dined on a shared fried rice and stir-fry in the small, but busy L-shaped restaurant that they met at most Tuesdays. They had been seated at a table meant for four, so they were able to spread out a bit more and Hettie was using her hands widely as she provided Tony with a rundown of events. "Then she beat Karol Fageros, three others, and finally it was the showdown between her and Shirley Fry—the clear favorite of the year."

"If I didn't know any better . . ." Tony began languidly but paused as he reached for a carrot with his chopsticks. Tony always used chopsticks. Hettie had felt his silent judgment for weeks until she too relinquished the fork for chopsticks. It wasn't the easiest way of eating but she could now consume a bowl of rice without too much struggle. "I'd say you're loving the sports beat."

"Harmon loves sports. It just oozes out of his pores. He can recount someone's stats at the drop of a hat. He can run through a list of every game Althea has played since before the Second World War. He's aware of old injuries and new injuries and doubles partners and so on and so forth. It would take me years to reach his level." It would all be overwhelming if she was taking on the sports mantle for the rest of her life. But she had to give it just one solid year. "No, I don't love it. But I have found a new respect for sports in general."

Tony rolled his eyes before reaching for his small cup of tea. Tony was a very handsome man in his early forties. A member of the New York City council, he never walked out of his house looking anything less than immaculate. He'd removed his suit jacket, tossing it lightly over the empty chair next to him. Even with the sun having set, his dark clothing was still pressed and creased from that morning, not daring to reveal a wrinkle. "I heard Althea fell apart at the end."

"I wouldn't say that," Hettie said carefully, although that was pretty much how Harmon had described it. For reasons Hettie couldn't even begin to fathom, in the middle of her match with Fry, Althea's serves hit the net fifteen times. By the end of the game, Harmon had counted over twenty errors. She was her own worst enemy, Harmon had whispered in Hettie's ear. In just fifty-two minutes, Althea's hopes for Forest Hills had been soundly dashed. Harmon's article had been scathing. "She did make it to the final. That was the furthest she's ever gotten at Forest Hills."

"The *Boston Herald* said she doesn't have what it takes to

be a champion." Hettie felt her nose wrinkle up. Perhaps it was because she was new to this tennis business but Althea had seemed like she had what it took to her. Hettie was willing to bet that the sportswriter at the *Boston Herald* couldn't play tennis half as well as Althea. Eyeing her expression, Tony picked up his chopsticks once again. "The *New York Post* article wasn't so bad."

"I didn't realize you followed sports."

"I don't," Tony said flatly. But then his face brightened. "Except for baseball. I try to never miss a game. I will say that without Jackie playing, it's no longer as exciting as it was."

Hettie was not in the mood to hear about baseball. "I did see the article. Milton Gross said Althea played poorly because she was nervous and she carries the weight of her race on her shoulders."

Tony shrugged dramatically, not buying this excuse. "Okay? And? She's been doing that for almost a decade. Althea is no young teenager. If she still can't carry those burdens then she needs to go sit herself down. In case you were wondering, I disagree with that article. There has to be another reason she fell apart."

Hettie was inclined to agree with both Tony and the article. Althea had been nervous but Hettie had doubts as to whether it was because she suddenly realized she was a Negro in the midst of the finals. "Syd Llewellyn, her coach, said she just wanted it too badly. I could see that. This was her seventh try. And she's already on the road again. I believe she's headed to Toronto as we speak and then down to Mexico. Then she's defending her title at a tournament somewhere in Asia. She'll be back in New York in January." The time that they'd scheduled their table tennis rematch. "I wish I could tell you why Althea thinks she lost, but she refused to give an interview to the double H." Harmon had raced to meet Althea after the loss and was soundly rebuffed.

Tony waved a distracted hand. "Hettie, I appreciate your enthusiasm but this is ridiculous. You see that, don't you? You're trying to learn a whole genre for a single year just so you can stay at the double H. You should just take my friend up on his offer and become a freelance journalist for his paper. Then you can write about what you're passionate about rather than what Edgar is passionate about."

Hettie had provided Tony with a much-abbreviated turn of events regarding her switch at the double H. The one that went along the lines of Edgar summoning her back to New York to write on sports. She left out the part where she'd gotten in trouble. Everyone didn't need to know that.

"I'm not doing freelance."

"All of those people that you love and admire? Hughes, Wright, Hurston, Brooks . . . they were starving artists, love. Literally. We would have rent parties and whatnot just so people could eat and live. And yet they were so inspired, they created. They wrote out of their struggles. Rare is the person who becomes something great coloring within the lines."

They'd had this discussion more times than Hettie had fingers. "No," she said simply as she reached for her tepid cup of tea. "I grew up struggling. I'm not going back. And I have a much greater chance of being noticed if I'm writing for a paper where my articles might make the front page."

"You have no children and no husband. If you don't take the risk now—writing what you're passionate about—you'll never reach the heights you claim you want to reach."

"Would you prefer to discuss how you plan to run as a Democrat next year?"

"Do I want to talk about how the Republican party is increasingly welcoming the Dixiecrats? I . . . no, you will not distract me with work. I actually came here this evening excited to talk to you about something and it wasn't tennis or politics."

Hettie, finally eating her dinner, just raised an eyebrow in question.

"Let's talk about Lewis."

Hettie coughed into her fist, almost choking on the rice in her mouth. "Who?"

"Don't play me for crazy. While I do not have a membership at Shady Rest, I have enough friends who do. If I want to get in, I can. If I want the latest on-dit, I get it. Imagine my surprise when I learned that Lewis put a young, unmarried woman on his tab at the club."

"Ridiculous."

"There's nothing more exciting than scandal, particularly the scandal of a young woman leaving her husband for someone who, in comparison, looks like they fell off a dumpster truck. Anything related to Lewis is news."

Hettie chewed very slowly. "I could see if he was a politician or something, but—"

"He's rich, young, handsome, and now divorced. It was the quietest, coldest divorce I've ever seen. And I have seen my share."

Hettie placed the smaller end of the chopsticks in her mouth, now properly distracted even though she'd sworn she was not giving two thoughts to Lewis ever again in life. "How so?"

"There were no screaming matches, no face slaps, no loud accusations." Hettie leveled a look at him. "People do that in public," Tony said defensively. "All I know is, one day Lewis and Laverne were together, the next day Lewis was serving Laverne divorce papers."

"Wait a minute. *He* served *her* divorce papers?"

Tony jerked his head back slightly. "You didn't think it was the other way around, did you? This is Lewis we're talking about. He served her and the reason I know that's a fact is because it all went down at Shady Rest. She left his house and moved in with Humpty-Dumpty. Then he filed the paperwork and had it delivered to her at the clubhouse because Laverne had the nerve to keep going on his dime. It was very stressful. Laverne wanted things to be the same but when there's a divorce, people have to choose. Everyone chose Lewis."

"Because she left him?" Hettie whispered, after taking a quick look around the restaurant.

"Because he's Lewis!" Tony snapped as though she was an idiot. "Why would you stick with Laverne? For friendship? Please. Morton Smalls was, by all accounts, a successful accountant. The day people learned he was the reason for the divorce, his business dried up like a raisin in the sun. He had to leave New York if he was going to make any money."

Hettie reached for her cold cup of tea. Lewis hadn't said all of this.

"Lewis had someone else serve Laverne right there on the patio where he was reading his papers and drinking a cup of coffee. He never looked in her direction once. I know. I was there, I was watching. He's like ice, that man."

Hettie blinked once, long and slow. But Tony didn't notice.

"Ever since that day, women have been lined up in the pew behind his at church, wearing their Sunday best and waiting for the final papers to go through, and the week after they do, here you come."

"You go to his church?"

Tony nodded as he played with the rim of his teacup. "When I go to church, yes. We're AME."

That did not surprise her at all. The African Methodist Episcopal Church was an old Negro denomination that attracted the educated, the wealthy, and the traditional.

"Lewis doesn't talk. He's extremely close-mouthed, even when he and Laverne were together. No one ever knows what's on his mind, but Morton Smalls never shuts up. Once I knew the finalization of the divorce was on the horizon, I started going to church." Tony held up two fingers. "Best gossip is at Shady Rest, second at Bethel AME. Lewis attends service without fail—every Sunday—with his miniature doll at his side. Laverne switched to Morton's church months ago. They're married now, by the way. Some quick two-bit service at the courthouse. She keeps trying to act like it's romantic but there's nothing romantic about living from paycheck to paycheck. Mark my words, that girl is going to wake up one day next to Morton Smalls and regret her life choices."

Almost, Hettie asked for more information but she stopped herself from taking that route. "You've seen Hyacinth?"

Tony leaned forward. "You haven't met Hyacinth?"

Hettie lowered her chopsticks. "We're not in that kind of relationship. Why would I meet his child?"

"What kind of relationship are you in?"

The question was tossed out lightly but there was a gleam in Tony's eye. Whatever she told him was going to be spread around to somebody. "We're just . . . acquaintances."

"Lewis doesn't open his bank account for acquaintances. He gives to the church, to his own personal charity, his wife—ex-wife—and daughter. And no more."

Hettie scoffed. "How would you know that? Some people do not announce when they give."

"Fair point. But I've never heard of him inviting anyone to Shady Rest. Not one single soul. Except for you."

"You're making it bigger than what it is. We had something to discuss. It was more convenient to speak there."

"How do you even know him?"

"A friend of a friend. I don't know him that well. I don't even know what his first name is. Just acquaintances," she said firmly. "And not even that, really. What we discussed wrapped up and we'll probably never see each other again."

Tony sat back in his seat, his eyes narrowed as he watched her for a long minute. Then he pushed back from the table. "You made me drink all of that tea and now I have to use the restroom. I'll be back in a second."

Hettie took a moment to eat some more rice. She didn't want to think about Lewis, but her mind couldn't help but go back to those first few dinners where he'd done nothing but share his heart.

"Is this seat taken?"

Hettie almost choked once again as S. A. Lewis filled Tony's empty seat.

CHAPTER 16

Ace—a winning serve where the receiving tennis player is unable to return the ball

"You!" It was the only word that she could release in that moment but she thought it carried all of how she felt about his presence.

"Me," he said as he removed a dark blue hat from his head, lowering it onto an empty spot at the table. Lewis sat back in the chair, comfortable-like, as though all this time, she'd been waiting for him. She watched him cross one long leg over the other. Wearing dark pants and a white collared shirt that was mostly covered by a navy blue sweater buttoned neatly down his chest, he looked like a professor. Hettie stared open-mouthed at the man sitting across from her. "Who is it that you're meeting with tonight? Tony?"

"Um . . ." Lewis's thin-framed glasses slid a centimeter

down his nose as his eyes narrowed at her. She felt momentarily like a student who had failed to deliver an assignment on time.

"Hello." Tony's voice was cool as he approached the table. Lewis turned his head. Tony came to a stop. "Mr. Lewis." His eyes darted to Hettie's and she saw two words revealed: *you liar*. Her eyes flashed wide in response as she tried to quickly but silently convey that she didn't know why he was here. But Tony had already looked away, miffed.

"Anthony, it's good to see you again."

"Uh, you too."

"This is very, very rude of me, but I need to appropriate your date."

"No," Hettie said, finally finding her voice. "You and me, we're done." Hettie ignored the little fire that was now dancing in Tony's eyes. It took a second for her to realize that mere acquaintances didn't say things like that to each other.

Lewis folded his arms over his chest. "No, mockingbird. We've only just begun." He reached into his pocket and pulled out his silver case. Removing a card, he handed it to Tony. "Give me a call when it's time for you to run for re-election and don't worry about dinner—it's on me."

Hettie gaped as Tony practically bowed over the card. Tony was the politician and more likely to have power and authority in his hands rather than a man who sold sporting goods. "Thank you, Mr. Lewis. Much appreciated. You don't have to pay for dinner. I've eaten most of my fill."

"No, no," Lewis said breezily. "I'm being rude. It's the least I can do."

"Can you hand me my jacket?"

"Absolutely."

"Tony and I are having dinner. Lewis, you can't just—"

Tony walked away fast, his feet carrying him to the nearest exit. Saying no more, Hettie merely hiked a pointed finger in Tony's direction.

"Do you know who you remind me of?" Lewis was fiddling with the card case in his hand, opening and closing it.

"I don't care."

"My mother."

"The same one who made you flee the state of Tennessee? The one you didn't want to pick up from the train station?" Hettie stopped speaking and lowered her utensils to her plate. "You know what? As I've said already, I don't care." Hettie reached for her purse. She would pay for her own meal, thank you very much.

"The day I announced my engagement to Laverne, my mother told me that I was making a horrible mistake." Lewis opened the card case and then snapped it shut. "She said Laverne brought out the worst in me and one day I'd look at Laverne and I'd hate her. Naturally, that was all I needed to hear to rush the wedding."

"Your mother sounds like a very wise woman to me," she quipped, hoping to offend him.

Lewis glanced up from the card case, a smile written in his golden eyes and tugging on his lips. "My parents' store is only successful and still running because of my mother. My father is the warm one of the pair, the gentle one. But he's horrible at business and terrible at making the hard decisions. He was the parent we ran to when we wanted to be held and comforted, and the one more likely to tell you what you wanted to hear rather than what you needed to hear. It was easy to resent her when I was young—still is, truth be told—but I learned after a particularly stressful run-in with the Klan, where it was Mama and me on one side of the store's door with a shotgun and a bunch of Satan's followers on the other side, that Mama always has a reason for what she does. Always. But if I don't ask her why, she'll never share it with me."

"Lewis, I'm leaving." Hettie stood up, dropping several dollar bills onto the table.

Lewis leaned forward, one hand held up in supplication. "Sit, please. Give me two more minutes to plead my case. If you don't like what I have to say, I won't keep you."

She'd never seen this earnest expression in his eyes before. Two minutes, he said? She returned very stiffly to her chair and pretended not to hear the whooshing sigh of relief that exited his mouth. She reached up around her neck, digging out the necklace that had disappeared under her blouse, and played with the charm as he began to speak. "First off, I am that person who—when surprised—says aloud exactly what he's thinking without filtering it almost one hundred percent guaranteed. A gift, I think, from my mother. Laverne used to tell me all the time that it was probably best that I just kept my mouth shut. I said all of that to say that I wasn't trying to push you away with my words when you were confiding in me. I was talking without thinking and it came out very critical. I would like to apologize."

Hettie opened her mouth to speak, but he wasn't done yet.

"That leads me to my second point," he said quickly, as though to stave off another refusal. "I would like to understand if you'd be willing to explain. And to make up for my blunder, I would like to help you if I can. You were right. We did—we do—have a friendship of sorts but I've been the one doing most of the reaping. Let this be my turn to extend a hand of friendship to you."

Hettie stared down at the small swirls indented in the surface of the wooden table before her.

"Can I take this?" the waitress asked, appearing at Hettie's side and pulling her out of her thoughts.

"Yes, please. Thank you." Nothing was said as the waitress quickly cleared the table.

With nothing between them, Lewis lowered his arm and slid his hand across the surface toward her, palm up. "Hello, my name is Shadrach Ashley Lewis. I am thirty-five years old. I have a six-year-old daughter who is sometimes the only reason I can get out of bed in the morning, because my wife of twelve years—whom I've actually been with for twenty years—has left me for a man who I once considered a dear friend. I studied engineering in college just so I could learn how to tear things apart and put them back together again. Since I love sports of all kinds, it was baseballs and catcher mitts, and basketballs, and tennis rackets that I started fiddling with. Now I own four stores that sell sports gear and am planning to open a fifth next year. I'm often far more blunt than a situation calls for, which is why my favorite Bible verse is: 'The words of the reckless pierce like swords, but the tongue of the wise brings healing.'"

Shadrach. It fit him. It really did. Hettie looked down at his hand. She didn't know about this. It was in her to move on once hurt, but . . . it was Lewis. Hettie placed the palm of her hand in his before meeting his gaze. She watched him bite down on his lip, but his only response was to wrap his long fingers around hers. When she hesitated to speak, it was not because she didn't have words to say. "I am Hester Jolene Carlin, called Hettie by most, although those who knew me as a girl still call me Hettie Jo. I have never married. I have no children, although I'd like to walk those paths one day. I am twenty-nine years old and I was born with the greatest desire to leave my mark on the world. For me that's through writing. There's a lot I'm willing to do to get my hands on a good story like, say for instance, dine with older, educated men so that I can keep a finger on the pulse of what is happening in the world." Hettie watched a light go off in his eyes. She squeezed his hand to recapture his attention. She made sure to look at him when she said, "But that was not my motivation for steak nights with Shadrach Lewis."

A bemused expression crossed his face. "Really?"

"Lewis . . . Shad. I just learned your profession a few weeks ago. For all I knew you were a mailman. No offense to mailmen but they're not usually who I seek out when writing a story."

"Then why on earth did you meet me for months every Friday and put up with my whining?"

Hettie pulled her hand out of his and sat back, debating how honest she should be. "Because, in all my years, I've never come across a man so thoroughly committed to the vows he'd made before God." Shadrach closed his eyes, wincing as though she'd pressed on a wound. "It was intoxicating, listening to you speak this language I'd never heard spoken before. It wasn't simply a blanket commitment." Her parents, after all, were committed to each other. Morgan and his wife were committed to each other. Sort of. "It was something else entirely. You not only loved Laverne, you also strived to like her."

Hettie watched him bring embarrassed hands to his face. When he dropped them, he could barely look her in the eyes. "My father used to tell us that a man marries for his feelings but stays married by choice. He'd tell my brothers and me to remember to choose your bride every morning you wake up beside her. I tried, Hettie." The words were released with a sigh. "I really tried."

"I know." If there was one thing Hettie was certain of, he had not filed those divorce papers until he'd been absolutely certain it was over.

"We're not going to do this. It isn't Friday. I came here to hear about you. I find you . . . fascinating. What are your limitations?"

Fascinating? That one word—that look in his eyes—should not have thrilled her as it did. She was not over him. She was well and truly caught by him. "What?"

"You said there's a lot you're willing to do to get a good story. Where do you draw the line? Where do you say, I go this far and no further?"

They were very good questions to which she had no answer. She was sure there were boundaries, she just didn't know what they were or where they landed.

"I'm probably speaking out of my divorce but something outside of yourself should define you. People should be able to rely on the fact that at the end of the day you're trustworthy not because of who you are but because of what you stand for," Shadrach said quietly, gently.

Hettie dipped her head. "You're right. I . . . agree." It was something to think about. "My goal with Althea is to help her . . . as I help myself." She winced a bit. It sounded bad when put like that. "This is my job, Shadrach." Hettie hated that she sounded defensive.

Shadrach waved a hand. "I'm not here to tell you what to do or not do. You know better than me what's required of a journalist. I just think it's very difficult to change people's minds, and Althea seems the stubborn sort. I will say, since sports are near and dear to my heart, your plan caused me to nearly have a stroke. How did you cheat years ago?"

Hettie tapped several of her fingernails against the table

before leaning forward. "All right, have you ever been in a situation where one person was serious about something and the other person thought it was a joke?"

Shadrach nodded once, his lips twisting a bit as though he could see where this was going already.

"There was a table tennis game setup in our neighborhood and Althea would play all day on Saturdays, challenging every kid in the vicinity each weekend and forever winning. The rules were if you won, you could keep playing. This was a bit frustrating because it never seemed to cross Althea's mind that other people would like to play with someone who was not her. Well, one day, after watching her play for more hours than I could count, I realized that the only way to beat Althea was to cheat. I justified this because she was not being considerate of others. At the time, I thought, she's not going to be happy but maybe she'll have a laugh at my cleverness."

"Which was . . . ?"

"I added a second ball when she was distracted and won by a single point. She thought I had missed the ball—which I did—and turned away triumphantly, but a second ball slid down the sleeve of my sweater."

Shadrach held up a hand, silently asking her to pause as he tried to picture this in his mind. "The timing . . ."

"A gift from God, yes. But I practiced it too. For weeks, with my uncle Morgan."

Shadrach's eyes went wide for a second. "You could have practiced . . . getting better . . ."

Hettie waved a hand, dismissing his words. "It could not have been more perfect. She was very angry. Just when I was about to tell her what I'd done for laughs and giggles, her paddle goes flying past my head." Shadrach's lips pressed very tightly together. "I couldn't believe it."

"In her early days on the tennis court, she used to threaten to beat people who laughed at her." Shadrach's voice was very solemn, as if he was only realizing now that maybe Althea had been serious.

"Well, I didn't think she'd come at me. We were friends, weren't we? But I'd clearly crossed a line. I see that now. There is no such thing as 'just a game' with Althea. Anyway, you've had a taste of what I'm like when I'm angry."

"I'm guessing lots of words exited your mouth."

"Lots of them. I told her about herself and I told her about her mama, too." Hettie wiped her hands together. "That was it. We didn't speak to each other for sixteen years."

"So, what's the plan now?"

Hettie shrugged and looked away. "You'd have to be there really. I don't reveal my tips and tricks ahead of time."

"I don't know where you're planning to host your challenge but I do have access to several table tennis courts."

"I will accept nothing from you for free ever again." The look that crossed his face nearly made her laugh, except she was serious. "There's a perfectly good table tennis set at the youth center down the street from my apartment."

"But does it come with a personal table tennis coach? No," he said, answering his own question and clearly offended that she was not jumping at his offer.

"Sir."

"Ma'am. Listen, if you insist, just write an article on my stores and give me free advertising. Christmas is right around the corner." Hettie considered this. She probably could swing an article about his stores by Edgar and get approval for it. The double H did like to support Negro businesses. "And I will help you so that you can play a game of table tennis without embarrassing yourself in front of Althea. I keep a table tennis set in my office. We can practice there," he said as though it were a done deal. He extended a hand. Hettie hesitated only a second before bringing her hand up to take it but just when she nearly laid her palm against his, he jerked his hand back, laying it neatly in his lap.

Hettie, very slowly, pulled her arm back as Shadrach blinked at her behind his thin-framed glasses.

"I forgot to say something," Shadrach said quickly after a long pause. "You brought up a topic at Shady Rest that we have to remember to discuss at an appropriate time." Frowning, Hettie eyed him warily, wondering what he was referencing, because she was fairly certain they'd covered everything. Tugging on the collar of his shirt, Shadrach's eyes were somewhere just past her head. "I'd like to talk about it now honestly, because I'd be lying if I didn't say that I have been pondering your words since the moment you said them. They've been spinning round and round in my head like a phonograph record."

What on earth was he talking about? "Shadrach—"

Shadrach looked down at himself and pinched an inch of his sweater. "I'm even sitting here wearing my favorite outfit—despite warning myself very sternly not to."

"Shadrach, what are you . . ." Hettie paused, a sudden, mortifying thought occurring to her.

"Yes, that. That is what is on my mind."

Heat flared up her face, under her arms, on her chest. It was her turn to look everywhere except his eyes. Hettie waved a hand. "Just ignore it. I only said it because I thought I'd never speak to you again." What kind of woman admitted aloud that she lusted after a man? If her mother were here, she'd faint dead away. Hettie wanted to faint dead away. Why on earth would he bring this up?

Shadrach leaned forward, elbows on the table. "No. Absolutely not. I am in a fragile state of being at the moment and those words have bolstered me. We will discuss them when the dust of my life has settled."

"Shadrach . . . please." Hettie brought her hands to her face. She was beginning to see just the sort of person Shadrach Lewis was.

"The first time I saw you, you were laughing at something Howard was saying as though it was the funniest thing in the world and I remember thinking, that is one beautiful woman." Hettie's fingers parted. Shadrach's golden gaze was very much on the table. "I was still legally married but a man's got eyes. I sat with you that first day because . . . because . . ."

"Laverne and Morton were at the restaurant dining and you wanted to show that you had moved on."

"I wanted Laverne to see me with a woman who is prettier than she is. And far more sophisticated. Laverne's originally from some hick town in Mississippi where there are more cows than people. She's always been insecure around educated, career-minded women. I used you," he said apologetically.

Hettie released a small laugh, returning her hands to her lap. This conversation was so awkward. "Shadrach, I know."

"I'm afraid that if I acted now on any of those sorts of thoughts . . ."

Hettie knew exactly what kind of thoughts he was referencing.

"I'd still be using you. Inviting you to Shady Rest? That was me showing you off. Look, there's a beautiful woman who wants to be around me."

Shadrach was worried no woman would want him again and if Tony was to be believed—and Hettie believed him—the women had already lined up. Hettie could not work up an ounce of anger or annoyance. For one, she was extremely flattered. And for two, she'd used him too; the only difference was that he'd known it up front.

Eyes now focused on her, Shadrach lowered his voice and said, "I will not play with you, Hettie. My mama thinks I need to get remarried tomorrow. She's afraid I'm going to run amok and sow wild oats or something but I've never been a person who acted on impulse and I'm not going to start now. I'm not an animal." He tapped two fingers against the surface of the table. "I refuse to put you in a position of constant comparison to my ex-wife. One day I'm going to wake up not thinking about her at all and when that day comes, you'll know . . . if you're willing to wait . . . which you don't have to . . . although I'd be very disappointed if you didn't because I cannot seem to get you off my mind." Shadrach lowered his hand onto the table, extending his palm in her direction once more. "So, friends for now. Perhaps more later."

Hettie reached for his hand and shook it.

CHAPTER 17

Game point—when a player is one point away from winning the current game

On one of those warm, wet, winter days, Althea Gibson sauntered through the door of Shadrach's store. Hettie had been waiting for her, playing with the charm around her neck, as the clock ticked above her head, and so it was easy to see the delight that flooded the other woman's eyes as she paused on the threshold and took in the baseball bats that lined the walls, the catcher mitts, the bicycles tucked under racks. Footballs, basketballs, baseballs were stacked neatly on shelves as though just waiting for someone to pick them up and toss them around.

"You look like a kid entering a candy shop," Hettie called out lightly as she stepped out from the shadowed corner she'd been loitering in. It was now January. The Montgomery Bus

Boycott had wrapped itself neatly up with a bow—the perfect gift to American Negroes everywhere and just in time for Christmas. The Supreme Court had very kindly agreed that the 14th Amendment guaranteed all citizens equal rights and equal protection, and segregation on buses was no longer allowed. Of course such a victory was followed by four church bombings in Montgomery. A separate bomb—defused—was left at the Reverend Dr. King Jr.'s home. Every step forward could only mean an uptick of violence. But progress.

With it being the Lord's day and all, Shadrach's store was officially closed and thus the lights in the front of the building were turned off. Shadrach had only unlocked the door to let her in ten minutes ago. He'd told her to make herself comfortable while he wrapped up something and then disappeared into one of the many offices in the back ten minutes ago, leaving her to wander around, eyeing his inventory.

"You *would* be standing there like a creepy little goblin." Althea shrugged off her coat and pulled off her hat. Looking very different than the woman who had walked out onto the courts of Forest Hills just a few months ago, she was wearing a pair of blue jeans that had seen better days and an old T-shirt that Hettie would probably sleep in rather than wear out and about. Althea's short hair was pulled back into a small ponytail and she looked remarkably as she had sixteen years ago.

Hettie looked down at her skirt and blouse. She, too, probably resembled her younger self. All she was missing was a bow and a few barrettes. It was fitting, she thought grimly, that they meet like this again.

"Welcome back." Hettie forced herself to sound cheerful. It was not lost on her that even though she might win, Althea would be as unhappy as she had been the last time they'd played each other. Hettie's next few months could be miserable.

Althea sliced a hand through the air. "Hettie Jo, let's be nothing but ourselves here. You ain't no more happy to see me than I am to see you."

"Now, that's where you're wrong. I see you, I see dollar signs, I see good things. The sight of you makes me very happy."

Althea released a loud snort that sounded like she was both amused and annoyed.

"Miss Gibson." Shadrach appeared from around a shelf. "A pleasure and an honor to have you here at my store."

"You're *the* Lewis of Lewis Sporting Goods?" Althea extended a hand and Shadrach shook it with both of his.

"I am. I'm a huge fan. I know you're here for a showdown with Hettie, but I've got to show you the tennis racket I designed after watching you win the ATA tournament two years ago." Shadrach's words filled Althea, straightening her spine. An expression crossed her face that looked something like pure joy. "Let me take your hat and coat. I want you to be comfortable."

Hettie walked over and took Althea's hat and coat from Shadrach and went to hang them up in his office as he guided Althea deeper into his rectangular-shaped store and over to his wall of tennis rackets. Having fallen into the habit of meeting Shadrach three times a week for a game of table tennis—in his office—Hettie felt almost at home as she entered his workspace, which held a desk, chairs, awards, a filing cabinet, bookshelves, and the table tennis set.

There was also a small closet within his office and Hettie hung up Althea's outer garments right next to hers. With Shadrach playing the host, Hettie meandered over to his desk and only hesitated a second before picking up one of the framed photos that stood sentinel along the corners of the table. When they'd first met in his office, there had been no pictures in the room at all. It was his secretary who had let it slip that he'd removed all family photos. But now, very slowly, they'd been replaced. There was an old black and white photo that included Shadrach—who had to be approximately ten—his striking parents, and his younger brothers who all looked to be around the same age as one another. It was one of those pictures were no one smiled at the camera and everyone was wearing their nicest suit. The remaining photos were filled with Hyacinth at different ages. Hyacinth was her father's mirror image, although she was missing his golden brown eyes. But the newest photo was Hettie's favorite because Shadrach was in it. Shadrach had spent the holidays down South with his family and in this picture, he was sitting on a fallen log, in the woods, with Hyacinth in his lap. His daughter's arms were around his neck and they were both smiling at the camera.

Releasing a sigh, Hettie replaced the photo. She was distracting herself from what was about to come next. Forming her hands into fists, she whispered the word, "Focus." Then she left Shadrach's office, closing the door behind her.

"I designed this one for beginners so they can feel where they're supposed to grip the racket when playing," Shadrach was explaining to Althea.

Shadrach had set up a tennis table in the very center of the store. He'd had all of the other shelving moved away from it so a game could be played without fear of running into the merchandise—assuming you weren't playing wildly. He'd had the store displayed this way just in time for Christmas, he'd explained firmly. Sometimes people needed to be reminded how fun it all was before they pulled out their pocketbooks.

Hettie walked over to the table where two paddles already lay next to a couple of balls that were strategically trapped to keep from rolling. Hettie tapped her fingers against the surface of the table as Althea and Shadrach spent the next few minutes discussing the pros and cons of the tennis racket. Shadrach moved to stand by Hettie's side as Althea swung her arm wide, practicing a few moves. "You've heard that nature sings of God's glory? I see proof that there is a God when his people move as he designed them." There was nothing but awe in his voice as Althea took a few steps here and there, swinging the racket as though it were another limb that had always been attached to her body. "Her wingspan is something of envy and her legs are incredible. She was put together for the sole purpose of playing tennis."

"Basketball too, probably."

"I've never seen her toss a football, but with those arms, she'd be a heck of a quarterback."

"I was thinking volleyball."

"Anything." Shadrach's voice was hushed. "She could play anything."

Althea turned and held out the tennis racket. "This is nice, Lewis."

Shadrach moved to take it. "I know you have a contract with Harvey Lee, but perhaps your lawyer could speak with my lawyer and we can figure out a second endorsement of some kind."

Althea rocked back on her heels for a second. "I'm not so fancy I keep lawyers in my back pocket. How about you write something up and let me have a look over?"

"That works too but I don't ever want you to think I'm

taking advantage, so maybe I can provide you with the funds upfront for you to hire the lawyer of your choice."

Hettie cleared her throat. Loudly. Shadrach and Althea both appeared to have forgotten the challenge that was supposed to take place.

"Oh, for heaven's sake," Althea muttered before marching over to the table. "Which side do you want, Hettie Jo?"

"This one." Hettie scurried over to the side most familiar to her—the one closest to the door—and picked up a paddle.

"First one to get three points, right?" This was not going to be a long game. Hettie couldn't afford it.

"That's right."

Althea bent down, taking a moment to eye the table and the net. "When I win, you leave me the heck alone, right?"

"Yes. And if I win, you're stuck with me for nine months and you have to sit for interviews. Many interviews."

Althea's gaze met hers and Hettie could see that she did not like these terms but then another look crossed her eyes and she straightened. "Agreed. But," Althea said, "I need a warm-up. It's been a minute. You play, Lewis?"

"I do." Shadrach stepped into Hettie's space, placed a hand on her shoulder, and gave her a gentle nudge, pushing her out of the way. Hettie swallowed a moan of protest as Althea and Shadrach eyed one another. Reaching for his suspenders, Shadrach slid first the one and then the second over his shoulders, leaving them dangling at his sides. "We don't have to flip a coin. You can serve first."

That was all Althea needed to hear. She reached for the ball and slammed the little thing across the table. Shadrach met her serve. It was like nothing Hettie had ever seen before. The ball bounced back and forth, and back and forth; a tick-ticking sound that could have almost been the beat to a song, so steady did it flow. And then, Althea hit it and Shadrach missed and the ball flew over his shoulder and bounced off a rack of baseball jerseys. Hettie ran to fetch it and then brought it back to the table.

Shadrach lowered his paddle to the surface before him, his face flushed and his eyes dancing with emotion. "That was the loveliest game I've ever played."

Althea pointed her paddle in his direction. "I like you. Are you married?"

Shadrach placed two hands on his chest. "I am single. Very single."

Hettie rolled her eyes as Althea laughed. Her face, too, was flushed and she looked high in energy, as though she could keep playing all night.

"All right," Shadrach said, moving away from the table tennis set. He motioned for Hettie to take his place. "Should we flip a coin to see who serves first?"

"Hettie Jo can serve first." Althea jumped twice in the air and then she landed on the heels of her feet, rocking gently from side to side. She was trying to intimidate Hettie, first with the game against Shadrach and now all of this. And it was working. Hettie had half a mind to raise her racket in defeat right then and there. She glanced over at Shadrach. There was a steady look in his eyes. The same one she'd received the day before when they'd played and she'd managed to beat him for the first time. She'd earned that look. At their first practice, he'd told her he was not going to go easy on her and he hadn't. She did not score once in any of the games they'd played in October. But in November, things had started shaping up and she'd found herself a rhythm.

A rhythm she needed to remember right now. She did not play well at the pace that Althea and Shadrach had just played.

She needed to slow things all the way down. Hettie took a deep breath, exhaled and served the ball lightly over the small net. Althea hit it back with the force of a thousand suns and the ball flew past Hettie's head.

"Point to Gibson," Shadrach said unhelpfully, as he made a mark on a small chalkboard he'd dug up from somewhere.

Hettie started to search for the ball but Shadrach pulled one from his pocket and handed it to Althea. Althea served the ball with her trademark boldness but this time Hettie was ready. She hit it back. Althea hit it. Hettie hit it back and then reminded herself that she didn't have all day. Althea hit the ball and Hettie spoke. "I went to your parents' house and talked to your dad the other day."

The ball sailed right past Althea and landed neatly on a shelf next to an air pump.

Hettie turned and looked at Shadrach who was staring at her wide-eyed, and if Hettie wasn't mistaken, slightly appalled as a dawning realization crept over his eyes. He'd never asked her how she planned to 'cheat' at this game. Hettie had a feeling he'd been hoping she'd forget all about it if he trained her well enough. "Point to me." She turned to Althea. She was also wide-eyed. "I asked him if he was proud of you and he said he was."

Shadrach reached into his pocket and pulled out another ball. He handed it to Hettie.

"I think you need to not do that anymore." There was a mulish tone to Althea's words.

"Once upon a time we lived on the same block. I was just being neighborly." Again, Hettie served the ball, slowly. This time, Althea did not change the pace.

Back and forth and back and forth. "I met with Syd a few times when you were gone."

"I heard," Althea said through gritted teeth.

"He told me about how you almost joined the military a few years ago. You got inspired while in Missouri."

"Steady paycheck." Althea didn't like talking and playing at the same time. Hettie had to pause the conversation as the tempo of the game picked up.

"I took a train down to Missouri for a weekend trip. Dova Lee says hi." This time the ball went just under Althea's paddle and landed on the floor with a plop before rolling in Hettie's direction. Hettie crouched down and grabbed it.

Althea slammed the side of the paddle onto the table. "No talking, Hettie Jo."

"Dova Lee—"

"Leave him out of this." Dova Lee was Althea's former military boyfriend. He had been very kind and handsome and he still had stars in his eyes when he spoke of her. He'd also been a bit gray, leaving Hettie to wonder if it was his age that had played a part in ending their relationship.

Shadrach was practically hugging the chalkboard as his eyes darted from Althea to Hettie and from Hettie to Althea. Any other day, Hettie would have laughed. Shadrach Lewis was a nerd, plain and simple, who lived his life by the Bible and his parents' axioms. And Hettie loved the looks that crossed his face when she rocked his boat a little. Like now. But this was not the time to think about that. Very carefully, Shadrach added a second mark under Hettie's name.

Hettie lifted the ball and served. Althea slammed it back and Hettie jumped out of its way. She looked in the direction of where the ball had almost hit her and then she looked at Althea. Hettie flipped the paddle in her hand a few times, trying to calm herself down and knowing that Althea was going to try not to give her time to say anything else.

"It's a tie." Shadrach's voice was hesitant as he placed another ball on the table, this time in front of Althea. "Next person who scores wins the game."

Althea tossed the small white ball into the air and hit it, but Hettie was ready and her paddle met it. "Everyone has their theories as to why you keep losing."

The ball went way left and Hettie almost ran into some shelving but she hit it. "But I know the real reason why you only get so far and no further." From the sweat gathering under her arms and the fact that she was barely catching her breath, Hettie knew that she was not going to last much longer. She couldn't drag this out. But Althea spoke first.

"Someone's an expert now that she's been to one game." There was a bitter tinge to Althea's words as the ball sailed over the net.

"Not an expert on the game." Hettie hit the ball back over. "But I am an expert on you. And you—" Althea hit the ball over the net "—are lazy." Hettie hit the ball, Althea dove for it but was a second too late. Hettie lowered the paddle in her hand to the table in quiet triumph. She'd won.

CHAPTER 18

Break—when the server loses the game
to the returner

Althea's response was written in the stiffness of her limbs, in the jerky way she pulled back from the table tennis set. She started to leave, changed her mind, turned on her heels, and leveled a finger at Hettie.

It was because they were fully grown women that Hettie stood there unmoving. Had they been children, she'd have taken off at a dead run. "I can't stand you and your lying, cheating ways."

Those words, as always, made Hettie flinch but even more so it was the look in Althea's eyes. A fleeting thought passed through her mind: perhaps she'd gone too far. Althea turned away, her long legs carrying her through the store and out the door. Hettie took a step forward but was stopped by

Shadrach's iron grip. "Don't you go out there without a coat and hat. It's cold."

Hettie shifted toward him and he let her go. "What did you think?"

"I think you're a frightening woman and I'm glad you called that cheating 'cause it certainly wasn't fair." There was a bit of a pout to his mouth. Sports were sacred to this man and Hettie had definitely stepped on what he deemed precious.

"It was the only way to win the game."

"But was it the right way?" Shadrach held up his hands in surrender before she could say another word. "I leave you to your own devices, mockingbird. Take Althea her coat and hat—she ought not be wandering around in the cold either."

"Thank you," she blurted out. When the expression on his face turned to slight confusion, she said, "For coaching me these past few weeks, for letting us use your store, for . . ." She couldn't quite articulate the last one; she just stepped forward, wrapping her arms around his waist and holding tight for a quick second. So quick it was, Shadrach didn't have time to reciprocate before she pulled away and ran to his office for the coats.

Outside, heavy snowflakes fell at a snail's pace, slowly painting the city white. But Hettie still had no problems making out Althea's tall, slender figure as she stomped her way back toward the store with her head held high and her arms swinging at her sides as though the cold didn't bother her one bit. Hettie ran to meet her. "Here."

"You have some nerve," Althea said as she quickly slid on her outer garments.

"I don't think you're lazy. But I had to say something so wild, it would throw you."

Althea released a small humorless laugh. "I knew you were going to have tricks up your sleeve but somehow you still managed to surprise me."

"Let me treat you to a meal."

"Today? I'm not in the mood."

"We need to talk."

"Ain't nothing you could say—"

"I cheated sixteen years ago." Althea stared down at her, her lips tight, her eyes almost slits. "I added a second ball," Hettie told her. The truth after all these years was an apology of sorts. Althea's eyes flashed at this confession. "At least this time I beat you fair and square. Don't get mad just 'cause I know how to win a game. Have you eaten dinner yet? There's a burger place not too far from here. They've got great fries and I recommend their milkshakes even in this cold weather. Let's talk."

Althea muttered something unintelligible under her breath but she followed Hettie down the street and to the one burger shop that was guaranteed to be open on a Sunday.

With Hettie in the lead, they entered the warm and brightly lit-up diner. The place was mostly empty and around them Elvis was crooning a song about heartbreak. Hettie picked a booth and they sat down opposite each other. Hettie waited until they'd both ordered before pulling out her notebook and laying it on the table. Reaching across the table with one of her long arms, Althea gave the notebook a push and Hettie caught it in her lap.

"No. I meant it when I said I'm not in the mood. And I hope you know you're paying."

"I figured as much when you ordered two burgers and two strawberry shakes." Hettie returned her notebook to her purse. She had everything she'd written down earlier memorized anyway.

"A second ball . . . that is lowdown and dirty."

"And clever. Don't forget that word."

"You ain't ever think, let me try and win this the right way?"

Hettie nodded for a second. "It crossed my mind for about thirty seconds. But I can't beat you at what you do best. I can only do what I do best." Hettie sliced a hand through the air. "That's all in the past. Let's talk about now. I don't know what monster you've conjured in your mind when it comes to me writing on you but believe it or not I'm not here to tear your career down. I'm here to build it up."

"That is hard to believe."

"Let's talk about what it is that I want. I want to be in on your strategy for the tennis year of 1957. I want to attend your practices. I would like the option of attending your go-away games. I want to interview you before and after every game. If anything happens in your life that affects the game, I want to be the first to know." Hettie paused as the waitress appeared with a chocolate shake for her and the first of Althea's strawberry shakes.

"I've got a couple of rules I'd like to put in place," Althea said as she played with the straw in her shake.

"Okay, hit me."

"I don't want to talk about Will and whether or not we're getting married and when. I don't understand what any of that has to do with the game."

"We're single women, pretty much past our prime. Of course, we want to get married and the sooner the better," Hettie muttered aloud, purposefully including herself in the narrative to let Althea know that she understood.

"Speaking of men, you and Lewis are . . ."

"Just friends. Taking it one day at a time." But lest Althea get any thoughts, Hettie added quickly, "But we may be working toward something."

"So, like me and Will?" Althea's lips twitched.

"Exactly. We'll get to the finish line, if and when we want to." To Hettie's surprise, she was very much enjoying the slow pace that she and Shadrach were taking. They still met every Friday evening but he had nixed the steakhouse. Steak reminded him of his divorce and he was trying to get past that. Now, they tried a different restaurant every Friday and sometimes, to his horror, she paid for the meal. There was no pressure and no expectations. Just a gentle layer of understanding.

"I don't want to talk about my family. Where do you go off reaching out to my dad?"

"Just trying to gain an understanding."

"Don't do that."

"I'll remind you that I know your parents." Althea's mother had remembered Hettie and welcomed her right in.

"I play tennis. Me. Leave them out of it."

"Heard. But you ever think about how you could effectively use the media to work for you? That, too, is an option."

"You know what else is effective? Points on the scoreboard. My strategy for this year is winning and winning big. I'm stepping back from the little tournaments and putting all my focus on the big ones."

"Like Wimbledon?"

"Yep."

"What about the French one?"

Althea said nothing as the waitress arrived with their meal. Hettie snagged a hot fry and dipped it in her shake before eating.

"I've won at Roland-Garros already," Althea finally said. "I don't know that I need to do it again. It's Wimbledon and Forest Hills this year for me. When I win those, it'll shut people like you up."

"People like me? I haven't written a single article on you." That honor had gone to Harmon, thank you very much.

"You know what I mean. What's that you said about losing because I'm lazy?" Althea asked the question with some sass.

"I also said I didn't think that was actually true."

"But I bet you think you know why I'm losing." Hettie did have a theory and it had everything to do with why she'd won against Althea in table tennis a half hour ago. But she said nothing. "I'm tired of reading about how I'm no longer championship material, how I've gotten too old, how I fall to pieces in big tournaments—despite the fact that I consistently get into the finals. Everybody's got an opinion like they're any good on the field out there. I'm better than all of them on my worst day so who are you to sit there and tell me what a terrible talent I am?"

Taking her time, Hettie fixed her burger just the way she liked and then cut it into four pieces. "As long as you're in the public eye," she said slowly, "folks are going to have an opinion. That's life. No matter how much you'd like to change the rules of the game, you can't. Thus, you must learn how to play and win within the confines of where you've been placed."

"What?"

"The media is going to report on you, Althea, whether you like it or not. So give them stuff to report on that you like." Hettie pressed a hand to her chest. "That's what I'm here for. They'll speculate about your personal life, so tell me which part of your personal life you are okay seeing written in print. They'll discuss your training, so take me along so I can see how much hard work you're putting into it. And yes, if you lose, they'll say horrible things because that is how people are, but if you talk to me before and after, I can spin it so favorably to you that they look unnecessarily cruel. Make it work for you, Althea. You're drowning and only you think you don't need a lifeboat."

Althea's response was to take a big bite out of her burger. Hettie followed her example and they spent the next few minutes eating in silence.

"What's your thinking on fixing it?"

"Well," Hettie said as she dipped another fry into her shake. "We've got to change people's perception of you. We've got to make you America's darling before you start competing again. A love story can do that but, I get it, that's off the table." And Hettie did get it. The more the press wrote about Will and Althea, the more people expected to see an engagement ring and a wedding photo. If Althea had no intentions of marrying anytime soon, then to avoid that additional pressure, she needed to avoid discussing Will. "A family story depicting hard work with underdog themes will do it, but . . ."

"Off the table."

"Taking an interest in something that affects others may help. What do you think about meeting with the Reverend Dr. King Jr.? Rumor has it he's cooking up something else this year."

"No," Althea said flatly.

"What do you mean no?"

"I don't want any parts of the civil rights movement."

"Now, see, that kind of talk upsets people."

"I play tennis. That's it."

"No, that's not it. You don't just play tennis. You're a colored woman and you play tennis. Guess what folks see first?"

"I won't."

Hettie stared at Althea. "I know it's not 'cause you're chicken."

Althea rolled her eyes. Hard. "What's that you were saying about learning how to stay within the lines that you've been placed? I play tennis. I don't speak for you and nobody else with your skin color."

"Except that you do. If you walked out on the tennis court tomorrow and acted a fool, those white folks would point to every Negro person they see and say, 'Look, I knew it. They can't behave.'"

"I'm tired of carrying the weight of all you Negroes on my back. And I refuse to do it any longer. God bless the Reverend Dr. King Jr., and everyone working with him, but I am a tennis player. Not a crusader. Besides, personally?" Althea placed a hand on her chest. "Our best chance to advance in society is to prove ourselves as individuals. This way, when you're accepted, people will appreciate you rather than having you shoved down their throats."

Hettie stared down at her fries. So, this was a hiccup. People who read the same news as Hettie and continued to think that the slow and easy path was the way to civil rights were usually fairly settled in their minds at this point. Still, she found herself saying, "Individually? White people get the luxury of being treated as individuals. Not us. We're all the same in their minds."

"When I win Wimbledon—"

"Oh," Hettie said aloud, tossing her hands in the air. "Okay, that's what we've been waiting on all these years. If only Frederick Douglass had known. Wimbledon was the key."

Ignoring her, Althea continued, "People will see me and realize that Negroes can do and accomplish much. You can say what you want to say and think what you want to think, but I'm not budging on this. So, what else can I do to change my image?"

Hettie felt a creeping sense of dread wash over her. She was never going to write for *The Crisis* and Althea was never going to win over public opinion because there was nothing that was going to change her public image—unless of course, Hettie once again took matters into her own hands.

CHAPTER 19

Down the line—hitting a tennis shot from where the tennis player is standing

What Hettie told Althea was that she needed to think on things and try to come up with a plan. After they finished eating, Hettie paid for the meal, but knowing she still had a ways to go before Althea would feel even remotely comfortable with her, she asked Althea if she still enjoyed going to the movies.

"I still love flickers. I see every single one I can."

"A favorite of mine has returned to the Apollo. Want to go?"

"Which one?"

"I'll let you be surprised."

"Just so long as you're paying."

"Of course. Where are you staying, by the way?"

"With Will's family," Althea told her as Hettie left a few bills on the table.

"That's not awkward?"

"I met him through his sister Rosemary. His family is like my family. It's not awkward at all."

"Why not get your own place?"

"With what money?"

They left the store, waved to the waitstaff and stepped out into the snowy evening. "Do you play tennis 'cause you like it?"

Althea released a huff that materialized as a cloud before her. "Tennis is the door to other things opening up."

"Like . . . ?"

"I want to sing."

"Sing?"

"Yep. I've played around in a recording studio before," Althea said smugly. "If I do well this year, maybe I'll be on the big screen myself."

"You mean like Hollywood?"

"I'm suffering now to get paid later."

It wasn't the worst plan in the world, but there certainly was no guarantee that those doors would open. "What happened with you almost joining the military? That surprised me."

"The year I graduated from college was rough. Everyone was tugging on my sweater. The ATA, the USLTA, my coaches . . . they all had ideas for what I was supposed to do and all of that wears a body out. I just wanted some peace . . . and a steady paycheck. It'd be nice to be able to buy what I want when I want. It'd be nice to have my own place and maybe my own car."

"It didn't have anything to do with Dova Lee?"

Althea's former boyfriend hadn't just been in the military, he'd made it his career. "A little maybe," she said after a minute. "He was presenting another option, if you will. And at the time it wasn't a bad one. I was this close." Althea created an inch between her fingers. "This close to signing the paperwork but then I got that call from the State Department asking me to play in Asia."

"Did you make the right decision?"

"Absolutely. I've seen the world, Hettie, and in fine fashion. I wouldn't change that for anything."

They said little more as they marched the rest of the way to the subway in silence. It was a short ride to the theater and an even shorter walk to the building. Althea paused as she read the name of the film they'd be watching. "This would be one of your favorite movies, wouldn't it?"

"Sometimes people say I look like her." Hettie was pointing to the woman in the middle of the large advertisement outside the theater. "The colored version of her."

"Where are these people who say these things? You look like Marilyn Monroe just as much as I look like Lauren Bacall here."

Ignoring her, Hettie walked up to the glass window of the ticket booth. "Two tickets for *How to Marry a Millionaire*, please." Then, turning to Althea, she asked, "You know what's returning next week?"

"*The Day the Earth Stood Still*?"

"Please. *Seven Brides for Seven Brothers*."

"I think *Dial M for Murder* is coming back too." As if Hettie wanted to watch anything without some romance in it.

"So is *The King and I*."

"I'm sensing a theme here."

"If that theme includes good movies, you're right."

Both too full for snacks, they went straight into the hushed and darkened theater, where only a few people were scattered here and there. Althea chose two seats that seemed like they were in the very middle of the theater and Hettie sat down. Having been so busy in the past few months, it had been some time since Hettie had watched a film. The one that was beginning to flash on the screen before her reminded her of days past, when she and a few girls from school would come to the movies and pick an actress 'to be'. They'd go in blind, not knowing which woman on screen would be the heroine, the villain, or simply an extra (although if you watched enough films you sort of had an idea). They'd giggle through the whole movie as they slowly realized who the 'winner' and who the 'loser' was. This memory shook another one loose and Hettie recalled one of the few times—during the year of their tenuous friendship—that she and Althea had gone to the movies together.

"I'll be that one," Hettie had whispered, pointing to Joan Fontaine, recognizing the actress immediately. Her odds were good on having chosen the best character in the film.

"What?" Althea had whispered back, confused. Evidently, she had never played this game before.

"I'm going to be her," Hettie had said pointedly, as though that explained everything. It wasn't as if she could go into detail when the film had already started. "Who are you going to be?"

Althea said nothing and Hettie had sat back, shaking her head, disappointed that Althea was not familiar with this way of watching a movie. Ten minutes into the film, Althea had nudged Hettie. "I'm going to be famous like all of them."

"That's not how it works!"

"Shh!"

Hettie had taken a moment to turn around, glaring at the young man behind her. "Don't you shush me!"

"You just watch, I'm going to have so much money and everyone will know my name and I don't care what I have to do to get it." Hettie had shaken her head. Trust Althea to get it all wrong. But she wasn't done yet. "I'll have a house, a car, and new clothes all the time. And nothing and nobody will stop me from getting that."

A week after their trip to the movies, Hettie was sitting on cold metal bleachers and trying to ignore the chill that was soaking into her woolen skirt. Outside, the sun was shining and the sky was a brilliant, blinding blue. The snow from a week ago had not stuck, most of it melting by the next day. But still the beauty of the morning seemed confusing when contrasted against the invisible frost that hung in the air. Hettie wanted nothing more than to be inside a warm building somewhere—preferably next to a heater—and drinking something hot. Instead, she was doing her very best not to turn into an icicle as Althea ran this way and that, hitting balls served by her opponent.

"What kind of serve was that?" Althea called out to the other tennis player.

There were indoor tennis courts. But, Althea had explained, if she was going to win big this year then she had to practice on grass. She'd play on no other kind of court. Hettie shuddered as a cold snap tried to whittle its way past the buttons of her coat.

"Watch your footwork," Syd yelled as Althea ran to meet another ball.

"If Wendell could actually play, I could work on my footwork." If Hettie had been Wendell, they'd have been in the midst of a knock-down drag-out argument by now. But Wendell merely rolled his shoulders at Althea's words and whacked the ball over the net once again.

Althea usually spent the cold months of the year down South. Apparently, her old coaches, Dr. Eaton and Dr. Johnson, still opened their doors and their tennis courts to Althea, allowing her to visit anytime. But Syd wasn't able to take off for warmer weather just yet, so here they were.

Hettie stomped her feet and sniffed before checking her watch once again. She had a meeting with Edgar in a half hour. Two minutes had passed since she'd last checked it.

"Again!" Syd called out to Althea. Althea took a step back, and then leaped forward, serving the ball that Syd had tossed her way. Hettie might be freezing but Althea was not. Sweat was dripping down the side of her face and soaking into her shirt. The conditions seemed ripe for coming down with an illness of sorts.

Hettie snorted at the trail of her own thoughts. She was beginning to sound like her mother . . . or Howard.

The night before, she'd had dinner with Howard. "I don't see how she can stay here if she wants to train only on grass," he'd told Hettie as they dined on pasta. "Practicing in New York, outside, in the middle of January, is not wise. Weather conditions matter too. But Althea will always do what Althea wants to do."

Hettie had pushed back on that statement. "I don't think that's a fair assessment, Howard. Having seen her up close, it seems as though she spends all of her time doing what others would have her do." Howard's expression had taken on a stubborn, old-man tinge and having been raised by a stubborn old man, Hettie decided that their conversation would be better served with a slight change in subject. "Howard, what would make you like her? What would make you root for her?"

He'd shrugged. "She's just too standoffish. She thinks she knows best." He'd paused. "I suppose she'd have to come across as vulnerable. But she's never that way—even when she loses."

Come across as vulnerable.

Hettie had been thinking about those words all day. Hettie checked her watch and then slowly stood up, stretching. It was that or lose all feeling in her nether regions.

Wendell served the ball across the net and Althea missed it. Her response was to take her racket and slam it against the ground. The racket bent and cracked. Althea tossed it to the side with frustration. Apparently used to this sort of reaction, Syd merely tossed Althea a new racket. Hettie tsked under her breath. Some people really had anger management issues.

Stepping down off the bleachers, Hettie slowly walked toward the court where the tennis ball was being volleyed back and forth. Althea did not want to speak on civil rights but sometimes people who felt that way didn't actually know why civil rights were necessary. Althea arguably should know, considering that she'd spent so much time in the South training, but Hettie could see how she might have a one-track mind that was zeroed in on tennis only. Maybe Althea needed help seeing. Maybe she needed someone to point things out to her. Hettie winced at where her thoughts were taking her. Did she really want to go down that path again?

"Fifteen–love," Syd called out. "Let's take a short break."

Althea walked away from the net, coming to a stop about a foot away from where Hettie stood next to her personal items.

"If I understand correctly, you're here in New York, playing outside, to recreate the atmosphere you'll need for the tournaments, right?" Althea dropped down, crouching before her bag and ignoring Hettie.

Hettie extended a hand as though checking for snow. "I don't think it's going to be this cold in London. Imagine overexerting yourself for nothing."

Sorry, Syd, Hettie thought as she returned her hand to her pocket. But some things were more important.

"You'll be tired before March comes around and you won't have played a single game."

And with those lightly placed words, Hettie left and tried to ignore the guilt that whispered in her ear.

"Good afternoon, Miss Hettie. You make me think it might be cold out there," Isaiah Thompson teased as Hettie entered the office building. He left his desk, walking over to the elevators.

"Don't be ridiculous. It's perfectly balmy." There was a tremor to the last word that caused Mr. Thompson to laugh.

"I'd believe you if your nose wasn't so red." An elevator's doors opened and Mr. Thompson put a hand inside, forcing it to wait for Hettie.

"I'd believe me if I could feel my nose." Her nose could be running at the moment and Hettie would have no clue. She couldn't feel anything on her face.

"Have a nice day, Miss Hettie, and take care now. I don't want you getting sick." The elevator doors closed and Hettie slowly took off her gloves and began unwinding the scarf she'd wrapped so tightly around her neck that she was almost in danger of choking.

By the time the elevator doors opened on the floor of the double H, she was holding most of her winter things and feeling was returning to parts of her body. "Hello," she called out to no one in particular as she entered the office space.

"Hello, Miss Hettie." Tilly rose to her feet as Hettie reached her desk. "Mr. Edgar said he wants to see you as soon as you come in."

"Do I have time for a cup of coffee?"

"I say take it with you."

"Fabulous idea."

Minutes later, Hettie very carefully walked down the long hallway to Edgar's desk with a hot cup of coffee in hand.

"Just push the door open," Gayle told her. "He's waiting for you."

Hettie obeyed, encountering the cloud of smoke that filled Edgar's office. She closed the door behind her.

"Sit." Edgar's voice was gruff and heavy with tobacco. There were two ashtrays on his paper-filled desk and both were overflowing. Gripping her coffee cup, Hettie fought the urge to ask if they could open a window. She would face the cold again if it meant she could breathe. Instead, she took a seat across from her boss. "It's been a week since you got Althea's agreement and I've seen nary an article."

"She's not competing."

"That doesn't mean you can't write about other things. You think I'm paying you to watch her toss a ball back and forth?"

Hettie had known this conversation was coming. "No, I don't. But people don't just confide in you. You've got to build a foundation of sorts."

"Build a foundation while you write." He hissed the last word. "This would be a good time to write about her personal life. Is she marrying what's-his-name?"

Hettie shook her head. "She said no to the personal life."

"What do you mean she said no? When did we decide that she got to choose what gets written?"

Hettie pinched a small stack of papers and set them onto the floor. Ignoring Edgar's look of irritation, she lowered her cup of coffee onto the flat of his desk. "Let's assume that I started with this much grace with Althea." Hettie created a space of about ten inches between her hands. "I've burned half of it just getting her to agree to let me tag along. If I start writing about topics she's deemed off-limits, I'm out, Mr. Edgar, before she plays a single game this year."

Frown lines appeared on Edgar's face. "Do you know why her personal life is important?"

"Yes. It makes her interesting and relatable."

Edgar's frown deepened. "It's more than that, Hettie. Are you playing stupid or are you simply that naive?"

"Let's call me naive." Hettie's voice was cool. She appreciated being referred to as stupid as much as she liked being hit by a car.

"She's tall!" Hettie waited for him to continue. "Aggressive! They say the other girls are afraid of her. And I'm not just talking about white girls. She always wears shorts and pants."

Picking up her coffee cup, Hettie gave her drink a stir. "You sound ridiculous."

"Hettie—"

"I know what you're referencing. I'm neither stupid nor naive. I guess I simply don't cotton to unsubstantiated rumors."

"In her free time, they say she plays football . . . with men! Grown men!"

"Well, shiver me timbers! Not grown men!" She probably, definitely, should not have said that, she thought, as Edgar's face practically bulged with anger. "Yes, Mr. Edgar, she's not cute Lorraine Williams or the pretty Nana Davis. She's tall and tomboyish. That doesn't make her a lesbian."

"Have you even checked—"

"Of course I have. There was a cousin of a friend of a friend who lived on the same floor as Althea when she was at Florida A&M University. She mentioned that Althea was chasing all the girls. Not any girl in particular. All of them." Hettie paused so Edgar could realize how ridiculous that sounded. "Althea does not look like the average tennis player and she doesn't act like your average player so something clearly must be wrong with her. Give me a break, Mr. Edgar." Hettie refused to entertain such rumors. Refused. Althea's life was Althea's life but such a stigma would ruin her career; just burn it up in flames. And quite frankly, it was embarrassing that all they could point to was the fact that she had tomboyish ways.

Edgar reached for his smoking cigarette and brought it to his mouth. "Nevertheless, the stories about the boyfriend help her."

"I've already told her I would not write about her personal life. I was thinking that I would present a more in-depth focus on what it takes to be a tennis star. I don't think most people understand all the work that goes into it."

"That's maybe one article."

Hettie thought she could stretch it to three. By the time the third article came out she was hoping to be struck with inspiration.

"Why not write about the challenges of being a Negro in a white sport?"

"You know why that's off the table."

"Still?"

"Yes."

"You're supposed to change her mind if you want to keep your job."

"Thanks for reminding me, Mr. Edgar. I almost forgot. Listen, what if I can find another way to make her America's darling?"

"How?"

"I don't know yet. I just started shadowing her this past week, but I could find something." Wouldn't it be better if Hettie didn't have to manipulate the situation? Then maybe she could be a real reporter who wrote about what they saw as opposed to what they had created. Maybe then she could be assured that there would never be another repeat of Montgomery, where she walked away leaving destruction in her wake.

There was a moment of silence as Edgar turned his chair away from her, thinking. He removed his cigarette, tapping the remaining piece against the edge of the ashtray. Orange-red ash rose in the air before settling down on the surrounding paper. Hettie took another swallow of coffee as she realized she was going to have to wash her hair tonight. The stench of this room was probably seeping into her pores.

"It has to be civil rights."

"I'm telling you I might be able to think of another way." She didn't know what that way was yet but she was only getting started. She just needed time.

"And I'm telling you that there's too much money that's been put into this thing."

Hettie paused. "Too much what?"

Edgar wouldn't meet her eyes. "This is bigger than you and me. It has to be civil rights. In the meantime, find something about tennis to write about. I want an article from you every week. But by Wimbledon, I want an obvious shift to civil rights. I want an exposé on how the tennis world has treated her. I want stories that show the mountains she's climbed to get where she's at—with or without her permission. There's rumors that Dr. King is planning something big this summer. We want to be right there, riding the waves of it."

"Mr. Edgar—"

"None of that was a suggestion, Hettie. If you want to go your own way, you're always welcome to leave your double H credentials on the desk behind you."

CHAPTER 20

Lob—a tennis shot where the ball is lifted high and above the opponent

It was in the washing and rolling of her hair that Hettie was suddenly inspired. With half of her hair up, and the other half wet and dripping down her back, Hettie ran for the phone in the kitchen.

"No date tonight?" Faye called from the living room. "Seafood, isn't it?"

"Seafood is pondering remarriage with his new secretary. We're on hold," Hettie yelled back. Reuben had sworn he'd never walk down the marriage path again, but it just went to show that when men said it, it wasn't true. Hettie dialed the number she'd only recently memorized.

"Darben residence. How can I help you?"

"Hello, this is Hettie. Is Althea there?"

"Yes, please hold on."

"I'm leaving," Faye called out. Hettie heard the front door open and slam shut.

"What?" Althea answered the phone like she entered a room: with attitude, force, and the odd sense that your presence was annoying her.

"I've got an idea for the paper. Come on by so we can talk."

"And just why would I want to leave the warmth of this house to do that?"

"I'll braid your hair so you don't have to think about it for a week." Doing hair was not Hettie's favorite thing to do in the world but she'd learned how when she'd realized it was a form of currency that Miz Ce-Ce would accept in exchange for an outfit. There was a short pause. "You don't have any games, Al. No one will see your hair, especially if you wear a hat or cover it with a scarf. And just think, for at least seven whole days you won't have to think about it."

"I'll be there in twenty minutes."

Twenty minutes was enough time for Hettie to finish rolling her own hair and to set up her mini hair salon in the kitchen. There was a firm knock on the door and Hettie went to open it. Althea brushed past her, coat already in hand. "I suppose it's a good thing you called. I can't take another day like today. I'm leaving New York."

The words were not surprising. "When?"

"In two days."

"What kind of heads-up is this?"

"The only kind you're gonna get 'cause I just decided an hour ago. Where do you want me?" Althea asked the question as she ran her hands through her short, curly, dark brown hair.

"In the kitchen. You'll have to bend over the sink. Where are we going?"

"Wilmington, North Carolina."

Hettie shuddered. Wilmington was right up there with Tulsa, Oklahoma. But maybe for what she wanted that was a good thing.

"It's not so bad, so long as you stay where you ought. I'm only there for the tennis court anyway."

Hettie waited until she was soaping Althea's hair before asking any more questions. "This is Dr. Eaton you're staying with, right? Dr. Johnson is in Lynchburg, Virginia?"

"That's right. He's going to let us stay in his house. If you insist on coming, we'll have to share a room."

Hettie grimaced. She'd walked out of the college dorms promising herself she'd never share her bedroom with another person unless they were married. But they were both grown—perhaps it wouldn't be so bad. "How do you do your hair on the road?"

"I wash it just about every day."

"Every day!"

"I've got to. Especially when I'm in a tournament. Then I dry it, use a pressing comb, a curling iron, and Dixie Peach Pomade hair grease. You should see what I rig together when I'm traveling. I cut the top off an old soup can, light a fire in it, and use that to heat the comb and curling iron."

Hettie reached for a drying towel. "That's . . . pretty clever. I don't think I'd have thought of all that."

"You would have if you had to. Straight hair is a must."

"I'm done. Come on and take a seat. If what you say is true, that's too much heat on your hair on a regular basis. It won't grow."

"You see me trying to compete with Rapunzel? The very last thing I need is long hair anyway." Hettie reached for her comb and began working on Althea's hair. It was as she suspected, slightly brittle and a bit crispy. But when straightened, you'd never know. Using the fine tooth of the comb, Hettie began to part her hair. "You said you had something you wanted to talk to me about?"

"I met with my boss today. I'm going to need to write an article about tennis once a week. What do you think I should write about?"

"Uh-uh. That's your job."

"What do you like about tennis? Why this game when there are so many others?"

Using a clip, Hettie set most of Althea's hair to the side and began the task of plaiting a single row of hair.

"You know, I don't really play doubles a lot," Althea said, speaking quickly, as though embarrassed about this small fact.

"You play with Dr. Johnson in the ATA tournament."

"That's only 'cause we've known each other for years and can speak each other's language on the court."

"You played with that one girl . . . the British one . . . Angela . . ."

"Angela Buxton. She's great. She really is." There was a moment's hesitation. "She's Jewish and a bit of an outsider herself in the tennis world. We're two oddballs together, although I think she'd be who she is regardless. Angela's a one-of-a-kind sort of person but if there's one thing I've learned it's that I'm not a team player. People annoy me." Because she'd slipped a rubber band in her mouth, the only response that Hettie could make was a grunt. "I've got to take the lead and some folks don't like that. Tennis is a one-man sport. If anyone messes up out there on the field, it's me. If someone does something great, it's me. Some people can't handle the loneliness of tennis. But that's the very thing I love about it. Most times anyway."

Hettie reached for her comb, creating a new part. "What if we write about the . . . emotions of tennis?"

"What?"

"An article on the joys of tennis, the sadness of tennis, the loneliness of tennis. It would allow people insight into who you are, how you think, and what tennis is actually like behind the scenes. The main focus would be tennis but you'd also have a voice about your thoughts on the game."

Althea went silent as Hettie braided. "The emotions of tennis."

"I'll work on a catchier title."

"I like that." Althea's voice was soft. But then she straightened beneath Hettie's fingers. "Do I get to look at these articles before they go out?"

"Yes, I'll let you have a look but you do not get the final say. I don't tell you how to play and you don't tell me how to write."

Althea leaned back. "Fine. We have a plan."

Shadrach had several store locations but only one warehouse where he and others crafted the inventory that filled his shelves. When Hettie called his office to see if he was in, it was his secretary who told her that today was a warehouse day and then she'd given Hettie the address and told her it would be fine if she went.

Inside the warehouse, Hettie was greeted by the sight of wide-open space and what looked to be fifty separate tables. Men in overalls or dark pants worked at each one. She could hear Ray Charles singing as loudly as he possibly could about Mary Ann but he was being drowned out by what sounded like chainsaws and whirling machines. Behind the tables, shelves were stacked parallel to each other and holding sporting goods in various stages of life.

Hettie inhaled and got a whiff of fresh-cut wood.

"Hello?" The man at the table nearest her lifted the goggles off his eyes. "Can I help you?"

"Is Lewis here?"

The man set his goggles aside and began pulling off gloves. He pointed to Hettie's left. "See those benches over there? Go take a seat and don't touch nothing. I'll fetch him."

Resisting the urge to tell him that last time she checked she wasn't five, she carefully stepped over wires and boxes until she reached a long, backless bench. After taking a seat, Hettie watched as the man she'd spoken to crossed the room, stopping at a work table not too far from her.

Shadrach was wearing a white shirt—covered in dust and particles—and a pair of loose brown working pants. As the man approached him, Shadrach lowered the tools in his hands, lifted the goggles from his face and then raised the bottom of his shirt, pulling the fabric up to wipe at his eyes. Hettie had seen shirtless men before but none of them were Shadrach and so none of them made her stomach flip the way it did at the sight of his flat stomach and the dark hair on his chest and the . . . was that a tattoo?

Shadrach dropped his shirt and turned in her direction, surprise written all over his face. Leaving his table, he strolled over and, lifting one leg over the wooden bench, he sat down sideways, facing her. "Hettie Carlin, what brings you out here today?"

Up close, Hettie could see that he was filthy. There was

dirt crawling up his arms and streaked across his face. His shirt and his pants had an interesting red smear on them. But, as he folded his arms over his chest, she thought she'd never seen a more attractive man.

"About the tattoo—"

"What tattoo?" Alarm ran through his voice.

"The one right there." Hettie pointed to the spot where she'd gotten a small glimpse of a half-circle that seemed oddly familiar. She'd seen the symbol he had imprinted on his chest before. But she couldn't remember where, although if she had to hazard a guess it was a military emblem of some kind.

Shadrach grabbed her hand and placed it very gently in her lap. "I don't know what you're talking about." His voice was firm but she saw that flush in his cheeks. He was embarrassed.

"All right," she said slowly, humor infusing her voice. "There's no tattoo."

Not meeting her eyes, he nodded once in agreement. "What can I help you with?"

"Nothing. I came to tell you that I'm leaving and I might not be back until April."

Shadrach lifted his head and she saw a momentary flicker of dismay fill his eyes. He would miss her. Hettie reached for her purse, gripping the handle tightly. "Althea's going south to practice?"

"Yes. We're headed to Wilmington, North Carolina." He winced. "Have you been there before?"

"No, but didn't they massacre Black folks down there?"

"About sixty years ago."

Shadrach shook his head. "Be careful. That sort of stuff lingers in the air."

"I know."

"Don't make eye contact."

"I won't."

"Don't forget to step into the street if white folks are walking past. It just makes life easier."

"Yes." She'd learned all of these rules before she'd left for Montgomery. It might have been some months ago but she hadn't forgotten them.

"Do you have a green book?"

"Yes."

"If you two drive anywhere, always fill the gas tank up in the daytime. Never run out of gas at night. Ever." He was sounding like her father, only Oral always added a reminder to keep her mouth shut. "Do you know how to change a tire?"

"Yes, my dad has taught me everything there is to know about cars." He'd really been teaching Morgan but she'd been right there, paying attention.

"It's harder for you Yankee Negroes."

Hettie released a huff of air. "Not as hard as you think." There was something in the heaviness of the air below the Mason–Dixon Line that warned her intuitively how to behave. Only a fool ignored the silent alarm that rang unendingly in the South. She supposed that those born there were used to it but as a non-native, it was a wearing, tearing thing on her soul and she was not eager to return to hear it.

Shadrach patted at his chest and then paused. "Do you have a piece of paper and something to write with?"

"Of course." Hettie dug around in her purse and pulled out a small pencil and notebook. In careful letters, Shadrach wrote down two phone numbers and an address. "This is my home number." He tapped the first one on the paper. "Call anytime. I'm a night owl. I'll be up even when it's late. This second number belongs to my parents."

"Shadrach—"

"If you ever find yourself in trouble, Ash and Talitha Lewis will help." Hettie knew his mother had returned home to Tennessee for Thanksgiving and had yet to come back. "Wilmington is on the coast but if you two do any traveling, you might find yourself in my neck of the woods. That's their address."

Hettie slowly took the pencil and returned the notebook to her purse. "Thank you."

"You can write too, if you want."

Hettie fiddled with the strap of her purse. If he kept saying things like this, she might lean over and kiss him. "Do you want me to bring you back something? Like pecans or pimento cheese . . . fruit?"

Shadrach shook his head slowly. Then paused. "Well . . . sometimes . . . I have a hankering for pecan candy."

Hettie slapped the palm of her hand against her thigh. "Pecan candy it is." The warehouse felt hot, really hot. It probably didn't help that Hettie still had her coat on. A bead of sweat rolled down the side of her face.

"Be careful, hmm? And have fun. It's not all bad. But not too much fun. You still have to come back home."

Hettie shrugged off her coat. It was either that or melt. "Can I run something by you? A hypothetical of sorts?"

"I love hypothetical questions."

"Let's say there's a journalist."

"Uh-huh."

"And she's supposed to convince someone to take a certain path but when she informs her boss that that's not doable, he pushes back and says something along the lines of 'too much money has been put into this thing'. What do you think he means?"

Hettie heard Shadrach inhale and exhale. "It's been said before but the road to hell is paved with good intentions. Set your boundaries, Hettie. Figure out what they are or one day you'll wake up and not recognize the person looking at you in the mirror."

CHAPTER 21

Out—a ball that lands outside the lines

That evening, Hettie joined all the members of her family in her parents' tiny apartment and dined on her mama's fried catfish and spaghetti. It was Hettie's father's favorite meal—not hers—but she liked it enough not to be bothered.

"Mind yourself," her father told her in that deep gravelly voice of his when Hettie came to tell him bye. "And don't talk back."

"No, sir."

"Don't you forget to add sir and ma'am."

"I won't." She couldn't forget to say it in her own house. Nothing made her father more quietly furious than dropping a ma'am or a sir.

Her father reached out, squeezing her shoulder once, and then turned away to sit in his favorite armchair. His attention was already once again on the radio before him. Hettie carefully stepped over toy trains and small cousins scattered on the carpeted living room floor.

"Hey!" It was Morgan and he was standing in the doorway of the bathroom with his briefcase in hand. "Look."

If they'd been under the age of twenty, that would have been a dangerous command to obey but because they were both adults, Hettie walked over and glanced in his bag. A black gun gleamed at her. "Morgan Edward Jennings!"

"I'll let you borrow it."

"I won't!" She'd never been one who could stomach violence.

"It's better to die fighting than to die like a rat in a trap. Someone crazy come at you just pull this out and show them who's boss."

"Put that away! I'm not taking a gun with me!" If ever she were in such trouble, she'd unfortunately just die.

"Shh! You want my mama to hear?" Morgan closed up his briefcase but not before shooting her a look of rank disapproval. "Your mouth ain't gonna get you out of mess down South."

"Says the boy who's never been there."

"I traveled through it to get to California." California was where he'd done his basic training. "And who do you think I was in the army sleeping and eating and practically dying with? Southerners! My CO was southern. Educated, but country." A hint of a smile graced Morgan's face as he looked away, distracted by a memory. "He was from some backwater town in Tennessee."

Hettie's eyebrows lifted in surprise. "You sound as if you like him?"

"Well, he was colored and sharp as a tack with his fancy

college degree. Sometimes he got uptight but you could trust him." Morgan's words were jerky in the way they always were when he referenced anything from his time in the war. "He was father, brother, teacher, priest, friend."

"Was?" She asked the question timidly. She could not recall the last time he'd shared so freely without a bottle of something amber in front of him.

Morgan frowned at her. "No reason to look all sad. He made it back safe." He hesitated. "But he just disappeared once we were discharged. He doesn't come to anything and he doesn't respond . . . none of that is relevant. You call me if you ever need rescuing." He'd told her this too, last time. "But don't call on Mondays, Tuesdays, Wednesdays, Thursdays, Fridays, or Saturdays. If you call on a Sunday, I might be at church and you know that reverend will keep you in service all the day long if he thinks he's preaching good. That's why I'm willing to loan you my friend Fred here."

"Morgan, hush up. We don't live in the Wild West."

"They do down there. Everybody's got a gun. Even folks who look like us. Don't trust any old body just because they're skin kin. But fine," he said as he began zipping up his bag with more fervor than needed. "Don't listen to me." He was highly offended at her refusal of his offering.

"I appreciate the thought," Hettie said after a moment.

Morgan held up a hand. "Spare me. I don't want to talk about it anymore."

She'd really hurt his feelings. "It's just that—"

"Don't argue with me. Argue with your bald-headed granny."

"I beg your pardon." Hettie hadn't even seen Miz Ce-Ce walking past.

"Mama, ain't nobody talking about you. Hettie's got two

grannies, doesn't she? And by the looks of Oral, the other one is probably missing a great deal of hair."

Hettie clicked her tongue at this insult of the grandmother she'd never met before. "Morgan, shut up."

Miz Ce-Ce poked Hettie in the shoulder. "Come on, let us say good-bye to you in the kitchen." 'Us' referred to the women in her family.

Hettie nodded in response but dove forward, wrapping Morgan in a tight hug. "Stop touching me." His voice was gruff even as he lowered his chin on top of her head. "Don't up and decide to stay down there. You're my favorite niece."

Hettie rolled her eyes. "As if I would ever do such a thing."

Then she stepped back to follow her grandmother into the kitchen, where her mama was wiping at countertops that had already been cleaned. Carol, Morgan's wife, was sitting at the kitchen table and drinking a cup of coffee. Carol was smart and nice and kind, and they should have been friends except that Carol seemed to be under the impression that if she and Morgan divorced, everyone would take Morgan's side. She was sixty percent right in her assessment and thus there was always a hint of tension in the air.

"Where's Oral? He needs to pray for Hettie before she leaves," her mama said as she turned away from the counter.

"Do we want the prayer to reach higher than the ceiling? You pray, Rosa." Miz Ce-Ce pushed Hettie further into the kitchen.

"Trains are no longer segregated as of January 10th, so you won't have to change cars," Carol told Hettie, lifting her coffee cup in silent toast.

"I just don't know about this," Rosa Carlin said with a

sigh. "You need to get married and stay at home." Hettie looked at her mother but said nothing.

"Men are not the answers to life's problems." Carol's words were firm.

"That's not what I'm saying at all. But when Hettie wanted to open a bank account, what did she have to do? Come and get her pa." That was unfortunately true. It had been a toss-up between Morgan or her father being on her bank account. She'd picked her father because while he might fuss at her spending habits, he'd never steal from her. Morgan, God bless his heart, might take a 'loan'. "If she wants to buy property one day, she'll need her pa. Well, Oral won't be around forever. Can't fault me if I want to make sure my girl is looked after."

Put like that, Hettie felt a little guilty on the inside. "I wouldn't worry too much, Mama. I still might meet someone."

After a skipped beat, Miz Ce-Ce asked, "Does someone have a name?"

Why was she doing this to herself? "We're just friends," Hettie warned, making eye contact with her mother and her grandmother. "His name is Shadrach."

Her mother repeated the name softly as though God had answered a prayer. Hettie winced. She shouldn't have said anything.

"Shadrach?" Miz Ce-Ce made a face. "Stay away from men with Biblical names. And good gracious, don't let them be southern. My first husband was one of those. Remember Esau, Rosa?"

"Unfortunately, I do, Mama. I don't want to talk about Esau. I want to hear about Shadrach."

"Esau was a *godly* man," Miz Ce-Ce went on, too far along in her thoughts to hear anything else. "Couldn't listen to this music, couldn't wear this or that kind of dress. No makeup. No friends. Don't talk to a man that wasn't him. He had enough rules to choke a horse. I put up with it for three years 'cause he married me when I was nine months pregnant. A lot of men won't do that."

"Mama—"

"He hit me one time and that was the last time. When he went to sleep, I put on a big pot of grits."

"We've heard this story a million times, Mama. But do you know what we haven't heard? Hettie mentioning anybody special."

"He's just a friend, Mama," she stressed once again. She never should have said anything.

Rosa Carlin lifted her head to the ceiling. "You and these men friends."

"It's for the best. Shadrach sounds dangerous," Miz Ce-Ce offered knowingly. "That's right up there with Jehoshaphat."

"Well, he's not dangerous, he's not controlling, and he'd never hit me. He's opinionated but that's most men. Shad—" Hettie stopped talking, suddenly feeling everyone's eyes on her. "Maybe we can just pray so I can leave."

Hettie watched her mama and Miz Ce-Ce exchange a look. "Yes," her mama said after a minute. "Let's pray."

"But first," Miz Ce-Ce interrupted. "Let me tell you about my second husband. He too had a Biblical name: Nehemiah."

Settled on the train to North Carolina, Hettie slipped on her reading glasses and pulled out her notebook.

"Can we not?" Althea closed her eyes, leaning her head back against the seat rest. She was wearing the most tired-looking skirt Hettie had ever seen and an old rugged sweater. Althea had wrapped her braided hair in a bright red scarf and covered it with a hat. None of it worked. Hettie, on the other hand, was wearing a long-sleeved dark blue blouse with a pretty bow in the center and a blue and white checkered skirt. A lampshade hat completed the picture and also covered the French braids she'd put in her own hair. "I'd prefer to sleep."

"Just give me five minutes of your time and then you can sleep the whole rest of the way. One thing that we must do as I write these articles is strive for honesty."

Slumping down, Althea stretched out one leg, and kicked at Hettie's seat. "What's that supposed to mean?"

Flipping a page in her notebook, Hettie said, "When asked what your favorite book was to read, you said, and I quote, 'The Bible'." Hettie looked up, eyebrow raised. "Tell me, what's your favorite book of the Bible? Is it Ecclesiastes?"

Althea leveled a finger at Hettie. "I've read the Bible."

"I didn't say you didn't. You converted to what? Episcopalian, a few years ago?"

Althea straightened and leaned forward. "How did you know that?"

"I know all about the St. Michael & All Angels Church you attended when you were living in Florida." Hettie removed her glasses. "I am very good at what I do. Just because I was born yesterday, doesn't mean that I was born last night." She tapped a finger against the page of her notebook. "Don't feed me these ridiculous answers. What is your favorite book that you've read?"

Althea shook her head slowly, the look on her face like a weary lioness trying to figure out if she was amongst predator or prey. "That's not the way I pass the time. If I read anything it's the news or a magazine. The Bible probably is the only book I've read. Well, parts of it, anyway."

Hettie returned her glasses to her face. "I've got a title for the series we'll be doing together: 'How to Win a Game of Tennis'."

Althea rolled her neck first to the right and then to the left. "Some would say I don't know how to win a game of tennis."

"This is the year that we show them, right? Think of these articles as a road map leading to your success. I'll write on understanding and embracing the loneliness of the sport, capturing the moments of joy of the sport . . ."

Althea's sigh was deep and reflective. "Enduring the repetition of the sport."

"I like that. Let's start with that because from what I could see of your training, it's very repetitious and practice is where it all starts."

"You think this is really going to change anything?"

"I do think it will change things. You've got to try something. What's the definition of crazy? Doing the same thing over and over and expecting different results. If you keep ignoring the power of the media, they'll keep telling your story the way you don't want it told, so change the narrative." Hettie closed her notebook. "Tell me what I should expect in Wilmington."

"Mom and Dad Eaton are nice folks." Althea closed her eyes, but a smile danced on her lips. "Dad Eaton drives a big fancy car and they've got a maid and all that jazz. At dinner, there's always the fancy silverware and you've got to use the right spoons and whatnot. Very fancy people, but kind. And yet you've still got to follow their rules. It was bothersome when I was younger. But I'm used to them now."

"How are the locals?"

"Not so bad. The bus was segregated when I was last there but I'm not sure if that's the way of things now. The movie theater was segregated. Blacks had to sit in the balcony—which I prefer anyway, but who wants to be told they can only sit in one section? Not me. I don't see many flickers down South. The restaurants might sell you food but you have to eat outside. It's not the nightmare everyone paints it to be. Just a bit uncomfortable at moments."

"Didn't you finish high school out here?"

"Don't remind me," she muttered, opening her eyes as she thought on her past.

Hettie hesitated. "Were you bullied?"

Althea's eyebrows lowered. "Not in the way you're thinking. There's more than one way to bully a person."

"I believe that."

"Those Wilmington girls didn't like me at all," Althea muttered as she turned her head to look out the window.

"Future housewives, huh?"

Althea snorted. "Probably. I've never really gotten along with most girls," she admitted softly. "Give me boys, any day."

This sadness, this vulnerability was not something Hettie was used to seeing from Althea and as though sensing she'd revealed too much, Althea kicked at Hettie's seat once again. Hettie made a face. Althea made one right back. "Didn't you use to run the streets with . . . um . . . what's her name? It was Ellen or Anna or . . ."

"Alma Irving." Althea's whole expression changed at the mention of her friend's name.

"You two were always playing hooky and going to the movies. Remember?"

"I do."

"Although your partner in crime probably was Charles," Hettie admitted, thinking of a boy in their class who had gotten into one mess after another with Althea.

Althea brought a fist to her mouth to hold back her laughter, memories of the antics she and Charles used to get into dancing in her eyes. "I haven't seen him in a month of Sundays and a week of Junes."

"You were what, eighteen when you started high school? Of course those girls were going to give you trouble. That's what girls are like. Now, tell me what Dr. Eaton is like."

Althea looked out the window and didn't speak for a long minute. Hettie waited, allowing her time to think. "Well," she began slowly. "He's smart as a whistle for one. He has his own medical clinic. He went to the University of Michigan."

"Oh."

"Yep. He's not much of a talker. He loves his wife, his children, tennis, golf, and photography. In that order. You'll like him, I think." She waved a tired hand. "No more. I'm going to spread out and get some sleep." A veteran of constant traveling, she did just that, leaving Hettie to wonder how she could use this trip to open Althea's eyes.

CHAPTER 22

Doubles—a game played by four players, two on each side of the court

At some point on the train ride, Hettie too nodded off, but both women were awake as the train entered North Carolina.

"You've got to be careful out here."

Hettie waved a hand. "I've heard it all."

"I'm not talking about that," Althea said, with a shake of her head. "You were on the right track when you said the women out here are marriage-minded. They're different than the girls in New York. They won't like your hoity-toity ways."

"Hoity-toity? Such compliments, Althea."

"Once I went down to the local bar to play pool. I racked up some nice wins and was aiming to return again. But then someone called Dr. Eaton and told him I was there." Althea shook her head. "I couldn't play no more."

Hettie frowned. "Why?"

"Women don't play pool."

Hettie opened her mouth. Then closed it. The women in Montgomery had been quite traditional but Hettie had chalked it up to the fact that they couldn't take a step out of line in the midst of the boycott. "That's what I mean. Women live by different rules out here. They just cook and clean, have babies and go to church. Mind yourself," Althea said, shaking a finger at Hettie. There was a gleam in her eye. "They might not like you either, with that big mouth of yours."

Hettie's eyes narrowed. "I'll have you know that everybody likes me."

"They're gonna hear you're almost thirty and still not married. Boom, one mark against you. Then you'll start talking about your career. Boom, another mark against you. Don't come running to me when you realize there's no one to talk to."

"If what you say is true, I love that you decided to save these warnings until right before we got here."

"A friend in need is a friend indeed."

Hettie rolled her eyes. "Well, I'm not here to make friends. I'm here to write about you. And to show you just how professional I am, I am going to make you take that ugly scarf off of your head and I'm going to loan you mine. It's like you got up this morning and decided to put your hands on the most hideous things you could find." Hettie dug into her bag and pulled out a silk brown and teal scarf.

Althea removed her hat, revealing the red scarf that she'd tied around her head as though she were some kind of pirate. "I don't own that many skirts and dresses. I don't like the way they feel. The nice ones I do have, I save for church."

Still, she scooted over to the window, allowing room for Hettie to hop over and sit behind her.

"This doesn't match your outfit but at least you'll be able to remove your hat." On days when Miz Ce-Ce didn't leave the house, she always wrapped her hair turban-style as though she was the queen of something or other. Hettie had always found the look becoming. "Do you have earrings?"

"No."

"Are your ears pierced?"

"Yes."

"Grab my bag. I keep a spare pair in the inside pocket."

Althea didn't just grab the earrings, she also grabbed a mirror. "I look ridiculous. Dr. Eaton won't know what hit me."

Despite her words, Althea was primping in the mirror, turning her head from side to side to get a better view of her angles. Hettie returned to her seat. "You're a world-class athlete. You're allowed to look a little different than the rest."

"Huh." Althea handed her back her mirror and her purse.

As the train began to lose speed, Hettie put her reading glasses away, exchanging them for a pair of shades just before touching up her lipstick.

"Dr. Johnson is here! I didn't know he was coming!" Althea exclaimed. Hettie looked out the window for a glance but they'd passed the man. "I'm going to give you a warning about ole Whirlwind right now. He's not a man who cares about a wedding ring and by wedding ring, I mean his. I've known him since I was a girl so he's just an uncle to me, but he does think he is better-looking than he is."

"He's what? In his fifties?"

"Yes, but we still play doubles in the ATA and we win more than we lose. He's pretty spry for an old man."

"Hmm. Well, I know how to handle old men and church ladies." Hettie had a parent in each category and while she might have personally given up on trying to win either over, that didn't mean she didn't know how to.

"There's a part of me that says you can't and another part of me that called you a lizard for a reason."

"What does a lizard have to do with me?" Hettie's voice may have been a little sharp. The train jerked slowly, coming to a stop.

"You know the ones that change colors depending on where they're at?"

"A chameleon?"

"Yep. That's you, Hettie Jo. Don't think for one second that I'm fooled by all this." Althea motioned toward her hair and face. "You're trying to butter me up so I'll give you what you want. You don't actually mean any of it."

Hettie's smile was brittle. "Keep sitting there on your high horse like you don't pretend, day in and day out, so you can reach the top tier of your profession. The only difference between you and me is that I'm better at it."

Althea crossed one long leg over the other and leaned back in her seat, her hands clasped in her lap. "Would you like me to make you a trophy?"

Hettie started to speak but then made the executive decision not to. One of them had to act like an adult. Althea stood up first, reaching for their suitcases. Althea had brought only one bag, which looked as though it had once been an expensive thing and Althea was doing her very best to squeeze every penny out of it. Hettie had packed lightly, to her way of thinking, for a trip without a definite end date: three bags.

Althea easily grabbed her bag and two of Hettie's, as though it were a small thing. Hettie grabbed the remaining one and followed the other woman off the train.

"Althea!"

"Dr. Eaton! Dr. Johnson! Over here!"

There was a bit of a shuffle and then Hettie was standing before Althea's former coaches. "Althea!"

Hettie watched as hugs and words were exchanged. Althea finally took a step back and motioned toward Hettie. "This is the journalist I told you about, Hettie Carlin."

Making her voice as warm as possible, Hettie said, "Hello."

Both men were tall, although to Hettie it looked as though Althea had an inch over them. Dr. Johnson's skin was dark and his frame was a bit stocky, like a man who'd once played football and softened with age. Dr. Eaton was of a lighter hue and wore dark-framed glasses. It was Dr. Eaton who extended a hand in her direction first. "A pleasure to meet you, Miss Carlin."

"The pleasure is all mine, and please, call me Hettie."

"Where are you from, Hettie Carlin?" Dr. Johnson asked, a smile on his lips and a flirtatious look in his eyes as he slid his hands into his pockets. Althea had moved to stand next to Dr. Johnson and she rolled her eyes.

"I'm from New York."

"Is this your first trip South?"

"No, sir. I've been to Alabama." Both men groaned, comical looks of dismay on their faces. Hettie couldn't help but grin.

"We've got to take her to the water, Hubert."

"You're in for a real treat, Hettie," Dr. Eaton said firmly. "Let me grab your suitcase."

When everyone and everything was settled into Dr. Eaton's shiny Packard, they rolled all of the windows down and turned on the radio. Fats Domino sang 'Ain't That a Shame', while Hettie leaned back, enjoying the cool breeze and the smell of the ocean in the air.

They passed houses and buildings and overhanging trees, which had probably been standing since the turn of the previous century.

"Althea, I came up here just to help Hubert set up the grass field."

"I do appreciate it, Doc."

"You make your decision yet?" Dr. Eaton asked.

"I'm not playing in the ATA this year." Althea's voice was firm. "I've got my eye on a goal and I can't accomplish it if I'm being pushed this way and that."

"I told you," Dr. Johnson said, wagging a finger at Dr. Eaton. "I agree with you, Al. None of those other women are winning the USLTA and playing the ATA. It's too much."

"Baker's not going to like it," Dr. Eaton said with a sigh.

"Forget Baker! This is about our girl here. Not him! Hettie, you eat seafood?"

Hettie straightened in her seat. "Sir, food is the one language I speak fluently everywhere."

Dr. Johnson laughed, shooting her an easy grin. Next to Hettie, Althea shook her head. "Well, we're gonna get you fed, darling."

The doctors gave Hettie a slow tour of Wilmington, North Carolina, pointing out different buildings here and there. They parked the car and took her and Althea on a walk through an elaborate botanical garden. Then they were led across a walkway that paralleled the ocean. The tour ended at a small shack of a restaurant that served fresh oysters, shrimp and crab that was scooped right out the water. It was, in a word, lovely.

And then finally, they got back in the car and headed to the residential area, coming to a slow stop in front of a light green two-story framed house with an extended porch that held several rocking chairs, four pillars that supported the second floor, and an American flag that fluttered in the wind.

"Your home is beautiful, Dr. Eaton," Hettie said as she climbed out of the car. "I can see why you live here." And she could. Everything around them seemed peaceful and slow and inviting.

Dr. Johnson came around the car, extending his elbow in Hettie's direction. "Wait until you see the tennis courts. They're in the backyard."

"Let her go inside and meet the family first, Robert."

Dr. Johnson waved off his friend's words. "She'll meet them soon enough."

"Well, I'm going inside to greet Mom Eaton and the kids," Althea muttered as she fetched several suitcases.

Dr. Johnson patted Hettie's hand. "Come on. Let me show you where the magic happens." They walked alongside a beautiful flower garden, before two tennis courts made an appearance. Several college-aged boys were playing a game and a few were sitting on the side. The game stopped and the young men rose to their feet as Hettie and Dr. Johnson came into view.

"Hello." Hettie waved to the crowd. The boys waved back, although their eyes were on the doctor.

"This is Hettie Carlin. A reporter from New York here to write on Althea."

"Althea's here?" There was a small wave of excitement that emanated from the court.

"They all think they can beat her," Dr. Johnson whispered in Hettie's ear. "They're all delusional. When Althea's at her best, no one can beat her. When she's at her worst, you still had better know your way around a racket, and these children are still learning." He lifted his head. "She's in the house."

Rackets were dropped, tennis balls were discarded, and there was a mad stampede for the door.

"You see they're playing on clay? Hubert and I put together a grass court just for Althea in the back. No one will disturb her as she trains. This is Althea's year. Mark my words. You're going to see something special take place, Hettie Carlin."

CHAPTER 23

Backswing—the backward motion of a swing that positions the racket to swing forward and strike the ball

It was as Althea had said. They were sharing a small room that contained two beds, one small desk, one small drawer, and one small closet. But they each had their own lamp-stand. Hettie's last college roommate had thought that what was Hettie's was theirs. And Hettie, only child that she was, did not believe in sharing. By the end of the semester, there had been a distinct imaginary line marked down the middle of the room that they did not cross. There was an instinctive part of Hettie that wanted to lay down the same divider now.

"Don't touch my stuff," Althea told her as she tossed her suitcase onto her bed.

"There is nothing in your suitcase that is of any interest to me. I like to wear clothes made in this decade. It is I who should fear a thief." Hettie tossed her purse onto her bed and reached for one of the suitcases standing at the foot of it.

"Your clothes wouldn't make it past my thumb. I get the top drawers of the dresser."

"Hardy har har." After her tour of the place, Hettie had met Dr. Eaton's wife and mother and several of his children. She'd been introduced to the college-aged boys who were currently training for the ATA. There were eight of them and they shared rooms downstairs. All of them were attending colleges in the area, commuting each weekend for training and coaching. Like Althea once had, they'd then travel to Lynchburg, Virginia, and train with Dr. Johnson when the summer season came around.

Althea and Hettie took turns in the washroom and both turned in early, but despite how tired Hettie knew she was, she still could not go to sleep.

"What is that noise?"

"Bugs," Althea muttered from her side of the room. "Frogs. Animals. Nature."

Hettie's lullaby had always been police sirens, car engines, and the occasional street argument. Her night-light had been flashes of traffic lights flickering onto her bedroom ceiling every few seconds. It was both eerily silent and strangely loud in Wilmington and it was going to take her hours to sleep. It had been just this way in Alabama.

"I can hear you thinking. Go to sleep."

"How do people live like this?" Hettie whispered. There was something about having a roommate that invited conversations in the dark.

She heard Althea turn. "When I was in India, it was hard to sleep. Different animals out there."

"What's it like traveling the world?" Hettie asked, genuinely curious.

"I love it. You name a place, I've been there. It never gets old."

"Plane rides?"

"You get used to them."

"Hmm." Ten minutes passed. Hettie turned onto her back, staring up at the inky black ceiling. "Do you remember that poem we used to have to recite at school? The one written by William Holmes Borders?"

"I Am Somebody," Althea recited in a voice that was eerily similar to their teacher's.

Because she was so tired, Hettie laughed. But then she whispered the first stanza softly. According to the poem, she was a poet like Langston Hughes and Paul Laurence Dunbar, a statesman like J. R. E. Lee, and a diplomat like Frederick Douglass.

"I am somebody," Althea murmured, picking up the next lines, which referenced Colonel Young, Crispus Attucks, and Marian Anderson.

It was a long poem that outlined the greats of Negroes that had come before them. They'd had to recite it every morning after the first bell.

Althea finished her stanza and Hettie picked up the next one. At some point, she fell asleep.

Time passed quickly. January rolled into February, which rolled into early March. When Hettie wasn't watching Althea absolutely smash the college boys into the ground with her racket, she was working on an article. If she wasn't working on an article, she was writing a letter to Shadrach. If she wasn't writing to Shadrach, she was taking long walks down to the water and sitting on the pier, dangling her legs over the side but too citified to even think of allowing her bare toes to do much more than touch the water.

Based on her brief experience in Alabama, Hettie had packed mostly light cotton dresses. North Carolina was hot and Wilmington carried a heavy cloud of moisture that seemed to hang low to the ground. Sometimes just breathing seemed to take more air out of her body than allowing air in. And yet Althea trained and trained as though the weather were a mere annoying fly, easily brushed away.

She was headed back from one of her walks to the waterfront when she caught sight of Althea sitting on the front porch. It was not a completely unusual sight except for the fact that at this time of day, she was usually in the backyard whacking balls at anyone who was willing and able to give her a challenge.

Seeing Hettie, Althea rose to her feet and marched down the stairs, a newspaper in hand. Hettie didn't even have to guess what it was in the paper that had upset Althea. It was entirely possible that Hettie had taken that particular paper, opened it to a specific page and laid it where Althea would surely find it.

"Have you seen this?" Althea demanded, shaking the paper at Hettie. Her expression was murderous.

"I have read several newspapers this morning," Hettie said calmly as though she had no care in the world. "As is my practice. I would need to know which paper it is that you're waving around."

Althea unrolled the paper. "Supposedly, I am announcing

my engagement to Will when I return to New York! And the marriage will take place sometime this year."

Hettie pressed her lips together for a second. "Well, you have been writing Will an awful lot."

It had become something of a silent race to the mailbox to see who was getting a letter that day. It was, quite possibly, the most exciting part of the day.

"Hettie!"

"Althea, you've gone mute these past few months. Of course people are going to write to fill the space." Hettie leaned very slowly in Althea's direction. "If you want to change the narrative, give them something to talk about."

Hettie moved past Althea, leaving the other woman standing on the sidewalk. That paper in Althea's hand had also bothered Hettie but not for the same reason. President Eisenhower had apparently refused to travel to the South and give a speech on the importance of civil rights. Another disappointing coward of a president in a long line of them. Even Roosevelt for all his esteemed greatness had had to be begged and pleaded and bartered with to remember that he was president to Negroes too. Hettie clicked her tongue as she climbed the steps to the Eaton home and opened the door.

Althea caught the door before it closed behind her.

"Oh my gosh!" Hettie jumped away, startled.

"Doc!" Althea called out, not seeing her. "Is there a game I can play in the next week or so?"

Hettie sat alone on one half of the bench that was specifically set aside for the press. They'd traveled hours by train to get to this small tournament in Missouri so that Althea could change the narrative. That, and hopefully give Hettie something more interesting to write about.

"A lady reporter." A man sat down next to her. A colored reporter. It was a USLTA tournament, which meant that most of the players were white and so were most of the spectators. Segregation was technically over. Hettie should be bold enough to sit next to the white reporters. She was not. It wasn't fear that kept her in her seat. It would be more accurate to say that wisdom was holding her back. One had to be in the right mental space to be next to people who didn't like you. Hettie wasn't there. They'd rushed to make this game happen and as Hettie had to prep her article, sleep had been very low on the list of important things to do. It was better for Hettie to stay away when she was tired.

"What paper are you with?" They appeared out of nowhere, a cluster of Negro male reporters. Hettie recognized a few of them but none of them appeared to recognize her as they filled the seats next to her and behind. She felt surrounded. When Harmon had been with her at Forest Hills, most of the reporters had pretended not to see her. She'd been perfectly satisfied with that way of thinking. But she had no buffer now.

"*Harlem Heights*," Hettie finally said, since it seemed like the small collective group was waiting for an answer.

"What's your name?" a man demanded. "Are you Hester Carlin?"

When embarking upon her writing career, Hettie had debated for a very long time as to whether she wanted to go by her initials or reveal that she was a woman. Pretending to be a man got a woman very far in life. But what if she ever reached the top like she hoped? It was the name Hester Carlin that she wanted on everybody's lips. Hettie reached up, her fingers playing with the gold chain of her necklace. "I see you've heard of me."

Another man pulled out a newspaper: it was a copy of the most recent issue of the double H. "You're the only one Althea is talking to right now. Of course, we've heard of you."

"She would talk to a woman," someone muttered behind her.

"This isn't really all that interesting," another man pointed to the article.

"And yet, you've read it." Hettie kept her voice cool. She charmed *old* men. Not men who were her peers. "How about you worry about you and I worry about me?"

One of the men whistled. "That right there is probably why you're not married."

Hettie tugged on her necklace. "Gentlemen, I live by one philosophy." The little huddle went quiet as the men waited for her to speak. "If you try to make a fool out of me, I will make a fool out of you and then we will both be fools together. Consider this to be a warning."

There was a long moment of silence. And then laughter. "Okay, Carlin."

"Whatever you say."

They talked their talk but they also said no more about her writing or her personal life. Hettie reached for her notebook as the first game was announced. It was a match-up between two up-and-coming young women. Althea had spent the whole train ride reading up on her competition and explaining to Hettie her plan for taking each one out should she be matched up against any of them. Hettie was therefore familiar with the strengths and weaknesses of the women in front of her.

But it was not the way one woman rotated her wrist or the way the other woman already seemed to favor one leg over the other that caught Hettie's eye. It was the gentle swirl of their skirts. It was the way they smiled and softly waved to the crowd with sweet shyness. They were dominating sportswomen, but at the end of the day, women. Thus, they were expected to display flagrant femininity to prove that even in playing sports, they were still female.

Hettie wrote very little as the matches went on. She merely tugged on her necklace in thought. And then she felt it. Was it the way the linespeople straightened? Was it the hush of the crowd? Was it the tense, strained look on the other player's face? Althea's steps were slow and unhurried as she entered the arena wearing a white shirt and a pair of white shorts. Hettie had curled her hair the night before and Althea had pinned the curls back just an hour ago so no hair would be in her face.

"This is the best part," someone murmured behind her. "It's like watching King Kong entering New York City."

Hettie turned around in her seat and glared at the reporter behind her until he wilted, looking elsewhere.

"Do you need anything?" Hettie was close enough to hear the lineman ask Althea the question. Standing next to Althea's lanky frame, the lineman looked like a small child.

"I don't need anything but to beat this girl right here so I can eat lunch." There was no humor in Althea's tone whatsoever and Hettie watched as a slight repulsed look crossed the lineman's face.

After this game was over, Hettie should tell Althea to try and wear a skirt every now and then. Hettie should tell Althea to try and make up to the crowd. Hettie should tell Althea to speak in a more sportsman-like manner. But . . . this was Althea in all her glory. Why should Hettie tell another woman she needed to change in order to make others feel comfortable? Besides, if she were a man, they'd praise her confidence.

Hettie turned a page in her notebook because she did need to keep a record of how the game was played. She didn't realize she was smiling until she looked up and saw Althea frowning in her direction. Hettie's response was to give two thumbs up. Althea twirled the racket in her hand and then swung it out, stretching her long arms. It made Hettie think of Shadrach's awe at her figure. Althea had not just come to win today. She'd come to destroy hopes and dreams. And in little less than an hour, she did just that.

CHAPTER 24

Spin—rotation of the ball as it moves after being hit

"Was it a relief to win this tournament after not playing for the past few months?" Althea and Hettie were on the train returning to North Carolina. It seemed as good a time as any for Hettie to complete the interview.

Althea was once again dressed in her long, shapeless skirt and frayed sweater. Hettie was beginning to recognize it as her travel wear by choice.

"I wouldn't use the word relief. I wasn't worried I would lose."

Hettie's pencil paused and she adjusted her reading glasses. "Validating?"

"Yeah. I like that word better."

"Most of the crowd seemed friendly enough but there

were a few who felt it necessary to toss insults your way. One man called you a—"

"I don't listen to any of that. When I'm on the court, I keep my focus on the other player. The moment I take my focus off the game, anything can happen. I'm not trying to allow for surprises."

"Does it bother you when people you don't know call you something that is not your name?"

"My focus is on the game."

"I understand that," Hettie said gently. "But the game is over now. Does it make you angry in this moment that some people are so unkind?"

"I can't control other people. I don't think about other people. I think about me."

She was so irritating. Hettie flipped the page of her notebook. Tennis, tennis, tennis, she kept saying as though she were some kind of automaton. "Will you be playing any other games in the near future?"

"Yes. I am playing the tournament in Kentucky in a week."

"Is there any particular player you're looking forward to playing up against?" After a few more questions, Althea cried off, pleading exhaustion. Hettie closed her notebook, removed her glasses, and stared out the window. Nothing in this interview was remotely interesting to her as a layperson. It was a good thing she'd made a phone call and put plan B into operation.

"Where did all of these children come from?" They'd just entered the backyard of the Eaton home, where on the clay tennis courts were about forty children ranging in ages from five to ten. Like a bunch of puppies set free, they were everywhere.

"I arranged for them." Hettie's voice was nonchalant as she adjusted the bag on her shoulder.

"You arranged . . ."

"The Joys of Tennis. That is the subject of my next article."

"The joy of tennis is being alone."

"There are only so many articles I can write about you enjoying loneliness. For this article, we're going to say that you find great joy in putting smiles on children's faces." Althea's head dropped back in exasperation. "Don't you dare say you're tired—you slept ninety percent of the ride here."

Eyes still on the sky above them, Althea placed her hands on her hips. "Hettie Jo!"

"I thought you liked children? Didn't you work with kids in Florida?"

"I don't mind them every now and then but I'm not sure I'd go so far as to say they give me joy."

"They are going to give you joy today. Just go in there and teach them tennis things. And guess what? Lewis donated rackets and balls. Dr. Eaton is keeping them in his cellar." Hettie had mentioned her idea to Shadrach in one little sentence in a letter. Next thing she knew, there were two boxes sitting at the postal office with her name on them. After that, she'd had no choice.

"It'll be fun, Althea," Dr. Eaton said, coming up from the cellar with one of the boxes in hand. Dr. Johnson was right behind him with the second box. Both men had plans to sit Althea down and review the tournament with her in great detail. It was a meeting Hettie fully planned on missing. "Let's show them how to play."

"I've got a camera." Hettie slipped the small machine out of her pocket, holding it up. "Go have a good time, y'all."

Althea's expression was dark but it gradually cleared as she stepped closer and closer to the little mass of bodies that writhed with excitement.

To add to the mood, Hettie turned on an outside radio and 'That'll Be the Day' by Buddy Holly and the Crickets filled the yard.

For the space of two hours, children played and ran, and Althea fussed and laughed and taught. Hettie used all the film in her camera getting shots that she thought would go nicely with her article.

After the last ball was hit, Dr. Eaton and his wife passed out frozen popsicles to exhausted kids who were strewn across the clay courts like Raggedy Ann dolls. Althea joined them, lying stretched out across the baseline and listening to the conversation of one tiny person who had enough energy to still run at the mouth.

"Here you go." Hettie reached for the pink popsicle being handed to her and set aside her camera and notebook so Dr. Johnson could have a seat next to her on the back porch stairs. "I think this went well."

"I think so too, Doc."

"Did she tell you about the two other tournaments she wants to play?"

"She mentioned one."

"There's another she just sent the paperwork in for. Because of the location, there's no easy way to get to both in a timely fashion so we'll get you two a car. Miles will tag along," Dr. Johnson said, referencing one of the college students. "He'll play chauffeur and get to see some real talent at the same time. Y'all are young. You'll make the trip there and back quickly."

Hettie nibbled on the top of her popsicle. She was not

a fan of road trips but different locations offered different opportunities.

They left before the sun was up.

"I hope you drive better than you play," Althea told Miles from the back seat of the car. She'd insisted that because she was taller than Hettie she needed more room, thus Hettie sat in the passenger seat next to their college chauffeur.

"Well, considering that I play better than most—"

"You play better than Hettie. I'll give you that." Hettie chose to ignore this comment and then mentally patted herself on the back for doing so. She really could be mature at times.

"If you need me to help you drive, I can," Hettie told Miles. "If you get tired, just let me know."

Miles shook his head. "I won't get tired."

"But if you do," Hettie said firmly. "Let me know." Miles might be a decade younger than Althea and Hettie, but someone had ingrained in him early on that men drove and women didn't. That was fine with Hettie so long as he didn't fall asleep at the wheel. "Now, everything has been planned." Dr. Eaton had carefully marked out the roads that they were supposed to take, the restaurants they should eat at, and the hotels they'd be staying in at night. Hettie slipped on her reading glasses and unfolded the map. "I'm going to be following along to make sure you don't make any mistakes."

"She will," Althea warned.

"Listen, neither of you spinsters needs to worry about a thing. My grandma taught me how to take care of old women."

There was a minute of silence.

"I beg your pardon."

"Boy, we will leave you at the next rest stop," Althea said after giving his chair a thump from behind. "Old? Didn't I soundly thrash him yesterday?"

"Oh yes. He lost every set. I was embarrassed for him," Hettie offered.

Miles grinned. "Sorry," he quipped, except to Hettie's mind, he didn't sound very sorry at all.

"Althea, it's time for your pre-game interview." In the back seat, Althea released a groan. "How do you intend for the game to go?"

"I'm going to whip everyone's tail from here until kingdom come." In the driver's seat, Miles laughed. "It's going to be over before they know what hits them. Slam, bam, thank you, ma'am."

"Althea Gibson," Hettie chided, feeling like her mother.

"Well, it's true. And that's all I have to say on the matter." This was only Hettie's second tournament at Althea's side but she had a feeling this was all Althea ever had to say on the matter. Deciding that she'd get the meat of her article after the game, Hettie asked no further questions. Instead, she fiddled with the radio until she heard Chuck Berry's familiar voice.

They reached all of their destinations in one piece, arriving earlier than expected. In no time at all, Althea disappeared into the bowels of the tennis club where the players waited and Hettie and Miles went to find seats in the stands. Because of her journalist credentials, Hettie marched them both to the front.

"Why journalism, Miss Hettie?" Miles asked as he took a seat next to her on the bench.

Pulling out her notebook and something to write with, Hettie asked, "Why tennis, Miles?"

"It's fun. I'm not that good at it but I enjoy playing."

"That is not the attitude of a winner."

"It's funny you say that. Miss Althea told me the same thing last time we played. But if I've learned anything this summer, it's that tennis is not my ministry. I'm not willing to do what Miss Althea does to be a champion and I'm all right with that."

"Is there any room for us?" a voice asked.

Miles and Hettie scooted down as more reporters arrived. "You didn't answer my question, Miss Hettie."

Hettie reached into her bag and pulled out her fan. She snapped it open and began the arduous task of trying to keep cool on a day that made you sweat even when not moving. "I like to observe," she said finally. "And then I like to write what I see and share it with the world. If my writing introduces you to something you otherwise never would have learned or encountered, then I was successful."

"Or she did really well in her English classes." This comment came courtesy of one of the sports reporters she'd come across at the previous game.

Keeping her eyes on Miles, Hettie said, "I also like the idea of giving voice to the voiceless but last time I checked, my vocal cords and my pencil worked just fine. That person behind us does not speak for me."

"This lady is a trip," the other journalist muttered.

Hettie leaned back and looked at him. "Is this the part where I tell you about yourself? No? Then maybe . . ." Hettie held up a single finger over her mouth and then she turned around. She ignored the laughter that started around her.

Miles's eyes had grown wide so Hettie winked at him before reaching for her sunglasses.

As she predicted, Althea made mincemeat of her competition and then the three of them were back on the road. Watching the sun go down and the stars begin to populate the sky, Hettie leaned against the window. Her interview with Althea after the game had gone just like all the rest. Althea was not giving an inch and Hettie was running out of time. She didn't like to think that she was working against a clock. But she was.

Wimbledon was taking place in June. Hettie needed to change Althea's mind in a matter of months and literally nothing had happened that Hettie could use to do so.

"Miss Hettie?"

"Yes, Miles?"

"Can you pull out the map? I'd like to see how far we are from the hotel."

The map lay discarded between their seats and Hettie carefully unfolded it. Because it was dark, she also produced a tiny flashlight she'd found in the car on their way to the tournament. She'd been so lost in her thoughts that she hadn't paid attention to a single marker they'd driven past in the last hour. "Where are we at?"

"Well . . . um . . . I think I may have made a wrong turn."

"Okay." Hettie flashed light on the thin red line that Dr. Eaton had drawn. "Where do you think you made the wrong turn?"

"About an hour back."

"What?!" The voice was Althea's. Hettie had thought she was asleep.

"I only just realized it," Miles whispered.

"Fine," Hettie said, her voice clipped. "So long as we're not going west, it's not the worst problem in the world." West would mean going backwards. If they were in an easterly direction, they'd run into North Carolina soon enough.

"I don't think we're going west."

"Good."

"I think we're going south. I saw a sign for Atlanta. That's how come I realized we might not be where we're supposed to be. And that's not the worst of it." Miles paused, letting his words dangle in the air.

"I will strangle you." Althea's words were calm.

"We're running out of gas. We only had enough to get to the hotel."

Hettie brought a hand to her head but only for a second. "There's a sign coming up. Let's figure out where we are." It was not as bad as it could have been—they'd only strayed about a hundred miles in the wrong direction.

"The nearest hotel according to this book is . . . how many miles is that, Hettie?" Althea had the green book and was comparing the locations listed to those on the map.

"I'd say it's about 150 miles away." Math was not Hettie's strong suit but she figured she was somewhere in the ballpark. "So, about a two-and-a-half-hour ride."

"That far." Because his voice was low, the panic seemed loud.

"Look!" Hettie pointed. "There's a sign for a gas station." All three of them read the exit number. All three saw that it was twenty miles away. Hettie looked out the window again, this time for a different reason. There were no city lights in the distance. There were no businesses where they could easily stop for help. Only trees, grass, and tall hills looked back. There was not even another vehicle on the road. Hettie brought both hands to her face, rubbing her eyes gently.

"If we make it, will the gas station even be open?"

Althea said nothing and Hettie chose not to respond to Miles's question. She could only deal with one problem at a time. Fifteen minutes passed with a tense silence hanging in the air. With her shoulders high and her stomach tight with anxiety, Hettie sat on the edge of her seat as though she could will the car to move further down the road. But after turning onto the exit, the car made a few odd sounds, and then quietly slid to a stop. Hettie bowed her head. *Dear Lord, I know you haven't heard my voice in a while but it's your daughter, Hettie Carlin.*

CHAPTER 25

Break point—when the returner is one point away from winning the game

"Are you praying?" Althea's question filled the silence, making Hettie unreasonably angry. But she was so at her wits' end, even a cough would have filled her with rage.

"Of course I'm praying!"

As though Hettie hadn't just yelled, Althea calmly said, "This is not the best situation in the world but neither is it the worst. The gas station is maybe five miles away. It could be less."

"Althea—"

"We'll just have to walk there, get some gas, and then walk back. I'm assuming, Miles, that there are empty gas cans in the trunk that we can use?"

"Yes, ma'am," Miles said quickly. "But you shouldn't have to walk. I will."

"That's very kind of you to offer, but it's safer for us women to do the fetching."

Hettie dropped her head back against the car seat. "And if the gas station isn't open?"

"Chances are the owner of the station doesn't live that far away from it. We'll knock on doors until we find the right person," Althea said confidently. "Don't worry. It'll all work out."

Knock on random doors in a rural area where people had more guns than children? That sounded like something only an idiot would do.

"Alternatively, we sleep in the car and get gas in the morning," Althea mused. It was an uncomfortable proposition but not undoable. "But I'll probably miss the tournament. If we wait to get gas in the morning, there won't be enough time to make it to North Carolina."

"I'm sorry. I'm so sorry," Miles began, his voice breaking. "I got distracted. This is all my fault." He opened the car door. "I'll fix it. I'll go find the gas station."

"No," Hettie said firmly, feeling like she'd suddenly been handed a two-year-old.

"Shut that door! I just told you if anyone leaves it has to be us."

"This is all my fault," Miles repeated mournfully. Hettie said nothing. Every now and then silence was sufficient.

"Come on, Hettie. Let's go see if the gas station is open. Worst comes to worst, we come back and sleep in the car. The more I think about it, the more I want to play tomorrow."

That was not the worst that could happen but Hettie already felt a little as though she'd wished this situation upon them by mentally complaining that nothing exciting had happened. She wasn't going to now speak into existence the very fears that they were all trying to ignore.

Hettie released a long pent-up sigh, slung her purse strap over her shoulder, and then opened the door. Although the sun was currently level with the Earth's surface, it was still hot as Hades outside. Hettie tugged on her blouse, already beginning to feel a bit confined. She stopped when she caught sight of Althea. "You're wearing pants and that big ugly shirt. They'll think you're a man!"

"Fine! I'll change into a skirt!" While Althea dug around in her bag, Miles went to the trunk of the car and handed Hettie two empty metal tin-pail-looking things with lids.

"I'll pay for it."

"Child," Hettie began as she swung the cans lightly, "I am not angry with you. But I am in such a mood that if you keep talking, I will tell you where to go and how to get there."

Miles started to speak but then wisely kept his mouth shut. Althea slammed the car door, now wearing one of her long ugly skirts. "Let's go!" Shoving one gas can at Althea, Hettie started down the road. "Did you bring the flashlight?"

"It's in my purse." Hettie didn't know how long the flashlight would operate and so she'd wait to use it until they absolutely needed it. They passed the first fifty yards in silence.

"It's so beautiful out here."

"There are wild animals out here." Hettie liked animals so long as they were in the zoo. She warily eyed the shadowed trees that populated the small hills that lined up both sides of the road. She could hear creatures talking to one another. It was unnerving.

"Is a lion going to get you, Hettie?"

"Laugh it up but I'm willing to bet that there are bears and big cats and . . . snakes out here." There were parts of America that were still undeveloped. Hettie knew because she was looking at it right now.

"You're not scared, are you? Not Hettie, who's unafraid of everything."

"Althea." Hettie said her name, stressing each syllable. She was not in the mood. Every step forward she was taking was adding one more brick to the house of anger she was currently building.

"Are you bothered, Hettie? Does the sound of my voice annoy you? Is there a headache beginning to form in the back of your head 'cause I won't shut up, Hettie?"

"Do you know why you feel safe asking me all these questions?"

"Feel safe?!'

"'Cause you know I'm not going to take this can and ream you over the head with it. And I'm too frustrated to say more words than I need to."

"You know why you're mad, Hettie Jo?"

"There are so many reasons, Big Al. But I wait in all eagerness to hear your opinion on the matter."

"You're mad because something happened that you can't control but you think you could have controlled it. If only you had followed along with the map, if only you had made Miles fill up the tank at one of the gas stations we did pass, if only, if only, if only. I get that way too when I lose a game. Sometimes other players have better days than me but I've trained so much, so hard, I still should have been able to beat them. If only, I think."

Hettie gritted her teeth but within her began the burning of a small flame. The writer in her had another idea: the rage of tennis. Sentences and paragraphs began forming in her head.

"But you see, the difference between you and me is that I will place myself in that position of having no control, over and over again, just for the chance to see my name in lights. You take no risks. You just—" Althea waved her hand "—try to set up everything so that you know the beginning, the middle, and the end. That's no way to live."

Someone was remarkably chipper considering the circumstances they were currently in. "I don't recall asking for advice."

"That's no way to achieve anything great."

"Excuse me," Hettie said politely through a jaw clenched so tight, her teeth hurt. "But writing is not the same as playing a game of chance."

"Maybe not," Althea murmured, as though really thinking about it. "But I still say with no risk there is no reward."

"Okay, well. I'm glad one of us is happy that we're risking our lives out here in the dark."

"I'm not happy about this situation in particular but it is nice that for once it's you about to have a meltdown." Hettie decided not to dignify that with a response because she was not about to have a meltdown. She was just angry. "I'm in such a mood that I'm willing to hear why it is you think that I was losing last year."

There was a bit of a war raging on the inside of Hettie. A huge part of her wanted to give Althea the silent treatment and not say a word. But the journalist in her was interested in where this conversation might lead. That thought propelled her to speak. "I'm not an athlete," Hettie finally said.

"No kidding."

"But I think you approach the game with too much emotion. When you play, you're like a Coke bottle that's been shook up—all the time. If somebody pops that top and you erupt, anything could happen. It just so happens that I knew you well enough when we were younger to know what popped your top then and lo and behold, it still pops your top now. So, if I'm your opponent on the field, what I already know is that you're good at tennis, but I also know you can be unstable, depending on your mood. Do I wear you out so you're tired? Do I try to win the crowd over to my side so they freeze you out? Do I play up to the lineman so that you look ridiculous when you get angry? If I were a tennis player, this is how I would be thinking."

"Okay, Genghis Khan, but I don't think anyone approaches the game that way."

"See. That's why you lose." Hettie meant for that to be her closing statement but there was just one more thing she had to say. "When you walk out on the field, you intimidate just about every other woman who comes out against you. For your weaker opponents, you've already won. The stronger ones will do what they can to even out the field. You need—"

Something caught Hettie's foot and she flung forward onto the gravel road. She just barely stopped her fall by landing on all fours.

"You need help?" Althea was at her side, grabbing her arm.

Hettie pushed her away. "I've got it." She stood slowly, wiping at her hands and knowing she was bleeding. She didn't need to look down to know she'd ripped up the skin of her knees and torn holes into her pantyhose. It wasn't going to fix anything, but she really could use a good cry right about now.

"Hettie—"

"I just can't, Althea." Neither woman said anything more for the next half hour as their steps ate up the ground.

"Hettie." Having spent the last two miles keeping her eyes on the road before her, Hettie looked up. The sun was gone. It was not quite pitch-black because of the bright three-quarter moon in the sky and the stars flickering above, but it was still a bit disorienting to realize that at some point they'd stepped into night. "I think that's the gas station up ahead." It was a shadowy, hovering thing in the distance, clearly closed and locked up for the night. "And look."

Hettie took a step past Althea to see a farmhouse just off the road. Of course the house looked to be a mile back from the highway but it was something. Lights were on and Hettie could see someone's shadow as they passed a window.

"Give me the other gas can." Hettie passed it to Althea and took a step forward—she would be the one taking the lead here. The path that led to the door of the farmhouse was long. Hettie knew she didn't look her best. Her dress was probably streaked with dirt. Her stockings were ripped. She'd long since stopped fighting the battle against sweat, and so her hair was puffy and her blouse was damp.

The farmhouse had several steps, a wide-open porch, and a large front door. There was also a dog, but thankfully he was inside the house and on the other side of the door. That didn't stop the dog from growling and barking as it sensed Hettie's presence. Althea stood at the bottom of the porch steps while Hettie stepped forward and knocked on the door several times before taking a quick leap back.

"Would you hush?" a man yelled from within the house. The doorknob rattled and then the front door opened, revealing a white man about her father's age. He bent down briefly to push his dog away and Hettie caught a glimpse of a long hallway with a rather large cross nailed to one of the walls for decoration. It was the sort of thing her mother would have if there had been space in her apartment for it.

"Hello!" Hettie said quickly. "My name is Hettie Jo and that's my friend Althea standing over there. Our car ran out of gas a few miles back and we were wondering if you owned the gas station and would be able to help us? If not, perhaps you know someone else who might?"

Hettie had decided that a Southern accent would be better than a New York accent and so everything she'd said she'd made sure exited with Miz Ce-Ce's voice.

The man looked Hettie up and down and his nostrils flared as though he smelled something bad. There was enough light behind him in the house that Hettie decided to take a look at herself. Her knees resembled the same ugly mess that she had made of them when she'd first learned how to ride a bike. They had been aching slightly before but now that she saw them, she felt the sharp pain of her wounds. Her pantyhose was shredded, the rips having spread wider and wider, up and down her legs. But her dress wasn't stained with dirt like she'd thought it would be. "Uh-uh." He waved a hand. "Station is closed. Come by in the morning."

"Who's at the door, Bobby?" a woman's voice called out.

"Daddy, is it the reverend coming to pick you up for the meeting at church?" a young girlish voice asked.

"Nope. It's just a nigger."

It was said so casually, Hettie felt as though she'd been slapped clear across the face. No white person had ever called her that word in her life. *Ignore it,* she told herself firmly. "Sir, I am a young woman in desperate need of gas for my car. I do have money and you will be paid if the gas station belongs to you and if you can allow us to fill up the gas cans that we have brought ourselves. I recognize that this is an inconvenience for you, but my friend and I would be extremely grateful if you could help us." Was she begging? The voice in Hettie's head was bitter.

Behind the man, a girl in her early teens slid into view, there to watch the happenings.

"Gal, I done told you to get. Don't make me fetch my gun."

Fetch his gun! Was he insane? Hettie's foot slid back an inch, away from the door. Her stomach tumbled and she hated the fear that blossomed within her, spreading to the tips of her fingers and toes.

"Excuse me, sir!" Althea called quickly from the bottom of the porch. "Do you know the Oliphants? I think they live around these parts. They can vouch for our character if you're worried."

Vouch for her character? Was this man afraid they were going to rob him or something? Hettie's hands were shaking and she fisted them at her sides. *Calm down*, she told herself. *Get it together.* She looked past the man and the girl, and a cross-stitch hanging on the wall caught her eye. *Blessed are the pure in heart for they shall see God.* She was in such a wild mood, Hettie nearly started laughing.

"David and Katie Oliphant?" The man's voice was suspicious.

"Yes, sir. Those are the ones. Tell them it's Althea Gibson who's standing on your porch."

"The tennis player?" This came from the girl in the house.

"Yes, ma'am," Althea said, even though it was clear she was years older than the child. "That's me, the tennis player."

"A tennis player?" the man repeated.

"Yes, Daddy. She plays in all the big tournaments. Even the ones overseas." The girl pushed past her father to get a better view of Althea. She didn't see Hettie standing there at all. "Will you be playing at Wimbledon again?"

"I reckon I will. Look for my name in the papers in June."

There was a moment of silence. "I'll open one pump. I'll meet you down there in ten minutes."

The front door slammed shut.

"Hettie?" There was worry in Althea's voice.

Hettie turned on her heels and marched down the porch stairs. "Why didn't you say you knew people out here?"

"I don't. I've played against Theresa Oliphant who's a bigwig in these parts. I figured if he called the family, they'd at least recognize my name. But never fear, you needed to be the one standing in front of that door. He had to feel safe and you're tiny enough to do that. Although, for a second there, I thought you were going to lose it. Didn't they tell you before you came down here to keep calm and keep your mouth shut?"

Hettie pressed her lips together and started down the long driveway toward the gas station.

CHAPTER 26

Topspin—when a player hits the ball with an upward motion and the ball spins forward

While Althea filled the gas cans and chatted it up with Bobby the gas station owner, Hettie stood with her arms folded across her chest and staring out until something caught her eye. Tossing a quick glance at Althea, who stood under the sole gas station light that Bobby had deemed to turn on, she hurried along a rocky path that led to the thing she'd noticed: a payphone.

It was late. If they continued to their original hotel of choice, they wouldn't make it there until midnight and the truth of the matter was that it wasn't actually a hotel like those in New York. It was someone's home that had been turned, more or less, into a place where you could rent a room for the night. That someone was not going to be up and waiting to greet them. To Hettie's thinking, they should find a place to rest for the night that wasn't as far away, and then leave early for Althea's tournament the next day. Pulling out her notebook and her small coin bag, Hettie got to dialing.

"Lewis residence, how can I help you?"

"Hello, may I speak with Mr. or Mrs. Lewis?"

"This is Talitha Lewis speaking."

"Hi, Mrs. Lewis, my name is Hettie Carlin and I am a friend of your son Shadrach Lewis. I am currently in the state of Tennessee, traveling to North Carolina. However, we had some car trouble." As if Hettie was going to admit that they'd run out of gas. "And it'll be hours before we reach the place where we'd been planning to spend the night. I was wondering if you would, by any chance, be able to help me find a place that's close by?"

There was a pause. "I'm sorry, dear. Did you say that you were a friend of Shadrach's?" Shadrach's mother's voice was clear and crisp, and she sounded like the no-nonsense woman Shadrach painted her to be. Still, Hettie found herself gripping the receiver of the phone with both hands, oddly comforted by the voice of this woman she'd never met.

"Yes, ma'am. I'm from New York but I'm traveling for work."

"And he knows you how? Never mind—don't answer that. This call is probably costing you a small fortune. I'll call Shad later. Ash! Where's the map? There's a young lady on the phone who needs some directions. She's Shadrach's friend."

"Shadrach doesn't have friends," a low voice said from some distance. "And certainly not female ones."

"Well, he has this one. Would you hurry, please? She's probably on a payphone. Are you on a payphone, dear?"

"Yes, ma'am."

"Where are you exactly?"

Between Ash, Talitha, and Hettie, they were able to pinpoint the car's location and the nearest place where Hettie and the others could stay.

"Thank you, ma'am and sir."

"You're welcome. Hettie Carlin, did you say your name was?"

"Yes, ma'am."

"I've got my hands on a good book this evening so I'll be up late reading. Give me a call and let me know when you've made it in safe."

Feeling a bit teary, Hettie nodded even though Talitha Lewis couldn't see her. "I will. Thanks again."

When Hettie hung up the phone, she looked down at her notebook where she'd filled the page with all of the directions that Shadrach's father had walked her through. They were only a thirty-minute drive from where they needed to be.

Hettie walked back to the gas station where Bobby was jumping into his truck. The light above the gas pump flickered for a second and then whooshed off. Hettie blinked as her eyes tried to adjust to the night sky once again. "He's not going to give us a ride?" It was a stupid question to ask because the man was tearing out of the parking lot at a ridiculous speed.

"He's late to a church meeting," Althea said as she hefted both cans and walked toward Hettie.

"A church meeting?"

"He said we're only about four miles away from the car. Where did you disappear to?"

"I made a phone call and found a place where we could stay tonight. We'll just have to get up early to leave for North Carolina tomorrow. Four miles? It would have taken him thirty seconds to drop us off." A slight exaggeration but not by much. "Now, it's going to take us an hour to get back to the car."

"Maybe less than that if you pick up the pace."

"Give me one of those gas cans."

"I've got it," Althea said breezily. It was ten gallons of gasoline that she was carrying. Sure it might be easy now, but even for Althea it was going to be tiring. Especially with four miles to go.

"Give me one. If I can't carry it, I'll give it back to you." Hettie thrust out her hand, demanding the return of the gas can she'd carried this far.

"I know you. You'd die first before you admit you're struggling."

"That's not exactly true. If it gets that bad I'll definitely hand it back to you. They will not put on my headstone that she died because a car ran out of gas."

Althea slowly, reluctantly, handed her the gas can. Hettie nearly dropped it. They'd have probably lost half of the gasoline if the can hadn't come with a lid. Deciding that she was willing to sacrifice her dress, Hettie leaned down and scooped up the heavy tin pail, holding it against her chest as though it were a baby.

"You're stubborn."

"So are you."

It was faster coming this direction than heading back, Hettie decided. She felt each step she took. The gas can was slowing her down and her knees were aching. The palms of her hands were starting to hurt from where they'd been cut up by the gravel. And she was tired. Oh, so tired. If a fly landed on her that might be the very last thing. She'd break down and cry and refuse to move another foot.

To think that man could have given them a ride but he'd chosen to run out to a church meeting. Admittedly, Hettie hadn't picked up her Bible in a minute but she was pretty sure leaving young women to walk four miles in the dark when you could help them was not something Jesus would do. How did one get to the place where they were kindness itself to one group of people and cruel to a different group of people? History would tell her that it was a very easy dichotomy to make.

"Stop thinking about Bobby, the gas station guy," Althea said from where she walked next to Hettie, swinging the five-gallon gas can as though it were still empty. It wasn't lost on Hettie that with Althea's long legs and athleticism, she could probably be yards down the road. She was keeping pace with Hettie. "You can't focus on other people and how they think or how they act." Althea patted her chest. "You only have control over you."

Hettie's response was a grunt. That was true and not true. If people advertised themselves as something, they should be that thing. Bobby with his cross and his church meetings should play a certain role. How had Shadrach put it? *People should be able to rely on the fact that at the end of the day you're trustworthy not because of who you are but because of what you stand for.* Not that Hettie was naive; there were so many people who cloaked themselves with a religion they didn't even follow. She would not be the same way, she vowed to herself. She needed to establish what she believed, how far she would go and the lines she would not cross, or one day she'd be like Bobby the gas station owner, professing one thing but being another entirely.

Amidst the buzzing of flying insects, the croaks and groans of animals she didn't even want to try and identify, and the steady footfalls on the asphalt beneath her feet, Hettie began to draw borders encompassing who she wanted to be and promising herself that she would do the work to become that kind of person. She vowed that she would not change the parameters just because life got hard.

"You're very quiet over there and it's making me nervous."

"You ever set rules for yourself?"

"Rules?"

"How you'll live, move, and have your being?"

"You mean you haven't seen them?" Althea's question took Hettie back for a second, and then Hettie laughed, long and hard. "Someone has well and truly lost their mind over there. Hand me that gas can. I'll carry it."

If she let it go, she would not be able to carry it again. Pausing to heft it higher, she said, "I've got it."

"*Gonna lay down my burdens, down by the riverside.*"

"Are you singing a slave song?" Hettie asked Althea politely, as though she did not recognize the tune.

"*Down by the riverside. Down by the riverside. Gonna lay down my burdens, down by the riverside to study war no more.*" Althea's voice was deep. Not unexpectedly, she sang alto. But it was a pretty voice and Hettie remembered that she was hoping to become a professional singer after her tennis career concluded. "*I ain't gonna study war no more, study war no more, study war no more.*"

"I feel like there's a hidden meaning in this song just for me. Don't worry, I'm not planning to come back and murder Bobby the gas station owner in his sleep. I might think about it. I'm angry enough to do it. But I'm not that kind of person. I don't seek revenge."

Althea stopped singing. "I know you're inhaling those gas fumes same as me but it must be on account of the fact that you're so little that you're starting to already talk crazy. Remember that one girl you had me knock the block off? Hettie, you tore her up in school. Plain and simple."

"Sue Ann?"

"That's the one."

"I'm not that person anymore."

"Since when?"

"Since five minutes ago. *I'm gonna lay down my burdens,*" Hettie sang. It was Althea's turn to laugh. But she joined in with the rest of the song and they sang until they heard the rumblings of a car behind them.

"Dear God Almighty." Just when she thought she could not deal with another thing, here were the bright, shiny headlights of a vehicle.

"Step back. Off the road." Althea's command was low but Hettie heard it and stepped off the gravel and into the mushy, damp soft earth. Lovely. Her whole outfit was a wash. "If they're colored, we'll ask for a ride."

The car that passed them held a white man in the driver's seat. The car drove past them, slowed and then reversed.

They both released deep, weighty sighs. When Althea lowered her gas can to the ground and stood in front of it, Hettie did the same, all the while wondering if she'd be able to pick it back up again.

The car came to a stop, paralleling them. The driver rolled down his window and stuck his head out as he took a long moment to assess them. He did not appear to be old or young. He was probably around their age, but Hettie could be wrong. It was nighttime after all. "Girl, you are tall as a giraffe," he kindly told Althea before turning his head to look at Hettie. "What is going on here?"

A dozen responses flashed through Hettie's mind. None of

them were okay to release in this moment. So she just stood there, exhausted and staring, knowing that she was making a faux pas but not sure how to correct it. "Girl, I asked you a question. Don't make me ask it again."

It was the kind of threat her father would make to her as a child, which begged the question of just who this man thought he was. And what did he think he was going to do if he had to ask the question again? Hettie's body felt heavy and her fingers ached with a tension she could not release.

"Sir." Althea's voice was clipped and heavy with exhaustion. "We're just walking. Keep going on your merry way."

Hettie's eyes slid in Althea's direction before returning to the man whose face now held a pinched expression. When he started to open his mouth, Hettie pointed. "Can we please walk down this road?" Hettie didn't recognize the pitch of her voice. "Is that not allowed? Do you own this land?"

Trust Hettie to always take it one question too far. But her words caused the man to sit back in his seat, start his car, and drive on. When his car was almost out of sight, Hettie turned to Althea. "Did you see how I had to step in there and save the day?"

"Girl, shut up," Althea said, but there was reluctant humor there. She reached for the gas pail.

Hettie bent down and lifted hers, ignoring all the parts of her body that protested. Once again, they started walking. "I was worried you were going to start something. I had to step in and distract him. You know how you get when you're angry."

"You were about two seconds from saying, 'yo mama'."

Hettie's grin was fleeting. "It doesn't tick you off?"

"Of course it does. I'm just focused on the forest while you're snarling at the trees."

"Hmm. In this analogy, what is the forest?"

"A better way of life." Althea swung the gas pail, the liquid sloshing inside. "This won't be me, always. I can put up with nonsense now if it means I'll come from a place of height later."

"Interesting. Can I put this in an article?"

"Sure," Althea said flippantly. "Tell them I can take it all: the slights, the insults, the name-calling, because one day I'm going to be so big, none of this will ever have mattered."

They went back and forth, tossing out different components Hettie could add to the article, until they finally reached Miles, who was sound asleep in the car.

From there, they had no more issues. Hettie directed Miles to their accommodations, she called Shadrach's mother to thank her once again and let her know that they'd made it in safely, and they were all grateful to have not needed to sleep in the car.

The next day, they got up early to make it to the tournament. Althea played as though she'd gotten a full night's sleep the night before and managed to win the small tournament.

Hettie did find thirty seconds at another gas station—where she watched Miles fill the tank of the car until it nearly overflowed—to make a phone call.

"You ran out of gas?" Shadrach's voice was cool on the other line. His mother had managed to get that tidbit out of her and clearly the woman had told her son.

"I know. Believe me, I know. Please convey my thanks to your parents again. They were very helpful and also I hope I didn't cause you any trouble."

"Trouble? With my parents?" he asked as though the question was ridiculous but Hettie knew his parents had probably had something to say about a woman calling them and claiming to be his friend. "You're the one who was wandering around in a sundown town after the sun went down! But fine, there's no point in talking about it anymore." Hettie silently agreed, deciding to wait patiently for him to change the subject even though this phone call was getting ridiculously expensive. "When are you coming back?"

"I don't know yet but hopefully soon. I miss New York."

"Well, I hope you know I miss you," he said bluntly and Hettie grinned. Just hearing the words made every cent of this phone call worth it. "Where's the first place you want to go when you get back?"

"With you?"

"Yes. Dinner?"

"No. I want to go to the zoo."

If he thought the request was strange, he didn't say so. "Done. Let's go as soon as you return. Hyacinth will love it." Hettie was glad he was not there to see how she almost dropped the receiver. "If you're okay with her joining us, that is?"

"I'm okay." Did he hear the strange high pitch of her voice? She looked out the phone booth and saw both Miles and Althea staring at her, clearly ready to go.

"Good," he said firmly and she wasn't sure if he was trying to convince her or himself. "But I'm not going to keep you on the line. Take care, Hettie, and be safe for crying out loud!"

"I will. Take care of yourself! I love you, bye!" Hettie hung up the phone. She took one step out of the phone booth and froze. Had she just told that man she loved him?

"Mother of . . ." The rest of the phrase was rushed air because she preferred not to use the Lord's name in vain. But sometimes swearing really was the only effective way to communicate a feeling. First, she'd told the man she was in lust with him and now she'd told him she loved him. She was never returning to New York. She'd have to purchase a piece of land in North Carolina and settle down forever. Maybe she'd like growing cotton or rice or whatever they farmed out there.

"Hettie Jo!"

"Coming!"

This time Hettie sat in the passenger seat with the map in her lap and her reading glasses on, focused on the road and nitpicking Miles's driving. It was either that or think about her confession to Shadrach that was making her both overheat and break out into a cold sweat every time the memory crossed her mind. They reached the Eaton home in the early afternoon.

To Hettie's surprise, Dr. Eaton came running out the front door just as Miles pulled up outside the house. "Althea, Harold called! You've got to call him back right away!"

Althea rushed out of the car and into the house. Dr. Eaton followed behind, the screen door swinging shut behind him.

Hettie thought she knew most everyone's name who was anyone in the tennis world but this name escaped her. Either that or she was just tired. Walking to the trunk of the car where Miles was removing their bags and suitcases, she asked, "Who's Harold?"

"Harold could be anybody. But," he said quickly, noting the perturbed look on her face, "if it is who I think it is, it's probably Harold Lebair."

"And Harold Lebair is?" Hettie asked slowly. She liked Miles, she really did.

"The chairman of the USLTA's international play committee."

The front door of the house opened and Althea stepped out onto the porch. Miles and Hettie turned, waiting to hear what had been so important. "The USLTA is paying all of my fees for Wimbledon!"

"That's wonderful, Althea!" Hettie knew the costs of the tournament had been in the back of Althea's mind all this time. She was sure it was a relief not to have to think about it anymore.

"What about Fry?" Miles asked, bringing up the tennis player who had outplayed Althea the previous year.

"She retired. You two are looking at the USLTA's number-one tennis player."

CHAPTER 27

Crosscourt—hitting the ball diagonally into the opponent's court

With Althea now being the official number-one player, she no longer wanted to remain in North Carolina. Neither did Hettie for that matter, although the thought of returning and seeing Shadrach was a little bit terrifying.

"I'm not returning to France," Althea announced. They were in their shared room at the Eaton home and both were tucked in their respective twin beds.

"You don't want to defend your title? With Wimbledon taken care of, don't you now have money for France?" Hettie had been sort of hoping that Althea would return to Roland-Garros. She'd always wanted to visit Paris.

"No. I've won it already and this year is all about accomplishing what I haven't managed to do so far. I'll use that time to continue to train."

"How can you maintain your new status if you don't actually play at any major tournaments?"

"By winning the two I want to win. Besides, I did sign up to play the tournament in New Jersey. That will be the last one I play before London."

"Question."

"Yes?"

"Do you get free tickets to tournaments? I'd like to buy one off of you. I promised my uncle a seat at one of your games."

"I will get five free tickets for the tournament in New Jersey and you can have them all. No costs."

"What about your family?" New Jersey was not that far from New York.

"My parents have never been to a single game. They say tennis is too hard to follow and they feel uncomfortable at country clubs. I don't think my siblings care one way or another." Hettie started to speak but swallowed the words. She'd been living alongside Althea long enough to know that her nearest and dearest assumed she had money and asked her for it regularly. The least they could do was come to a game and offer support.

Hettie turned onto her stomach, pulling her pillow up against her chest. "I'm a changed person now, you know."

Althea released a tired laugh. "The rules, right?"

"Exactly. So, know that the old me would have said something but the new me is wisely keeping her mouth shut."

"Is the new you going to toot her own horn every single time she does the right thing?"

"Naturally. Althea?"

"Hmm?" She was losing Althea to sleep.

"You're the number-one tennis player in the whole US, probably the number one in the whole world."

Althea's hand appeared above the cover and she started snapping her fingers. "I love this song you're singing."

Hettie scooted over to the edge of the bed. "Miss Gibson, how does it make you feel to know that you have beat out hundreds of young women to attain this position?"

"Well, it hasn't been easy," Althea said, no longer sounding tired. "I've worked real hard squashing all of the little people beneath my feet."

Hettie grinned, made a fist of her hand, and then held it up to her face as though it were a microphone. "Knowing that you're number one, does that new ranking make you feel more or less nervous about the games up ahead?" Hettie extended her faux microphone so Althea could talk.

"I'm not nervous at all. In my mind, I've always been number one. I've just been waiting for everybody to recognize what is widely known."

"And what is your plan to stay number one, Miss Gibson?" Hettie moved her fisted hand in Althea's direction once again.

"Stay calm. Train. Eat right. Sleep well and then whip everybody's tail." Hettie fell back on the bed and they both were laughing the laugh of the tired. "We're about to do something big, Hettie. I can feel it in my bones."

"What do you think?" Althea was reading the draft of the article that Hettie had written. They were on the train headed back to New York.

Althea twisted her lips to the side as she laid one sheet of the article down on the empty seat next to her and continued to read the second page. Hettie forced herself to say nothing more until Althea finished the last paragraph. Scooping up all three pages of the drafted article, she handed it back to Hettie. "It's written very well."

"Thank you." Hettie felt that same warmth that flooded her every time she saw her name on the front page of the double H. A compliment from Althea was hard-earned.

"It really does bring that night back to life." Hettie had written about the issues that Althea faced as a tennis player traveling through the United States. She'd started the article with their experience in Tennessee. "But I don't know about this."

"I'm sorry?" Only a few days ago, Hettie had had Althea's stamp of approval.

"I don't think I want anything like that published about me." Althea sat back in her seat and turned her gaze to the window next to her.

"Althea, this story is not made up. Neither did I pull it out of thin air. This actually happened. This is a recording of events and how you felt about those events."

"It's trying to say something."

"Well . . . yes . . . there are words on the page." The look Althea sent her was less than kind. "Are you trying to tell me that you can talk about practice and games but you cannot talk about what it's actually like to travel to games in this country? You can't talk about the fears and concerns that you face as a colored woman?"

"Let me think about it," she said stubbornly.

Hettie looked down at the article in her hand. She was holding, quite possibly, some of her best work. She slipped the article into its folder and returned it to her briefcase. She wouldn't toss it out just yet. Events changed people's minds all the time. She just needed to wait for the right moment.

★

Shadrach offered to pick Hettie up and give her a ride to the zoo. Hettie knew this because he'd left a message with Faye. She'd made sure to decline the offer by leaving a message with his secretary. She wasn't ready to speak to him yet. She wasn't ready to see him yet, but there she stood outside the zoo's entrance on the unusually warm spring day, wearing a simple light purple dress and a ribboned straw hat. She'd labored over what to wear for hours before settling on something that she hoped Hyacinth would like.

Looking away from the parking lot and walking over to where a map of the layout of the park was, Hettie asked herself for the fiftieth time if she knew what she was doing dating a man who had a child. She was not exactly stepmother material . . . assuming of course that Shadrach wanted her to be the stepmother of his child, which he might not.

"Hettie!" Hettie turned to see the man she'd missed for the past few months. He was, surprisingly, wearing a pair of dark blue jeans, a white shirt, and a long-sleeved checkered shirt that was acting as a jacket. A dark cap covered his head. But the thing that grabbed her attention was the dark beard that covered the lower half of his face. He came to a stop about a foot away from her and placed his hands on his waist. He grinned, teeth flashing, eyes lit up. "You've been avoiding me, beautiful."

Ignore it, she told herself. Ignore the teasing glint in his eye, the way his words filled her with something deliciously warm, the way she desperately wanted to kiss him. Hettie closed the gap between them, reaching up to touch a hand lightly to his jaw. "This is new."

He leaned into her touch, brushing his lips against the palm of her hand. "Get used to it. I prefer it to being clean-shaven." This would have been the moment where he told her Laverne hated beards but he didn't mention his ex-wife at all. He took a step back and turned to look behind him. Several feet away a little girl stood, wearing a white and blue long-sleeved blouse, a blue skirt, white socks that went slightly past her ankles and black shoes. Hyacinth's hair was parted down the middle and she sported two braids that were mounted with white ribbons. A blue purse was slung over her shoulder and she was watching the pair of them with suspicious eyes. She stood straight and stiff, her body posture conveying her desire to be anywhere but here. Even still, she was a pretty little girl, prettier than the pictures Hettie had seen of her.

"I'll have you know that I've been telling her about you for months," Shadrach whispered. "So, I'm not sure where this reticence is coming from." Raising his voice, he said, "Cindy, come speak to Miss Hettie, please."

"Cindy?"

"Hyacinth to strangers. Cindy with friends and family." His explanation made her stomach flip. But she was not calling the child Cindy until the child gave her permission.

Without taking her eyes off of Hettie, Hyacinth took a few tiny steps closer. "Hi, Miss Hettie." The words were the barest of whispers.

"Cindy Arabella—"

Hettie crossed the few feet that were separating them and then she lowered herself to her knees, which no longer hurt but were still bandaged on account of how ugly they looked. Hyacinth now stood a few inches above her and the look on her face was one of confusion. Hettie stared up at the child. Hyacinth greatly resembled her dad, but she did not have his eyes. The little girl darted a quick glance to her dad and then returned her gaze to Hettie.

"I love the zoo," Hettie told Hyacinth. "Whenever I had

a few free coins, I'd catch the subway and ride out here. I'd sit for hours staring at the animals." Hettie reached inside her purse and pulled out a small stuffed lion that was only a bit bigger than her hand. "Sometimes I'd imagine that they reminded me of people I knew and it'd help me . . . relate to those people a bit better. When I met your dad, I thought, he reminds me of a cat."

Hyacinth's face took on something of a pinched look but Hettie thought she was trying not to smile. "He's watchful and alert but also likes to be alone because sometimes he doesn't know if he likes people." Hyacinth's eyes went wide for a second and her lips disappeared as she darted another glance at her father. This time when her brown eyes returned to Hettie, Hettie saw laughter there. "But then he's sometimes playful and he's begging you to pet him. I couldn't decide if he was a Siamese cat, a tiger, or a cheetah so I went with the king of the jungle." The king of the jungle also shared a similar eye color to Shadrach. Hettie offered up the cat and Hyacinth took it.

"Thank you. He's a house cat, not a lion, but I will still call this one 'Little Daddy'."

"What do you mean I'm not a lion?" Shadrach asked, appearing next to them. He leaned down to poke his daughter in the side.

She twisted out of reach, all the while giggling. "You're scared of everything, Daddy."

"No, I'm not!" Hettie brought a hand dramatically to her mouth and Hyacinth met her eyes, nodding once, slowly.

"Whenever someone rings the doorbell, you hide behind the couch."

"Because I'm trying to make you laugh." Hettie could hear the embarrassment in Shadrach's voice. He extended a hand

and she let him pull her to her feet. The expression on his face was one of pure gratefulness . . . and relief. "Don't listen to this one. She's the real scaredy-cat."

"That's not true!" Hyacinth ran between them and then paused. "What animal am I, Miss Hettie?"

"Ask me when we leave. I've got to watch you a bit."

Hyacinth seemed to ponder this. "What animal are you?"

"She's a mockingbird," Shadrach offered as he reached for Hettie's hand, entwining their fingers, and making her feel like a member of his family. "You know, those little, bitty birds that PawPaw's always fussing at."

Hettie elbowed Shadrach in the side as Hyacinth nodded, understanding this reference. "But," Hyacinth said quickly, her eyes narrowing in suspicion once again. "Cats eat birds."

"Not this time," Shadrach said, shaking his head sadly. "This cat is very much being eaten by the bird."

"Shadrach," Hettie protested, feeling more than a little self-conscious. She tried to pull her hand out of his. But he was holding on tight.

"The cat's just being devoured here." He bumped his shoulder against hers. "But the cat didn't say he didn't like it."

Hyacinth released a small, confused noise as though trying to make sense of this while Hettie was looking off to the side, unable to even look at Shadrach at the moment. Then Hyacinth waved a hand forward. "Can we go in now? Little Daddy wants to see the real lions!"

"Little Daddy," Shadrach muttered under his breath and Hettie released a small laugh. "All right, hold your horses, we're coming."

CHAPTER 28

Counterpuncher—a player who is a defensive baseliner and tries to return every shot

"Did you read the interview that Althea did with *The Baltimore*?" Morgan asked Hettie as they sped along the highway. She'd taken three tickets from Althea for today's tournament in New Jersey. Two of them she'd given to Shadrach for him and Hyacinth. She gave the last one to Morgan because she'd promised him a ticket to a game and because today was the day that she was going to begin introducing Shadrach to her family.

"I did read the interview. Mr. Edgar read it too and chewed me out for missing the scoop." One of the first things Althea had done when they'd returned home was a lengthy interview in the Darbens' living room with Will at her side. Together they'd dodged questions about their impending nuptials. The only thing Althea said during the interview was that at the moment she was going to focus on resting and preparing for Wimbledon. But because the interview was with Will, most everyone was taking it as some sort of pre-wedding announcement. "I told him that the reason we didn't get this interview is because she knows that I know that she has no intention of marrying Will anytime soon. There would have been no point in sitting with me. It was probably Syd's idea anyway. She's been trying to placate him since she left him in New York."

"Listen to you." Morgan was wearing a light brown spring suit but his jacket was in the back seat and his white shirt sleeves were rolled up to his elbows. He had one hand on the steering wheel and he was leaning far back in his seat. "If anyone heard you talk they'd think the two of you were fast friends."

"I don't know if I'd go that far. I think it's safe to say that we're not enemies." They passed a sign that displayed their exit. Hettie reached for her purse, pulling out her mirror and lipstick.

"What did you say this guy did for a living?" Morgan's response to hearing that she had wanted him to meet the man in her life had been disbelief and skepticism. It was as though he had thought she'd never show any interest in romance and marriage.

"He owns a store," Hettie said as she made her lips brighter and redder.

"What kind of store?"

"I'll let him tell you about it. I think you'll like him, Morgan. He's only a few years older than you and he's a veteran."

"Which branch?"

"Army."

"Which unit?"

"I didn't ask," Hettie said politely.

Morgan hummed. "I might know him already. What do you think about that?"

"I doubt it. He's not originally from New York."

"He still could be a part of a veterans group. Did he sign up or was he drafted?"

Hettie waved a frustrated hand. "Ask him. We talk about other things besides his time in the war." She paused. "His daughter will be there."

"He has a kid? *You're* trying to be a stepmother?"

"I don't know why you just said it like that. Your children love me."

"Because they have to. Is this an other-side-of-the-blanket child?"

"No, this is a right side of the blanket. He's divorced." Morgan clicked his tongue in judgment. "Are you joking? The only reason you're not divorced is because—"

Hettie stopped talking. Now was not the time to defend Shadrach by releasing her frustrations with Morgan on Morgan.

"Please, my favorite niece," Morgan said as he placed his other hand on the steering wheel. "Finish the statement."

"Nope. I will not."

"I'm not sure why you're getting all uptight with me just because I don't want you marrying some guy whose first instinct is to flee rather than fight," he said petulantly.

Hettie rolled her eyes but at the window so he couldn't see. Just because Morgan was still married didn't mean that he was fighting for his marriage. "Just meet him first. Reserve your judgment for after the game."

"Does he know I'm coming?"

"Yes. I told him my favorite uncle—who was more like a big brother—was bringing me to the game."

Morgan turned off the exit. "I'm going to drop you off at the door but then find a gas station to fill up for the way home and buy some snacks for the game."

This did not surprise her. Morgan had a sweet tooth that craved the kind of penny candy that discolored your tongue and made your mouth ache. "They sell candy at the stadium."

"Anything they sell at this country club is probably overpriced. Find your seat and I'll find you." It was a USLTA tournament so the Negroes in the crowd would be few and far between. She would not be hard to find.

"Don't take too long." Hettie pointed a finger at him as he pulled into the clubhouse parking lot. "Please, Morgan. This is important to me."

"Yes, yes. Believe me, I want to meet this guy. Now, get out."

Hettie climbed out of the car just as another car passed them. She recognized the driver and passenger immediately. While Morgan did a quick U-turn, Hettie went to meet Syd and Althea. It was Syd who noticed her first. "Hello, Hettie."

"Hi, Syd. Althea." Today, Althea was wearing a navy blue dress that was only slightly too big, otherwise it was almost becoming.

"Don't tell me, Will's coming."

Althea wrinkled her nose in Hettie's direction but didn't say nay as she reached back into the car for her bag. "Go scout out the field, Syd. We'll meet up. I need to change."

Syd gave Althea a two-finger salute and headed toward the

entrance of the stadium. Hettie moved to walk in step with Althea to the clubhouse. "The ATA is sponsoring a bon voyage event at the Birdland for you. The double H got an invite. I'll be going along with my boss."

Althea nodded, a tiny smile forming on her lips. "I heard Sammy Davis Jr. is coming in to sing. Sugar's gonna be there."

"Sugar? As in Sugar Ray? The boxer, Sugar Ray Robinson?" Hettie didn't watch or listen to boxing but she always paid attention when that beautiful man was on the cover of a magazine or a newspaper.

Althea's grin was wide now. She shrugged nonchalantly. "We're really good friends. He's like my fairy godmother. Him and his wife, Edna. They have helped me out a lot over the years. Whenever I'm short a few dollars and still have to make it to a tournament, he'll cover me." The words were said with a mix of pride and embarrassment.

"Well . . . I don't think he can make it any clearer that he believes in you."

Althea released a snort. "Is this Hettie Jo having a kind word to say?"

Hettie lifted her chin. "I have lots of kind words to say. I am filled with nothing but happiness and joy to spread amongst the masses."

"Careful. Christmas isn't for another eight months." Althea's expression changed, her face turning serious. "Did you see that interview I did with Will?"

"Of course I did." Hettie came to a stop, waiting.

"I didn't like that one bit," Althea said, looking very uneasy. "That article you wrote about Tennessee? I don't want it published."

Hettie bit down on her lip to keep from releasing a weary sigh. None of this surprised her.

"It's no one's business how I—"

"Okay, let's talk about it later." Hettie reached the door of the clubhouse first and held it open so Althea could go inside. This particular clubhouse was built more like an office building but it had the same feeling as all of the others Hettie had frequented over the past seven months. The entryway was hushed and quiet, and Hettie took a step back so Althea could speak to the older woman at the front desk first. "Hello, ma'am. I'm Althea Gibson and this is Hester Carlin." Both of them were given their respective passes and information pertaining to the games and the clubhouse.

Hettie placed a hand on Althea's arm. "I'll see you out there on the field. I'd tell you good luck but you don't need it."

Althea smirked before turning back to the woman at the desk as Hettie retraced her steps, headed for the door. "Can you show me where the locker room is? I need to get changed before I practice."

"Oh, I'm sorry, Miss Gibson, but the locker room is full."

"Really? I called ahead yesterday and was told that I'd be able to change here."

"I'm not sure who you spoke to but the locker room is full. I'm afraid we can't accommodate you."

Hettie watched as Althea's head dipped. She took a step away from the desk. Very kindly, she said, "Thank you, ma'am."

"The locker room is full of what?" Hettie asked from the doorway. Both Althea and the woman at the front desk looked at her. "What is it full of? She is asking to change clothes. She is not asking you to store several crates of bananas."

Althea's eyes flashed a silent message and she shook her head at Hettie. "Hester," the front desk lady said, her voice now cool. "If I say the locker room is full, it's full. She'll have to change elsewhere and that's all there is to it."

"Let's not assume that I'm as stupid as you think I am. Say it plainly. Why can't she use the locker room?"

"Hettie!" Althea's lips were thin as she crossed the few feet to stand next to Hettie. "That's enough." Her voice was low and filled with anger. "Let's go."

Hettie raised her hands in surrender. "Fine. The locker room is full." Hettie reached for the door handle, opening the door. She paused on the threshold. "Ma'am, when you die and go to hell and you wonder why you ended up there? Remember this moment, right here."

Hettie walked outside and nearly ran down the stairs. She turned on Althea when they were a few yards from the clubhouse. "You were just going to stand there and let that woman treat you like that?"

Althea's eyes were flint. "You should have just left it alone. I'm the one who will most likely return here. If I want to play on their territory, then it's their rules I've got to follow. They can shut the door anytime."

"Althea, I'm beginning to wonder about your god of tennis. He seems a very cruel and unconcerned one, what with the way you have to be walked all over to appease him."

"Hettie, hush!" Althea continued to stomp forward, her destination becoming clearer to Hettie: Syd's car. She was going to change in Syd's car.

"Is there literally nothing these people could say or do that would make you put a foot down and demand respect?"

Althea turned on her heels, staring Hettie down. "You say that to me as if you wouldn't do anything for notoriety!"

Althea patted her chest. "Unlike you, when it's all said and done, I'll have accomplished something great!"

"Go change or you'll miss your first set!" That was all Hettie allowed herself to say. She'd written new rules and Althea wasn't going to make her break them, even though Hettie was fighting the desperate urge to draw blood.

Althea opened the car door, slid inside, and slammed it behind her. Even though Althea had not asked, Hettie leaned against one of the windows to allow for some kind of privacy.

When Althea was done dressing, Hettie walked off toward the stadium entryway with her hands folded over her chest. It wasn't until she reached the court where Althea would be playing that she dropped her hands and took three deep breaths, one right after another, before forcing a smile on her face. Then she scanned the stands looking for Shadrach. Even though he was wearing a tan suit like most men around him, he was easy to spot a few seconds later.

"Hettie!" Her smile turned genuine as she climbed the stairs, scooted past a few people, and went to greet the one person who could make her forget about the past fifteen minutes.

He stood up as she approached. His smile started first in his golden eyes and then appeared on his lips before he pulled her in for a brief hug. Oh, but she loved the way he smelled and the feel of his hands on her back. "Be proud of me," she whispered.

"I am always proud of you but for what in particular?" he whispered back. She felt a sudden urge to cry and she didn't know why.

"I did not cross my boundaries." She'd told him about the

decision she'd made as they walked the zoo. "And I really, really wanted to."

Shadrach pulled back and the expression on his face was gentle as he cupped her cheek. "Then I am very proud of you. Do you want to talk about it now or later?"

"Later. Where's Hyacinth?"

"Right over there." He pointed to another Negro family a few rows down. Hyacinth was sitting in the stands and giggling with a little girl her size. "She said she'll return when the game starts. I've been tasked with watching 'Little Daddy'." He moved so she could see the stuffed lion that was next to his things.

Hettie grinned as they took their seats. "Do you think she really liked it or is she being nice?"

"She's six. 'Just being nice' is not a skill she's developed yet. The jury is still out but she doesn't dislike you. I've got popcorn." Shadrach picked up the bag next to him and offered her some. She took a few kernels, starting to feel a bit more at peace. "Is your uncle still coming?"

"Yes." Hettie reached up, tugging on the chain at her neck. She shifted to get a better view of the crowd. "He ran to the gas station but . . . there he is!" Hettie stood to her feet and waved. Seeing her, Morgan waved back before climbing the stairs.

"Hello," Morgan said cautiously as he reached them.

"Morgan, this is Lewis. Lewis, this is Morgan." Hettie knew that Shadrach still preferred to be Lewis to most people.

Next to her, Shadrach was already on his feet. He extended his hand. "It's very nice to meet you, Morgan. Hettie speaks of you often."

Morgan reached out and grabbed Lewis's hand. The oddest expression crossed his face. Hettie turned to look at

Shadrach as Morgan responded and that's why she saw Shadrach's eyes go wide and flash with something. They dropped each other's hand mid shake and both of them took to their seats.

Hettie carefully sat down and looked out over the crowd, unsurprised to see Will Darben enter the stands. The woman at his side appeared to be his sister, Rosemary. "Do you two know each other?"

"Never met him in my life," Morgan said flippantly as he began digging through his pockets, producing all kinds of candy.

Out of the corner of her eye, Hettie watched Shadrach shift away from her so she could not get a good look at his face. "All right," she said slowly. "You both know me. I'd like to think that you both know me well."

"Is there a point you're trying to make? Here, want some candy?" Before she could protest, Morgan stuffed a Mary Jane in her mouth.

"Morgan!" His name came out sounding mangled over the peanut-butter and molasses flavored candy.

"Shh. The announcer is speaking."

Hettie chewed in annoyance as she listened while they were told that everyone needed to take their seats quickly because the match would be starting in five minutes. She reached over and tapped Shadrach's arm. "How do you know him?"

Shadrach pointed at his mouth where he'd stuffed a handful of popcorn. Hettie lifted her eyes to the sky in frustration. How could Morgan and Shadrach possibly know each other? Had they had a bad moment at one of Shadrach's stores? Were their daughters on unfriendly terms? Morgan's middle child was also six. Speaking of daughters, Hyacinth raced up the stairs, excused her way down the row, and hopped into her father's lap. "Hi, Miss Hettie."

"Hello, Hyacinth." Hettie reached over and touched her knee. "You look pretty today."

"Daddy did my hair," the little girl said, touching one of the ribboned plaits.

"Your father did a good job." Shadrach was not looking at her but she could see the rise of color in his face. And that reminded her of another time he'd blushed, which reminded her of . . .

"You both have the same tattoo!"

CHAPTER 29

Backhand—where the player hits the ball with a swing that comes across the body, with the back of the hand facing the direction of the swing of the racket

Hettie felt Morgan shift in her direction but she saw Shadrach's head snap up. "I don't know what you're talking about."

"Why would you have seen his tattoo, Hester Jolene?" Morgan asked, demanding an answer. "All of this time I've been reassuring Rosa that you're not out in the streets playing it fast and loose, and here you are looking at men's tattoos."

On any other day, Hettie would have had words for Morgan but she was too busy grasping the situation.

"But Daddy, you do have a tattoo. Right here." Hyacinth patted his right pectoral. "The Blue Helmet, remember?"

"You were in the 93rd Infantry with Morgan?" Hettie asked Shadrach. It was a stupid question. Of course he had been in the same unit with Morgan. Why on earth were these two trying to hide it? So many questions danced on Hettie's tongue but Hyacinth was right there watching them. Or watching Morgan's candy in particular. "Hyacinth, this is my uncle Morgan. Morgan, this is Hyacinth, Lewis's daughter."

"Hi, Mr. Morgan," Hyacinth waved at Morgan but she eyed the Pixy Stix in his hand. Morgan, being a father, had no trouble recognizing who the real star of the show was.

"Hello, Hyacinth, would you like some?"

"Yes, sir. Thank you."

Before she could take his offering, he pulled his hand back. "You look like your dad, Hyacinth." He extended the Pixy Stix. Then pulled them back again. Hyacinth pressed her lips together very tightly.

Hettie elbowed her uncle. He ignored her. "How long have you lived in New York, Hyacinth?"

"My whole life. I was born here."

"You've been in New York a long time." The words were said pointedly. "Here you go." Morgan finally handed her the promised candy. Hyacinth turned to her dad. "Can I go give one to Sarah?"

"The game is about to start. You'll have to stay down there until the first set is over."

"Okay," she whispered just as Althea and her opponent walked out onto the field amidst clapping. Hyacinth jumped down and ran for the stairs as both women waved to the crowd.

Morgan leaned in to Hettie, brushing his shoulder against hers. "Remember my CO from Tennessee?"

"Lewis was your CO?"

"I don't know who that person is, sitting next to you over there," he said stiffly, clearly offended. Shadrach was the lieutenant who was father, brother, teacher, priest, friend. And Shadrach had been in New York all of this time and never reached out to him.

Hettie leaned in to Shadrach, who was steadily eating popcorn as though he hadn't eaten in days. "Are you a part of any veterans groups?"

"Why would I do that? That was three and a half years of my life I pray every day to forget," Shadrach muttered.

On the field, it was decided that Althea's opponent would serve first. Both women took their positions on each side of the tennis court.

"What did he just say?" Morgan's question was indignant. He'd heard what Shadrach had said.

"I thought you didn't know him?"

Morgan cut her a dark look before turning his gaze pointedly at the field. The ball was served, Althea ran for it—and missed. "Fifteen–love!"

"I could have done that," Morgan whispered.

"Hush, Morgan."

The ball was served over the net again. This time, Althea hit it back.

"I've recently learned that my CO is divorced." Morgan's voice was low, but loud enough for Shadrach to hear. "I'm not surprised."

Althea hit the ball. It went too far. "Out!" Althea's opponent smiled broadly. Around Hettie, the crowd cheered.

Hettie had been watching Althea play for months now. What was happening here?

"My CO would write these long letters to his wife. Outrageously long," Morgan was whispering. "And filled with ridiculous things like he couldn't wait to return home to drink his wife's bathwater." Next to Hettie, Shadrach sighed deeply before reaching up and adjusting his glasses. "His wife's letters would be shorter than an advertisement and filled with something stupid like: *I hope you're having a great time in the war.*"

Shadrach finally turned his head to look at Morgan. "I knew you and your little friends were reading my mail."

"We needed a laugh every now and then. Your ex-wife's letters were hilarious."

Shadrach shook his head as he reached for more popcorn. "Shut up, Morgan." The words were said as though he'd said them a thousand times.

They were quiet as Althea scored another point. Within her small group, Hettie alone clapped.

"Where've you been?" Morgan's sudden question made Hettie jump. "I wrote to you when I got home."

Gently bumping Hettie's shoulder, Shadrach asked, "Did he ever tell you what our role was on those Japanese islands?"

"He's been very vague." These men. How on earth was she supposed to focus on this game with these sorts of revelations happening around her? She was pretty sure Althea had just scored another point but she could also be wrong.

"We cleaned up. The military sent their best, brightest, and whitest to the islands first. Then, they sent us to bury the dead, straighten things up, and clean out the remaining Japanese that had been missed." Shadrach snacked on a few more pieces of popcorn. "I wasn't built for war. When I was discharged, I wanted nothing to do with my unit because when I see my men, all I see are my failures."

Next to Hettie, Morgan was fingering the candies in his hand. Not sure who to comfort, Hettie patted Morgan's knee but then reached over, grabbed Shadrach's hand, and squeezed it tightly. Shadrach's eyes flicked to hers and Hettie saw a deep sadness resting there. But then he blinked, and the emotion disappeared. "Anyway, your uncle and about seven other teenagers spent the entire war clinging to me like white on rice. It felt . . . undeserved."

"As always, you're overthinking, Lieutenant. I miss you. We miss you. That's all there is to it." Trust Morgan to boil it down to its simplest parts.

Althea's opponent served the ball. Althea hit it but the ball slammed into the net. "First set to LaBounty."

Althea's response to these words was to slam her racket against the ground. It cracked, breaking. The crowd hissed in disapproval. Something was happening down there and Hettie was missing it because of Morgan and Shadrach. "Excuse me."

Standing up, Hettie quickly exited the row and ran down the stairs to the bench where Syd was sitting. "She's distracted," Syd whispered. "I don't know what's on her mind but it ain't tennis. This isn't the game it should be." The game had momentarily paused to allow the women a drink of water before the next set began. Althea appeared just below Hettie and Syd, fetching a replacement racket.

"Hey!" Hettie called down. Althea did not acknowledge her and Hettie felt that same anger from the parking lot rise up within her. How could Althea be mad because Hettie believed in standing up for herself? Why would Althea—the one person who had never accepted disrespect as a child—accept it now as an adult, just to play a game? How could she allow something to change her simply because she wanted to reach a certain goal? As soon as the question raced through Hettie's mind, her anger receded. Her voice was gentle when she spoke. "The only person you're fighting out there is you. How about you let yourself win today?" Althea looked up, her gaze sharp. She'd expected some kind of rebuke from

Hettie. "You're the number-one player. Make it happen, Cap'n."

After what felt like a long moment, Althea dipped her head. Hettie nodded back.

Hettie turned around and began climbing the stairs, returning to her seat where Morgan and Shadrach were talking and laughing like, apparently, the old friends they were. She had not been waiting for a sign of any kind but if she had been, there it was. "Excuse me," she said, when she reached them, forcing them to create a space for her.

"What did you say to that girl?"

"Just watch. She's going to win."

"Your niece is very good at reading people."

"Survival instincts. Not much of a fighter. She's like Barney. Remember him? Tough at all the wrong moments. I spent half of my childhood trying to save this girl from this thing and that."

"How odd, Morgan. I have no such recollection."

The next set started and this time when Althea's opponent served the ball, Althea tossed it back like it was nothing. It was a surprise to no one when she won the match.

Hettie slipped into the last pew of the Baptist church. She was late but that was because she'd attended services at her family's Pentecostal church a few blocks down.

"Everyone, we have a very important guest with us today. Sis. Althea Gibson, why don't you make your way on up here," the reverend said excitedly from the pulpit. Hettie pulled out her notebook and pencil, happy she hadn't missed the main event.

"I don't know if any of y'all have been paying any attention, but Sis. Althea is a tennis player." There were a few excited whistles and claps. "And she is heading over there to Europe to play a few games. Sis. Althea, do you have any words that you'd like to share?"

The night before, Hettie had attended the bon voyage event at the Birdland Jazz Club in her capacity as a journalist. As Althea had stated, Sugar Ray Robinson was there. Sammy Davis Jr. toasted Althea. Althea sang 'I'll Be Seeing You' to the crowd. It had been a lively event that Hettie had spent mostly by Howard's side once she'd found him amongst the people.

"Thank you all so much for having me," Althea said at the pulpit. She had been dressed very smart the evening before and she must have decided to maintain that look because the dark gray dress she was currently wearing was very becoming on her. "I cannot even begin to tell you how excited I am to represent the American people overseas. I will return to you a winner!"

There were cheers and claps.

"Sis. Althea, we want to be a blessing to you." This was the real reason Althea was attending a church that was not her own today. "We're going to pass around the offering bucket and give you a gift that we hope you can use while in Europe."

Hands clasped neatly before her, Althea dipped her head. "Thank you, Reverend. I very much appreciate it."

"Before we take up the offering, let's pray. If you all could bow your heads and your hearts."

Hettie started to obey when she felt a pair of eyes on her. Rather than lowering her head, she looked up and saw a face from Montgomery that she'd hoped she'd never see again.

CHAPTER 30

Flat—a shot with minimal spin

Hettie led Casper Linwood to the same diner where she'd treated Althea for dinner, simply because she knew it would be open. They entered the restaurant to Doris Day singing 'Que Sera Sera'. Her voice should have made the atmosphere feel light but all Hettie could feel was the weightiness of it. She ordered no food, although that didn't stop the man sitting across from her from ordering everything, complete with dessert.

"Never thought I'd see your face again," Casper said as the waitress walked away from their table. Casper Linwood was in his late twenties, neither handsome nor unattractive, tall or short, heavy or thin. He was an altogether unremarkable man that most people would have passed over, including Hettie. His mother, on the other hand, was different. "Thanks to you, my family's been run out of Montgomery. Mama won't be buried amongst her kinfolk."

Hettie had apologized when everything had gone so very wrong. She would not apologize again and certainly not to Casper.

But Casper didn't appear to be waiting for her to respond. For one, he was too concerned with all that was going on around him. The passing cars caught his eye, the bright red plastic seats of their booth were distracting. The white gleaming counter where you could sit on a stool and watch the chef cook was engaging. This was someone's first trip up north. For two, this was something he felt he needed to get off his chest, whether she was listening or not. "I'm the only one who decided to move to New York. Mama is settled in Missouri. She's got a sister there. I—"

The waitress reappeared with a Coke for Hettie and a vanilla shake for Casper that he stared at in awe. Inserting her straw in her ice-filled glass, Hettie poked at an ice cube for a bit before finally speaking. "What do you want, Casper?"

"Fifty dollars a month will do."

Hettie's first mistake was in admitting how much trouble she was going to be in when everything had gone wrong. Her second mistake was allowing Casper to be there for the conversation. Hettie took a sip of her drink. "You must be out of your mind."

"Thirty dollars."

"You could walk it all the way down to a penny and the answer would still be no. I'm afraid you're out of luck, Casper. My boss is already well aware of every single detail of what happened in Montgomery." Hettie folded her arms over her chest and watched as disappointment flooded the young man's face. "I'm afraid you'll have to find some other way to live an easy life."

Casper slammed a fist against the surface of the table and the few people in the restaurant looked their way. When he spoke, his voice was lowered. "You ruined my family's life!"

Hettie had had a lot of time to think about this. "I will admit that the idea was mine. I will even admit that I very much wanted to put your mama's words in print. But I didn't force your mother to talk. When she sat down with a reporter, she made a choice."

"You said you wouldn't tell anybody what she said. You said it would all be anonymous. You lied."

It was far more complicated than that but Hettie decided to nod in agreement. "I have fallen on my sword already, Casper. I gave your mother money to relocate." Money Hettie had been hoping to use to purchase something more permanent. Now, she would have to wait for several more years before she could buy a home.

The waitress appeared, placing a burger and piping hot fries in front of Casper before slipping quietly away.

Casper grabbed a fry, and winced as he took a bite. "What you gave was not enough."

"Then tell your mother to sue me. I'm not providing you with a dime." Oh, how she wished she hadn't attended the Baptist church today. Of course, if Casper was looking for her, he'd eventually have found her at the double H. Perhaps this meeting was inevitable.

"You're going to regret turning me down. I'm going to tell your friends—"

"They are few and far between. Good luck finding them."

Casper paused. "Your family."

"They don't care." Her family was not the best family in the world but the moment Casper opened his mouth to say something about Hettie, they'd move on about their day. He was coming across as desperate and untrustworthy and if they wanted to learn more, they'd ask Hettie themselves. Hettie shifted a bit in her seat. "What is it about me that tells you I would be okay with being blackmailed and threatened? Is it because I'm a woman? Because I'm short? Mr. Linwood, let me remind you that you are no longer in Montgomery but New York. You are in my backyard and you tread on dangerous ground."

Casper's nostrils flared. "After you ruined my family's life you would try to come after me?"

"Casper, I only attack if bitten first." Hettie reached for her purse as a wave of exhaustion rolled over her. How draining it was to see the very thing that represented your greatest failure. "All I'm saying is think before you act." Hettie opened her wallet and tossed enough bills onto the table to cover his meal and her drink. It would be the last thing she ever did for the Linwood family.

"Wouldn't it have been nice if you had done so."

"Casper? Kiss my grits."

Hettie left the diner feeling far more despondent than she would have liked. She greatly regretted ever meeting the Linwood family. But she could not go back in time to change what had already happened. Checking her watch, Hettie kicked her feet along until they brought her across town and to Miz Ce-Ce's apartment.

Her grandmother's door was not closed. Hettie started to push it open further but it was hindered by someone. "Hello?"

Her mother pulled the door from the other side. Her jacket

was on and her purse was in hand. She was carrying a pie and she looked ready to walk out of the door. She frowned at the sight of Hettie standing there. "Where did you run off to after church?"

"Something for work," Hettie answered. "What are you doing here?"

"I felt like baking," Miz Ce-Ce called from the kitchen. "I made one too many sweet potato pies and told Rosa to come get one. I've got two for Morgan. You want one?"

"If I hadn't come by you wouldn't have saved one for me."

"Oh, hush. You told me to expect you, remember?"

"What were you coming by for?" her mother asked, her eyes squinting with suspicion.

"I'm going to Europe with Althea. I've come begging for clothes." They wouldn't be leaving for a couple of weeks but if Hettie needed time to rework a dress, she needed to pick it out now.

Her mother turned, looking about Miz Ce-Ce's living room, and finally settled on lowering her pie onto a hatbox. She dropped her purse onto the floor. "I'll stay and help you pick something out."

Hettie did not make a face but she thought about it.

"Let's start with the ball gowns. They're in the closet." Hettie took her jacket off and tossed it onto Miz Ce-Ce's couch, not bothering to care that she dislodged several rolls of fabric.

"Why would she need a ball gown?" Rosa Carlin grabbed a handful of blouses, scooped them out of the way, and took a seat on the lone armchair.

Miz Ce-Ce walked into the living room. "This one claims she might be invited to a real ball over there in England. She says she might meet the queen. I don't understand why you'd want to meet the queen when you could meet the king."

"First off, there is no king. There is only a queen."

"Are you telling me even she can't find a husband?"

"She's married, but he's a prince not a king. Don't ask me why," Hettie rushed out. "Besides, even if Althea wins I probably won't meet the queen but I'll be in the near vicinity. And if Althea wins, I will be able to attend the Wimbledon Ball." Althea had shared this bit with her only a few days ago.

Both Miz Ce-Ce and her mother looked a bit flustered. "Don't they have dukes and earls and counts over there? Are any of them single?"

"Miz Ce-Ce, none of those people could handle me. Now, I'm going to go try on a dress."

The first dress was a short, light blue sleeveless tulle dress with a boat neckline.

"Absolutely not," her mother said from her seat. "No sleeveless dresses. The queen or whoever will not want to see your armpits."

"Not my favorite. You look like a stuffed sausage. When did your breasts get so big?"

Because Hettie wasn't sold on the dress, she didn't bother to argue. The second dress was a tea-length black and white number, which Hettie thought was quite sophisticated. "No black and white," Miz Ce-Ce declared. "They'll confuse you with the help."

The third gown was a deep emerald green that brushed the very top of the floor. There was a tight bodice and the skirt overflowed from the natural waistline. It was sleeveless but it came with a matching wraparound. Her mother and grandmother were silent for thirty seconds.

"I think it works," Miz Ce-Ce finally said.

"You don't think it shows too much . . . ?" Her mother motioned toward her own chest.

"She's not married. She needs to advertise something."

Rosa Carlin tsked and shifted away from her mother. "It's a pretty color. I suppose it'll do." Feeling confident and pretty, Hettie swayed from side to side, allowing the skirt to twirl around her. "Do you have gloves?"

"Yes, ma'am." Would she wear the gloves? Probably not.

"What's Althea wearing?"

"I don't know. She said she'll buy the dress in London and not before." It was the closest she'd ever heard Althea get to a superstition.

"She's very tall. Hopefully they have something in her size. Can you believe this Rosa? This girl might meet a queen."

"Same space as the queen is more accurate."

Her mother released a deep sigh. "I will say that this writing job is taking her further than I ever thought it would."

"What if I quit?" The question was out before Hettie could think about it. But she'd asked. She turned to face her mother and grandmother. "What if I never see my name in lights?" Hettie's voice broke on the last word and she brought her hands up to cover her face. She couldn't believe she was falling apart in front of these two of all people.

"What is she talking about?" Miz Ce-Ce clucked her tongue and then came to stand next to Hettie. She pulled Hettie's hands down and sighed when she saw the tears on Hettie's face. "So dramatic." She reached behind her for a blouse and began wiping Hettie's cheeks.

Her mother was looking at her with that familiar expression of confusion on her face. Then, Rosa released a deep sigh. "Hester Jolene, I swear, you're always worried about the wrong things. I'd like to think that I raised you to fix your eyes on that which is unseen. What is seen is temporary. I've got to go. Oral's keeping an eye on dinner for me. Don't go off to wherever without letting me pray for you."

"Yes, ma'am." Hettie's head was dipped back in an effort to stop the tears. Meanwhile, her grandmother danced around her, pinching and pulling at the dress, searching for areas that might need the touch of a needle.

Hettie heard the door open. She heard her mother's pause. "Hettie, the only person you're trying to prove something to is yourself." And then the door shut.

CHAPTER 31

Groundstroke—a forehand or backhand shot executed after the ball bounces once on the court

The crowd gathered in front of the tall, stately white brick Hotel Theresa was filled with men and women, boys and girls. There were so many people there waiting that if you weren't careful, you'd confuse the sidewalk with the street and be hit by the oncoming traffic that was moving back and forth at a steady pace. But Hettie wasn't worried about being able to see the man of the hour because a small black stage had been erected, along with a podium of sorts. The Reverend Dr. Martin Luther King Jr. would be speaking shortly and everyone who wanted to hear him was going to be able to do so.

Hettie was supposed to be packing and putting the finishing touches on an article but instead she was here, waiting to listen to Dr. King just like she'd been at the Abyssinian Baptist

Church the evening before. She'd wisely sat in the last pew of the church. Chances were, the man would not remember her but she had wanted to play it safe—just in case. She'd asked Morgan if he was planning to come out today but pessimist that he was, he'd said no. He was of the belief that it would only be a matter of time before the other shoe dropped. Shadrach, on the other hand, wanted to be there, but his new store was opening next week and he was beyond swamped with work. He'd turned down her invitation with much dismay and the hope that he wasn't going to regret it.

"When's he coming out?" someone muttered next to her.

"I'm sure he'll be here," another person answered. "But I hope it's soon. It's getting hot." It was a cool day outside—so cool, Hettie had grabbed a jacket on her way out of the door but there were so many bodies packed together that heat was festering.

Dr. King would be there because he was on a mission to recruit bodies. Bodies that he wanted to march in Washington D.C. at what he was calling the Prayer Pilgrimage for Freedom. What better way to petition God than to do it before the Lincoln Memorial, where the President and Congress would have no choice but to see.

Gutsy, Hettie thought. The reverend wasn't backing down from any of the threats being tossed his way. And there were threats. Even in Harlem, Hettie had seen more than the usual number of police cars circling the block and Hettie didn't think they were there to offer protection.

Someone tapped Hettie on the shoulder and she almost didn't turn around to see. There were so many people that it was inevitable that someone would accidently touch someone else. But she did turn and then had to do a double take. "What?" Hettie placed a hand over her chest. "Do my eyes deceive me?"

"Oh, hush," Althea hissed. She was clad in a pair of blue jeans, a cotton blouse, and a long, stiff leather jacket.

"Not you. Not here." She was going to be obnoxious, Hettie decided.

"In case no one has shared with you that you are annoying, you are annoying."

"No one has ever said that to me before." Hettie shifted, returning her gaze to the empty podium. "Nice jacket, by the way."

"A gift from Sugar Ray. He always gives me something nice before I leave for Wimbledon. Have you ever met this reverend?"

"Huh?"

"You were in Montgomery, weren't you? Before you returned to New York?"

"Who told you I was in Montgomery?"

"Pretty sure you mentioned it at some point. Why? Is it a secret?"

"No." Hettie hesitated. "I met him once. I doubt he remembers." She prayed he didn't.

"I'll admit to being a little bit skeptical about this fella but I thought I should come. I don't know that I'll ever get another chance to hear him speak in person."

Hettie leaned in to Althea, brushing her arm against hers. "I'm willing to bet that if you wanted to, you could arrange to speak to him face to face."

A dark cloud slowly covered Althea's face. Althea had enough fame, whether she performed well enough at Wimbledon or not, to have any civil rights leader at her beck and call—assuming she decided to join them in the war of dismantling injustice. "I just want to hear what the man has to say."

As though her words conjured him, the doors to the hotel opened and there stood the small, slender reverend dressed in a dark suit. People began clapping and whistling excitedly as he took the stand.

"He's a lot smaller than his pictures."

"He's younger than us but he's got an older face."

"Younger? Really?"

"Yep. Not yet thirty."

"Good morning, people of Harlem, New York." The crowd got louder for a few seconds but when Dr. King raised his hands, everyone went silent. The speech was not a long one but Hettie didn't feel like he wasted one word in the time that had been allotted, because she now had a sudden urge to march in D.C. Dr. King took a step back and someone else replaced him. Feeling a tug on her jacket, Hettie turned to see Althea walking away. After a few seconds, Hettie turned and pushed through the crowd after Althea. She only had to jog a little bit to catch up with her.

"What did you think?" Hettie asked.

"I think he made the right decision in becoming a reverend. He can sure make you ponder a matter. I'm still not sure what to think about this pilgrimage. What's it going to change? Who is it going to help?"

"Historically speaking, whenever we have walked or threatened to walk in D.C., things *have* changed. Case in point Executive 8802." Althea looked down at her, her expression blank. "The Fair Employment Act of 1941 that banned discrimination in war industries." Hettie remembered that moment vividly because her first job had been working in a factory building weapons for the war. "That happened because a march on D.C. was planned. America likes to look good before the world. That's hard to do when you have an entire population of people showing up on the White House doorstep claiming that things are bad. Dr. King is trying to force change."

"You can't make people accept forced change."

"Actually, you sort of kind of can. Lots of people wanted to hold on to their slaves. They had to be forced to set them free. And behold, we were no longer enslaved."

"Whatever," Althea said dismissively with a wave of her hand. "I'm not going to pretend like I know all the answers. That's why I'm going to stick to tennis."

Hettie said nothing, even as an article began forming in her head. A lot of people would be happy to hear that Althea had come to hear Dr. King today. Even if she was still working out her own opinion.

"I will say that he's not afraid and that's admirable. If you're going to stir the pot, then you've got to be responsible for the consequences. He'll be an interesting one to watch. That's for sure. Well, I'll see you around," Althea said, already stepping into the street. "Don't be late to the airport."

Hettie turned, hand in the air even though Althea couldn't see her, when something caught her eye. It was a man slipping into the dispersing crowd just to her right. It had only been the briefest of glances but she was almost certain it was Casper Linwood. Was he following her now? *Good*, she thought, as she slipped her hands into her jacket. Let him watch her board a plane to Europe. Hettie headed straight home, pausing only to purchase a colorful bouquet of flowers.

It was an hour later when the panic crept in. She was in the middle of packing when it occurred to her that Casper had most likely seen her with Althea. What if he chased Althea down? What if he told her all that had happened in

Montgomery? What if Althea called and made it clear that Hettie was no longer allowed to personally report on her? What if she lost her job? What if? What if? What if?

There was a knock on the door. "Hettie? There's a man here to see you. He says his name is Lewis." That pulled Hettie out of her thoughts. She was supposed to be dining with Shadrach later this evening. And he was here now? She hadn't even realized that he knew where she lived. "Coming!"

Hettie hesitated and then looked in the mirror. Her hair was pulled back into a ponytail, and she was wearing a pair of jeans and a button-down shirt. Having grown up with Miz Ce-Ce, it was not ideal that a man she was dating would see her so . . . relaxed. But, it was what it was. Hettie left her bedroom and instantly saw Shadrach standing awkwardly in the doorway next to Faye. He was dressed in a dark blue pinstripe suit, which meant he'd been in the office today. Debbie was sitting on the couch. Both she and Faye were watching them intently. Hettie waved Shadrach forward. "We can speak in my room."

Ignoring the sharp looks her roommates shared, Hettie pushed her bedroom door back open. She glanced around the space, noting the emerald dress hanging off the back of her closet door, her drawers opened and askew, and several suitcases on the floor that were in the process of being filled. Again, not ideal. "Are you sure?" Shadrach asked. Clearly a bit uncomfortable, he pointed behind him. "We can talk downstairs."

Hettie waved Shadrach forward and he obeyed slowly, hesitantly. It might have had everything to do with the way her roommates were staring. When he entered her room, she shut the door behind him.

"Ignore the mess," she said even as she saw him shifting

slightly so he could get a better view. She wondered what he thought. For someone who had been living in this very room for almost seven years, the space was rather plain. A bed, a dresser, a desk and chair in the corner, a closet. There was nothing hanging on the walls. There were no pictures stacked neatly on surfaces. When she got her own home, she would decorate. Until then, there was no reason to settle in. The only thing she had that was specific to her liking was her bedspread. It was outrageously pink but she wasn't going to apologize for finally being able to buy something she had wanted most of her childhood. "How did you know where I lived?"

"Morgan. He's been coming by the store nearly every day."

Hettie shook her head as embarrassment creeped up her neck. "I apologize."

Shadrach took his eyes off of her bedspread and placed them on her. He grinned. "Don't. It's good to see him again. It's good . . . to talk about it."

There was much Hettie would have liked to say but war stories were tender and she wasn't going to poke and prod. Instead, she put his mind on something else. "I got you a gift."

She was going to miss the inauguration of his fifth store. She crossed the room. Passing her dresser, she too ka quick moment to push in all the drawers. Then she reached for the bouquet that was on the floor beside it and extended it in his direction. "Congratulations!"

Shadrach blinked. He looked at the flowers. Then at her. Hettie glanced down at the bouquet. "Don't tell me you have allergies."

He shook his head. "No." He dragged the word out as he took slow steps to her side. He reached up and laid his hat on her dresser before relieving her of the flowers, carrying them like a newborn. "No one has ever bought me flowers before."

"I was thinking that if I had just opened a store, wouldn't I like flowers? But it's only appropriate if a man buys them for a woman," she said slowly, figuring out her misstep as she spoke. Naturally, she would mess this up. Why did everything she did with him have to be so backwards? Thanking God that she could not turn red, she held out her arms. "Give them back. I'll get you something else."

"No." Shadrach held them tighter against his chest, his golden eyes intensely focused on her. "My flowers," he said like a two-year-old. "I got you a present too."

"Shadrach."

"Not giving them back." He lowered the bouquet onto her bed before reaching into his suit jacket and pulling out a long, rectangular box. "Morgan said the necklaces you currently wear have no special meaning. So, I got you one you could tug on when you're nervous that does mean something special." Hettie leaned forward as he opened the box, revealing a gold chained necklace. The charm was a gold bird flapping its wings and holding a branch in its mouth. At the bottom of the branch was a pearl. Hettie knew two things instantly: the bird was a mockingbird and the pearl was real.

Shadrach sat down on her bed. He patted his knee. *Gosh*, she thought as she lowered herself onto his thigh. *Gosh*. She turned her head so he could slip the necklace around her throat. She felt the softness of his fingertips as he lightly touched the skin at the nape of her neck. She felt his warm breath on her cheek. The pearl landed just above her chest, visible from the top of her blouse. She would wear this necklace always. "Would you like to know something else that seeing Morgan reminded me of ?" Shadrach didn't wait for an answer as he reached into his pocket and pulled out a piece of paper that was creased, and yellow, and stained. He handed it to her. Hettie unfolded the paper and gasped as familiar words appeared before her.

"Those boys were always reading my mail so I stole a letter from Morgan." Hettie's eyes filled with water, making it near impossible to read her own scribbling from all those years ago. She made out her signature, which was simply H. J. C. "Morgan was right, Laverne's letters weren't worth . . . crap. But I liked yours. I kept that on me the whole time I was away and I keep it still in the back of my Bible. I've read it so many times, I can recite it word for word." He reached for it and she protested. "I don't think so, madam. That's my letter." Lightly snatching it from her, he folded it once again and slipped it in his pocket. "Can you write to Hyacinth while you're away?"

Her stomach clenched. He had yet to tell her that he loved her and yet he said it in so many other ways. "Yes."

"And you'll write to me?"

"I'll think about it." He placed his hands first on her shoulders, then down her arms, and finally resting on her waist.

She said nothing as his grip tightened, and he pulled her up against his chest. She felt him rest his head on her shoulder. "I'm going to miss you." She was going to be gone for nearly two months. She reached up behind her, cupping his cheek and touching the softness of his beard. After a few seconds, he lifted his head and leaned back. Hettie looked over her shoulder in time to see him remove his glasses, laying them next to the bouquet. "You can kiss me if you want."

She was already hot but now flames were ratcheting their way up her body. "I can do what? Sir, this whole relationship I have been the one—"

"Or you can talk instead."

Hettie leaned forward, pressing her lips against his and wrapping her arms around his neck. Hettie had been kissed before, but Shadrach was by far the more experienced kisser, taking full control in seconds. It was everything she'd ever imagined and more. And then without any warning whatsoever, he pulled away and reached for his glasses. "Shadrach—"

"Distract me." He unwrapped her hands from his neck and gave her a gentle push. Hettie stood up, feeling more than a little disorientated.

"Distract you?"

"You've always got something to say. What's on your mind?"

"Besides you?"

He grabbed the bouquet of flowers, once again cradling them against his chest. "Tell me about that dress."

Hettie turned around to see what he was talking about. She could barely process a thought. "The dress . . . is for the Wimbledon Ball if Althea wins." Saying her name, all the worries she'd had before Shadrach had come over hit her. "Oh, Shad, something terrible may have happened."

Hettie sat down on the bed next to him. "Let me tell you what happened in Montgomery." Predictably, her beau's eyes grew wide a few times and at one point he looked shocked. But when she was finished telling him the story, the expression on his face was thoughtful.

"Hettie, have you ever given any thought to just telling Althea all of this outright? It would erase the power that this Casper person has."

"She wouldn't let me anywhere near her ever again. Edgar would then fire me."

Shadrach tilted his head to the side. "Possibly."

"No possibly."

"At least she'd respect you. And no offense but you're already in danger of being fired, aren't you?"

He was speaking of the looming deadline that Hettie had been ignoring for months. She had two months left to convince Althea to let her do a civil rights piece that was dictated from Althea's mouth and thus far, not even Dr. King could convince the woman. "You're right," she said as she met his gaze. "I'm running out of time."

CHAPTER 32

Set point—when a player is one point from winning the set

Hettie looked out of the window of the plane expecting to see the ocean beneath them, but all she saw were clouds. They were too high to see the waves of the Atlantic Ocean. Man's ingenuity would never cease to amaze her.

"I see the stewardess. She's coming around with drinks," Althea explained to her. She'd been very happy to be the one with airport and airplane knowledge, and she'd been sharing what she knew generously.

Hettie eyed the other woman intently once again. Casper had not chased down Althea and fed her horrible tales of Hettie. There was no way that had happened if Althea was still this happy, still this friendly. Hettie reached for her purse and pulled out her reading glasses, notebook, and pen.

"That was not an invitation for an interview."

"You said when we get off the plane, we would hit the ground running. I can't think of a better time for an interview." Hettie flipped to a blank page. "We're headed to London now but Wimbledon doesn't actually start for several weeks out. Where will you be staying?" Hettie asked the question, already knowing the answer.

"With my good friend Angela Buxton."

"You two have played doubles before, correct?"

"Yes. Last year, we won the women's doubles at Wimbledon and the French Championships. But we won't be playing together this year. Angela's wrist is in a brace."

"Why don't you play doubles regularly with American players? Did you have to cross an ocean to find a partner?"

Althea was silent so long, Hettie looked up from her notebook to see the other woman's tight, narrowed expression. "You already know the answer to that question. I don't care for doubles anyway. I'm a terrible team player. But, I do have Americans that I can partner with if needed, like Karol Fageros and Darlene Hard. In fact, Darlene and I are playing doubles at the Queen's Club. And I'm playing mixed doubles at Wimbledon. Stop trying to force a story."

"Have any of the other American women ever invited you for a meal?" Eating together was one of the clearest indications of genuine friendship and respect. So long had her people served white people that she did not trust those who called themselves friends of colored people and yet had never eaten at the same table with a Negro.

"Hettie."

"I heard that on the tournament circuit, players will often pin up weekly stories about each other and sometimes they give each other nicknames. It's a solo sport but also like a sorority."

"I have nothing to say about this."

Hettie rubbed her hand over her chin and then dropped it. No matter how many times she tried to show Althea the mirror, the girl refused to recognize the image that greeted her. "Fine." Hettie turned a few pages in her notebook. "Do you recognize this handwriting?"

Althea leaned forward and then sat back in her seat. "Is that Syd's writing?"

"He formally knighted me as your coach." It cost too much money for Syd to come to London and so he'd sent his notes along for Hettie to read to Althea before each game. Althea would have no coach and no friends and family from home by her side. If Hettie hadn't been there, it would just be her taking this long ride alone. "Prepare yourself. I will not go easy on you. Why wasn't Will at the airport?"

Morgan, Shadrach, and Hyacinth had escorted Hettie to Idlewild. They'd helped her get her suitcases checked and then sat with her as she waited to board the plane. Morgan had gifted her with a camera, telling her to take lots of photos because she didn't know the next time she was going overseas. Hyacinth had given her a bracelet she'd made with a red ribbon and beads. Hettie had it encircled around her wrist now. Shadrach had said little, although he'd held her hand for much of the time. He'd pressed a kiss to her cheek and whispered about them having a talk when she got back.

Tugging on the chain of her necklace, Hettie looked out the window so no one would see the expression on her face. Was she ready to get married? Was she ready to be a stepmother? Was she ready to birth her own children? Would she have to give up her job? Should she give up her job? There would be much to talk about and yet, a part of her already knew there was a lot she'd give up for Shadrach. How very scary it was to fall in love.

"Will's not happy with me." Hettie looked up, startled. She'd forgotten the question she'd asked. "I think," Althea began slowly, "I think he really thought I'd marry him this year. I am finally the number-one tennis player. Am I just supposed to give it up?"

It was eerie how similar their thoughts sometimes ran. "Does Will want you to give it up?"

"He has never said so, but . . ."

"But?"

"One of those reporters from *The Baltimore* called him Mr. Gibson. He didn't like that at all. I like Will. I love him, really. But I won't give up tennis for Will Darben. We argued yesterday. That's how come only Syd and Buddy Walker were there." Hettie had learned that Buddy had been the person who had first seen Althea playing tennis on the street. He'd been the one who invited Althea to the Cosmopolitan Club, changing the whole trajectory of her life.

"What about your family?"

Althea wagged a finger. "I told you I don't like to talk about them."

Hettie released a sigh. "When we get to London, what happens next?"

"I've got to run out to Surbiton. I'm playing in the Surrey Grass Court Tournament. There are four pre-Wimbledon tournaments I'm playing in. I'll be at the Queen's Club and Beckenham but not the Queen's single matches. I've got to conserve some of my energy."

"Who's your biggest competition?"

"Shirley Bloomer, who won at Roland-Garros this year. Louise Brough, who has won Wimbledon four times; Angela

Mortimer, who has unfortunately beaten me a couple times, and then a couple of young ones like Christine Truman. I haven't played against any of these women all year long by focusing solely on small American tournaments. I haven't got to see what kind of shape they're in."

"Do you feel confident that you'll win?" It was Syd who had told Hettie that it was easy for Althea to win the smaller 'local' tournaments. It was the bigger tournaments that tripped Althea up. She could win but it was his theory that she often lost the battle in her mind before she even stepped out onto the court.

"Yes," Althea said without hesitating. Every single time Hettie asked this question, she got the same answer told the same way. "I can beat every single one of those girls. Just watch me. Now, want some tips for England?"

"Lay it on me."

"Tea is dinner. Not tea. Angela invited me for tea once and I ate before I went to see her. Don't do that."

"Why is tea dinner? Tea is a drink."

"I don't know."

"So, if I want to do one of those high tea things, I should expect food to come with it?"

"I'd say that's a good bet. And they've got more than one type of tea. I always thought there was only one flavor but there's a whole bunch. If you buy a cup of tea, be sure to know which kind you want. Black tea is always the safest choice. Also, when you've got to go, ask to use the toilet. They don't really do washrooms and ladies' rooms and bathrooms."

"That seems a bit rude." Hettie was not going to be telling anyone she was about to use the toilet. Quite frankly, it was none of their business.

"They drive on the wrong side of the street."

"I've seen pictures."

"They use twenty letters to say two-syllable words. The word is never as complicated as you think. Food's pretty bland."

"The British were in India, China, Africa, and America and the food's bland?"

Althea shrugged, confused. "It rains all the time. Did you bring your umbrella like I told you?"

"It's in my bag."

"Everyone sounds like they know what they're talking about. If you're not careful, the accent will fool you." Althea tilted her head slightly, thinking. "They're nicer than the French. Those jokers will knock right into you and keep on moving."

"Do they have a lot of . . . non-white people there?"

Althea shrugged again. "I'm in England to play tennis. Tennis is a white people sport. And before you ask, no one has ever called me a name or anything like that. They're just . . . cold . . . stiff . . . polite."

"They make you feel like you don't belong there?"

"Yes."

"Then I'll guess you'll have to show them."

"I plan to."

Several hours later, the plane landed at Heathrow Airport. They both hurried to fetch their bags from baggage claim. Hettie was carrying her purse and Althea was carrying her tennis rackets, refusing to allow another person to hold them. Althea had one suitcase that she laid her hands on easily enough. It took ten minutes for Hettie to get all three of hers. But she was too busy being charmed to care.

"They all sound so . . . educated," Hettie whispered to Althea.

"The first time someone asked me for a pound on the street, I almost said it should be the other way, chap."

"A pound? Oh, right. We should find somewhere to switch the currency."

"Althea! Althea!" Both Hettie and Althea turned.

"Oh, no."

"What?" Hettie asked as a young white woman in a flowing white dress ran toward them. "Do we not like this woman?"

"It's not her. That's Angela. It's the men behind her with pen and paper and cameras. Your kind of people."

"My kind of . . . paparazzi? They're here for you?!"

"Althea!"

Althea turned around and opened her arms just as Angela ran into them. "It's so good to see you, my friend! It's been too long!"

There were pops, flashes. "Althea Gibson. Angela! Over here!"

Hettie took several steps away from the other women as reporters ran over. "Miss Gibson, it's said that you're playing in the Surrey Grass Tournament. Do you expect to win again this year?"

"Miss Gibson, how was your flight over here? Were you happy to learn of Shirley Fry's retirement? Is she, perhaps, the better player?"

"Miss Gibson, please smile for the camera over here."

Hettie had never seen anything like this before. She had to do a double check. Had Althea morphed into Elizabeth Taylor and she'd missed it? Hettie had loaded her suitcases onto a cart and she pushed it away from Althea and Angela.

Althea was staying with Angela's family for the duration of the tournaments. But Hettie not only had not wanted to presume, she also did not wish to stay around others and so it had already been planned that she would take a separate taxi to her hotel and meet up with Althea later. Thus, she did not feel bad at all when she walked past the paparazzi, and out onto the street to find a cab to take her to her accommodations.

It was in Hettie's tiny hotel room that she and Althea reconvened the next day. The room was clean, and nice but Hettie had the sense that it had once been a house and someone had been sleeping in the room since King George I.

"Look at these," Althea said, as soon as Hettie opened the door. She began tossing newspapers onto the floor, one right after another.

"I thought you didn't care about the media," Hettie said as she crouched down to read the headlines. They were headlines she'd already read that morning. She had copies of the same papers in one of the dresser drawers. She had been debating all morning whether to use them to try to get Althea upset and then ultimately decided not to. She had drawn her boundary lines and would stick to them, even to her own hurt. Not that she wanted to hurt. "This isn't bad. The *Daily Mail* says that the only person who will beat you is you because you are the best woman player. That's right on the money, Al."

Althea tossed more papers on the floor.

"What did you do? Buy every paper you saw on the way here?"

"Yes."

Hettie picked up another paper. She didn't have to read it to find what she was looking for. "Look! The queen is going to be there. We're actually going to see her in person! It says she will present the trophy to the winner so I hope you know what that means."

"Look at how they describe me."

Hettie's eyes scanned the different papers quickly. "A Negress," she read from one paper. Hettie wrinkled her nose. She did not like that term. "A Negro. Okay, very original that one. You are 'a coloured favorite'. This one describes you as the 'long-limbed ebony opponent'. You know they thought long and hard about that one. According to this paper, you're 'brown and lean'. This one says that you have 'supple brown muscles'. Listen, how about those 'dusky shoulders'?"

"None of this is even remotely funny to me."

"Oh, but this article was written by your friend. Angela Buxton is a writer? It says, 'Go to it, girl! Knock that brown chip off your shoulder. You can do it this time!'" Hettie paused. "I don't know what that means but it feels nice."

Althea sat down on Hettie's bed and the thing squeaked under her weight. "I am a tennis player," she said flatly. "Not a Negress, a Negro, or a dusky whatever. Just a tennis player."

"No." Hettie circled a hand above the papers. "You're most definitely Black."

Althea brought her hands to her face. "I'm not ashamed of being Negro. That's not the point!" Hettie knew what the point was but Althea may as well rage at the sky for being blue. "I know I can't change anything. I know I'm like a monkey in the zoo."

"Nope. We are never comparative to monkeys. I will, however, accept tigers." Hettie was strangely light hearted when she should have been panicking. She should have been stoking Althea's rage at these people who harped on about her color. Hettie pushed herself to her feet, in search of her purse. "Syd gave me instructions on what to say when you're in this kind of mood."

Althea dropped her hands. "What instructions?"

Finding her notebook, Hettie flipped a few pages. She cleared her throat. "When Althea is down or sad or angry, read from the book of Ecclesiastes." Hettie hummed. "That seems both specific and vague." Hettie set the notebook aside and walked over to the lampstand where her copy of the Bible rested. "It is as I thought," she said as she flipped the pages. "Ecclesiastes is longer than a few chapters. What exactly am I supposed to read? The whole thing?" Hettie closed the Bible. "I think the point is that you should not take this so seriously." Althea blinked once.

Yes, that did not sound like a good answer. Perhaps Hettie needed to reread Ecclesiastes at some point. For now, she could only give Althea what she had. "All right, you're colored and they care and you don't care, but there's nothing you can do to change it. Thus, embrace it. Get out on that court and show them what Black girls can do."

CHAPTER 33

Follow through—continuation of the racket's swing after the ball is hit

Hettie sat in the portion of the stands that was designated for the press. Surrounding her were old white men who spoke in an English she was trying very hard to comprehend. She could understand it if they deigned to speak slowly enough. But, as they were not talking to her, they felt no need to. She felt awkward and it seemed as though every decision she'd made that day had been the wrong one. Her dress was tan and not white, and she wondered what she was thinking in wearing it. Her hair was crown-braided in the front with the rest pulled back into a bun because it had been drizzling that morning. But she felt as though she should have tried to straighten it.

She crossed one leg over the other and then uncrossed it.

She sat with her legs tucked to the side and then set them solidly beneath her. She sat up straight, so straight her shoulders were aching from holding the pose. She got it now, what Althea had said. Something about this place feeling cold.

"Oh, look who's here." The voices were American. Hettie turned around to see several of the Negro reporters that she'd met in the few tournaments that Althea had played in the States arrive in the stands. She picked up her purse, her notebook, and her pen, excused her way out of her row and walked up to theirs.

"Did you miss us, Sugar?"

Hettie hated nicknames, especially from male colleagues, but the smile that appeared on her face was genuine. "My dear fellow Americans."

They laughed and hooted, drawing looks of disapproval from people around them but these men did not seem to care one bit. Their lack of attention to protocol calmed her mightily. "Scoot over." Once she was safely cocooned between two American men, she said, "It's a bit quiet, isn't it?"

"We're not supposed to talk while the game is being played and don't clap too loudly even when she does well. They don't do that over here."

"These British games are different, Carlin. Respect the sport," one man said, rolling his eyes. "It's been around since King whoever, you know."

"I thought it was invented in France?"

"Shh. Don't tell them that."

"There's so much white out here, it's almost blinding. White shirts, white pants, white shoes, white socks, white people." Back in the States, the men had sometimes rooted for Althea and sometimes not. But here in a foreign country there was only one player they wanted to win.

"I swear if this woman makes me lose all the money I bet on her . . ."

"Ladies and gentlemen," the announcer began. They quieted as Althea walked out onto the field with her trademark swagger as though she were back in North Carolina about to play a game against one of the college students. She was wearing white shorts and a matching shirt. Even from where Hettie sat, she appeared tall and lanky, and borderline thin. Her racket was attached so comfortably to her hand, it was as though she'd been born with it.

"I bet you she's going to win this one. She always wins the ones that don't matter." And the comment was right. Althea won the singles finals in the three tournaments she had entered and she won doubles with Darlene Hard.

In between games and Althea's practices, Hettie bought a tourist book and roamed London, doing all the possible touristy things that she could squeeze in. She walked around Buckingham Palace and Trafalgar Square. She saw Big Ben and Westminster Abbey. She borrowed a car and learned how to drive on the wrong side of the street. She nearly met God twice but was otherwise successful. Whenever possible, she purchased postcards and tried to send one off to Hyacinth every other day. She wrote the little girl a letter once a week and she wrote the little girl's father thrice a week.

She was in a bit of a pickle. She missed Shadrach desperately and was wishing the tournaments moved faster but the ticking clock was also a constant reminder of her looming deadline. She was down to mere weeks of trying to change Althea's mind and she was no closer than the first day they'd started 'working' together.

And then the first day of Wimbledon started. The All

England Lawn Tennis and Croquet Club held several courts, and several games were being played on the day that Althea was making her reintroduction. Following a paper map, Hettie turned this way and that, getting stuck in one crowd after another as she maneuvered her way to the locker rooms. She did noticeably draw some attention—there was a decided lack of Negroes in the place—but she ignored the people who stared a bit too long or whispered a hurried question to her.

After confirming with the security person at the door that she was allowed in the women's locker room, she navigated a few more twists and turns and then she found Althea sitting on a bench in an area that was far from where other players were dressing and talking and laughing. Her elbows were on her knees and her hands were tucked under her chin. One of her knees was sporting a bandage, still healing from a spill she'd taken at Beckenham that had left her knee torn and bloody.

"Your coach has arrived."

Althea lowered her hands to her lap. "I can't wait to hear this."

Hettie pulled out her notebook and flipped to the last page that held Syd's words. It would have been nice if Syd had titled his notes with something like, 'Say this before the first game at Wimbledon.' But that would have been too much like right. As it stood, there was just a jumble of words that Hettie had been trying to make sense of since she'd arrived in London. She snapped the notebook closed. "The battle is here," she said, touching a finger to her head. "Not on the tennis court. You already have the tools needed to win."

"That is so profound, O, wise one. You can leave now," Althea said with no heat to her words. In fact, Hettie could tell that Althea was only giving her half of her attention anyway. The battle really was taking place in Althea's mind and it just seemed so dang odd to Hettie. The woman kept winning. Why was this tournament even a worry?

"Hey!" Althea blinked up at her. "I don't know the right way to coach but I will be able to tell if you're losing. These British people are not keen on talking during the game so this is how it's going to go. If you see me do this?" Hettie poked a hard finger at her head twice. "It means get your head in the game. If you see me do this—" Hettie pointed at herself and then at the floor. "It means we didn't come here for that. If you see me do this—" Hettie mimicked placing a crown on her head. "That means, I came here to see the queen, so do better."

Althea rolled her eyes.

"You got this. I know Dr. Eaton, Dr. Johnson, and Syd wish they could be here. I know your closest friends and family would love to be in the stands cheering you on. I know I'm probably the closest reminder of home and that's a scary thing in and of itself, but win or lose, you've got folks in your corner. You've worked hard for this, fight for it, but don't forget to have fun. Tomorrow's not promised to anyone so live this moment." Speech concluded, Hettie dipped her head and left.

Sitting in the stands of Centre Court—the main court at Wimbledon—which was fully packed with spectators, Hettie was surrounded by the other American reporters, who were quietly talking trash amongst the few British reporters who sat nearby.

Despite being June, it wasn't very hot at all. Gray clouds were covering most of the sky and Hettie could have sworn that she felt a few raindrops splash across her arm. Fortunately, she had brought an umbrella but she dearly hoped it would not rain. She had never felt any pleasure in getting soaked. Hettie ignored most of the chatter around her as she slipped on her reading glasses and scribbled nonsense on a blank notebook page until the announcer began talking.

From then on, she didn't have to wait long for Althea and her opponent, a Hungarian girl named Suzy Körmöczy, to walk out. Suzy was possibly an inch or so taller than Hettie, which created a sharp contrast against Althea's long, willowy figure as they entered Centre Court together. The pair of them waved to a crowd that quietly cheered them on before they each took their spots on opposite baselines. Althea was allowed to serve first. She tossed the ball in the air and bent back gracefully, momentarily reminding Hettie of a ballerina. Then, she brought her racket up to send it over the net. Suzy ran fast, her racket catching the ball and returning it Althea's way. Althea ran, hit the ball, and the ball hit the net, giving Suzy a point. Around Hettie, the crowd erupted into a loud, unexpected cheer that startled her.

Hettie leaned into the shoulder of the man sitting next to her. "What was that?"

"You know what that was. Did you see this cartoon?" The man dropped a folded paper in Hettie's lap. In the cartoon, Althea had been drawn with exaggerated lips as she shook the hands of a smaller, daintier, whiter opponent. The bubble above Althea's head read: 'Do I shake hands with the 17,000 spectators? Ah sure was playin' against all of them too.'

Hettie tossed the paper back into the man's lap. "I saw it."

The cartoonist was trying to be kind by acknowledging the racism in the room but had clearly very much missed their own prejudice. Earlier that day, she'd dismissed the cartoon. But now, the sight of it set off a burst of instant rage that flooded her body. But mixed within it was the oddest feeling of sadness. Hettie loved the color of her skin, she loved her people, she loved everything about being a colored American but at times, it was overwhelming to be a Negro.

Next to her, none of the men said anything. Like her, they were quiet as they processed their thoughts and emotions because suddenly this tennis match didn't feel like a game anymore. It wasn't fun. Watching as Althea took her place at the baseline again, Hettie felt a sharp sense of regret for the speech she'd given Althea. How could you have fun playing a sport when it felt personal?

The tennis ball bounced back and forth over the net. At one point, Althea slid across the wet grass. Despite the thousands of people who filled the stands, the stadium was so quiet, Hettie heard her grunt as she slammed her racket into the ball. This time Suzy missed it and Althea got a point. Hettie clapped, loudly just like the men around her did. There were other people who clapped but it seemed muted.

Althea served the ball, it crossed the net, hit the ground once and Suzy returned it. Back and forth and back and forth. Using her forehand, Althea hit the ball and it went too far. "Out!"

The crowd roared in excitement. Hettie reached up, tugging on the chain of her necklace. On the court, while Althea had seemed disappointed about the point, she seemed otherwise unbothered. She just crouched down, waiting for Suzy to serve. When the ball came her way, Althea seemed to almost fly off the ground as she dove right, left, right again. Nearly spinning on her toes, she hit the ball with a backhand. Suzy couldn't catch up and Althea scored another point. The only indication of her happiness was a small fist pump.

The crowd was once again unenthusiastic in their clapping. The game went on until the announcer finally called out, "Set point." Althea hit the ball, Suzy missed, and Althea won the set.

"This is so stressful," one of the journalists whispered. "I feel like I have to use the toilet."

"Hopefully, Althea will win this second set." If Althea won the second set, then she'd have won the match, since the winner of women's singles was the best of two out of three.

The second set was worse than the first. For one, it started raining. Hettie opened her umbrella, protecting her hair, but there was no such protection for her backside, as water was sliding down the bench and soaking into her skirt. Hettie felt like a circus act trying to juggle the umbrella, the notebook, her pen, and watch the game. A game in which Althea double-faulted, hit the ball out of bounds, and missed easy shots. Was she going to lose in her first round at Wimbledon after all she had put into it? The question danced in Hettie's mind as the crowd went wild in their approval of Suzy from Hungary. While Althea might have been the taller player, she seemed smaller and smaller with each point scored on the other side of the net. And yet, when they finally reached match point, it was Althea who scored the final point, winning the match.

"All right boys and girl, let's do this another time, shall we?" one journalist quipped before rising to his feet to leave. Hettie shoved her glasses and notebook into her purse before standing. She offered quick good-byes to her peers before running down the stairs and retracing her steps to the women's locker room.

She hurriedly passed conversations and women in various states of dishabille until she found Althea in the same lonely part of the locker room where she'd been before. Still dressed in her tennis outfit, she was crouched down before her locker, with her head bowed to the ground.

A thousand thoughts flashed through Hettie's mind but sometimes words weren't sufficient. Hettie lowered her purse and umbrella onto the bench and then carefully sat down onto the floor next to Althea, resting her back against someone's locker. Althea was taking in large, steady breaths of air as a few silent tears rolled down her cheeks. Several seconds later, she fell back onto her bottom and then lowered her head to Hettie's lap. Slowly patting her shoulder, Hettie whispered, "You did good."

The following day, Althea beat the next player. And then she beat another and another until, finally, she won Wimbledon.

CHAPTER 34

Chop—a shot with extreme backspin and meant to stop the ball where it lands

The airport was packed. There was no other way to describe the crowd of people that met Hettie and Althea as they stepped off the plane and into New York. Not wanting to be in a single picture, Hettie carefully slipped away as Althea was mobbed by some people Hettie recognized and more that she didn't. Althea's mother was there and two of her siblings. Syd was there with Buddy Walker and even Fred Johnson, Althea's first tennis coach. Reporters seemed to fill every empty space and everywhere Hettie turned there were flashes of lights from cameras. They'd both figured it would be this way and so Hettie didn't bother to even try to communicate to Althea over the host of people. Instead, she went in search of a payphone.

"Hello? This is Hettie," Hettie said, informing one of the secretaries at the double H. "Is Mr. Edgar in?"

She didn't have to wait thirty seconds for Edgar to pick up the phone. "Where's my article, Carlin?"

"Give me until Forest Hills."

"Hettie!"

"We've been moving so fast since Wimbledon. So fast." There could be no greater truth. After Althea had won, it had been one waterfall moment after another. First, there was tiny Queen Elizabeth II who presented Althea with the Venus Rosewater Dish, a silver salver that was engraved with the names of previous Wimbledon champions. Althea had curtseyed perfectly after she and Hettie had hilariously practiced the night before. Hettie had then played the role of messenger, as telegram after telegram poured in from all around the world congratulating Althea.

That same night, Hettie had attended the Wimbledon Ball, which took place just down the street from Buckingham Palace. Wearing a floral print strapless gown with a bow under the bustline that she had purchased just before finals, Althea sat at the head table between the men's champion and the Duke of Devonshire, who was the master of ceremonies. Hettie had sat at a table with two of Althea's friends who were captains in the Women's Army Corps but had played in the ATA years ago. They'd come to London expressly to cheer on Althea. Hettie spent the evening transcribing the speech Althea gave and making notes of things like Althea dancing with the male winner of Wimbledon, and Althea singing 'If I Loved You' and 'Around the World' to the crowd.

Amidst all of the happiness and excitement, Hettie tried to drown out the words of the tennis officials around her that were murmuring that Althea's win was a fluke and unlikely to ever happen again.

"Did you get my article about the ball?" She was one of the few American reporters who had attended so she knew her article would probably be received well. Plus, her article had included things like Althea's visit to the Astor Club afterwards. The others didn't know about that because they hadn't been invited.

Edgar sighed, deeply. "It was a good article, Carlin, but the wolves are circling. Do you know why they're circling?" Hettie did know why but she kept her mouth shut. "Did you hear the answer she gave that one British reporter before she got on the plane to New York?"

"I was there, Mr. Edgar."

"He asked her," Edgar began as though Hettie hadn't spoken, "whether she had faced any difficulty as a result of her race. Do you remember her answer?"

Hettie had been stunned by Althea's answer. So stunned that she'd said very little to her on the long ride back to the States. "She said no."

"No. There is not a single Negro in America who believes that. Not a single one." Would it have been so hard for Althea to admit that it hadn't been easy? Did she have to outright lie and claim that race didn't matter at all? "Do you know what every colored person in America is thinking right now?"

"That she's trying to get in good with white people. That she doesn't care about us." There had been too many people around Althea at that time, otherwise Hettie would have stopped and forced a come-to-Jesus moment right then and there.

"How about her answer to that one paper's question—the

one who asked if she liked being compared to Jackie Robinson?"

"I saw it."

"What did she say? She doesn't consider herself to be a representative of her people. She is thinking of herself and nobody else. Carlin, I love me some Althea but I'm struggling to remember why right now. You have one job." Actually, she had more than one job but she understood his point.

"I have articles. Several articles about Althea's run-ins with racism. They're written and they're ready to be printed. They're just sitting in my briefcase. Give me until Forest Hills."

"Hettie, why on earth are you sitting on them?" She could hear Edgar's rage. She wondered if her co-workers could hear it. "We need to change the narrative now!"

"She hasn't given me permission to use them."

"We don't need her permission."

"Give me until Forest Hills to convince her."

Edgar's sigh was once again deep and heavy. "You have until Forest Hills." Hettie heard a click and then a dial tone. She hung up the phone, feeling more tired than she could remember. But there was some reason to be happy and she was reminded of that fact when she went down to baggage claim and Hyacinth Lewis came running to greet her.

"Miss Hettie!" Hettie reached down and picked up the girl even though, at seven now, she was no light feather.

"I thought you would have forgot about me by now!"

"No, ma'am. Look!" Hyacinth had a purse wrapped around her and she opened the small bag to reveal dozens of postcards.

"Hyacinth, you're getting too big to be picked up," Shadrach said as he grabbed his daughter by the waist and lowered her back to the ground.

Shad's grin was tender and shy as he gently pushed his daughter to the side. "Hello, Miss Hettie."

"Mr. Lewis." And then she was in his arms.

"I've missed you."

"I missed you more."

"I'm glad you're home."

Hettie hummed.

"What's that mean?" Shadrach asked, as he pulled back so that he could see her face.

"In three days we're flying to Chicago." Hettie reached up, her hand cupping Shadrach's chin. "But then I'm back in New York and I'm done." One way or another, she'd be finished.

In Chicago, sitting on a fancy armchair in a fancy hotel lobby, Hettie was reading the *Michigan Chronicle* article, which was entitled 'Althea Gibson Answers Senator Russell'. Senator Russell was a senator from Georgia who was starkly opposing the proposed Civil Rights Act of 1957, claiming that if there was a law put in place to protect Negroes' right to vote there would be bloodshed in months to come. The author of the article was arguing that Althea's win in Wimbledon proved that Negroes could measure up to whites and were fit to vote. The whole thing gave Hettie a headache.

"There's no room?" Althea was saying. Hettie looked up from the paper and folded it. Althea was supposed to be getting their rooms. She had not been in a good mood when they'd met at the airport that morning but Hettie understood. Who wanted to go and compete in yet another tournament when one could be resting and soaking up all the benefits of being a Wimbledon winner. When Althea had insisted that she'd get the hotel room, Hettie had wisely taken a seat and let her have at it. Except it looked like she was not having at it. "I'm competing in the Clay Court Championship tomorrow at the River Forest Tennis Club. I called yesterday to secure a room. I spoke with someone named . . ." Althea paused, digging through her purse.

"I'm not sure who you spoke to but we don't have room here." Hettie rose to her feet and crossed the room.

"Hello, my name is Hettie Carlin and I'm a reporter from the *Harlem Heights* in New York. Are you telling me that you—little hotel in Chicago—have no room for Althea Gibson? The number-one tennis player in the world?" Of course, Hettie made sure her voice rose with each word that exited her mouth. Of course, she made sure to garner the attention of every person on the first floor of the building.

"Hettie!" Althea hissed.

"Are you telling me that this woman—who was just celebrated in a parade that shut down New York City two days ago—is not eligible to get a room here? Is that how you would like to present yourself?"

"Excuse me. I will go get my supervisor."

"Do that." The man at the desk walked away, disappearing into a room behind the front desk. A few other hotel clerks looked down, unwilling to meet Hettie's eyes.

"There are dozens of other hotels around here," Althea said as she angrily zipped up her purse. "There's no reason to cause a scene."

"You're getting angry with the wrong person here."

"You never listen to a thing I say. I'm not even sure why I bother talking to you in the first place. You're just going to do what you want to do."

Hettie was not in the mood to listen to a speech on Althea's politics about being nice today. "There's a payphone over there. Go call one of these dozens of hotels while I tell these folks about themselves."

"If they want to be nasty it's their problem. Not mine. I don't want to stay in a hotel that doesn't want me here."

"Me neither. I still have things I'd like to say!" Shooting her a fierce glare, Althea did not walk over to the payphone. Instead, she left the hotel.

The supervisor, an older white man, came out of the back room with the hotel clerk behind him. "I'm sorry, but we are filled to capacity."

"You're not filled to capacity and you're not sorry." Hettie pointed a finger at all of the staff behind the counter. "None of you are any more special than I am."

"Do I need to call security?" the man asked, his face carrying a cold, stony expression.

"No. I don't linger around trash."

Outside, Hettie saw Althea at a phone booth and started to walk over when a familiar man peeled himself off the wall of the hotel. "What's going on?"

"Gosh, you keep turning up everywhere." It was one of those Negro sports reporters that Hettie had started to reluctantly get to know. This one's name was Percy. Hettie pointed to the hotel. "No room at the inn."

The reporter looked at the hotel and then at Hettie, a frown appearing on his face. "They don't let Black folks in?"

"Nope. Althea's trying to find us another place to stay."

"This is Chicago," Percy said as though the city should make a difference.

Hettie shrugged. She had run out of explanations for such behaviors. With a click of his tongue, the reporter pulled out a notebook and started scribbling. "I've heard a rumor."

"What's that?"

"The luncheon that the USLTA was supposed to hold in Althea's honor at the Ambassador East Hotel is canceled." The man leaned forward. "Supposedly the room set aside for the event has flooring issues but the floors are working just fine for some swanky event tonight."

It was Hettie's turn to frown. This luncheon was definitely something Althea was looking forward to. In fact, Hettie knew of a rare shopping trip that had taken place that had made Althea nearly late for the party the ATA had thrown her. "No Negroes allowed?"

"No Negroes allowed. Of course, I could be wrong but if I were you, I'd have Althea call and confirm before she shows up."

Hettie placed her hands on her hips. "This is such a . . ."

"Mmm-hmm. Well, I'm staying at a smaller hotel about twelve miles from here. It's not ideal but I know they accept Black folks. Check it out if you can't find anything."

The hotel Percy recommended was the hotel the two women ended up checking into that evening. By the time Hettie settled into her room, she was so angry, she had lost her appetite, which was a rare feat in her world. Choosing to get ready for bed, Hettie kicked off her heels and removed her pantyhose. Then she began unpacking the lone suitcase she'd brought for the tournament. Oh, how she missed her apartment and her bed. How did Althea live like this, year in and year out? After Forest Hills, she knew Althea was headed to Australia and probably to Asia. Thanks, but no thanks. Hettie's mind drifted back to the few days she'd spent with Shadrach and Hyacinth. They'd attended Althea's parade together and then took a long walk through Central Park, talking and enjoying each other's company.

There was a knock on the door. Hettie pulled a dress out of her suitcase. This one she'd have to hang up. "Who is it?"

"It's me."

Barefoot, Hettie crossed the hotel room and let Althea in. Her expression was thunderous as she pushed past the door and entered the room. "Did you call about the luncheon? Is it true it's canceled?"

Althea's frown deepened. So, this was not what had her angry? "It's canceled," she said after a long minute. "That's not why I'm here to talk. I'm here to tell you that you're fired."

CHAPTER 35

Match point—when a player only needs one more point to win the match

It took a long minute for Althea's words to register in Hettie's brain. "I'm sorry, what?"

"You're fired."

"You can't fire me. You don't pay me. Are you referencing the partnership that you agreed to? The one where I get to tag along and interview you before and after every game until Forest Hills because I beat you in a game of table tennis?" Talking was the best way that Hettie worked through things but even as the words exited her mouth, the only thing that raced through her mind was confusion. "Is this because I said my piece to the hotel manager? I refuse to apologize because it wasn't just you he was saying no to. People don't get to treat me that way and then walk away feeling good about themselves."

Althea folded her arms and stared down at Hettie through narrowed eyes. "He said I couldn't trust you and it turns out he was right."

"He?" As soon as Hettie asked the question, she knew. She tossed the dress she was still holding onto the bed. There were other more important matters to think about.

"I forget his name. Some man from Montgomery."

"When did you speak with Casper?"

"You know who I'm talking about?"

"I do. When?"

"Before we left for London. He chased me down after we listened to Dr. King speak in Harlem. I didn't give his story much thought because he seemed the sort who'd make a mountain out of a molehill."

"You must have given him some thought." Hettie spread her hands. "Because here we are. What did he say?"

"He said you tricked his mama into giving you a story. You told the mama you weren't going to print the story until after the boycott was over but you had it printed beforehand. As a result, the Klan came by and set fire to their house and they lost everything. They had to leave town out of fear of further, deadlier repercussions. He said you're a liar and you can't be trusted. He said that chances were you had already written the articles you wanted published and I could find them if I looked hard enough. On the plane home from London, you fell asleep and I decided to write out the speech I had to give at the ATA party. I went through your bag looking for paper and what do I come across but the articles I explicitly asked you not to write. When were you planning to backstab me, exactly?"

"Backstab you with articles about events that actually happened?"

"I'm not Dr. King. I'm not Jackie Robinson. I'm not

whoever it is you're trying to paint me to be." Althea slammed her hands against her chest. "I am Althea Gibson and I play tennis and that is all that I want to be said about me. And I think that's pretty good compared to the liar and cheat that you are."

Hettie reached up to tug on the chain around her neck. "Would you like to know what actually happened in Montgomery before you go around tossing out names? 'Cause last time I checked those articles were still in my briefcase, not published. Did you see the date from the first one? And do you think it does me any good as a reporter to have those printed, only for you to turn around a few days later to refute my writings?"

Hettie was proud of herself. Look, she had not chosen violence with her words. Instead, she'd recognized that Althea was mad, and she had something of a right to be mad.

Althea considered this for a second, tilting her head to the side. Then she sat down on the edge of the bed. "What happened?"

"I went to Montgomery to cover the bus boycott, which lasted three hundred and eighty-one days. I was there for approximately ninety of those days. After a few articles about what it was like, I was quickly running out of things that would not be the same as what was already being written. That was when I learned about other women besides Rosa Parks who refused to get off the bus or were terrorized in some way by these bus drivers. I began collecting their stories." She had pitched the idea to Edgar over a phone call. Wouldn't it be more impactful to personalize the women of the bus boycott? To talk about the grandmothers, mothers, the wives, the daughters, and the sisters who often had taken bus rides that led to events that were now etched on to their souls? Edgar had loved the idea but he didn't want repeat stories.

Hettie needed to try and find the unique ones. She needed to tell stories that had yet to be told.

"In doing so, I came across a woman named Mary Linwood. She was about Miz Ce-Ce's age and she was very much gung-ho about doing anything for the movement. By this time, I had gathered all of these stories from women within the movement, but none from women outside the movement. Would it not be fascinating to see what white women thought about the boycott? Mrs. Linwood was a cook for a wealthy white family and she agreed to pass along to me anything she heard while in their home—so long as I made it clear that I was receiving everything from an anonymous source."

Althea's gaze was sharp. "You put that poor woman in danger."

"If you're asking me whether I regret it, the answer is yes. But let's make it clear that I didn't force that woman to do anything."

"You took advantage of her desire to be a part of something great. You took advantage of the fact that she wanted to be remembered for contributing to something bigger than her. You always walk that fine line of following the rules and manipulating them."

For once in Hettie's life, it was not rage that rose up at hearing such accusations. It was sadness. "I do have a tendency to find others' weaknesses and prod at them until they do what I want. I will admit that much."

Althea's nostrils flared as she eyed Hettie. "You published the articles and didn't make them anonymous?"

Hettie did not think that she and Althea were friends, but she did think there was some ounce of respect there. Perhaps, she'd thought wrong. "I did not mention Mary's name once. But some of the things Mary mentioned to me were so specific that they could have only come from her." She'd told Mary that she'd let her read the article before it went to print but then decided that since Mary's name wasn't on it, it would be safe. She said as much to Althea. "This is where Casper blames me. This is where he calls me a liar and a cheat. The man Mary worked for was a Grand Imperial Wizard or something, so he roused the Klan and they burned down her home and threatened to kill her and her children. Mary packed up that evening and fled into the night. She was a valued member of Montgomery and a longtime secretary of a prominent church.

"The incident reached the ears of Dr. King and he asked me to return to New York. He said the people of Montgomery were struggling enough without having me trying to convince different ones to create stories that weren't needed at this time." Edgar had not been mad about the way she went about things. He'd been mad that she'd gotten caught—so to speak.

But seeing the damage that Hettie's thoughtlessness had wreaked on this family that had been living in Montgomery for generations had shaken Hettie. It shook her still when she thought about it.

"I wrote those articles, yes. But I have no intention of publishing them without your approval. I have learned my lesson, Althea."

Althea looked away, quiet. "You're trying to make me some kind of civil rights activist, aren't you?"

"Yes and no. This whole thing started in part because my boss is a huge fan of yours. He doesn't like articles that paint you negatively. His thinking is that if you come out as a proponent of civil rights, the people will love you."

Althea rubbed the palms of her hands against her thighs. "I told you that that is not what I'm interested in doing."

"I was hoping to change your mind."

"Did you at any point try to play around with a situation to get me on board?" Everything Hettie had done was subtle, so subtle that even Althea couldn't pinpoint a specific moment. She could talk her way out of this. But she considered the lines she'd drawn, she considered the person she wanted to be. She would rather keep to her vows and be known as someone who was not moved by circumstances, even if it was to her detriment.

"I did," she said, knowing that she'd signed her own death warrant.

"Then I want you to leave. I think we're done here." Althea's words were cool, not hot. There was no burning anger on her side of this conversation either. Look at them, two grown women at last.

"Fine," Hettie said after a moment. "I'm leaving but you should consider the fact that you are doing yourself a grave injustice by refusing to take a stand. No one is saying that you have to organize marches or give speeches. All they want from you is acknowledgment that you see their pain and agree that America has to change."

"I don't see you doing that."

"You know so goodness well I don't have the platform that you do."

"You also only work with Negroes. You're surrounded by Negroes. You only enter spaces with white folks in them if you have to. Tennis is white, Hettie. I'm not going to end my career to say what's already being said."

"Then give the money back."

"What?"

"Why have people invested in you, Althea? Why do people give you money? Why did the doctors take you into their homes and give you free coaching? Why did the ATA make sure you had the memberships needed to play tennis? Out of the goodness of their hearts? You know like I know that the whole point in lifting you up was so that you could turn around and help the person behind you. You can sing and dance about me being manipulative all day long but you're just as bad. Worse, even, because with every handout you take, you silently agree to something you have no desire of doing."

"I didn't agree to anything."

"Yeah, well. If that helps you sleep at night, you keep thinking that."

Althea rose to her feet. "I am giving back. Every time I win, I do something for our race."

"And every time you say with your own lips that race has nothing to do with your success or failure, you lie." Hettie clapped her hands. "Congratulations, we're the same."

There was a flash of pure rage on Althea's face. "I don't have to stay here and listen to this."

"Riddle me this, Althea. Who is going to remember you ten years from now? Twenty years from now? Fifty years? Will it be the ladies who won't let you in the locker rooms? The people in the crowds who cheer for your opponents because they're not Black? The officials of the USLTA who pray to God that you're the only person of color who ever reaches these heights? You keep right on ignoring the plight of the ones most likely to speak your name over and over to their children and one day you'll be lucky if you're a footnote in history."

When Althea left the room, she slammed the door behind her.

As Hettie began tossing things back into her suitcase, she thought that perhaps she still had some growing up to do.

★

Hettie caught the first flight back to New York, which meant that she got home at some ridiculously early time the next day. She should have been exhausted—and maybe she was—but she couldn't sleep. As soon as it was reasonable, she left her apartment. An hour later, she stood in front of a home she'd never seen but whose address she'd written nearly a thousand times over the past year.

Shadrach lived in the only cream and tan rowhouse on his block. His house did not have any elaborate stairs that led up to the first floor. The front door was practically level with the street. But his four-storied home followed the typical architecture style of the rowhouses around it. If you split his house down the middle, half of the building was flat but the other half protruded a bit, rounding out part of the house in a way that Hettie was fairly certain was for looks rather than function. His front door was red and when she knocked on it, she wondered if a butler would answer.

A butler did not answer the door but a man who looked remarkably like Shadrach did. "Hello," this stranger said politely.

"Good morning, is Shadrach home?"

The stranger's eyes widened for a second. "Are you Hettie? The journalist?"

"I am. Is Shadrach a twin?"

Shadrach's brother frowned, although his eyes were light and teasing. "Oh, come on. I look better than Shad," said the brother who must have heard often that they looked the same. "My name is Shack." He took a step back and yelled into the house, "Shadrach, Hettie's here to see you. I guess you do have a type." Lowering his voice, he said, "Shad's upstairs. I bet he'll hurry himself on down now. Come in."

Hettie entered Shadrach's house, immediately noting the gleaming wooden floors that were partially covered by a thick, plush rug. Front and center was a wide, curving, wood staircase. To her right was an open door that led to what looked to be an office. To her left was the living room. She caught a glimpse of a piano, bookcases, and an elaborate fireplace. Behind her, Shack closed the door. Hettie turned. "I don't look like Laverne."

"Sure you do. You're prettier. But you're probably the same height. And you have the same—" Shack made some kind of weird gesture with his hands that Hettie figured had to do with a woman's shape. "I guess he *likes* bending himself in half to kiss someone."

A door on the first floor opened and another man who looked eerily similar to Shadrach appeared. "What's with all the yelling?"

"That's AB. AB, this is Shadrach's girlfriend." Hettie looked at Shack. Despite their courtship, she and Shadrach had never referred to each other as boyfriend and girlfriend, although she supposed that was what they were.

"Shadrach." Hettie's finger went up. "Meshach." She pointed to the man beside her. "Abednego." Her finger darted to the new arrival. Almost she laughed. Almost. What were their parents thinking? "Is the youngest one named Daniel?"

Meshach and Abednego wore similar expressions of annoyance. Above her head, Hettie heard a door slam shut and feet on the stairs. "Yes, the youngest is Daniel."

"You're not triplets, are you?"

"No." This answer came from Shadrach himself as he jogged down the last few stairs of his house barefoot. Shadrach waved a hand. "Go away."

His brothers were smiling as they made themselves disappear. Shadrach came to stand right in front of her, his eyes searching.

"Did you just get out of the shower?" She reached up, touching the small line of lotion that lingered on his cheek.

He captured her hand but didn't take his eyes off of her. "You're here early and I'm not talking about time. Let's talk in my office."

Shadrach's home office was a little bit different from his work office, in the sense that trophies lined his bookshelves. Baseball trophies, Hettie saw, as she went to read the inscriptions. "Did you try to play in the minor leagues or major leagues or something-else leagues?"

"Something-else leagues," he said with a straight face as he leaned against his desk. "But then Pearl Harbor was bombed. When I got out of the military, I no longer had any serious interest in pursuing a professional baseball career. What happened to you? Come here." Shadrach grabbed her hand, pulling Hettie to him.

Wrapping her arms around his waist, Hettie closed her eyes and inhaled. "I quit my job this morning." She'd known Edgar would be in the office even if no one else would. He'd been shocked when she'd handed him her resignation. So shocked that she had robbed him of his speech. He'd said nothing as she quietly said good-bye and packed up her things.

Shadrach's response was to lean down, lowering his chin onto her shoulder. Hettie very quickly, very quietly told him the story of what happened. When she finished, she pulled back so she could see whether there was disappointment in his eyes. What she saw was an odd look of wonder. He touched a hand to her head, lightly running it over her hair before meeting her gaze. "I'm honestly surprised this partnership lasted as long as it did. I will never forget that table tennis match for the rest of my life."

"Shad."

His hand cupped her face, his golden eyes meeting hers full-on. He hadn't taken the time to slip on his glasses. "I'm serious. I'm proud of you for all that you accomplished this year and for making the hard decision to pivot even when it cost you."

"I'll never write for *The Crisis* now." The thought made her sad but it was something she could live with. She could not live with the reporter she had been slowly turning into.

"You don't know that. Just because your path is different doesn't mean that it won't get you to the right destination. Look at Althea. How many times has she tried for Wimbledon? How long did it take to get her on the winner's podium?"

Hettie sighed. That was another thing that made her sad. "I could have handled that last conversation better."

His smile was tender. "I think Althea knows you and she hears you. The decisions she makes are her own. But if she ignores everyone else, it's your voice she listens to."

"You still admire her, don't you?"

"Althea Gibson is my hero. My love, she was simply born in the wrong time and it's so unfortunate that she can't just play tennis like the rest of the women in the USLTA. It's not fair that the focus is always on the color of her skin and not on the fact that she can destroy any player out there on the court. Wouldn't it be nice to live in a world where every Negro who rises to prominence didn't have to then turn into Moses? Kudos to her for refusing that job."

Hettie blinked a few times. "You're supposed to agree with me."

Shadrach pressed a soft kiss to her mouth. "Half the reason I love you is because we think so differently from each other. You weren't completely wrong. Althea has chosen a very hard road for herself. But that's who she is. That's who she always has been. She has fought every day of her life to get where she's at and she'll continue to fight for what she wants. It's her life to live and who are we to make further demands upon it? We have so many other people who are willing and ready to jump into the fight. Let her play tennis. And mark my words, one day, people will look back and they'll see what I see: that she is a once-in-a-lifetime athlete who deserves all the laurels."

There were a lot of things that Hettie wanted to discuss further but only one thing was on her mind. "Half the reason why you love me? Are there other reasons?"

"I love how determined you are," he said before pressing a kiss to her cheek. "I love how fiercely you defend yourself and those you love." He kissed her forehead. "I love who I am when I'm with you." He pressed another kiss to her forehead. Hettie closed her eyes. "I love how kind you've been to my daughter." He kissed her other cheek. "I love that you chase after what you want." He kissed the top of her nose. "I love your laughter and your smiles." This time he kissed the corner of her mouth. "I love you, Hester Carlin." But he didn't kiss her this time. Hettie opened her eyes. "Will you marry me?" Hettie's eyes went wide. "I had to ask now before you asked me."

She poked a finger in his side, feeling a little bit embarrassed even as she grinned, happier than a person who had just given up their dreams ought to be. "Yes, I will marry you. I love you, Shadrach. I'm pretty sure I loved you first."

"Maybe, but I love you more."

"I don't think so." They put their argument on hold as he leaned down and kissed her.

EPILOGUE

1964

If someone had ever told thirteen-year-old Hettie Carlin Lewis that one day she'd be tired of country clubs, she'd have adamantly denied it. But she was tired of country clubs.

"I'm not sure if you can use the telephone here," the woman behind the front desk said nervously. A look of pain was etched on her face and Hettie suspected that the woman was hoping for a supervisor to come along, because she kept glancing over her shoulder.

"Forget about it." Hettie's voice was so cool, the young woman's shoulders tensed and her face bloomed red. "Is there a payphone around?"

Excited to answer this question, the woman leaned forward, pointing. "It's just outside that door and to the left."

"Thank you. I would love to say that you've been very

helpful but I try not to lie these days." At her words, the young woman's eyes widened, but Hettie did not have patience for people who were determined to follow rules that kept her in her place.

The only reason Hettie didn't leave was because she and Shadrach were guests, and Shadrach was currently on the golf course being courted by some wealthy white businessman who wanted to invest in Shadrach's corporation. Deciding to turn the meeting into an excuse for a getaway, they'd been in Maryland for nearly a week and had driven to the country club from their hotel earlier that morning. Shadrach had asked her if she wanted to caddy. If it had just been the two of them then she'd have done so, but she wasn't interested in spending hours listening to topics that would probably put her to sleep.

Instead, she'd opted to find a quiet place to work on her article—which she had done—until she'd checked her watch and decided it was time to see what her children were up to. If only she'd known that asking for a phone was akin to starting a war.

Hettie left the main building, stepping out into the bright summer day. Before her was the parking lot where dozens of vehicles were lined up neatly in a row. Slipping on her sunglasses, Hettie turned left and found the phone booth.

"Hello?"

"Cindy?"

"Hi, Mama! Mama's on the phone!" Hettie could hear the scrambling in the background. "Are you guys having a nice time? I wish I could have come!"

"Next time! How are y'all getting along?"

"Mama?" It was her baby. And it sounded like she'd found another phone in the house so she could join the conversation.

"Hi, Celeste. Are you having fun with Grandma and Grandpa?" Her parents had volunteered to stay at the house with the children. Oral and Rosa were, in fact, insulted if Shadrach and Hettie didn't ask them to stay with the children at least twice a year.

"Grandma and I are baking a cake!"

"I'm helping them," Cindy interrupted. "Grandma's been teaching us to knit. We're working on a blanket for when the weather cools."

"Mama!" This was her boy.

"Ash, where are you?" Hettie asked.

"Daddy's office! When are you coming home?" her five-year-old demanded.

"Tomorrow. You're not having fun?"

"I am having fun," Ash said, sounding very much like he wasn't having fun even though he loved spending time with his grandfather. Hettie would never not be surprised by how patient and gentle and kind her father was with her son. He was a whole new man with his grandson. Hettie was jealous. "But it's funner when you and Daddy are here."

"Funner's not a word," Cindy told her brother.

"It is too if I just said it!"

"All right." Hettie's voice was stern, but she was smiling. Being a mother was the absolute hardest thing she'd ever done in her life but moments like these filled her heart. She looked away, her gaze drifting across the sea of cars. She took a step forward as a car door opened and a familiar, tall, lanky form emerged.

"Mama?"

"Huh? Listen, I have to go but I just wanted to call and check in."

"Grandma wants to know why you're checking in. She said she raised you, didn't she?" Cindy said, clearly repeating Rosa's words.

It *was* Althea, using the side car mirror to run a comb through her hair. Had this place forced her to change in the parking lot? "Tell Grandma I was calling because I love my babies. I've got to go but Dad and I will call tonight when we get back to the hotel. I love you."

A chorus of 'love yous' rang out and Hettie hung up the phone. From where she stood, Hettie watched as Althea opened the trunk of her Coupe de Ville and pulled out a bag filled with golf clubs. Hettie had watched Althea win Forest Hills in 1957. She'd watched Althea win Wimbledon and Forest Hills in 1958. She'd been a bit sad when Althea announced her retirement from tennis shortly thereafter. She'd seen Althea on *The Ed Sullivan Show*. She'd purchased Althea's debut album, which hadn't been as successful as Althea probably hoped. She'd dragged Shadrach to the theaters to see Althea in the film *The Horse Soldiers* despite his great dislike of John Wayne. Althea had had some high highs in the last few years, but she'd had some lows as well.

Althea crossed the parking lot and she must have felt Hettie's eyes on her because she stopped and turned. Did Althea recognize her? Hettie had cut off most of her hair after her second pregnancy and so her hair was short and curly. She was a size bigger than before, as she was still trying to lose weight from carrying Celeste. But otherwise, she was unchanged.

"Hettie Jo."

Hettie stepped out of the phone booth, her arms swinging at her sides. "Big Al."

Althea looked away for a second. "You still writing?"

The question wasn't a surprise. It wasn't as if Althea had ever seen Hettie on the sports beat again. After her wedding, Hettie was hired as a freelance journalist and immediately asked to write restaurant reviews. Seven years later, she was still writing restaurant reviews. Shadrach claimed it was because she loved to see the fear in the waitstaffs' eyes when they realized who she was. That was not true. She'd just found this very odd niche that worked for her and gained her recognition in certain circles. In fact, a week ago she'd bumped into one of the editors at *The Crisis* who wanted to meet to discuss one of her pieces. She was trying not to get her hopes up too high. "Some. I see you're destroying barriers and changing the game once again."

Althea's smile was slow to appear but it was genuine when it did. "You know me. I'm never satisfied unless there's a challenge." Althea was the first Negro woman to receive membership to the Ladies Professional Golf Association. In other words, she was now a professional golf player. As always, she was making a difference in her own way. Althea shifted. "Are we headed in the same direction?" Hettie glanced at the country club doors, knowing a sneer was crossing her face. Althea laughed and then waved her forward. "Come on."

Hettie closed the gap between them and together they walked inside. When she almost started humming, she realized that she was happy for this chance to see this once-in-a-lifetime athlete again. Happy to be in the presence of this woman, this game changer.

ACKNOWLEDGEMENTS

I work with a great team. I am grateful to everyone at HarperCollins UK for the time, energy, and assistance they provided in getting this book off the ground. I would specifically like to acknowledge Rachel Hart. It's been wonderful working with you again.

I've mentioned them before, but I have been truly blessed with a wonderful family who—for months—patiently listened to me talk and talk and talk some more about Althea Gibson, race, tennis, and the 1950s. I think it's fair to say that we all learned about her together! Thank you, Mom and Dad, for answering my questions about your personal experiences growing up in a time where segregation was technically outlawed but also still reigning as king. Thank you, Jannett and Victoria, for your support as always. I could not ask for better sisters. Thank you, Tee Jannett for always being willing to take the time to invest in this passion of mine.

And to my readers, I hope that you were both blessed and entertained!

In the City of Light, one woman will stand against darkness.

Inspired by the incredible true story of Josephine Baker and her role in the French resistance during World War Two, don't miss CODE NAME BUTTERFLY!

Available now!